Time is the Fire

Joseph Phillip Natoli

"Come here and sit with me, Joe"

What will become of you and me
(This is the school in which we learn ...)
Besides the photo and the memory?
(... that time is the fire in which we burn.)
Delmore Schwartz

BOOK ONE

CHAPTER ONE

FALSE IDENTITIES

Whether I am to be the hero of my own life -- and my twin's -- this tale will show.

Probably not.

Nevertheless, in the beginning was the word and years later what the last auditor heard was unintelligible noise. When I find it's a dreary November in my soul and I'm trailing funeral processions, I know I've been re-reading *Moby Dick*.

Don't call me Ishmael.

Actually, it's a bright crisp day in April and the clock is set to ring. Really, you don't know anything about me unless you've read a book titled *Between Dog & Wolf,* though what's between a dog and a wolf I don't really want to know. The lower orders are entitled to their privacy.

What you have before you now is the testament of a man who was slandered, by whom I don't know, but I woke up one morning without ever having done anything wrong beyond mischievous tricks played, acerbic mockery, false witness and cockeyed testimony, wicked verbal abuse in the Romance languages, salty repartee, making soul sucking sounds in quiet zones, and inappropriate smirks at Episcopal high mass, to find myself arrested.

The next morning awaiting trial I woke up in bed to find myself changed into a monstrous vermin. I tried for months to find out what I was on trial for and in between struggled to rock my hard, round shell over so I could get to my feet, all eight of them.

My name is Theodorus Maximillian Bratter, called Theo by all. My Pater named me after Theodorus the Mathematician, but I grew into the identity of another BC Theodorus, the one called The Atheist. He brilliantly decided that in life one should avoid grief and maximize joy. I wonder how much objection he got to that. Ignorance would bring you to grief, eventually, while intelligence would fashion you a joyful life. And vastly superior intelligence such as my own fashions the greatest joy.

All that being said, the man was an atheist which means no matter how many gods how many people believe in when they die and turn to dust, Theodorus failed to see that dust on a journey anywhere but into the mouths of worms.

Do worms have mouths?

So much for false identities. I don't have eight feet. Now to my family. I am committed to telling you all that lousy crap because if I don't, it will fester inside me and erupt as endless falsehood and preposterous revelations stolen from Kaka assuming the identity of both Joseph Ray and Karl Sandsung.

This is not a middle-brow narrative so keep your super bright cell phone handy. I will seldom say anything you already know or feel comfortable with in any warm, ontologically confirming sense. Most difficult is my trying to reach beyond what I know and with which I am comfortable. Most of that is in the voices of other people but it is not easy to listen outside my receiving channels. Every reader is a better listener than I.

See?

My Father has a boat, not a ship in which a boat can go in while a ship cannot go in a boat. When he's not in the Lab he is on his boat. It's called *The Lee Shore*, which Father says is a latitude and longitude you don't want to be. Dirk, my twin, has a hand puppet with that name.

Dirk's the anti-anti-hero naïf-slob of good heart of *Between Dog & Wolf* while I am a bit player therein though noble. The strongest proof of reality for Dirk is in these hand puppets he makes. Father says what Dirk does is not a hard science but very well may be on the path to such, as lunacy is on the path to more lunacy.

Father thinks everything Dirk or I do is a sign of a hard science coming to life in us. For instance, Father believes that my language precocity, by which I mean I speak all the Romance languages and can carry on a conversation with a Catholic Cardinal in Latin, is a movement toward La Place Transforms. And the fact that Dirk has a French hand puppet he calls La Place Transforms is what Father calls a very promising sign in terms of a future in the hard sciences.

However, Maître Rectum, who is one of our tutors, told Dirk that a soft mind is not conducive to a hard science. Maître Rectum insists that I should call him the Very Reverend Richard Rechter and not Old Rectum, but I tell him the Latin neuter fits a neutered man and that rechter is an ancient misspelling of rector which itself is a barbaric bastardization of the Latin, rectum, rectorum.

Now I'm tired of talking and for Chapter Two shall take a respite from relating all this crap. This book is about inconceivable loss and deep grieving. Like the socially insecure and inept, I enter tragedy like a standup comedian.

I mean I've had some peculiar dreams.

When all you love in the shape of one person leaves the Earth forever, you yourself enter an afterlife, though you are still breathing, talking, writing.

CHAPTER TWO

DREAMSCAPES

I have shards of memory that appear as dreams. I call them dreamscapes not in the landscape or seascape sense but in the sense that I'm having them and at the same time trying to escape them.

I think they are more important than DOB and DOD, social security, driver license number, age, weight, vax record, passport, and what answers you give when you are interrogated, and you will be in the course of your life interrogated countless times, mostly on a Smartass phone by a computer Inquisitor. And no one will know who you really are because they don't ask about the dream-escapes.

My dream-escapes have revealed that I am not who I say I am though I believe what I say about me. Put it another way: I'm naïve, which is a surprise to me. Put it another way: What I know is far less than what I should know about me. My dreams have been revealing to me that someone I knew and loved is gone and I don't know how to find her or even retrieve what I knew about her. And what she knew about me.

For instance, was I a naïf in her view, or a full-blown narcissist as Eve Solly, Dirk's partner on radio smashmouth, says I am. Truth is even if Eve appeared in a potent dream, I wouldn't pay any attention to her. I may not know in the dreamworld who I am, but I know she's not a Virgilian guide around those circles.

What my dreams revealed to me was disconcerting, to say the least. Maybe if I said the most it would all be clear to you. But dreams, even those a Mensa has, are not clear. It's as if they are touching on what I don't know but did happen and I need to know. I'm quoting Dr. Fraud although I don't pay any attention to him either. He's in the pocket of Big Farmer. He won the most pills prescribed in one day award. Several times.

Even though I always record my dreams, I give them no credence. I mean it doesn't seem that I can do anything about what they show me because she's already dead.

She's already dead? That seems to be a given somehow although she is always so very alive in my dreams.

Having these dreams in multiple languages doesn't help. Different words spoken do not help. I groan and moan, cry and gasp in pain, but no dream has mercy on me.

My brother, Dirk, says he has lucid dreaming where he takes control of his dream but as he cannot take control of his life when he's awake, I doubt he has more success when he's asleep.

When all you have are shards of memory which only appear as dreams. . . And as the Bard says 'for in those dreams who knows what foul and fucked up things may appear . . . you don't really have a childhood, do you?

Or is it when you have a normal childhood, you don't dream, and you don't remember anything about being a child? Normalcy does not inspire dreams. Normalcy has memories that show up, for instance, at birthdays, baptisms, marriages, divorces, promotions, evictions, terminations, and funerals, at dinner time and football games, job interviews and picnics. Never in dreams. Your Smartass phone is ready to take a Pict but dreams don't pose for them.

I don't know if normalcy is not having dreams or ignoring them as abnormal when you do have them, so as to preserve normalcy.

There is a high price to be paid for normalcy. I mean you may wind up believing you are who you say you are.

One of my dream-escapes:

"What is your earliest memory, Theodorus?"

"I'm looking at a very large fetal ass for nine months. It's my fetal twin's ass. Dirk's."

"That's absurd. How did you know so early on that your twin would be called Dirk? And besides. fetuses have no fetal memory."

"I didn't know his name was Dirk. He told me."

"You know of course how upset I was when I was told I was to deliver twins?"

"I have no memory of that."

"Of course not. Why would you? One fetus was a personal and private event. Two or more so very obscenely public. But your father loved the number two. It was a prime or primal something or other. According to your father, I was giving birth to two factors, and he thought that was a good thing. Random but good. Then he went back to the Lab. He entered me once and then entered the Lab for the next forty years."

"I'm going to know how to predict prime numbers when I grow up."

"What? Who told you that? That is an absurd life goal. As it happened, I had asked that one fetus be removed for decency's sake, but it couldn't be done. I so regret having had relations in your father's Lab when I was so young and foolish. He said chances were six million to one I would be impregnated. He said he knew his probabilities. Intercourse at that time was not stow drastic. Idiot."

"Stochastic. It is. Everything is. The Mathematics failed him."

"You don't know how many times I wished he would just vanish as my mother did."

"You had a mother? I mean, she vanished?"

"It was very convenient. But she was like that. She thought if she lived much longer, she would be a burden to others. Do unto others first, matters like dinner and clean clothes for myself and my sister. . ."

"You had a sister? Did she vanish too?"

"No, dear. You've met her hundreds of times. Your Aunt Finesse."

"The name sounds familiar."

"We had so many needs right at home, but mother didn't see us as others, or sufficiently other to fit her peculiar morality. It was those others, swarms of the unwashed, virulent, nasty public she never met, she just loved them to pieces and she decided to vanish for them. The family could find its own way."

"She just one day up and vanished?"

"I think so. Then I met your father. And he didn't vanish.

Another dream-escape with the same lady, The Mater:

"How did you boys behave during your therapy session?'

"Theo told him that there was no such thing as a spiritual indigestion advisor with a name like Mister Tums."

"And the poor man's name led you to lead your brother astray?"

"I had my reasons, mother. Do you think it's a good thing or a bad thing that everyone has their reasons?"

"Only the public refer to things, Theodorus. A sign of a weak mind is the continual reference to things."

"That's why the Pater uses profanity and numbers, right, Mother?"

"I haven't the slightest idea, Dirk, why your father uses numbers. A marriage based on numbers is not a marriage. Words are the bond for any sane, successful marriage. I make allowances, however, as did my own mother. Your father has his memories."

"Do you have memories, Mother?"

"Yes, of course. Dust thou art and to dust thou will return. Comes immediately to mind. I don't know why but I remember it, especially at funeral services. It's not very uplifting. I wouldn't remember it if I could control my memories, but you see you can't. It's like that jingle about soap. It's so much better a memory than your father's, though. He remembers going in search of his biological mother, who, according to what was said, was a very lustrous young woman who was there one day and gone the next."

"She vanished? Like your mother?"

"Totally different. No one went in search of my mother. Your father went in search of this lustrous woman like a loitering pilgrim as the poet says. *What leagues are lost, before the dawn of day, thus loitering pensive on the willing sea, the flapping sail haul'd down to halt for logs like these!* That's Lord Byruin. He was sad, bad, mad and he had a clubbed foot. Somehow I suppose it all was for the best."

"So, where is she now? Father's mother?"

"He dreams about her, you know. Other than that, she's quite out of his mind. She's for the ages now, as they say. I abominate death. We are snowflakes on the long continuum of time. So public. So many dead. A huge faceless horde of dead people. I ask you, what kind of end is that? The dead are all equal. I mean equally dead. No distinction. That is my definition of Hell."

"Why was the Pater's mother lustful?"

"Biological mother, Dirk. Lustrous, not lustful. The words are similar though. She was radiant, glowing, soft brown eyes so fascinating that you stopped and looked at her. There's a picture of her some place."

"Like a photo?"

"A painting. Your father's father did it. He was a painter. And of course, a voluptuary. He called it 'Numina.' He painted himself right alongside her."

"I'd love to see it."

"It was sold at auction. To strangers. It went up at a public auction. That is such a terrible memory for your father to have."

"Will our own things go to strangers at a public auction?"

"What things do you have, Dirk? We don't have things. But if we did, they would go to a private auction. The public adores things. Memories, however, die with us."

"I'll remember Theo when he's dead."

"I don't intend to die, Dirk. And if you die, I won't remember you. Besides, I'm going to find a lustful young lady of my own and marry her. Death won't part us."

"Of course, you will, and it won't. But you might not know her when you find her. Your father found me, and he didn't know he had. Idiot."

My most confusing dream-escape:

I don't tell her I'm going. I start walking up a very unremarkable street, a long uphill in clear air but empty. I turn and look back and see her with the others. I don't know them, but they are all busy talking. I'm tired of that socializing. They're busy networking. They don't notice I'm gone.

After a long while I realize I don't know where I'm going. I don't know the building I'm heading for. Our hotel. We checked in earlier in the day. No, I didn't. The hotel now stands before me like a tall, gaunt skeleton. When I enter the lobby there's a rush of noise and people. The guests, a milling crowd all knowing where they are going. I had not seen one person in all the longish time I was walking and now this place is a hive of them. I am not moving. I don't know what room we are in. I never saw it. I've never been here. If I go over there to the busy desk, they will know I don't belong here. I think I'll go back to her, but I am full of fear that I won't find her now, that everyone is in a different place, including her. So stupid to have left her.

I feel myself waking up, angry. Why am I now buying something? Fruit in a bag. It is being sold in the lobby. I need to buy a lot. Why is fresh fruit being sold in the lobby of a five-star hotel? Nevertheless, a man who looks like my father holds the bag while I fill it. You are a good something he says but I don't catch it, so I give him the bag of fruit and walk away. I want to ask him why he's not in The Lab, but it doesn't seem to fit the occasion. The fear returns when I say nothing though the man thanks me profusely and offers me some fatherly advice. Don't lose my way.

But I've lost her. I feel the emptiness of that deep inside me just as a woman ahead of me in the queue turns and I say to her "Do you know me?" "Yes, I do," she says, and I see at once that it's her, that I've found her though she is wearing a huge red blouse with small star like designs. I don't think she would ever wear that. It is so different. I tell her I don't know the room and she goes to a door, opens it and tells me that this is it. "It's here." I peer in. A small, brown room no bigger than a closet. "I don't recognize it," I tell her, puzzled but she is smiling at me. I remember that she would look at me with a steady gaze not saying anything. I've never known what she was telling me.

"I don't recognize it," I tell her. "Of course, you don't. You've never been here before," she tells me. I admit that at first, I didn't recognize her, and I apologize. "Because it's different now," she replies. "It's timeless now."

I began to look for her in my dreams and wondered if I would know her when I found her. I wondered if being with her, being together with her would be eternal or whether what was found would somehow be lost.

I was looking for her before I ever knew her and when she was gone, there was no time left in me at all.

That was a dream-escape. I didn't know it could become true. But it did become real.

CHAPTER THREE

THE FAMILY

Something is rotten in our Father's Lab. Always. Terrible smells. These are the times that try those who have souls while everyone else seems to be enjoying themselves.

More about my family.

My family, which is Pater, Mater, Dirk, and myself, and the family retainers by which I mean the tutors, the shrinks, Juanita the upstairs/downstairs twice a week maid, and the Lab Post-Docs. We are all unhappy together in a hapless way that Father, from his perspective in the Lab, calls happy. The Mater sits at her desk in her Office and stares at a piece of white cardboard. No. That was Miss Lonely Hearts. The Mater is out in her flower garden. In all weather. She finds the winter rest of flowers comforting, a message that though all is dead now, it will flower in the Spring.

Flowers are more like zombies than resurrected souls, by which I mean she does not see spiritually. She sees the spiritual world as a kind of public toilet in the NYC subways system. All the wrong kind of people use it.

She has other odd ideas such as believing that once you speak Italian, complications set in. I tell her that Commendatore Spinalzo, another of our tutors, teaches Dirk and I Italian behind her back. I also told her that he steals her undies and wears them. I totally made that up. No matter. She wasn't going to fire the Commendatore because that would put us all on a slippery slope to The Public, in this case public school.

Did I tell you that the Mater's greatest fear in life is The Public, any appearance of the word drove her toward suicide. The Public was the enemy of The Private and she felt that robbed of the sanctity of her privacy she would wind up sitting in her Office staring at a piece of white cardboard.

I use the word Office in a non-commercial, no wages paid, no royalties made, no output or productivity, no benefit to society at all sense. The Office was the place where she sent out missives into social media the way Emily Dickinsad threw poems out of a second story window in Amherst. Mother made daily counterattacks against the invasions, corruptions, and perversities of The Public. She campaigned for the end of Public schools, water parks, libraries, phone booths, library cards, parking, water fountains, rest rooms, park benches, beaches, health services, prisons, legal aid, housing, transportation, sidewalks, aid to mothers with dependent children, and any activity which all could partake without cost, like voting. She held that all public charity destroyed the will to go red in tooth and claw in one's dealings with one's fellow creatures. Out of struggle came a few winners in private compounds.

The most effect she had was on Dirk, who had no dislikes and certainly no hatreds in his life, but he did react like a pit bull to the word public, which he heard as pubic. He in fact had only one bad guy in his life, a villainess hand puppet, Miss Street Toilette, who was in Dirk's mind the great malefactor of The Public, coming to that view after the Fam took a short vacation in Europe and Dirk connected the street urinals and the street walkers around the Place Pigalle to The Pubic.

As my wont was to extend my own ego into the world, I had no issues with The Public. To me it was like conquered space. I walked frequently into The Public and when I was old enough to drive, I drove recklessly into The Public. In the Mater's mind The Public had raped and ravished the private womb of Mother Nature. The Public was tacky, poorly educated, noisy, exhibitionist, unclean, shifty, fecal, and lazy. I think she was quoting Marie Bassinette but I'm not sure. Eyetalians with their churning cement trucks paving over Mother Earth and killing the flowers, the seasons, the worms and so on should be arrested.

The Public should be arrested by Private Police, hired I suppose by people funding The Private Good. The Common Good of the Constitution was something to be ignored as it was the absurd product of senile semen. "The Public has a stench" was a meme in her life.

Dirk, as I say, always heard that as "The Pubic" from a very young age which was an explanation according to the family psychiatrist on life-long retainer, Dr. Emil Fraud, as to Dirk's attraction to the region of the pubes, which Dirk connected with The Virginia. He thought entering the whole state led to an orgasm.

Yes, there is no end to my twin's misrecognition and malapropism, but Dr. Fraud believes that in time Dirk will "reprehend" the true meaning of what he hears and speaks. You see in that very sentence why Dirk will never be cured and why I call our family psychiatrist on retainer Dr. Fraud.

My Pater, P.T. Bratter was a brilliant theoretical, abstract mind but the Mater thought him a perfect fool, a type she was more familiar with than geniuses. She liked his Post-Doc Lab People even less though I found them very amusing and great fun. They, like my tutors, provided me with endless hours of amusement, not consciously on their part but it was in their nature to be so.

The Pater spoke of The Mathematics the way The Mater spoke of The Public, but as she spit the word out as if it was poison, The Pater spoke of The Mathematics the way a Holy Roller speaks of The Jesus.

While The Public was working daily to erode the quality of The Mater's life, The Mathematics was working on the same day to fit everything into a smooth and elegant algorithm. Morality was a matter for The Mathematics to deal with. Marriage was an arrangement of The Mathematics, which, from what I could see, meant that The Pater worked and slept in The Lab, dined with The Fam, and kissed The Mater on both cheeks upon every occasion they ran into each other. As The Lab was in The Annex which was in previous centuries a stable for carriage, coach, and horses, and so bore in The Mater's mind deep association with the ancient filth of an ancient Public, she never stepped foot in The Annex. And so, in short, what The Mathematics and The Public did for their relationship was sufficient to require the services of a family psychiatrist on permanent retainer.

The Lab and all its hi-tech equipment were on the first floor of The Annex and the Post-Doc Lab People, all four of them, lived on the second floor, much in the way rats live in tight spaces.

They were all young men and women, brilliant geniuses of narrow focus, and had come from all over the world to work in The

Pater's Lab. When The Pater told us they were Post-Docs, Dirk's eyes went wide in wonder, fear, and excitement. I have no idea how that word connected to what was in his mind, but I can say it was in no way normal.

They were Post-Docs who were devoted to The Mathematics. The Mathematics which would end world hunger, flatulence, wars, bar fights, death, taxes, seat belts and red lights, fibromyalgia, cardiac arrest, fertility, paper and pen, phone booths, the need to work, and embodied sex.

I don't know why but I felt my precocity demanded a sexual dimension, so I hinted to Dirk that I was having a modest amount of embodied sex at about the age of 11 with Juanita who came twice a week to do "deep cleaning" of both the Manor house and the Annex. That really impressed him. "Juanita? Damn!"

"I can handle Juanita as easily as I handle integral and differential calculus," I told Dirk.

CHAPTER FOUR

THE TUTORS

"Who made the world, Master Theo?"

"God made the world, Rev. Rechter."

"And who made God, Master Dirk?"

"The Pubic?"

"No. Who made God, Master Theo?"

"The Mathematics?"

"No. No. No. God made God."

I had a frown on my face.

"But who made the first God?"

"There is no first God, idiot. There is only one God. We are monotheistic."

I saw the word frightened Dirk.

"I just don't think God made himself. Or herself. Or itself. Nothing comes out of nothing."

"Are you saying God is nothing, you fool? Are you an atheist, Master Theo?"

As Dirk thought the word has something to do with eating, he asked for a jelly sandwich. The Rev. Rectum ignored him.

"I think the world made God," I said, winking at Dirk. What fun.

"You have that backward, you young jackass. How could the world make God?"

"By thinking him up."

"By thinking him up!" Dirk shouted, laughing.

We both couldn't stop laughing.

"Jesus is not laughing," The Rev said. "Jesus is frowning."

On these many occasions I was busting his balls, an expression Juanita taught me, She used it a lot. It seems everyone in her life was always busting her balls. Her ex-husband did, as did her new boyfriend who she said she was about to dump. Her early childhood was filled with relatives who busted her balls. "But you don't have balls, do you?" I'd say to her, grinning. "You're busting them right now, kid," she'd say.

Back to The Rectum. When I had been sputtering, he'd pick up his Gibson, strum it and sing "I've Never Been to Heaven But It's Where I Come From." He had a good twang of Hank voice, and Dirk and I would sing along. The song refuted all logic.

"So, how can you come from a place you've never been?" I'd always ask after the song.

Rev. Rectum would mumble "shitheads" and then announce that he was prepared to accept that it was God's will that I was a ball buster. He didn't use that expression but said "a soul lost in self-adoration."

"Is it God's will that I'm a genius and Dirk is an idiot?"

"Sin comes through the pride of Lucifer. Your brother has the humble spirit of Jesus."

"I do?" Dirk said, pulling one of the hand puppets he liked to sew together. I think it was supposed to be Commendatore Spinalzo.

"Put that heathen idol away," Reverend Rectum told him sharply.

Later, at dinner, I told The Pater about the God discussion. Just to wind him up. I knew what he would say. We had heard it about a trillion times.

"The idea of God is contrary to The Mathematics. The Mathematics disproves such an existence. I will instruct Rev. Rechter. . ."

"Theo calls him Rev. Rectum," Dirk said. "He calls us shitheads."

"Watch your language, young man," The Pater told him.

"Tell me, Father, is it logical to say that you've come from a place you've never been?"

With that simple sentence I primed The Pater's rant on logic.

And so, he began. I had it all memorized and mumbled it along:

"We begin with the direct forerunners of Leibniz himself, especially his methodological principles and the three stages in the development of his Logical Calculus. Next, of course, we find the Logic of Relations of Johann Lambert and the intentional Logical

Calculuses of Maimon and Castillon. We must realize of course that the work of Theotham, Hamilton and Drobisch is seen as an anticipation of that of Boole. I refer to Boole himself, and his Calculus of Classes. Lastly, any discussion of mathematical logic must review the contributions of Jevons, Schröder, Peirce, the father of semantics, Frege, and Peano."

Then he'd clear his throat.

"Peano!" Dirk shouted in full gaiety.

The Mater who ignored any and every word coming out of The Pater's mouth, said:

"Keep that drivel to yourself. I want our sons to have a personal relationship with Jesus. He was quite a man, never mind the superstitious rot and nonsense. Blessed are those who put a gate between them and others. Blessed are the poor who keep to themselves. Blessed are those who laugh at the meek. And so on. Jesus is the most remarkable brand of all time. They need to learn how to network that. And they need a personal tutor for that."

"Maitre Patawalla is a Hindu," I said, nursing my peas with knife into spoon.

The Pater was losing himself staring into his own plate.

"He's a Sick," Dirk chirped.

The Mater looked at him and then at me as if The Public had invaded.

"He's a Sikh. No Jesus," I told her. "No personal identity. Just a public one."

That brought the color to her face. She looked at The Pater.

"Is this true?"

That authority didn't come up from his plate.

"I'm asking you. Is Theo telling the truth?"

The Head of the House meekly looked up.

"Has this one ever told you the truth about anything?" he moaned.

She looked at me. Her eyes narrowed.

"Go to your room."

I went to my room gladly. Juanita was doing the bathroom next to it and proximity aided the imagination.

The Mater feared that if Dirk and I did not establish a personal relationship with Jesus, we would establish a personal relationship with Karl Schmarx, that devil of Public sharing. I told Dirk that every time we entered a Marx & Spender, we were entering a world where everyone took what they needed. If he felt he had a great need for those brogues or that Walter, he should just help himself. It was all there to be shared. He pulled a lot of stuff out of a few stores before being caught but as he was 11 and I told the officer he was brain damaged, they let him go.

At the age of 11, Dirk and I were 5' 11". By the time we were fourteen we were 6' 4" and weighed about 15 stone. We took after The Mater, whose whole family were, as The Pater put it, Garancula and Pantsarecruel.

Size mattered. I mean in our dealing with our tutors. While I used my superior intellect and wit to wind all four of them up, and had done so from the earliest age, Dirk had been clay in their hands, a victim of their instruction. But now at gargantuan size, things changed. I advised him when upset to just stand up, walk slowly toward the tutor and then stand towering over them and say, "Would you mind repeating that?" "Could I bring a hand puppet along for support?" he asked me. "Certainly," I told him. "You can let the puppet do the talking." My thought was that while his physical presence would intimidate so also would intimations of mental instability.

For that instability, I mean Dirk's own, and my own variety -- too superior a mind and personal immortality confidence -- we had weekly sessions with Dr. Fraud.

"He says the unconscious cannot be reached with The Mathematics," I told the Pater when I was 9, after a Dr. Fraud session.

I was hoping to get the Pater on my side because I saw the time I spent with Dr. Fraud as time taken from dreaming about Juanita, who by the way was terminated for unspecified reasons, after several of my sessions with Dr. Fraud.

I'm sorry to say the reason to be specified was the fact that I gave the shrink long and detailed accounts of my sex life, mostly fraudulent but inspired by my imaginary trysts with Juanita. I fed the good doctor what he was after. All problems were sex connected. So, I obliged him, taking him down that path he wanted to go. I find that the best way to deal with people is first to find out how they think and what they think, jump on that train and along the way jump off, which startles the hell out of them, have a laugh, secretly, and jump back on.

Doing so with Dr. Fraud, unfortunately, put him on the trail of

Juanita and he outed what he called her debauchment of my psyche to The Mater. So, the fantasy sex partner of my life Juanita was gone.

Other terrible things happened when Dirk and I became sixteen. The Mater divorced The Pater and married a billionaire, "Gunner" Farnsworth, who lived out on Long Island in Fitzgibbon's East Egg kind of place. Real Batsby digs. The whole family entourage, minus The Pater, The Lab, and the Lab Post-Docs, moved into this vast domain of luxury. Dirk was happy because he could take all his hand puppets with him and I was certain, as I looked at this 20,000-square-foot main house, 12 beds and baths, and both indoor and outdoor pool with its 14 acres stretching from the ocean to the bay, providing access to both Hamptons waterfronts and with its amenities including two golfing greens, tennis courts, with smaller houses designated for each hobby that there had to be a Juanita for every thousand square feet.

So, moving to Billionaire's Row was not one of the terrible things that happened to me. The Fartsworth Confound, which is what I told Dirk to call it, was a whole lot better than a lab smelling of rotten eggs, odious gases day and night, small, controlled explosions -- all of which I guess had something to do with The Mathematics.

Gunner wasn't a bad guy, by which I mean he was friendly enough, but it didn't take me long to find out he was a bad guy in the law-and-order sense. It didn't take me long to figure out that he was a shady guy. For instance, he said his money came from his father who had inherited it from his father and so on, going back, I guess to The Primal Cash Source.

"He invests other people's money," The Mater told us, "lender sort of people and then he uses that as liverwurst to get even more money from other lenders. And so on. It's called finocle or pinochle, Theo. You could learn a lot from Mr. Farnsworth. You shouldn't think he or I will support you or your brother for the rest of your lives. You need to find your own finoculars. Mr. Farnsworth doesn't believe in inherited wealth. Every generation needs to find their own victims. You want to be part of the effete Merrydousury, don't you? Do you understand, Theo?"

There it is. One of the terrible things. I felt like all my ambition had been crushed.

"Jésus veut-il que je fasse beaucoup d'argent?"

"What was that about Jesus? I do wish you'd speak American

when speaking to me. Did one of your tutors teach you to speak foreign?"

"Commendatore Spinalzo."

"He sounds awful."

"You hired him when Dirk and I were 8. He's the one who wears your lingerie."

"I won't have a pervert in this house," she told me angrily. "He's to go immediately."

I shook my head.

"That won't do any good. You fired him about five years ago."

"And he's still tutoring you boys?"

"He followed us here. Before that, he was living in The Lab. None of the Post-Docs notice him. Pater either. They don't look up from their electron microscopes. I can tell you that a lot went on in that Lab that nobody in that Lab noticed. They only notice sub-atomic particles."

I thought about telling her the imaginary trysts Juanita and I had in that Lab but by this time I was feeling guilty about that phony story and the unjust end it had laid on Juanita.

"And if he's here, where is he?"

"He lives on the property. Somewhere on the 14 acres. Sleeps sometimes on Gunner's yacht. He gets by. Dirk brings Devil Dogs and greasy fries out to him. They're buddies."

"I shall see to it that our private security chases him off this property."

"You can just call the Hampton police department. Your taxes pay for that public service."

I had to get that one in there.

"Where are you going?"

"Farò sesso con Anna, il sous chef," I told her.

"Don't speak foreign in this house!" she shouted at my back.

"Dite a Gunner que me compre un coche," I shouted back. "Tell Gunner to buy me a car."

There was no Anna. I made her up. But I didn't make up the loveliness Dirk and I were soon to meet.

Here's what is: We had a visit from some other billionaires living on the row. Some guy named Dickel, like the Tennessee whiskey, and he may have founded the company. He looked old enough, somewhere just short of burial, I think. But he had a trophy wife, sixty years younger than him and there were parts of her in certain light that looked it. The sixty. There was a fifteen-year-old daughter.

By fifteen I mean I asked her, and she said fifteen.

Dirk blushed, shook, and stuttered when he met her and then pulled a hand puppet out of his pocket and talked through the puppet. That set her back a bit but then she smiled.

"I'm Bettina Parisi."

"This is Mr. Patawalla, Miss Parisi," Dirk told her.

"You can just call me Bettina. And you are?"

"He's an idiot. I apologize for him. I'm Theo. The better looking one. Dirk, go get me my camera. I want to take a photo."

She looked at me closely and then at Dirk.

"You have exactly the same face," she said. "But you don't do the same things with it."

I thought that profound. A fifteen-year-old Juliet, walking in beauty at such an early age, and all that's best of dark and bright meet in her aspect and her eyes. She was all that Byruin had imagined. And only fifteen.

"I've learned from Mr. Patawalla to hide my feelings and thoughts," I told her. "Not doing so makes you vulnerable. I'm sixteen. I know I look older given my size. I'm 6 feet 4. I don't like my hair cut. They put a cereal bowl on Dirk's head and clip the uncovered. His shoe size is bigger than mine. Don't ask me how that is. I suspect his brains are located there."

She studied me some more. I couldn't stop cataloguing her mesmerizing beauty. She had long burnished copper colored hair and soft brown eyes almond shaped. I could understand why a long war was fought over Heloise. I was looking at her right now.

"No, you don't sound more than five," she told me coldly. "A very nasty five-year-old."

"Maturity is hard to see."

"I wouldn't wait to see."

"Brilliance is even harder. I've been in Mensa since I was four."

"Does that, whatever it is, give you license to call your brother an idiot?"

"Well, because he is. One egg. Divided. But not evenly. I got the yolk, and he mostly got the runny white. I'm presence. He's absence."

She sighed deeply.

"I think you're the negative end. The dark end. I've just met you, but I regret it already. I'm tired of listening to you. Actually, you make me a little nauseous. I think my mother will be looking for me."

"Your mother is gorgeous, by the way. Depending on the light.

But your Pater looks like he's ready to be planted."

"He's not my father. He's just a man my mother married after my father died in a war."

"My condolences. Parisi was his name?"

She nodded.

"I was four. I don't remember much of him. Here comes your brother with your camera."

"Can you hold so I can take your picture?"

She hesitated.

"I'm not going to do anything untoward with it," I told her, smiling.

"I don't think I've ever met anyone for the first time who was so obnoxious," she said, shaking her head, turning, and walking away quickly.

I regretted not telling her I spoke all the Romance languages.

CHAPTER FIVE

PEOPLE DON'T FLOWER

Toward the end of the week, there was small cocktail party in honor of Bettina's family. I took the opportunity to invite her for a swim.

I whispered the invite in her ear, coming behind her as she was speaking to some homely birds I didn't know. Did you ever notice that stunning girls surround themselves with a pack of homely birds?

"What?" she said, turning to me.

I smiled at the attending birds and drew her away from them.

"A swim. Now. Private. You and me. It will be joy. Perfect day."

"Does it look like I'm here to swim? And with you no less."

"Brilliant. This is a no bathing costume pool."

"You know I think you're crazy."

"And you're blinding. In your eyes I see all that's best of dark and bright."

"What?"

"You can't tell me you're enjoying this party?"

Right then a wandering fool about my age came up to us. He had starched black hair and a starched white, smug face.

"Everything okay, Bettina?" he asked her but looked at me. Looked up at me.

"He's a Farnsworth. He lives here. I'm trying to be polite."

"Oh, a Farnsworth," he said. "I'm Michael. Why is Bettina trying to be polite? You are harassing her, my friend?"

"Get lost. Blow."

I towered over him like a bad angel visiting.

Michael lost the smug and went petulant.

"Sorry?"

"He's a joker, Michael. He wants me to jump in a pool with him."

"Why not?" I spoke. "But Michael is not invited. You're not going to throw a wobbly over that are you, Michael?"

"What the hell is with this guy?" Michael asked Bettina.

"He's the crazy half of twins," she told him, smiling at me.

"You mean there's another one. Isn't one enough of this guy?"

"His twin is the one over there wearing two hand puppets."

I looked in the direction she was pointing, and sure enough Dirk was in the middle of a group, hand puppets and all and most likely thinking he was cleverly throwing his voice into the creatures. He had a how to be a ventriloquist book he read like a hard-shell Baptist reads the Bible. All he ever did was mumble and throat gurgle.

"And you're crazier than he is?" Michael said, smirking.

"Did you ever get smashed in the face by a six foot four 15 stone guy?" I asked him.

He stepped away from me. Bettina told us not to start anything. She walked away.

"I'm trained in martial arts," Michael said, just before I kneed him in the bollocks, caught him as he slumped toward me. I held him up and while laughing and chattering away brought him to a chair and dropped him in.

I found Bettina wandering in the garden.

"I think that wanker was about to micro-aggress," I said, running up to her. "And he was nicking stuff too. I saw him. Gunner doesn't like his stolen treasures stolen. By the way, I'm a Bratter. Not a Farnsworth. I have absolutely no connection to Farnsworth sperm. The Mater married him. I've got nothing to do with him except enjoy the fruits of his bankruptcies. Illegal I'm beginning to think. And when I think, the clouds part. If you know what I mean."

She turned angrily to me. Puzzled, troubled, annoyed, exasperated, angry. Magnetic above all.

"Swim?" I asked.

"I don't understand you. What you say. What you do. What you want. And I don't want to. Leave me alone. You're so full of yourself. And abrasive. Just disgusting is what I mean."

"Funny. I thought there was a definite spark when I saw you and you saw me."

"You should have seen the instant dislike. You are very, very unlikeable."

"Don't talk tosh. You and I could be Albert and Ava in a pool right now."

"Tosh? I don't talk tosh, whatever that is."

"Rubbish. Americans say crap but Mr. Patawalla has been teaching us Oxbridge since Dirk and I were babies."

"You don't make any sense," she said, shaking her head.

"That's probably on you. You're blindingly lovely but still only 15. So much doesn't make sense at that age."

"You mean you can remember last year when you were 15?" she retorted, her eyes happy with the coup.

"I was never 15. It seems I was born knowing everything."

She went scornful, but still radiant. In the garden, among the flowering flowers. People don't flower. True enough. But she was in that very process.

"There's nothing I hate more than a know it all," she snapped at me. "Especially one who is also a huge ego, overbearing, rude, loud. Totally annoying and disgusting. Are you getting the message now? Leave me alone."

"We can get beyond first impressions. We'll have years and years. I love your name. Bettina. Don't you know names come out of the stories we live in."

"I don't know that. I don't know what it means."

"That's because at 15 you don't have a life story yet. But I could make one up for you. And a name. Shall I tell you?'

"I couldn't be less interested."

"This will rouse your interest. I think of the name Ease for you."

"What? Ease? What kind of name is that?"

"You would be even more fascinating than you are now if you had a name with a louche story to tell. Something you'd want to hide. Very disreputable. Or, maybe quite innocent but the world will see as scandalous. Or just naughty."

"And what kind of story do you have in mind?" she said, still angry but curious.

"Well, let's say, a friend one day said to you 'Let's get naked and jump in that pool and what fun! When you saw yourselves naked in the pool, you both felt like you had returned to garden of paradise. You were a very tempting Eve."

"And the name Ease brought that disgusting story to your disgusting mind?"

"Chapter Two. Your mother came out to the pool and saw you

both naked and she yelled `An easy girl is headed for a bad end.'"

"And you want me to be that girl?" she said and slapped me hard.

"My brother told me that tale."

"Somebody one day is going to shoot you," she told me, her whole head kind of trembling. Anger. I inspired that.

"If I have you with me, I don't care," I said, enjoying my part.

"You don't. You won't. You won't ever."

She then did what I had read about but never seen. She stormed off.

"No swim?" I called after her.

I don't know if you can tell a story without at least one likeable character but as I'm not about to fill that role, no one is to worry. Bettina Parisi is a very likeable young lady. You can identify with her.

Let's face it, reader. You want someone you can think is you. You want someone who makes you feel comfortable living as you do, someone who makes you feel comfortable being you and thinking and feeling as you do. Why do you think that in those sci-fi flicks the alien is almost always shot on sight? It's simple. You can't pretend to be It, so It has to go. It is why we have guns.

At the same time, you know being you sucks, that you don't see what is really there, that you miss the best parts of what life has to offer, that you read within the box of your own mind and can't read what's outside it, that you found the female Anima and that brought both of you together and somehow you lost her. And all that sucks and you suck, and I know that because my dreams tell me I suck.

Now, there are several terrible things about my first encounters with Bettina.

One, the words I used could have been better. Two, that she found me very unlikeable when I wanted her to find me very likeable. Three, we didn't get to swim naked together. Four, that her real father was dead and gone and she was within the reach of Mr. Dickel, who was clearly as shady as Mr. Farnsworth. I was now fated like the monogamous octopod to find no happiness, no pleasure, no love with anyone but Bettina, for I could see that she would flower.

CHAPTER SIX

SIREN CALLING TO MY SOUL

I was leaving the garden, pursuing this terrible thought that this young girl had totally fascinated me, when Dirk, one eye half closed and holding a tattered puppet, sprung out from behind a hew.

"What happened to you, bro?"

"Two guests punched me in the eye," Dirk said, sniveling. "And they smashed the guts out of Iron Mike."

He held up the puppet for me to see the extent of the damage.

"You should change his name to Marshmallow Mike. They happen to tell you why they knocked you around?"

"They said if I didn't keep away from Mr. Pickle's daughter, they'd be back to punch me some more. That was Bettina they were talking about."

"Not his daughter. Stepdaughter. Meaningless relationship. She hates him. And then they punched you? Or did you give them some lip and then they punched you?"

"I didn't give them any lip, but Iron Mike did. He told them to fuck off and then he sucker punched one of them."

"I see. Look, Dirk. If they ever bother you again, tell them they've got the wrong twin and they should come around and see me."

"Then they'd come and punch you. And you wouldn't have Iron Mike to defend you."

"Not to worry. I've got this."

I pulled out the Beretta I had started to carry ever since I sensed that the Mater had brought us into a criminal compound. I was observing. There was some dark matter here for sure. The best way to respond to a gun was with a gun. It also scared off people who didn't have a gun. I'd snatch the gun out of Charleston Headstone's cold, dead hands and shoot somebody. Just kidding. I attended NRA meetings to incite violence, to storm the capital, to start another war between the states. Just kidding.

"It's like the one James Blond carried," I told Dirk, handing him the gun.

"Does it have bullets?"

"They're hard to come by," I said, taking the Beretta from him.

"Have you been making out with Bettina?"

"What's it to you?"

"You like her?" he said, giggling.

"She's a Siren calling to my soul, brother. Took me by surprise I can tell you. You don't do teenage stuff like making out with a siren."

He began to rock back and forth, which was his way when he got excited, kind of like a kid putting off a pee.

"You know what? I'm going to make a Bettina doll for you?"

His eyes were jumping for joy, and he had the kind of smile that took *Facebotch* by storm, all bright veneer tooth work. Handsome dude, for sure. I could never strike the innocence and goodness of that smile. I was told not to frown at a photo op even though I thought I was smiling. I settled for a neutral look. I had the face of two Golden Age screen stars, a Tyrone Bogart face. Of course, Dirk had it too, but his face took all the smirk and circumstance out of it.

"Okay. Good. Fine. Just don't give her a blowup doll blow job mouth. I'm not attracted to her in that way. I'm more into courtly love kind of thing. Which I have no experience in."

"Juanita gave me one of those."

"What a blow job? Get off that."

"Somebody pulled me into a dark closet and pulled down my pants. I said what's going on? and a voice said, Juanita's, 'Don't tell me you don't want a blow job.' I didn't want to say no but I preferred oral sex."

"None of that happened. And you're dumbass to think anyone is going to be impressed by lying about any of that. Don't be imitating what you think I did. You're not me. Besides Juanita is Catholic. She probably wanted you to kneel down and pray with her."

"I just wanted to impress you."

"Well, don't. You know they punched your face because they thought you were me. I punched a wanker friend of theirs into a snooze. Anyway, keep your doll looking pure and lovely like my

Bettina."

"Sure. She wants to be your Bettina?"

"I've got no chance with her, bro. I've already deep sixed myself. She thoroughly dislikes me."

We were walking along slowly. We could hear the rumble of dividend recipient cocktail voices coming from the other side of the house, about two acres away. Nothing buys grandeur like thieves' money.

"Maybe Cag, your parrot, could help you? You don't have a puppet like I would show her. Rupert Vaselino. He's always a hit with females."

"Cag? No, the only stuff that parrot picks up is profane, obscene, and nutso. He mimics me. And I don't need that greasy puppet Mr. Vaselino to woo her."

"You said Cag was a genius parrot that learned a lot of languages from you."

"Okay. So, he's a dark side parrot from hanging around me. Exactly why I can't bring him around Bettina. One of me is enough. It would be like two devils being sent to the garden when one was more than enough to do the job. There's only one Eve here, brother."

Dirk began to look around, nervously.

"Not this garden," I told him. "The Biblical one."

"Who's Eve?"

"It's an old story. Never mind. But I did stupidly tell Bettina a stupid story."

So, I related the whole story about how Bettina went skinny dipping with a guy and was caught by her mother. She was 13 but obviously precociously sexual.

"And that's how she became an Eve," Dirk repeated slowly, mulling over the nakedness, the swimming, the guy, the mother, the sexual precociousness. God only knows what was going round in my strange brother's head. This is a good time to say you shouldn't believe anything I say about him. I tear into him, which is natural for leading players, the self-empowered and Leviathan types, who, by definition, can't have a twin.

"Look, I just made up that story. Kind of introducing my sex game with her, which I don't have. Didn't work. She froze me out, brother."

Ever since Dr. Fraud had been sent up for sixteen charges of sexual felonies, such as hustling his balls while listening to a patient's anxieties, Dirk and I had been working with another shrink.

It was Dr. Fraud's couch method that brought him to jail. He had this method he called Anxiety, Depression and Grief Groping Release. What it came down to be was a massage of the vaginas of patients, bringing them to climax and asking them if that made them feel better than what they felt when they walked in. That all came out on *Instagrab*. I actually testified in analog Court.

My testimony was exemplary.

"Tell us in your own words, please."

"Well, Dr. Fraud said I was a sociopath and there was no sense talking to me because I wouldn't listen, so I just read Caesar's Garlic War on the couch. In Latin. Dr. Fraud would send Dirk out for beer and sandwiches, order Dirk to take his clothes to the dry cleaners and things like that. Menial, degrading chores. He was a Fraud. Hence the name."

"The defendant's name is Shostokovici. Not Fraud."

"Same thing, Your Honor."

Anywho, they put Fraud away for couple of life sentences and Dr. Constance Nutley Wong Wrong took his place. She was in the same New Age group The Mater was in, one specializing in communicating with the dead and foreseeing the future in olive oil dropped in a plate of water along with the traditional irrationalities of reading your daily destiny in the stars, crystals, and a Ouija board, the rewards of lucid dreaming, and empowering yourself by shouting out what you want to the whole universe, the whole universe always seeming to be outside your front door or a kitchen window ready to listen to you. You do it more easily in the Metaverse on social mania.

So, Wong-Wrong became Fraud's replacement. I had one session with her thus far and it looked promising. I went with the sex game right off.

Roses are red, violets are blue, the shorter the skirt, the better the view is what I sang for her. I, myself, had concluded that I could get her to join me on The Couch by the sixth session. But now that I had given myself, against my will, to this Don Peyote quest to win the heart of the purest, finest creature on the planet, Bettina Parisi, the thought of wooing Dr. Wong-Wrong or indeed any of the servants bustling about the Mansion with feather dusters in hand had absolutely no attraction for me.

CHAPTER SEVEN

SESSION WITH DR. WONG-WRONG

Dr. Nutley Wong Wrong wasn't Chinese or any Asian at all. She had married and divorced a Wong. She kept the name because as she put it a diverse bi-racial background trumped old fashioned just being a woman. Her husband hadn't been Chinese or any Asian either and so not diversity representative. He had changed his name from Wrong, David Wrong, to David Wong but soon found out that the Ivy League was bursting with high achieving Asian applicants and were doing all they could to remain not an Asian Ivy League. They preferred a Wrong to a Wong.

When Dr. Nutley-Wong-Wrong found out she had married a Wrong and not a Wong, she divorced him on the grounds of Miss Representation. He wasn't who he said he was. Her own family, the Nutleys, had come over on the Mayflower and were very White, Conservative Republicans dedicated to giving the poor, not a salary raise, but an incentive to be rich. She had been in the process of getting the Wong and the Wrong out of her life when she took an interview at a major East Coast psychopharmacology startup and was straight out told she was a diversity hire. She had been about to tell them the Wrong in her Wong but withheld. So, now here she was doing some private gigs on the side as Nutley-Wong-Wrong.

The first time I saw her I wondered why anyone would think a woman about six feet tall and looking very Dutch with their fine Flying Dutchmen features could pass as a Wong. When she told me

David Wong looked like Roland Rump, Jr, I began to wonder if hearing a name, say Wong, made you see a Chinese face? Did words make you blind?

We went over all this at my very first session, sparked by her very first words to me.

"I've read Dr. Shostokovici's notes. He assesses you to be a pathological liar and affirms a therapist must take this foundational obstacle into account when treating you for a malignant sociopathy."

She looked at me and waited.

"Your response?"

"I might be lying here but who's Dr. Shostokovici? Wasn't he in *The Brothers Karamasovici*?"

"According to his notes, you called him Dr. Fraud."

"Oh, that guy. A helluva liar. Pathological. Liar. Clear case of malignant sociopathy. Do his notes tell you about how he caressed vulvas as therapy? He got sent up for it. So, I would ditch the notes."

"Pathological lying, Theodorus, or mythomania, is not a risible matter. It's a mental disorder in which the person habitually or compulsively lies. It was first described in the medical literature in 1895 by Anton Delbrück."

"Oh, that Nazi? They're still looking for him. You should call me Theo by the way. And, for truth's sake, I should call you Dr. Wrong. Or Constance if you want to get familiar. I mean you're not divorced from that wanker, right? And his truthful name was Wrong. Right?"

"I am divorced. Do you realize that lying to your brother further destabilizes his very tenuous hold on reality?"

"Give me an example of how I do that. The destabilizing part."

"Did you not tell him that Mr. Farnsworth is a member of a club of billionaires who are engaged in a variety of financial crimes?"

"Well, yeah, but I think I was more specific."

"Feel free."

"I've only known the wanker a few days less than The Mater knows him before she married him, but he was an easy read. For me. He had only one language. Twitter English."

"May I pause you there? Do you hold some ressentiment regarding your mother's marriage to Mr. Farnsworth?"

"I could tell you things that would scare you."

"But you didn't mind telling your brother. He's fragile you know."

"Some packages say Fragile. Some say Pericolo. Dangerous. The

Mater put us in a dangerous place here. Dirk needs to know that."

"Of what is it you're accusing your step-father?"

"Of what? The whole deal. Check fraud, credit card fraud, mortgage fraud, medical fraud, corporate fraud, securities fraud, including insider trading, bank fraud, insurance fraud, market manipulation, payment point of sale fraud, health care fraud, theft, Ponzi scheme, tax evasion, bribery, extortion, sedition, embezzlement, identity theft, money laundering, forgery, counterfeiting, and DUI."

I could see her eyes widening and then narrowing into slits as I catalogued. Walt Whiteman would have been proud of me. What fun.

"Is that all?" she said, clearing her throat.

"I'm not excluding cyberattacks, elder abuse, robbery, kidnapping and drug dealing."

"You can't be serious."

"I could by lying," I said. "Maybe the wanker and his peers just know how to seize the day."

"Let's get back to your brother. Your twin."

"Because I'm hopeless?"

"Why did you tell him that you both needed to surround and storm the Beach House?"

"Citizens' arrest. They were stashing tons of cash to be laundered in the Beach House. In the walls. Between studs 16 inch on center. Straight out of that stream *Odzark*."

"I presume the They refers to Mr. Farnsworth and his peers?"

"Independent contractors. Actually, with guns, so they're more like mercenaries. Private military company. They worked for a Prince."

She was making a lot of notes. She looked up.

"You know none of this is real, don't you? You do but your poor brother doesn't."

"Constance, we went there. Surrounded, besieged, and stormed the place. Shots were fired. There was more firepower than I anticipated. Dirk and I barely got out alive. We jumped on *The Lee Shore* and sailed into the Sound."

She looked dumbfounded.

"Ask Dirk. He'll tell you."

She stuttered.

"You are so much more a pathological liar than Dr. Fraud ...I mean Dr. Shostokovici imagined."

"Dirk brought Mr. Patawalla and Mr. Spinalzo along. They can confirm how the action went down."

"Your tutors were with you?"

"Hand puppets," I told her. "Dirk thought they'd like the change."

"Hand puppets?"

"A storm brew up and I got swept overboard."

"That's a lie," she said, calmly but I could see I had swept her mind overboard.

CHAPTER EIGHT

STORMING THE BEACH HOUSE

"You saw lights on when we walked up here from the beach?"
Dirk shook his head.

"I dropped Mr. Patawalla. I was looking for him."

"I'm pretty sure they're in there. Probably laundering money."

Dirk didn't know who they were or why they would be washing money, but he had learned not to question me because he knew I was always several jumps ahead of him.

"A wanker with Dobermanns makes the rounds," I whispered.

""Whoa!" Dirk let out, swiveling around quickly, and looking into the darkness behind us. "Where are they?"

"Calm down. If they were behind us, they'd let us know. No sense in sitting out there watching us. They'd have been all over us by now, wondering what we were doing here in the middle of the night."

Dirk too was wondering but said nothing.

"That's what made me suspicious about this place. You know, Dirk, the wankers in there might be dangerous. Where there's loads of money being hidden in the walls, there's powerful people. And powerful people have guns. Power is in guns then the money and then the guns again. What I'm saying is that there might be gun play."

"What kind of wankers are there in the Beach House?"

"Exceptional. Wankers. I think our new Dad is breaking the law big time."

"We should tell The Mater."

"What is she going to do? Divorce this wanker and marry some other wanker? Why are you laying down?"

"I'm tired. It's hard to walk in sand."

I stretched out beside him.

"You don't like The Mater much do you, Theo?"

"I judge people by their actions. She's a light weight indulgent. Hence, the stupid marriage decisions. The only reason I think she's our biological mother is the size. Gilgamesh."

"She's not an angel, for sure. If I didn't protect the puppets, she'd burn them. You think she was like Bettina when she was her age?"

"Bettina? What do you mean?"

"She's an angel. You like her, right?"

"Let's just say I'm drawn to her."

"Like Juanita?"

"I told you before. It's different. I'm not happy about it. I'd like to get her out of my mind. She's 15. How interesting can she be?"

"She's not going to like you, right?"

"What do you mean?"

"When she gets to know you."

"That's probably not going to happen. Her getting to know me. So, I'm not going be hurt about it."

"Remember that barmaid you told me about? The one you told you were twenty?"

"I don't remember. Let's go. We have to take some photos of what's going on in there."

"We're going in there to take some photos?"

"What did you think we were going to do? We can't just barge in there, guns blazing."

"We have guns? I mean you have a gun? I mean that gun? You found some bullets?"

I ignored the question.

"If we barge in there, guns blazing and a shootout occurs, shoot for the knees."

"But I don't have a gun."

"Let's say one wanker in there starts pumping an Ed Brown special forces and another wanker has got a Smith & Wesson shorty."

"You know I saw Bettina on the beach today," Dirk told me. "Maybe she's in the Beach House now. You don't want to shoot her by accident. You would never get over it if you accidentally killed the girl you're in love with."

"It's not love. It's some kind of magical attraction. Anyway, I was watching her when she was on beach earlier. She went home."

"You were stalking her? Did she have that bikini on?"

"Yeah. She calls it a two piece. Two pieces too many really."

"I think she's staying here for the summer. Wait. I heard voices just a second ago. Behind us. Maybe those private conductors you told me about."

"Private conductors? And who might that be, Dirk?"

"Train conductors that drive private trains and moonlight as private cops to pay the monthly nut. You said Mr. Fartsworth had an army of them on the place. To keep the thievish out. And The Pubic."

I did want Fartsworth to know I was on to him, but I didn't want my brains knocked out listening to Dirk.

"Just concentrate, Dirk. If you recall, I have a plan. Get up. Let's go."

"So, what's the plan again?"

"We assert the Natural Law which states when all others are shot to hell and what is coveted remains, you, a passing stranger, are entitled to all of it. Like a salvage at sea."

We were several yards from the Beach House when a shot was fired at us. I pulled Dirk down, face down in the sand.

"Whoa!" Dirk exclaimed. "What the fyuck?"

"That sounded like a Moss Long 500," I said, crouching low.

"Is that a gun or a guy?"

"Then again Moss Long doesn't fit the profile. I mean the profile of the Moss Long does not fit that Beach House. The whole damn estate. Private contractors wouldn't fire once from a window and then duck. They'd rush us pumping those automatics with a lot of hoopla like they did in that Nisour massacre in Iraq. Besides, a Moss Long 500 with a magnum load would have torn up the sand. What we got here is a .32 S&W long cartridge. Or maybe a Smith & Wesson Shorty. Besides, it fits the profile of a Wall Street inside trader, which is what we've got in that house. Or maybe a millennial tech billionaire with 5G. A whole pack of them doing their laundry. We could be facing a private equity mob."

"Are they bad?"

"Not as bad as the Hedge fund mob."

"They're in there too?"

"Who do you think would be in a place worth say 50 million? These people shoot from cover. No reckless advance. Wait us out."

"I don't know. I keep thinking about Bettina being in there."

"Bettina? You're kind of stuck on her too, aren't you? No, brother, that's poor profiling, no offense. If she knew we were out here, she'd shout to us to come on in and join the fun. But guess what? There's no fun in there. Only dark, evil stuff. So, she's not there. Someone so lovely as her would not be in a place like that."

"Maybe she's like that siren you said sang people to their death?"

"Calypso? She'd have to be a naughty 15-year-old. That ain't real, brother."

"She's not real?"

"She's 15. How real can she be? We need to go to plan B, which is to kick the door open and go in shooting."

"That's the plan? I mean the B one?"

"Figure it out. Whoever is in there shot at us which means they could shoot anybody who just wanders along the beach. I don't have to tell you that the country's seriously divided. Am I wrong here?"

"You mean in that house?"

"All over. Dirk. We're on a coast. Long Island Sound. We're surrounded by Coastals. What if some Rust Belt people wandered in? Or Red Necks? Or Fly Overs? Or Montana Militia or any of the survivalists living in bunkers out there in the desert waiting for the Communist Coastals to show up?"

"So, the people in there . . ."

"Let's just say what we've got in there are several thieves from Wall Street. We've got to accept the fact that the Metaverse has created a neuro-totalitarianism and the financial sector's domination of ordinary life pulls us all into murder and destruction in the name of Le ROI. The King."

"When did we get a king?"

"Those people in that mansion the Mater trapped us in are all heavily beveraged. Inside traitors. I tell you, Dirk, it makes me sick."

"You didn't like The Lab much either."

"Well, I don't like anything much, Dirk. I find more to dislike each and every day. Can you handle the safe?"

"The safe?"

"They've got a safe loaded with goodies. A safe is mandatory in the Hamptons. You can't leave the family jewels back in the penthouse. We are here to loot, brother. Which is not looting because it was already looted. We are re-districting. We fill up that sailboat and make our escape."

"You mean *The Lee Shore*?" Dirk said pointing to the sloop tied to the dock about a quarter of a mile away.

"We are not giving up, Dirk. What we have here is a kind of chess game in which we figure out the sequence of elimination. We must figure that given the state of animalosity in the country that those people in that house have drawn guns. If we wait long enough, they'll all eliminate each other."

"Maybe it was an accident," Dirk said. "The bullet."

I was about to answer when another shot whistled over our heads.

We both ducked, sticking our faces in the sand. It felt damp and cool.

"I'm scared," Dirk whined.

"A crippled effort at best, Dirk. I say we work our way from either side of the house, get to the windows and have a look see and then play it by ear from that point. You've got the gun I gave you?"

"The one you gave me for my birthday? That broke."

"I think we might have opened the safe in there. Where they keep the money they're going to launder."

"You think there's a lot?"

"They're billionaires, aren't they?"

As I headed in one direction and Dirk the opposite, Dirk stopped.

"What's Plan C if things go to shite?"

I pointed to the sailboat.

"Get to that."

Before I let Dirk respond, and he was pondering those words, I was crouching my way to one side of the house. Dirk crouched and made his way in the opposite direction, fully expecting a bullet whistling over his head.

Honestly, I was surprised that there were people in that Beach House and that they were shooting at us. Uncanny stuff. I was out here on a spoof just to see Dirk shite his pants. Now it seemed we had stepped into the real, the alternative real.

And so, as Dirk predicted things went to shite, but Plan C did work because we got to the boat. In a hail of bullets. Just as a storm was brewing. There was no storm in the forecast. In fact, there hadn't been this kind of storm since The Great Gatpeas had a party.

CHAPTER NINE

RUNNING WITH THE WIND

Dirk's brain may be a little shaky on land, but if you put it in water...nothing weird. I mean on salt water, preferably blue water...and he's a better sailor than that bloke who sailed around the world in *The Spray*, no more than a 37-foot boat, which, oddly, is the size of *The Lee Shore*, the one Dirk and yours truly are being tossed around in right now.

"You realize, Dirk that we're not sailing along the coast but being blown out to sea?"

"Whoa!" Dirk yelled. "We're running with the wind! This will take us all the way to Europe!"

Ever since he was a kid, Dirk went kind of what we called water crazy, among other craziness.

"This is a serious storm blowing up, Bro'!" I yelled back, looking up at him through the open doors of the berth.

Minutes before I had been making fast but unsteady runs to the starboard side and retching and then an icy wind swept across my body. Then my whole body was wave washed.

"We're going to capsize!" I screamed.

"Not today," Dirk shouted back. "Let's die at sea! It's the best!"

He rushed up to me, running like a half back down a crowded field.

"I slowed us down with a 45-degree rudder angle to windward," he yelled in my ear. "Kind of a heaving to. Like telling the sea gods Whoa! Time out. Let's just rest here a bit. Smoke down time. Which turned out alright because we got picked up by lee shore winds sweetly blowing us to all those lights getting brighter and brighter."

"You realize, Dirk, that we're not sailing along the coast but being blown out to sea?"

I paused.

"I said that already, didn't I?"

"Whoa!" Dirk yelled. "We're running with the wind! This will take us all the way to Europe! Get ready to fill a cajoli, brother!"

I let my mind ignore the Deja Vue of things. We were about to drown so reruns didn't matter. I think Dirk meant cannoli. He liked them.

I took myself to the security below deck where there were two disheveled bunks, a propane stove, and no stores at all, not even water.

I lay back on one of the disheveled bunks and imagined Bettina hearing that I had drowned at sea. I imagined her lovely eyes filling with tears.

"I should have told him I loved him," she moaned.

I heard Dirk yell for me to get on deck. My fate was in his hands. Can you believe it?

Dirk was at the stern, holding tight to the tiller, wind and waves battering the boat with water now sloshing over the gunwales at a terrific rate.

"Bail!" Dirk yelled to me. "We're taking on too much ocean! Not good, brother. Not good!"

I stepped on to the deck, quart pot in hand and was immediately flung to starboard, hitting the gunwale hard and clawing and banging the deck with the pot in my hand.

"You need something bigger! Take the tiller while I furl the jib."

In response, I leaned over the side, took a wave right in the face and retched. The pot in my hand went overboard. Dirk made his way to the jib sail, released the halyard and pulling in jerks managed to pull it down and slid it out of its groove. With the sail top in hand, Dirk disconnected it from its halyard fitting. He then scrambled his way to the main mast, grabbed hold of its halyard, wrapping it to the winch and lowered the sail half-way.

You see, I had taken sailing classes with Captain Joey, and I knew everything there was to know about water, wind, and sail, but I never got my sea legs. I had what Captain Joey called Permanent Landlubber Limbs. I also had Chronic Mal de Mer. I had this thought: I should have stayed there taking bullets from whoever was in the Beach House and not jumped on *The Lee Shore*. Plan C.

Plan Capsized.

When Dirk made his way back to the tiller, he found me sitting in water up to my waist, one hand stretched out holding the tiller. Dirk took the tiller from me and shouted:

"Bail!"

I looked up at him. I was drenched to the bone as was Dirk. I waited for a capsizing wave to sweep across both of us, before I yelled back:

"We're going to die!"

"Less sail in the jib," Dirk shouted, laughing. "Full sized main. Brother, we're gonna ride these waves. Bail like a son of a bitch! Whoa!"

I sat there, jaw dropped, amazed at how my inferior brother was kicked up to heroic levels by wind, sail, and waves.

CHAPTER TEN

TIME IS IN THE SKY

I woke up in total darkness. I heard water sloshing all around me. I took a deep breath. Air. I was alive. It was night.

I found Dirk on deck, smoking some weed. He passed to me.

"We're alive," I croaked. "How come?"

"Mr. Patawalla was swept away."

"What? Oh, the hand puppet.

"Maybe it was just his time. Now he's timeless. Makes me less sad."

I noticed lights in the distance.

"Lights."

"Shore lights."

"England?"

"Montauk Point."

"Any water? I mean drinkable."

Dirk shook his head.

"We kind of launched in a hurry. No booze, sandwiches or water."

"We don't have any alcohol, do we?"

Dirk shook his head.

"We left without it. Why was it we left?"

"Plan C," I told him.

"And Plan A and B were?"

"We go to the windows for a looksee. And then we play it by ear depending on what we see."

"So, what did you see Theo?"

"You mean in the Beach House? I had my face in the sand. Bullets were flying."

Dirk had another hand puppet out. I think it was Juanita.

"I think that's the point, Juanita. See? Montauk Point. Or it could be the light from a buoy. Or another boat. You know if that was a rocky coast with sand bars and reefs of rock, coral and sand and no harbor and riptides smashing you into jagged sea wall and breakwater jetties. . ."

He paused.

"Can you swim, Juanita? Mr. Patawalla was swept overboard. He drowned."

"What did you see back at the Beach House, Dirk?"

"I might have heard a Mexican asking a Cuban to raise his hands and hit the floor, face down. I don't understand Spanish. Then I heard a Neo-Nazi from the evening news tell somebody to shoot somebody. It might have been a woman's voice."

"What the hell are you talking about? What woman?"

"Not German. She sounded kind of Southern belle type. Like a Dixie chick kind of chick. Sweet natured more than harsh and nasty. Kind of naïve, like an engine knue. Not mean at all. Sounded like Bettina."

"You mean an ingenue? Look, I told you. She wasn't there. What we ran into was Fartsworth's crew warning us off. He knows I'm getting into his illegals. I'm ready to go to the FBI with what I know."

"I remember you yelling out something like that."

"What? I didn't yell anything out. Except let's make a run to this boat. Tell me, was it a fat or thin voice you heard?"

"Fat but muffled. No, wait. Thin, but meaty. Kind of a hash rye, lower East Side voice. Like Dr. Wrong has."

"You're thinking of a sandwich, aren't you?"

"Yeah, a Rueben. With mustard."

"Listen. Don't tell that Dr. Wrong squat. She'll get me sent to prison and you to a looney farm."

"Did you hear somebody shout, 'Get Alphonso!'"

"No, I didn't hear that. I told you I didn't hear voices. Just shots. Who's Alphonso?"

"The Puerto Rican."

"So, you heard a Mexican, a Cuban and a Puerto Rican? How come I didn't hear any of that back there at the Beach House? In any language. Not one voice. Tell me, Dirk, did you take your meds anytime in the last week?"

"The Pater always said you hear what you want to hear. He meant you."

"And you never hear the bullet that gets you," I snapped back. "And it's not over until the fat lady sings. If you want to go fast, go alone. If you want to go far, go together. I told you a hundred times. All those Post-Docs do in P. T's Lab is smoke dope and make up wise ass shit. Listen, you say those lights ahead are a big boat?"

"Or land. If it's land, we're on a lee shore, which is dangerous. If it's a big boat, we need to go around it."

"Can you handle any of that?"

"You know, Theo, I'm kind of attracted to Bettina."

"Yeah, I know. You think she's an angel."

"I could see back there at the Beach House that you were thinking the same thing."

"If I was, it flew away. I was on the run to this boat at that point. At which time I ran into you, and we set sail for a storm in the middle of the Atlantic."

"You know the closer we get to those lights, the more I think those are shore lights. A lee shore is a terrible danger to a boat. If a boat drifts too close to shore, tide and wind could run it aground or on a jetty of rocks."

"I could use a drink, Dirk. I've got full confidence in you. You know why? Because I sure as fuck don't know why."

"Not to worry. We've got Captain Joey with us."

He pulled a hand puppet out of someplace. Yeah, it did look like Captain Joey. Beady eyes, red cheeks, white whiskers. Another fucking drunk.

"Look there!" Dirk shouted at the helm. "Looks bad."

"There? Where? It's bad everywhere."

"Wind, waves and time," Dirk shouted.

I scrambled to him at the helm.

"Time is in the sky. See that darkness. There."

I looked up at the sky. Night sky. No Moon. Stars.

"Lie ahull," Dirk whispered, conspiratorially, still looking at the sky. "We need to drop the sails and let the boat fare for itself."

"What? Hey, Dirk, these waves here seem to want to be big. Very big."

"We're far enough from land and shipping channels so that it doesn't matter how far the boat drifts downwind."

"What's that?"

"We are far enough. Time maybe to get closer to land and anchor. If we lie ahull and the waves are large and breaking, there's a risk of the boat being rolled and capsizing because we'll be lying broadside to the waves."

"This is one of those perfect storms?" I said, wondering what the fuck was perfect about something that was going to kill us.

"I need to turn her close to the wind," Dirk shouted. "Furl and backwind the jib. Theo, stand by the helm and lock it into position."

"What?"

"We need to keep the boat pointed close enough to the wind so that it is less likely to be rolled by a breaking wave."

"Breaking wave?"

Dirk ignored me. He was already busy furling the jib. I didn't think he could move that fast. Or think that fast. It was like the waves, the storm, and the boat kicked up his IQ.

For the second time, I realized I was doing a lot of Deja Vue. I had PTSD.

"Dirk! Listen. I don't understand. What are you doing? What am I supposed to do?"

"The downwind sliding motion of the hull produces a slick in the water that makes it less likely for a wave to break on the boat," Dirk shouted.

I was configuring the physics here when a heavy true storm-force wind suddenly rose, smacked me hard like a Man Mountain Dean full body slam and swept me overboard.

BOOK TWO

CHAPTER ELEVEN

THE FOUR UNIVERSAL UNWHOLESOME MENTAL FACTORS

I think from the beginning Bettina saw me as a self-inflated ego, tall variety, even though I did what I could to convince her that what she said was all justified, that I agreed with it all, but that I would change. The more I tried to change, the deeper the hole I dug.

The birthday card I sent her today respected her wish: "No gifts, no money, no promises -- Just what you wanted --- a thought." Theo. And inside I wrote "To Bettina on her last teenage year."

I had been studying classics and ancient history at the Sorbonne for the past four years, taking time off frequently to bum around Europe. Fartsworth would never have supported me, but that wanker croaked, and The Mater married his accountant kind of financial adviser slime ball who cooked the books for "private equity," a slum fund manager consortium of slimeballs fully loaded cartel syndicate. I think the accountant, Richard Port, whom I dubbed Jabba because he really looked like that alien blubber in *Star Wars*, married my mentally disheveled Mater to nullify her as a witness.

Why did Jabba pay my freight in Europe? He wanted to nullify me as a witness. I promised to keep quiet about what I knew had gone on at the Beach House. Of course, I knew nothing of that but imagined much.

However, I ran the whole catalogue of what I imagined. Told him I was MENSA and so the authorities would believe I had the facts, the evidence, all the details.

I rolled out my usual Walt Whiteman catalog:

"Cheque fraud, credit card fraud, mortgage fraud, medical fraud, corporate fraud, securities fraud, including insider trading, bank fraud, insurance fraud, market manipulation, payment point of sale fraud, health care fraud; theft; scams or confidence trickery; tax evasion; bribery; sedition; embezzlement; identity theft; money laundering; and forgery and counterfeiting, including the production of Counterfeit money and consumer goods."

We were in his private study. He was on a Louis Quatorze, and I was rocking an overstuffed that Wilston Churchchill had dozed on.

"You get that off *Wickedpedia*?" he blubbered. He had the kind of lips that had to blubber, collagen rich.

"I've got a lot of evidence," I told him. "I've got the mind of Sheetrock Homes. I've followed the clues. Deductive. Inductive. And so forth. I've been in this household a long time. Two three years. I bugged the whole house. Got six million photos on my phone. I robbed the mail. In short, I got factoids. I could go to GPS right now and send a delivery to the Adenoid General's office.

He laughed.

"I got a better idea. Why don't you go off somewhere, get lost and I pay all your bills? Consider it a lifetime pension. Just don't come back."

I came back. Later. How much later I can't tell you because ever since I washed up on shore at Montauk Point and no one could tell how long I had been in the water, time telling went screwy with me. When I looked in the mirror, I sometimes saw a guy short of thirty and sometimes a guy on a pension. Time was no longer in the sky. It was in my face. Variably.

I had been calling and texting and emailing and snail mailing Bettina in all that time. Certainly years, not decades though. Never got a message back but I didn't deflate. Time had elapsed but my love was still strong. I wondered if time could elapse without you being aware that it was elapsing?

"What are you doing back here?" Jabba blubbered at me on my first day back.

Same chairs. He looked very old. I might have been in the water longer than I had figured. He definitely looked like he had been in the water, dragged out and toe tagged.

"I graduated. I'm post."

"You can't be post over there? You have to come back here to be post? You can't be post in Paris?"

"I've been living in Hondarribia, pais vasco.

"That's where people catch it," he replied, rubbing his groin.

"It's not an STD. It's a geographical location. Tell me, why is my mother still called Mrs. Farnsworth?"

I was going to say and not Mrs. Jabba.

"Because I'm Richard Farnsworth. We decided to keep the name. My name Port doesn't mean squat. Like Bratter. Doesn't mean squat. Insignificant names."

"My Pater has got some patents pending," I told him, not knowing whether this was so but figuring The Pater probably did have some patents pending. "He could win a Nobelly."

"You know, kid, everything's changed around here. What you think you had on us? Don't mean a thing now. All our assets are squeaky clean."

"So, you're cutting me off?"

"Yeah, and stay away from Dickel's step-daughter. She's gonna marry a sludge fund manager. Kid about your age plus twenty. Plus, twenty million."

He laughed, a kind of slobber laugh. Still too much lip collagen.

I must admit that news about the love of my life and a sludge fund manager was totally deflating.

I found Dirk living in the *pied a terre* in the New Utrecht section of Brooklyn. I had funneled some of Jabba's money to pay his rent as well as the beggarly lifestyle that was his. Jabba had kicked him to the curb years before. Either Dirk commits himself to an asylum willingly or hits the road.

Dirk was the same. I mean we were twins. But I hadn't seen him in four years. We measure a straight six foot six now, but he was a couple stones heavier than me. The *pied a terre* smelled like feet, unwashed laundry, fried cod, and urine. There was entirely too much *terre* on the shredded rugs. Dust hung on everything but the hand puppets which he kept active.

"Where's Cag?" he asked, from his location on his bed. I had the overstuffed chair with the stuffing coming out.

"He's in quarantine. He's in jail. He told a Custom's guy to go fuck himself."

"I thought parrots had freedom of speech? Aren't they like

persons under the U.S Constipation?"

"Only if they incorporate. He'll be out soon. I see you got a parrot hand puppet."

"That took me awhile," he said, looking over at the multicolored widget beak perched on a shelf alongside about fifty others. "You think a person can transmigraine into a puppet?"

I thought about that.

"You don't see Dr. Wrong anymore?" I asked.

"She got departed, I think. I do talk to Padre Balsio over at *The New Pompey*. He was a Cadlick priest but they defrogged him."

"What's he say about transmigraining into a puppet?"

I was genuinely curious.

"He doesn't say anything about that. Mr. Patawalla was the one. Remember when he told you that in the next life, you might not make it into human form."

"I think he was talking about you. Besides, who would listen to a guy who wears your mother's underwear?"

"Padre Balsio says there's only one God, but he's divided into three other gods."

"I can see why he got defrogged."

Dirk and I were twelve when Mr. Patawalla gave us a religion, not the same one for the both of us is what I found out because Dirk was on a totally different reception path than me.

"What are the four universal unwholesome mental factors, Mizra Doke?"

He meant Dirk; he called me Mizra Wiseass or just plain Theode.

Dirk racked his brain. He had a hard time memorizing words. He had an action memory. Such as: "Then I went there and after that I saw this and then it started to rain and then I went inside." Or "The thing of it is when the thing gets bigger than some things, that thing goes away.

"The first is seclusion," Dirk finally came up with.

I started to giggle but I put a hand over my mouth. These exchanges between tutor guru and my brother were priceless.

"And what the gotham mudderfolk is that?" Mr. Patawalla shouted. He had two levels of interrelationship. Sweetly enlightened and raging profanity. He crossed over from one to the other quicker than a bi-polar with a thin borderline.

I could see Dirk looking over at one of his puppets hanging on a hook nearby. They weren't allowed in the classroom.

"That's when you believe you are alone but you're really not."

Mr. Patawalla's face was contorting.

"And why the gotham mudderfolk is that a universal unwholesome mental factor, Mizra Dork?"

"You called it that," Dirk mumbled.

I came to Dirk's rescue as I often did.

"I'm stuck on the what the difference is between torpor and sloth, Mr. Patawalla? Which one is more unwholesome?"

Mr. P. turned his attention to me. Mizra Wise Ass. He also knew that I knew he was wearing the Mater's underwear.

"You are going to reappear as a cockroach, Mizra Wiseass," he said to me, cobra venom spitting.

"Why would that happen? I possess the 25 beautiful mental factors."

And then I recited them, to Mr. P's great loathing of my superiority.

"Faith, mindfulness, shame a doing evil, regard for consequence, lack of greed, lack of hatred, neutrality of mind, tranquility of mental body, tranquility of consciousness, lightness of mental body, lightness of consciousness, malleability of mental body, malleability of consciousness, wieldiness of mental body . . ."

"Mudderfolk! Shut up!" Mr. P screamed. "You are mocking the Theravāda Abhidhamma tradition. This will be reported to your parents."

"Not to the Mater. She won't like you wearing her panties. And the Pater won't like you teaching us a religion. You're supposed to be teaching us The Mathematics and not wearing the Mater's panties."

That sent Dirk into a paroxysm of laughter as was proportionate to the lightness of his consciousness.

CHAPTER TWELVE

TOTAL BOLLYWOOD

"Want to come to a play with me?" I asked Dirk on one of my visitations after I had gotten back from my Oxford outing. "Get you out of this dump."

"We can stop off at the *Pompey* afterward," he said, happily.

I don't think he got out much. The Angeloni's, who owned the building, seemed shady to me. Especially the wife. She looked like she wanted to snuff her husband out with a pillow. Just an impression I got. Dr. Fraud had said my globular lobular whatever was filled with dark affinities and dark imaginaries. In short, I darkened the landscape, a kind of twilight filter built into my cornea.

That was a fateful night out.

Dirk met a small, fiery demon there. Evangeline Solly. And for the rest of his life, she twisted his balls in the winds of time, chance, and fuck all.

She did a smash trash mouth radio show and she got Dirk drawn into it. Turned out, he had an over the air waves vocal presence. Rich, deep, sexy baritone was the way Eve Solly put it. She used him like a punching bag, and I suppose the listeners loved all that.

Things had changed in Bettina's life too. Dickel had divorced her Mom and moved in with a girl about Bettina's age. Her mom got shafted by Dickel's lawyers and thus kicked to the curb. Along with

Bettina. So, at nineteen, Bettina had plunged into working class Brooklyn's world of hard knocks. Of course, the gentrified Brooklyn was busy knocking back Aperol Spritzes.

As I stood in the street looking up at the third floor where I knew she and her Mom lived, a section of Boro Park not ever to be gentrified, I thought the poor kid was so down on her luck, though I knew she had that job on Wall Street.

I had heard from others who worked in the same building that avid and horny young brokers and traders were drawn to her like bees to honey. I imagined she was game for those pussy wankers as well as her bosses or any tottering slime fund manager who came along. What I imagined now was that she was engaged to one of those rich wankers looking for a trophy wife.

I would have to rescue her.

"Remember me?" I said, getting in between her and the Uber at the curb. I figured she had called it.

She stepped back, surprised.

"Theo Bratter," I said, smiling.

She looked up at me. Not that she was short. She was tall. She had also filled out, as they say, nicely.

"What are you doing here?"

"I was at Oxford. For a while. Then bumming around Europe mostly. On Jabba's dime. Port. He married my mother."

"Right. Right now, I have to meet my fiancé."

"He'll keep," I said, like I was talking about last week's chicken salad. "Maybe not for long but he's got some time. I don't think you should get involved with him. He's about to be indicted for insider trading."

I didn't know that, but I figured he probably could be if he wasn't passing along inside info to the indicters.

"How do you know that? Why are you saying that?"

And then she rushed to the Uber and got in.

I don't know when that was, but she looked fine, *pace* time. It could have gone better but then again who seizes the present without any next day regrets?

The next time I saw the lovely Bettina she was older and more beautiful than ever. She hadn't married the elderly slime fund wanker. He had been sent up for insider trading.

I had been making a living touring budget grade, elderly pensioner Americans around Europe. I did none of the wet nursing but hired interns as needed from various universities that had hospitality management programs. In lieu of salary, I gave my interns sparkling recommendations signed by Theodorus Bratter, Une Maitrise, Sorbonne, Paris, France.

I also owned a *laverie automatique* near the Institut Pasteur in Montparnasse. I had lifted some valuable *objets d'art* the last time I was allowed in the Farnsworth domain which when fenced brought me the laverie. Why that? I don't know. I was confused. I was totally in the grip of *la belle dame* sans *merci*. Bettina. Bettina Parisi. I thought she would admire my clean living, hence the laverie.

At some point in time, I realized it was futile trying to seek her admiration. The thought came to me that all I needed was a girlfriend in Paris. To break the enchantment. As soon as that thought came to me, I instantly rejected it and I flew back to the States, to Brooklyn. To Bettina. At twenty-two.

"Did you get the five hundred post cards I sent you?" I asked her, as I stood there as she exited the bank where she worked on Wall Street.

"I gave them to an antique dealer," she told me, walking briskly passed me.

"You hungry? I can take you to a French restaurant where you can watch me order in French."

"You don't change, do you?"

"I know the food. They wouldn't take a chance and serve us a faux dish. Come on. I flew four thousand miles to see you."

"I'm meeting someone. Fly back."

I ran after her.

"Was it you shooting at me and Dirk from the Beach House?"

She stopped. Stunned.

"What are you talking about?"

"I didn't think so. It was years and years ago. By the way, don't meet him. Whoever he is. Come and have *confit de canard* with me. You'd rather eat a duck than listen to him, no?"

She took off again. This time I just stood there and watched her go. I was not very good at seizing the moment. I would lie awake all night writing the lines I should have used.

I was once again waiting for her outside her bank. I don't know what she did there, but I was sure she did it compassionately. Not like a compassionate conservative but face to face sweetly. I had all manner of beautiful personal traits with which I imaginatively endowed her. It's what you do when you hunger. When you yearn for what you've seen once and now deprived, imagine there with you.

Right now, I see her come out of the glass doors, down the monument like steps and down to the street where I am waiting. I wasn't surprised to see she was being accompanied.

But I was annoyed. Three men. Tall, dark overcoats, no hats, all young wankers, all smiling, chattering away on both sides of her. She was smiling, talking, laughing. It wasn't what I expected. I thought that away from me, she'd be sad. Triste.

I confronted them at the bottom of the steps, big enough to block their way.

"Come with me to Paris, Miss Parisi. You've got the name for it."

"I wish you would please leave me alone," she said, her smiling face gone.

"Who is this?"

"He follows me."

One of her escorts, put out an elbow shutting me off from getting closer to her.

"What are you doing?" she asked.

"I'm looking at you, Bettina. Even when you're not here, I'm looking at you."

She started to say something and then just gave one shake of her head, such an unsure shake of her head. A movement only. I could see in her eyes as she then looked at me that we'd go far because, as been said, you go far together. You go fast but you're alone. We both didn't want to be alone. We wanted to be together.

"I wish you would please just go away."

Two of the men on either side of her put their arms around her and said, "Let's go then Bettina."

The other one put himself squarely in front of me.

"She said please," he said to me. "So, leave her alone."

She walked away.

"We used to be in love," I told him. "We couldn't be apart. When we were apart, we spent all our time hungering to see each other again. We spent more time locked together on the beach at the Beach House than you can imagine. The tide was low and then came in and we were still there. Locked."

He was looking at her and his friends crossing the street.

"I envy you," he said. "And then you lost her? What happened? She grew up. You didn't?"

I was looking at her and her escorts crossing the street.

"I got taller."

"I guess you got to put your big boy pants on and get over it. Or get a better game. Every one of us can take her to Paris for a weekend."

I redirected my attention to his face. It had no diversity in it.

"Take her?"

"Invite her. To lots of things. She doesn't accept. So far, we're like you. But then again, we didn't love her when she was a teenager. I can only imagine."

"They're getting into a cab. Your friends."

"Not a problem. I know where they're going. We're celebrating her birthday. I'll catch up. So, you want to bring her back to those days on the beach?"

I hesitated, then nodded. I guess that was the whole of it. Besides showing her I was better than I had been, though I couldn't swear to it.

"I know she thinks about me. But it's very difficult to figure out what that lady is thinking. She's not an open book. In fact, if she were a book, she'd be encrypted."

"Seems to me her message to you was pretty clear."

The words didn't say what her eyes revealed. I didn't tell him that.

"I was in the water a long time," I told him. "Then they pulled me out."

I didn't wait for his response to that but just walked away.

There was a big party at The Beach House on her sixteenth birthday. I wasn't invited but as the Beach House was part of the Farnsworth estate and I was a scion of that privilege, I just showed up.

I persuaded Dirk to dress exactly like me so while attention was on him -- and it would be if I knew Dirk -- I would wander off with Bettina.

She was bare foot playing with the tide coming in when I found her, hair blowing in the breeze. She was also tipsy.

She told me I hadn't been invited.

"You know," she said, pointing a finger at me and at the same time losing her balance a little as the tide swept and swirled around her ankles.

I reached out to steady her.

I started to say some very unmemorable stuff. Total Bollywood.

"I would never wind up with you," she told me, defiantly, kind of vehemently. "If I did, I would not know why I wound up with you. I would say 'How did I ever wind up with you?'"

"You're sixteen," I told her. "Why are you talking like fifty years ahead?"

She sputtered. I should have come to the party sooner before she drank the punch.

"That's when it starts," she then told me.

"What starts?"

"I don't want to talk about it."

"Okay. You want to go in for a swim?"

"I'm not taking this dress off," she told me, backing away, toward the ocean, the water now up to her calves. She had beautiful, shapely calves, the rarest gift of Eve.

At that moment, a clown came from nowhere, the kind Shakesbeer calls lunatics. A short, muscle man, the kind who inhabited the Hamptons the way horseshoe crabs did.

"Were you trying to rip her dress off?" he said to me, coming up close to me. his head my abdomen height.

I pushed him off.

"I'm black belt, kiddo," he yelled and sprung a foot up and into my chest. I grabbed his ankle and twisted him off balance and he fell in the sand and was instantly breaded.

When I turned to see how Bettina was taken it, I saw her jogging, knees high into the surf and in no time, she was under water.

I rushed into the surf. When I reached her, she threw her arms around my neck, coughed, laughed and spit water in my face, all of which naturally led to my kissing her. She had her legs wrapped around my hips, and her mouth pressed on mine. I would have let her go if I felt any resistance but there was none. I was enchanted but I wasn't a creep. She was drunk enough to kiss any rescuer. She might even have mistaken me for that clown, even though I couldn't conceive how that could be possible. But then she looked at me as if she were searching for something in my eyes and at the same time telling me something with hers.

After that one time, we found each other almost every day, our hideaway dunes near the Beach House. Even back then I wasn't so much of a know it all not to realize that the Goddess Fortuna played a big role in our lives. I accepted it. I hadn't done anything special to win the love of Bettina and from the very beginning I thought there was more about me that Bettina didn't like than she liked.

There was nothing much to like about me was what Dr. Fraud had told me, but I never cared. Now, I was thrilled that Bettina liked me, loved me.

It was as if I had gone to Heaven, by which I mean the place where I projected Bettina, myself, and my love for her. You know, the eternal place. That's all it's ever been. Not pie, a thousand virgins or harps playing, or basking in God's presence, but no more than what Dante wrote, "Love, that moves the sun and the other stars."

Then that summer was over, her mother got divorced and left penniless, they both vanished, I blackmailed Jabba, went off to Europe, came back and searched for her. Found her many times, some of the times I've told you about.

By the time we were both in our twenties, there was distance between us. But also, there was something I've never been able to understand, no less explain. She was a mystery to me, and part of that mystery was knowing what I was to her. But I think now there was something that neither of us could grasp and she could never dissolve. I never tried. It wasn't anything either one of us could dissolve alone. I came to see it as a numinous intertwining. You can see it on the cover of this book.

CHAPTER THIRTEEN

WHAT IS REAL AND WHAT IS ILLUSION

I was back in the States, pursuing Bettina without much luck, and basically falling apart. I was in a Wallow state. I feared Bettina would marry someone else, have kids, get absorbed in their lives, give herself totally to someone who wasn't me, and so forget my existence totally. The only thing worse would have been if she had died before we had spent our lives together.

I was staying at Dirk's *pied a terre* not because I had a fondness for the aroma of food having gone bad or laundry composting under the bed or my twin's company.

What I liked was the convenience of the wallow. I could wake up around noon, not shower, go out and walk a couple of blocks to *The New Pompey*, drink a breakfast, listen to the dead souls coming in and out of the bar, listen to my brother's moronic radio talk show where the tormented and demented called in, asked those categories of questions, Eve Solly would rip them a new asshole each and every time, and my brother would voice any of his countless handmade hand puppets, all of which was supposed to enlighten but actually darkened lives quicker than sudden death.

Dirk and Eve drank themselves into the kind of morose sobriety that lies on the other side of drunk. I usually left *The Pompey* when they rolled in. I could take just so much. While I was staying at the *pied* the rule was, she wasn't allowed in the place. He could bang her in whatever hole in the ground she lived. I was paying the rent, so my word was the word. Besides Mrs. Angeloni didn't like Eve Solly. She called her a Circus Person and they were all thievish, degenerate, and hateful and there were a great many antique furnishings in the *pied* that Eve would walk away with.

I told that blow torch, Mrs. Angeloni, to shut up and as long as she was getting her rent, she should let my brother bring whoever he wanted into the *pied*. I told her she should decide if she wanted to be paid or be a fucking bigot. She didn't like me at all, but I didn't give two fucks. I told her husband not to turn his back on her. He told me he didn't, but she'd get him anyway. He was resigned to it. I never saw such fear, not even in a handful of dust.

Tonight, Dirk rolled in early. I was surprised and asked him what had happened to interrupt his degeneracy. He was sober too. The normal sober that comes naturally if you don't consume shit loads of alcohol.

"Mr. Maya and I went to see her."

"What? Her? Who? And who the friggin' is Mr. Maya?

I wasn't surprised when Dirk pulled a hand puppet out of his pocket. The puppet wore a tunic and had a towel around his head.

"We went to see Bettina. She thought I was you at first and she said there was no way she was going to let me in and then I introduced her to Mr. Maya, and she knew it was me and she let us in. We had tea. We had a long talk. Mr. Maya explained everything to her. Well, not everything. And he doesn't always tell you the truth. He only gives you as much truth as he thinks you can handle at that time."

"Let me get this straight," I said, sitting up in the bed. "You knocked on the former love of my life's door, held up that hand puppet and it talked to her and then she let you in and you had tea and the puppet explained something but not everything. And he doesn't always tell the truth. What part of this had to do with me?"

Dirk held up Mr. Maya in front of his face and began to do his voice throwing thing.

"Put that rag down or I'll put a match to him. What did you tell Bettina?"

"Mr. Maya told her . . . "

"Last warning."

Dirk hid Mr. Maya behind his back.

"She heard a story about this man who didn't know what he was doing was what he should really be doing and when he went to see an old relative of Mr. Maya who could say what was real and what was not, this old grandfather of Mr. Maya sent the man to get him some water because he was thirsty. Which he could find in the kitchen. When the man went into the kitchen, he found this beautiful young woman he immediately fell in love with, and she returned the favor, and they had a young romance so they both got married and twelve years went by, and they had children and lived on a farm way down in a hollow in the southern Appalachians. But in that twelfth year a torrential downpour that wouldn't stop flooded the whole hollow and the house was swept in a whirlpool of water with the man and his family on the roof until one and then the other child was swept off and then the beautiful young woman, who reached out to him to save her, was swept away also, as was he, born away on the swirling waters, struggling, drowning, and then disappearing into a dark unconsciousness. He wakes up on land, his arms wrapped around a log of wood, and seeing that he is alone, that he has lost everything, he wails and screams and cries in despair. Then he hears a familiar voice. The old grandfather of Mr. Maya: "Young man, where is the water I sent you for? I've been sitting here waiting for a half hour." The man is mystified and doesn't know what to say and the old grandfather of Mr. Maya says `Now you know what is real and what is illusion. One slips away, the other you live with.'"

I sat there. Perplexed. Stunned. Mind fucked. First of all, I didn't think Dirk could string together so many sentences. And for all the rest, this was the craziest narration that had ever come out of anyone's mouth, sane or not. Maybe the hand puppet had been talking?

"And this . .. this story . . . I mean how did Bettina react? What I'm trying to say is, she knew what the hell you were talking about?"

Dirk nodded.

"Mr. Maya thinks she has a very deep but quiet independence of mind able to see into the heart of things. He says she is very together."

"Words too? Because I have to tell you, bro', that story makes the Biblical Begettings look like it has a plot."

Dirk got up from his overstuffed and went to the tiny frig he kept on the floor.

"You want a sandwich? I think the bologna is still fresh."

I shook my head.

"Okay. She likes this whatever it is you tell her. And then what?"

"She said you should call her."

I swung my legs around and sat on the edge of the bed.

"Just like that? I should call her? Doesn't make any sense. How did she go from the nonsense you told her to tell me to call her? How did I even get into the conversation?"

Dirk brought a bag of rumpled bread, some old cold cuts in a plastic bag and a jar of mayonnaise to the small table, mostly occupied by crumbs and a circle of sitting, observing hand puppets. He had them all sitting there with their heads up and their big eyes looking at you. It was freaky I can tell you. He sewed them super-sized eyes because he said that Patawalla had told him that eyes were the windows to the soul. He wanted his puppets to express that. They didn't. They all looked like nightmare freaks resting their butts in nightmare alley.

Sometimes when I think I shared an egg with this guy, I get queasy.

"I don't know. When I asked Mr. Maya, he said he thought she liked the way you tried to save her when she was being swept off the roof in the flood."

My eyes opened wide. She liked the way? . . .

"She's probably thinking of the time I saved her from drowning," I said and then told Dirk that tale.

Mr. Maya wanted to know what happened to the fanatical I knocked down in the sand. That puppet had reappeared. This time I didn't mind. That rag had done me a good deed.

"Really?" I said, shaking my head at my brother. "You got to stop focusing on the chaff, brother "

"You should probably call her. I mean if you want."

"Yeah, that sounds about right since I've been trying to get back into her life for, like, ten years."

"I would call her. Take her to dinner. A romance language bistro."

And that's how Bettina Parisi got into my life again. I kind of expected I would wake up and she wouldn't be there, but it didn't happen. No illusion here. She loved me. She was mine. I was hers.

That took a bit more time and effort though. When I think I'm ready to hear the truth, I admit that I never knew to this day whether our time together was when I went to get that guy a glass of water --as that cockamamie Mr. Maya story went -- or when I got back and found out how time had passed in my life, not with Bettina but within an illusion that I had passed my life together with her.

That thought of illusion hurt me badly, deeply, nonstop.

CHAPTER FOURTEEN

ENCHANTMENT

The restaurant date didn't go well. You see, she was in the real world, and I was in the world I made.

To me, that didn't make a difference if the two of us were somehow bonded beyond any world. I wasn't mystical but there was something numinous going on when I looked at her.

"If I don't think your brother is crazy, then I'm crazy too? Is that it?" she said after I had given her a really comical account of the bullshit Mr. Maya had laid down filtered through the insane mind of my bro.

"Why are you staring at my bosom?"

"I wasn't. I was deep inside my own head. Was I? Apologies."

It was full. Her bosom. It had been fine when she was sixteen but now it was splendid. Maybe this wasn't true love. Maybe it was just Dimitri Karamazov's voluptuariness. But I wasn't imagining. Enchanted though. Pathetic but what can I say? You pursue your enchantment regardless of how much of a lying, self-deceiving piece of shit you are.

Bettina had soft brown eyes that were now staring at me.

"I think you are destroying your life," she said. "And you want to destroy mine too."

"Ready to order?"

I looked up at the waiter. He had told us his name was Jason. Or Jared. Justin. That was it. A J name. Maybe not. It might have been Zed. I always thought more people fit the name Zed than they themselves thought.

I was kind of surprised Bettina had accepted my dinner invitation because I didn't believe Mr. Maya had persuaded her. I mean what persuasive points had that puppet made on my behalf?

This restaurant was called *Animale Cattivo* but judging by the menu it was what I called Fusion-Tweezer-Squeeze Bottle Plate Garnish-Mediterranean, where Mediterranean meant no place and every place not Indiana.

After Aaron took our orders, some kind of salad for Bettina, scampi for me, I told her that I really couldn't get her out of my mind. All I thought about was that summer at The Beach House.

"The shooting?"

"No, not that. Was that real? I thought I imagined that. No, our secret hideaway. I think it was all pleasure in those beach days."

"I was a teenager. I had a crush. That happens. I regret it. End of story. We're opposites. The ones that fight and hate each other. Not the ones that attract."

She had on a soft yellow blouse, open neck and her honey-colored hair just touched her bare shoulders. She had a beautiful mouth. Her teeth showed stark white when she smiled. Her eyes shone when she laughed. I was seeing all of this right in front of me. I wasn't imagining it. But, still, I was enchanted. Enchantment is a strong filter of reality. It makes it sweeter like anisette in coffee.

I felt I needed a coffee.

"Arthur, could you bring us some coffee?"

"Of course. It's Axel, though. My name. Gender neutral."

My mind should have stayed with Bettina, with reaching her and showing her how much I liked her. But it didn't. It gets drawn to the dark side.

"Neutral? And when do you get into gear?"

He didn't like that.

"Ignore him," Bettina told the waiter.

"It's a personal choice," he told me flatly.

"Your biology goes along with that?"

That disgusted him.

"Biology is not determining, sir. It can be indeterminate."

"Drop it," Bettina pleaded.

"Look, don't get angry but I'm trying to think it through here. You're neutral in regard to who you want to fuck?"

Bettina stood up.

"I'm leaving."

"Don't. I apologize"

Kind of too late. She was going out the door.

I looked at the kid,

"Sorry. I'm in therapy. I'm told I have what's called a dog with a bone mind. It gets a hold of something, it doesn't let go."

He looked at me blankly. Behind that was real genuine loathing.

"It's also called a Scottish philosopher's mind on account of the way they worked an idea to death."

"Your lady friend left, sir."

"Yeah, I know. I'm out of control. I'm an unlikable guy. I can't drive the narrative of my own life in any way that would attract a reader. I mean one who only puts up with what they like. And that's normal I guess."

Let go I told myself.

The kid had already walked away.

I caught up with Bettina outside.

"This was a big mistake," she said, pulling away from me.

"I fucked up. I'm sorry. Look, Dirk must have said something that made sense, that brought you here. With me. The sarcastic guy."

"That boy, that waiter, he has a job. Do you have a job, Theodorus? What gives you the right to insult anyone? What did you do with all that Latin and Greek you learned wherever? It didn't make you human."

I laughed.

"You're right. It's all promising until it's clear no promises have been fulfilled. Too much time had elapsed I suppose and then sarcasm and nihilism slip in."

She had hailed a cab.

And then she was gone.

After countless attempts, I finally reached her days or maybe years later by phone.

I recall some of it, shards.

She told me why she had agreed to have dinner with me on that very unfortunate occasion.

"Your brother, who is so much not like you at all but so genuinely good. He convinced me."

"Mr. Patawalla said he was as good as bread. Common staple not stable."

I laughed at my own witticism. Dead air.

"Your brother said he was afraid you were going to miss

everything in your life, and it made him sad."

That kind of threw me back.

"He said that. You know he was thrown out of Princeton. And Jabba won't give him a dime. All he's got is that stupid radio show with that Circus person. I've been supporting him out of the largeness of my heart. I was at Oxford, you know."

I hear her laugh.

"I think all you did was give your sarcasm an English accent. And that circus person is Eve Solly I take it? Well, I like her."

"I haven't found that part of her to like," I quipped.

"That's malice. Your whole attitude is hostile. Cruel to others."

"I have nothing against her except she'll ruin Dirk's life."

"You just told me he doesn't really have much of a life. What is it that you do that's so much better?"

"Me? I live in Paris."

"You own a laundromat."

"I own more than one, actually."

"Eve told me you launder money for your step-father."

"What does she know? My brother thinks Jabba is a crook. I don't know where he got that idea. The man just kept the books for Fartsworth. He was a crook too is what Dirk thinks. I've come to see that millionaires may be crooks, but billionaires go way beyond being crooks. They've got superpowers. They exist in a meta-moral domain. The rest of us are clods compared to them. They go way beyond being beyond the law."

"One of those supermen kicked my mother to the curb."

"I will avenge you. Meanwhile, don't think badly of me."

"Actually, I don't think about you. But tell me. Why did you attack The Beach House? Eve told me that story. You were going to expose the man your mother had married after she left your biological father. You wanted to avenge him."

That made me laugh.

"You sound like my old shrinks. Fraud and Wrong. That Beach House stunt was just a teenage frolic. Good fun was all. Besides I thought you were there. That's all I remember doing that summer was look for you. And when I saw you, I had this yearning to just kiss you and hold you forever. Of course, then we did. And then it was like you died and were totally out of my life. One doesn't cease being enchanted when the enchanter is no longer present. One seeks. Continues to seek."

"And you're that one?"

"That's me. I've got a deep yearning. It's like always a *carpe diem* yearning. But I haven't been able to do that. I don't fully see the moment until after so it's more like re-see the day and just cry over not having seized it then. Just like you were there then, sitting across from me, and then you were gone. And I missed it. The moment. The day. You. We had that summer but now when I want it again, I can't have it. We had that dinner together but didn't go well. And I can't seize it now. But I re-see it repeatedly and I regret what I've lost."

"That's something like what your brother told me. You have delusions you think are a life. One with me. And then none of it will be true because you'll wake up."

"Yeah, I'm a sad case."

"Will you promise me something?

"To leave you alone?"

"To change. You need to change. Right now, you don't have an ounce of love and compassion for other people. It's all reserved for you. I don't see how you can say you're infatuated with me."

"I was infatuated when you were sixteen and we spent those afternoons in The Beach House. I'm into something now with you that's . . . It's like a kind of worship. And you're the idol. I can't get too far from you. It's sick. I'm not crazy about being like this. You don't think I'd rather have my life back? I'd leave you alone if I could."

I imagined she was giving me the kind of cold-eyed look Margaret Flatcher would give a welfare recipient.

"You don't talk about any of that with your friends, do you?"

"About what? Why would I? It's too damn embarrassing."

"The Beach House. I was a teenager. It's what teenage girls do. I let my emotions make me think you loved me, and I loved you. I regret that time. I had a lot of dream fantasies in my head."

I was impressed at how she kept coming back to the Beach House in her mind. I did too. Time didn't matter. We were both still there in our minds.

"Don't forget the hormones," I told her, trying to lighten things up. "I was nineteen. Mine were raging. You were super-hot in that bikini."

"It wasn't a bikini. It was a two piece. You told me you were seventeen. A year older than me."

"You were months away from sweet sixteen. I was months away from the two-decade mark. I had more game than you could resist is what it was. I was also 6'4" and I could lift you high out of the water and throw you into the waves. I had a lot of twenty-year-old male charisma. I was tanned like a Greek god. You couldn't resist me."

"Are you serious?" she said. "Really? You have no self-awareness at all. You were skinny and pale, and you had a sunburnt nose."

"I was tall though."

I heard her laugh.

"You're insentient."

"I know. It's not good, is it? I like to think of myself as like the guy who doesn't die, who doesn't lose his hair, whose face doesn't go potato. I like to think there's a certain charisma in my abrasive wit."

"Nobody enjoys it. I'll tell you that for your own good. You just seem so sad and lost. I wouldn't be talking to you now if Dirk hadn't told me that story. I don't want you to think your delusions are a real life. You need to become real and dis-enchant yourself.

Dead air as they say on my brother's stupid radio show.

"You can't have me. Again, if you think there was a first time. You need to move on."

CHAPTER FIFTEEN

CARPE DIEM

There are really a finite number of story plots.

Pay attention.

Love/Loss.   Together/Alone.   Present/Absent.   Right Now/Oblivion.

They all seem to be the same, or at least circle like sub-atomic particles around some nucleus, most important, but which I can't see or describe.

I didn't move on but somehow, we moved toward each other.

"I'm sorry about lying about my tour guide business in Europe. It wasn't anything like a business but more like a hanging around bus and train stations with a sign in the proper language that spelled out "Need a Tour Guide?""

Bettina seemed interested in that, more so than the launderettes. If she didn't marry one of the many Wall Street players, young, middle aged, single, married, old, divorced and so on that wanted her in their life, she would one day hire me as a tour guide in Europe.

"I don't think I will marry anyone like those you mention," she said, curtly. "That's all in your head. Not in mine. That's your big problem, isn't it? Assuming what's in your mind must be in others? First, I'm not a gold digger. You say you were infatuated with me and now I'm like the center fold of your life, but the truth is you don't see me at all. I'm like something you create in your own mind. And I can tell you that I'm different than any of that. I've always been different than what you thought I was. Even at 16. I wonder what kind of tour guide you can be when you don't seem to see what's there to be seen?"

I realized then that there's another story plot: Perception/Blindness.

Also, I always thought she was fifteen when I first met her.

I spent a lot of time thinking about seizing time as it was passing. Actually, before it passed. I can't even do it with a sentence.

You never seize the day. You may go back later, much later, and see the day for what it really was. Or you may not. But no one seizes the day as it goes on second by second, minute by minute, hour by hour to the last, the 24th. You seize it fifty or so years later when she's died and so you don't seize it at all. You get seized with regret and with a soul crushing awareness you let everything that wasn't there block your view of what was there. You weren't there to seize the day. Or your own life.

This was a Deja Vue thing with the *carpe diem* and the two piece but at some point in time, if time has a point, I thought Bettina had died, that she was dead, after a long life together. That she was dead, and I had her in my life but somehow missed noticing it.

At that point in time, I had a sense that I was losing it. I had lost her and now I was losing my mind. I had Perpetual Concussion arranged when my head hit those stones on a lea shore near Montauk Point.

You keep circling in one orbit, repeating the same stuff, revelations that like souffle have no shelf life.

"You could learn something from the twin brother you think is so much less than your glorious self," I now heard her say.

"You had something in mind? I mean besides him showing me how to sew a hand puppet together?"

"Here's a story for you," she said, "A young boy, very young boy is given a doll so when he has a baby someday, he'll know how to dress it, put diapers on and gently caress it to bring up a bubble and care for his baby as every good father should learn to do. The young boy has a doll because someday he is going to be a father, too and he has to learn how to do what fathers need to do."

I thought about that. I mean I thought about how that fit into our dinner conversation during our "I will make amends" dinner, which like the first hadn't been going well.

"I think you're right. Dirk had a hand puppet at a very early age. Commendatore Spinalzo gave it to him. A store bought one.

Spinalzo said the doll's name was Nosferatu, but Dirk just called it Tutu. I don't think he's planning on being a father though. I mean he might, but he told me that Eve Solly told him that if she got preggers, she'd abort the fetus and my brother at the same time. She's a cold-blooded little witch. He asked me how she could do that to him, and I told him I didn't know the details of that way of killing somebody, but she looked to me like she could manage it and then go for coffee, so he better stay alert."

"I would never have children with you," Bettina said, calmly, looking me in the eyes, all business as if I had asked her to have children with me.

"We could marry and see how it goes," I suggested.

"To bring your children up as compassionate, loving, aware humans I'd have to keep you out of their lives. It would be a struggle because your noise, your voice sucks the oxygen out of growing minds. You can't make a nihilist out of a two-year-old."

"I would love them as much as I love you," I told her sincerely. "If they were precious to you, they'd be precious to me."

She laughed.

"And you see how far our relationship has gotten. Why don't you just imagine me living a life that I can enjoy with someone I enjoy being with? And you just wander off and have fun with your ego, wandering all over Europe, guiding pensioners to catacombs and cheap hotels."

"I do more of a wander off by yourselves tour and then meet me at 20 hrs. in a pub kind of tour. Will you marry me?"

That kind of came out of the blue.

"It would be illegal," she snapped back. "I mean you're married already. To you. "

I couldn't accept that though part of me was wondering how marriage fit in with infatuation.

"That doesn't work. I hate me. I don't believe a word that comes out of my mouth. The interminable nihilism drives me crazy. I'm trying to listen to a person I love -- you -- and all I hear is my own interior annoying voice interrupting. I hate my own thoughts. They cut, slash, and burn on sight. I swear to you I don't learn anything. Sure, I know all the Romance languages, plus Latin and Greek. I don't know if I mentioned that to you before. But I translate. I don't listen. I don't empathize. I don't care what the hell anybody is saying. I write dialogue for them so I can keep my own mind fed with its own wit. My own thinking gets in the way. I don't see the glass half full or half empty. I see it preternaturally cracked. "

I paused for breath.

"Actually, I don't have much of a life there. It's just one laundromat."

"You just said you have several."

"Did I? I told you I lied about that. I meant it was very busy. Well, the one I have is near the Pasteur Institute. I spend a lot of time there talking to people waiting for their clothes to dry."

"Do you lie and fabricate as well in French as in English?"

"Truth is, I mostly listen. I find it calming. Soothing. I'm not interested in what they're telling me but I kind of lose myself in the stories about their life they tell. I lend a friendly ear. French is a very soothing language. Not frenetic, like English and German. At the same time, I'm always looking for the hard consonants in all Asian languages. I know it doesn't make sense."

"You must make a lot of conquests there in your laundromat. I mean with the bored French housewives. They probably appreciate a man who does his own laundry and lends a friendly ear while his clothes are drying."

She had a way of throwing digs that I found just magnetizing.

"My height is kind of impressing. But I don't follow up on any of that. I tell them that I have a sweetheart, a *la belle dame sans merci*. Then I show them a photo of us."

"You have a photo of us?"

"Yeah. I set the camera on timer and you and I hugged. We were in our private spot near The Beach House. We were both wearing towels. Soaking wet after a swim.'

"So, it's a photo of me at 16? They probably think you're a child abuser."

"Fifteen, actually. You weren't going to be sixteen for several months. Anyway, the French have a more expansive view of what's sexually abusive than we have. Abuse to them is maltreatment of a kid. Héloise was between 15 and 17 when she had the fling with Abelard."

"I don't think I like you showing that photo of me to your girlfriends at your Paris laundromat."

"They said you looked great in a towel. A la Bardot. Les grandes dames. I just talk to the old ladies. They're my friends but not in the girlfriend sense like we were. Are."

"It was puppy love. Besides, it wasn't a bikini. It was a two piece. You see what you want to see."

"Whatever you call it, I did enjoy the seeing. I can't apologize."

When we parted after this dinner in which I didn't make amends, she told me she didn't want to see me ever again and I should rip up that old photo of her.

From this point on, I can't be sure if I ever did see her again, or, worse, whether I saw her at all at any time. Was I there with her, or wasn't I? Is she someplace or no place? Enjoying life with her husband, not me, and her family, or lost in the oblivion of eternal death? I thought I could find her but then the thought that she had died stopped me cold.

There are only a handful of story plots. Well, one. She lived. She died. I lost her. I lost knowing I ever found her.

CHAPTER SIXTEEN

SHE'S MAKING A PIE

*"[W]hat is not connected with her to me? And what does not recall her?
I cannot look down to this floor, but her features are shaped on the flags!
In every cloud, in every tree -- filling the air at night, and caught by
glimpses in every object, by day I am surrounded with her image! The most
ordinary faces of men, and women -- my own features -- mock me with a
resemblance. The entire world is a dreadful collection of memoranda that
she did exist, and that I have lost her!"*

Emily Bronte, *Wuthering Heights*

*"When I come home, I can think only of her. When I come in our room,
I expect to see her. I catch her shadow on the screens and curtains. Her
letters are the most precious examples of calligraphy. Her perfume still
haunts the bedroom. Her clothes still hang there in the closet. She is always
in my dreams. I wake with a start. She vanishes. And I am overwhelmed
with sorrow."*

P'an Yueh.

Where did she go?

If Bettina has entered a space something like the one anesthesia
puts you in surgery, a void you are not conscious of, a void in which
consciousness never enters, then she cannot know she is dead, but
I know it. But I cannot know anything really. I don't know death.
It's not a language I speak.

She cannot be reviewing her life, crying that she is dead,
yearning for those she will never see again, wondering where she
is and what will happen to her. Time will not be passing for her
because that requires consciousness. But there is no movement.

Nothing will get better or worse or advance or retreat.

I am nowhere if she is nowhere. Oblivion is the most inhabited part of our world, and we know nothing about it, not only because we cannot experience it and return to talk about it but because it has nothing to do with knowing. It is its absence.

She may be waiting for the Last Judgment, but where is she meanwhile?

Where indeed are all those who died before Jesus redeemed them and opened the chance to reach paradise? Why was there so great a time between the Fall and salvation through Jesus? Some 6000 years from Mesopotamia to Jesus whose arrival is to re-validate the opportunity for humankind to reach paradise. He delivers letters of transit. Judaism was in place 600 years before Jesus. Why wait so long for such an important delivery, a mission of redemption?

My cosmogony and theogony plan would have had Jesus pop up in the Age of Pericles. He would have been greatly assisted by Plato and found an obliging ear in Pericles. Honestly, if redemption required blood wouldn't any time after the Fall have obliged? History's most reliable theme is blood. Blood before Christ, blood after Christ.

And how long are we tainted with a sin committed by a couple we didn't know? Weren't they like hokey tourists from Kansas visiting the Big Apple? They were overwhelmed out of their gourds in that garden. How hard was it to hustle them?

And did I personally pay any reparation due if any were due? Jesus paid it all. If I'm a lousy crumb eternally tied to that comedy couple in a garden, am I less a lousy crumb for letting Jesus take the bullet for me?

Did you personally massacre Native Americans? Did you own black African slaves? Did you send Jews to Auschwitz? Did you drop bombs on Nagasaki and Hiroshima? Did you take a bite out of that apple Eve handed you? Your Everyday Christian Human says no to the first four but apparently yes to the last.

Very selective conscience. You personally choose to be free to personally choose only on those matters you personally choose. The rest you have nothing to do with, all the stuff that should make it clear to you that conditions and chance mock your free to choose bullshit illusions.

See? Not what you like?

Cheer up. The good news is that whatever choices you made or didn't make or think you made can be wiped out with a pill. If you don't think this is good news, then you probably think Big Drugs won't keep up with Big Tech. It will probably be difficult in the future to keep everyone with an AI device hard wired to their cortex drugged enough to avoid schizophrenia.

But why isn't death a part of that big inherited homo sapien sapien memory? We drop off a cliff into total darkness on that one. No memory.

I am lost in the plot of death. I began to put Bettina into it and wondered: Where is she now?

I close my journal, an old school composition book that didn't seem familiar. I think it was Dirk's.

I have been reading. I look up. I hear a voice.

"I'm only listening to this script, Brother Theodorus, because you're Mr. Farnsworth's kid."

The voice surprises me. I look around. I don't see anyone. I also don't know where I am. I look back down at my written thoughts. Funny stuff.

"Heretical, Brother Theodomus. Hair-retical is never funny in church, temple, mosque, or the one size fits all non-denominational, non-Celestial Entity gathering."

This voice reads my mind. So, that's it. I'm in a dialogue with myself. I'm going with it.

"Who are you?"

"You call me Dan. You white folks dream up some crazy names."

"I dream for therapeutic reasons. Actually, I'm just putting it out there for therapeutic reasons."

"I understand totally but do you want the truth? It doesn't sound real to me. Which means we could go in the superhero direction. Therapy wise."

"How's that happen?"

"A character that can go back and forth between life and death. On missions to help people what's hurting."

"What's hurting? Like a superhero doctor?"

"Not necessarily. Do you partake in the health services, Brother Theodorus?"

I shook my head. Why had I dreamed up someone who sounded like a southern Black holiness preacher?

"She left you and you're looking for her."

"I was but then I had this dream that she died."

"Yeah, you see that don't play. It's a downer. You don't want to mention somebody dying. Peoples has to be living. Dudderwise, the screen goes blank. And you don't want that, does you, Brother Theodominus? Walking around with nutin in your haid?"

"Well, no," I said, aware that since I thought this was a southern holiness preacher voice in my head that the voice had gone full tilt Black southern holiness preacher.

"Dat's the spirit, Brother Theodorcus. Put sumit in your head. Like she's making a pie. You hold on to that, brother, and it's a rock of the real and ain't nobody daid."

A rock of the real? My own voice was knocking my brains out.

"Wat's the matter? You ain't never seen her making a pie? You know, Brother Theodoloris, I have to tell you that you one big ass mudderfucker of a honkey to deal with. What's the matter? You look like you're going to spill your grits."

"I...I think I'm going to wake up. Who are you exactly?"

"Xactly? Der ain't no xactly no more when she daid. "

He started to laugh so loudly it felt like I was being attacked. I had to run. I had to wake up.

Bettina is rolling out a pie; swift, dexterous pulls in a few directions then the dough is rolled on the pin and unrolled on the pan. Pie making is all about prepping the pastry cloth, she tells me. You get that right and it all rolls out right.

What pies do I want for my birthday? A peach, certainly. Blueberry. Too early for apple. They are to come in the Fall when we wait for Ida Reds. No one sells them anymore. We look everywhere for Cortlands. And Northern Spies. They make the best pies. We relish our enjoyment and talk about apples.

I shall never again have a pie made by Bettina for my birthday.

I find this impossible to understand. It cannot be but it is what it is.

No, I think what it is nobody knows.

Death, I mean.

CHAPTER SEVENTEEN

LOCKED ROOMS

I began to go deep into the idea that Bettina and I had lived a long life together.

At the same time, I began to go deep into the idea all that was an illusion.

Multi-temporally, I felt that at the end of both reality and illusion, she had died. If her death was real, I'd never find her. If her death were an illusion, I needed to search for her.

I chose to think our life together was real, so real, that death, which was nothing but a fog of absence, couldn't stand up to it.

You know that the only steadfast possession of a lunatic is reason? The lunatic is more firmly attached to his reason than you are. You know what the one true reveal of a collapsing mind is? It can write scripts for illusion just as well as reality. You have to be very careful in believing what you tell yourself, about what you think you're seeing and what you think you can't see. You must be especially alert when your mind begins to give you the dimensions, the height, length, and breadth, of a surround designed by the illusionary manufacture of your own mind.

Things that never were can yet be detailed, skillful mimicry of what never was.

"Bring out number, weight, and measure in a time of illusion," to vary a theme of Blake's.

It's very unfortunate but when you are balls deep in the throes of passionate conviction you may be just balls deep in something that never was there, like the pea under a shell you throw down all the cash you've got because you know that pea is there under that shell and no place else.

At some point, uncharted, I began to toe across the Twin Towers of reality and illusion on a tightrope in my mind. That those towers were now gone was not a factoid unknown to me.

I can't see how she can vanish forever from sight. So much fineness in her, so great a loving, a giving spirit, a warm welcome and embrace of others, such fine concern representing the best our tortured, spotty, and confused humanity can achieve. So much forbearance, so much tolerance for my arrogant ego.

Why should so much fineness disappear so completely and suddenly?

I believe her presence replenished the goodness of the world while she lived and though the tiniest memory of her racks my soul to the core and has me cry Oh God! How can she be gone? I must remember every moment of her in the moments left to me. She fills my heart and soul. I cannot be alive otherwise.

The center is everywhere and it's unfortunate but there it is. I had a center and lost it. Or worse: I never had a center but dreamed I had one and lost it. Or worse yet: my center was real, but I didn't center myself there.

The center is a place to rest, to feel at home, to feel from that safe and sacred spot you can make sense of the flux and flow around you.

As a child will rush out exploring right and left, here and there but always look back to see if a mother is watching, I have lived looking back to see if Bettina was there.

I could climb the Lauterbrunnen in the Jungfrau region of the Alps, or walk solitary across Spain in burning heat, or hold a snag line in the North sea on a small boat pulling in bright mackerel, walk across the Pyrenees, rail all over Europe without knowing what lay ahead. I could roam into every kind of adventure because at the center of it all was the anchor of my being, the magnetism drawing my soul back to her, never leaving her. In countless years of travels all over Europe I have met beautiful, fascinating women...and I have told them all about my love for Bettina.

On every outing, I would reach a panic moment in which I had to get back to her and I couldn't do it fast enough. I was afraid that somehow that journey would be blocked. Until I saw her face again in our home, which I did not fully respect, I was full of fear that I wouldn't return, that I would never see her again

Our life together was a journey, an adventuresome outing of more than half century and that journey was one destined to end. I can return now from countless number of places, but she will not be there. She no longer can be found but the center remains, and she is there, in the heart of that center. So deep in my heart that I no longer need to panic. I am calm now with her in our journey.

Am I mad to think this is all true, that it happened, that it was real? Am I mad to doubt that it was? I burn within a knowing that I failed to bond with her in so many ways that could never be contested and never doubted. I burn knowing that I let the reality of her blur within the selfish idiocies of my own mind.

From around Thanksgiving to the first week in December we would both sit in the cozy living room she had designed and furnished. The largest bookcase in the house directly across from where I sat. It reached the top of the 8-foot ceiling and was three feet wide. Like the huge headboard upstairs in our bedroom, Bettina had built this huge bookcase.

I started the fire just before the *PBS Newshour* went on, sometimes rushing down from my writing in the small dormer area we called the computer room. As I set the kindling and brought armloads of firewood into the room, she would watch me. She was skillful in setting a fire in that fireplace, disagreeing with me as to whether the cardboard toilet cones she saved just for this purpose belonged below the wood or nestled within.

When the fire was crisply and noisily burning, I'd turn to where she was seated and say, "Nice fire." "Yes, it is." When one evening I noticed she was eying me mysteriously I asked "What?" And she said, "I'm waiting for you to say nice fire."

If you travel back many years when Bettina was 27, which was how old she was when we moved into Oxley Hollow, Mercer County, West Virginia, you could see how clever she was in banking coals in our kitchen wood burning stove so the next morning when I got up, as I did so that the house was warner when she and the babies got up, I always found enough burning coals to get a blaze going without lighting a match. She did that for a whole winter. One match.

Nice fire.

"How could I have these clear memories, not only of her but of her family. The dead ones."

"One possible explanation is that these memories were implanted."

"By whom? By what?"

"By your mental illness."

"You make me laugh, Groin."

"Grew. Dr. Grew."

"I'm here for help and you start with the worst. I'm mentally ill. Is that so obvious?"

"I said it was a possible explanation. So, you never lived in Fox Hollow, West Virginia? Or did all that Europe stuff?"

"I never started a fire in a fireplace. I never watched the whatever news show."

"But you know about the dead in her family?"

"Yeah, all tragic. How do I know that unless she told me?"

"Well, they could be not her dead but yours. That's how you know. Give me an example."

"Okay, way back. There's Aunt Finesse. She never marries, takes care of her aging mom and dad and then in her forties she gets a stroke and drops dead on the kitchen floor."

"Bettina told you about her?"

"How else would I know? She died eons ago. Al Green was the New York governor."

"Give me another."

"Cousin Bread. He's got a business just starting to make him big money. He strays from the desk he's always behind, does some pick and shovel work and gets a fatal heart attack. He's not even fifty. Then there's another of her cousins. Cousin Sweets. He leaves the city and goes to live in the woods where he can drink in peace. Car goes off the road. He jacks it up, gets under it and it falls on him. He's half in the bag and now he's dead. In his forties."

"Dead and tragic. All of them?"

"Yeah. A second cousin. Going to work in a storm. Tree falls on his car. He's dead. Just thirty years old. Then there's ...."

"She told you about a lot of tragic deaths in her family. Doesn't that seem strange to you."

"No, it doesn't. We were together for years and years.

Lots of time. Stories come up. More stories about the dead than the living. There was some comedy, but I don't recall. It seems like all these dead people cut out the comedy."

"So, she ever tells you stories about people who were alive and happy?"

"Not that I recall."

"That doesn't seem strange to you? Was she a morbid, death fearing person?"

"Not more than you or me, Groan."

"Grew."

"How do I think I know all this stuff but if you ask me, I don't remember any of it?"

"The human mind has many rooms, mostly locked. Would you object if I put you under hypnosis?"

"I wouldn't object to you trying, Grope. What are you looking for? More dead and tragic stories she told me?"

"I'll take what I can get."

"She's in one of those locked rooms in my head?"

"Well, we're hoping to find her someplace."

"What if she's dead or never existed?"

"One hundred and ninety sessions of therapy should clear that up. Plus, a targeted array of psycho-pharmaceuticals."

CHAPTER EIGHTEEN

EVERYDAY SLIPPAGE

"He said I needed 190 therapy sessions and lithium daily. I ended that bullshit."

"Who exactly is this man you're talking about. Doctor Green?"

"Dr. Green?"

"You made him up, didn't you? You were telling yourself you needed to see somebody, so you made him up. You fell asleep saying to yourself 'I need to see somebody' and so you did."

"I made up the 190 therapy sessions? That's scary."

"Look. I don't care. But why come to me? You're not my pupil anymore. And I'm an old man. What was the session fee?"

"What session fee?"

"In your dream with this Doctor Green."

"Five hundred for forty minutes. I made that up. Look, you're a Hindu, Patawalla. You're the closest thing to knowing about ... what's going on with me."

"Which is?"

"I think I'm a reincarnation."

"We all are. Who or what do you think you were before your present incarnation?"

"I know I wasn't a What. I think I was a guy married for fifty years to a marvelous, courageous, alluring, quietly independent woman. I call her Bettina."

"You call her Bettina? What did she call herself?"

"I don't know. That didn't come over. How would you call it?

In the reincarnation process. I expect you're familiar with that process?"

"I'll need five hundred to continue."

I nodded.

"Of course, my dear boy, I am a long-time student of reincarnation. A worm becomes an ant or a bee. That takes a moderate level of processing. Think of it like entering the country after 9/11 and going through Customs. An ant or bee to a dog is more like proving who you are to Google. Dog to cat is like being stopped permanently between floors. Cat to human is like waiting to win the lottery when you only buy one lottery ticket and you've never won anything in your life. I'm leaving out a great deal of reincarnation between roach and human. It's a process as they say. Indeed."

"Yeah, but I was clearly a human before I became what I am now. Why are you laughing?"

"I beg your forgiveness. You were always a cocky, conceited, presumptuous pupil. You thought very highly of yourself, but you were not so clearly a human for all that self-praise. And I would now rate you as an adult as only partially human. But yes, I think you were a human in another life. A better one. You are going down in the reincarnation process."

"You never liked me, did you, Patawalla?"

"I am merely observing the clues. The residue of memory from your previous incarnation by which I mean fifty years of marriage to a celestial woman tells me that you were a far better human than what I now see before me. Why would any woman remain married to you for a half century is what I ask you? No, she did that with a far better incarnation. So, I say, you have processed downward. Where you will go from here, I cannot say. Perhaps to your twin brother's level."

"That retrograde?"

"Who can say? Much depends on what you do in your final years of life in this incarnation. It doesn't look very good to you, does it?"

"I suck. I'm crap. Why am I in search of a woman who was this other guy's woman?"

"Not another guy. You. But in a different incarnation. The bee does not forget it was a worm. It has memories, dreams, signs, and signals. It dreams it is covered in dirt. The processing is not a total soul and spirit wash. More of a total brain wash."

"Nothing of this special lady got washed out of me. One minute I'm sure we had a life together and then the next I think I did but I didn't grasp just how beautiful and fine she was. And then in the next minute, I think I'm a fool and somehow, I let her go and she's somewhere waiting for me. And then the next minute I think she's not because it's all over now and she died. She'll never be found again. I'll never talk to her again. I'll never hold her again. And then I think, well, I never did because for me she was never there. It's like I missed her. She was there but I was looking the other way. Then I think --- and this is the worst -- that if it were true and I had been such a big part of her life. No, not big. Just consuming. I consumed most of her life by being there. And when she died and looked back at her life, she saw me standing there like a block in the road she could never get around. I mean, if all she had in her life was me, I feel so bloody sorry for her. No joy there for her."

"Because you're crap?"

"Yeah, I think so. What was I in that incarnation where this guy … I mean me but in a far better incarnation … really loved her and lived with and didn't have to panic to find her? Why I couldn't have been crap then. But don't you see? Then it couldn't have been me because, like you said, I've always been a nasty piece of work."

"A devolved form of life, I think for sure."

"But can't it be possible that the guy she knew was actually me? Devolved but someone she loved? Could it have been me and not some better incarnation? Maybe I did live with her all those years and fucked up her life and I'm not remembering because I can't live with that. I'm telling myself; we never had a life together. I'm defending myself in my subconscious but doing a lousy job. Maybe I'm not in process and never was. I'm just that same piece of crap guy. I was never better than what I am now. And she accepted that."

"In not too long, it will be over, and the process will continue."

"It's all the process with you. isn't it? I was better in another incarnation. That's the me she loved. But it wasn't me because in the next life I devolved into crap but there was slippage and some stuff got carried over to me and I think I'm the one who had her. But I can't be sure. There's the rub right there. The punishment. Time isn't a cure. It's the torture ground. I think it's like one time I had some surgery but not enough anesthesia to knock me out. I went into the slippage between life and death, light and dark."

"Very awful for you. How long did that go on you ask. Timeless. So unfortunate that this surgery went wrong. "

"You think I'm in the process of reincarnating now and something went wrong, and I shouldn't be awake during the transition?"

"Imagine what a man who is reincarnating to a worm would feel if the anesthesia mask was loose."

"What the fuck? You never did like me, did you, Patawalla?"

"I saw devolution in you when you were a young punk talking Latin and Greek. I looked at you and I saw devolution."

"Maybe you were looking at my twin, Dirk."

"No, your brother clearly has not evolved or devolved in very many cycles of birth and rebirth."

"So, there's no slippage in his life? Memories of his other lives?"

"No, not that. Just the ordinary variety of everyday slippage."

CHAPTER NINETEEN

UNDERSTANDING THE PROBLEM HERE

"Pogawally said you were a cockroach in another life? Maybe you should believe him. Your brother here was definitely some form of insect."

She made a motion with her head in Dirk's direction. Eve Solly. If the Eve in the garden was like her, the Big Fall was definitely in the cards.

I don't know why I was sitting here with my brother Dirk and Eve Solly, but I guess I was confused, scared, desperate a little bit lonely and overall fucked up since talking to Patawalla. Otherwise, I would have rather taken a bullet to the head than seek help from these two.

"Patawalla did say Dirk had devolved."

"If I did, brother, I had to," Dirk said. "My feet were killing me."

"That word has nothing to do with your feet, dear," Eve told Dirk. "You know, Doris, you could have asked your brother or me if you had a long marriage to a woman who is now dead. We would have said no, you didn't. We would have run into her. Case closed."

Eve Solly got a kick out of taking my name Theodorus and twisting it into Theodoris and then just calling me Doris.

"You're a lot like that bitch in the garden. Eve. Your namesake. You're fucking up my brother's life."

"He does that on his own. But at least he's not nuts. Just easily confused. You on the other hand think you lived with a woman who you think is both dead and alive. Tell me, Doris. How did you miss being sure one way or the other?"

"That's just it. I had her for such a long time, but I didn't fully realize what I had."

"Sounds like a soundtrack to a RomFarce. I'm tearing up."

"I know exactly what Theo means. Something happens a lot and I miss really knowing what ....what happened."

"Yeah, you forgot just now how that sentence ended. The cause of your confusion? You were drunk. Go get me a tissue. I'm tearing up for both of you."

I saw I wouldn't get much help here. My brother was in process and Eve was nothing good. But maybe she was what I needed?

"I somehow got outside of the best years of my life. And I'm still outside. I still don't know it happened, but I get so sad when I think it did happen and I just wasn't there."

"Tell me, was Dirk at your wedding to this woman? Were you, Dirk?"

"I don't know. I don't remember the details. I think I was there but maybe not. Did I give a toast?"

"Yes, I think so."

"Then I wasn't there."

"Big help. Give me details, Doris, like what she looked like?"

"She looked different over the years, but she was always beautiful. Quietly independent, alluring."

"Maybe she was so independent she was independent of you. You weren't there and neither was she. You were both missing."

Dirk laughed and slapped me on the back.

"I told you Eve would figure out what's going on. She wasn't in your life, and you weren't in hers."

"And you see that as giving me joy, brother? Having nothing? Not her. No memories. No life together. Don't you remember Bettina?"

"You were talking about her? I remember her."

"Those are the memories, brother, that are killing me."

"Those memories, Doris, aren't worth two horse dumps if you're remembering somebody else's life."

"You know, Eve, you are set on not understanding the problem here. There's no somebody else. It's just me in a previous incarnation."

"Oh, now I understand. That's easy to understand. Previous incarnation. So, who were you when you were in a previous incarnation?"

"I've been thinking about that."

"And? A man thinking. Lay it on us."

"I think I was a guy like Headcleft in *Wondering Heights*."

"You were Lawrence Oliverio?"

"He loves Cathy so much that he won't give her up even when she dies. Intensity of their love. It never died with him. And in the reincarnation process. . ."

"Headcleft becomes you?"

"In that process, that intensity, all that power that held the two as one, kind of seeped into me. There was slippage in the incarnation processing."

"Is that what Pagawally told you?"

"Yeah, I'm looking for a woman I never really knew. Didn't even meet. But I'm drawn to her, nonetheless. Living or dead I must find her. It's like a guy loses a foot but he still feels it."

"She's a foot? High?"

Eve was triggered. She was sensitive to height references. I could see she wanted to kill me. That was okay. I didn't feel much like living.

"She's everything to me."

"I'm trying to understand here," Dirk told us.

"Stop trying. I see your forehead bulging. So, the foot was amputated. It ain't there as the litterroti say about LA."

"But it was there, and it feels like it's still there. I mean her. Not the foot."

"Okay, Doris. I've heard it all. My advice. You're several drinks ahead or behind your own brain. You need to catch up. Or what would be my choice, just pack it in and admit you're a douche and this lovely lady probably thought so too and showed you the door. And reincarnation? I wouldn't worry about what you might have been. You've got enough to worry about with what you are now. Did I say douche?"

"I don't really believe in the reincarnation stuff."

"Now you say that? You've been in that pit for an hour now."

"I think she happened in my life and that she died, and I can't get over it and now I'm in a space, a time escape, the only one I can live with."

"The post-quantum one?"

"I can find her and apologize."

"For what exactly?"

"For taking up so much time and space in her life."

"That's what men do to women, Doris. I'm here waiting for your brother to apologize to me. He oppresses depresses and suppresses me, but does he apologize?"

"She could have had a happier, less anxious, less distraught life without me."

"I don't really want to make you feel better but go back to thinking she never knew you and you never had a chance to fuck up her life. She never knew you. You didn't live together long enough for you to affect her life. You didn't live together at all. Think of yourself as a nothing in her life. A total zero. A vacancy. You'll feel better."

"I can't. I keep seeing her face. It's different all the time, but it's there. I keep apologizing to it."

"You don't have to apologize. You weren't there. Think of it like a paternity suit. Take the vodka out of the freezer, Dirk."

"I somehow prefer to think she and I had a long romantic relationship that I somehow wasn't fully aware of or didn't fully appreciate and being the oppressive, dark, cynical presence that I am, I preempted the laughter and joy in her life. Not all the time but enough for her to beg me to stop. I hear her now begging me to stop."

"Don't say that when the #Metooed police are around. So, you'd rather have her alive and with you and suffering because of that and you suffering because you made her suffer. You'll go with that rather than accept you didn't hurt her because there was never a her and you?"

"Sometimes somebody wants something whatever the conditions," Dirk told us.

"Right now, I want the vodka. Is your brother right?"

"Yeah, I have to have her. What does that make me?"

"Well, first, what I heard from the start, you're nuts. Second, you are also one selfish son of a bitch."

"She says that about me too, bro."

"Let me conclude here, Doris. And what I conclude is that all that reincarnation shit is shit. Because if it were true, I'd be stepping on two cockroaches right now and not listening to them. There's no way you or your brother could have migrated into any human form. So that belief is just belief in the face of the factoids. Like the sun rises."

"I guess the fact that I am human, six foot six and healthy means I haven't devolved."

"You're a tall guy that's lower than a cockroach is what it means. If I were you, Doris, I'd dig that six-foot six hole in the ground and throw yourself into it. Or you could hang yourself from a really high branch. If your big fat feet are touching the ground, you're not high enough."

None of that helped I can tell you, but she had a point.

"You're right. I can't find her here. She's in the After Life. We'll meet there. Again."

Eve laughed.

"I'm sure if she's there in the After Glow, she'll be thrilled to see you. Plus the fact that why the hell would you wind up in any place where she is? You said she was a lovely, pure soul?"

"She was. Is."

"I rest my case."

CHAPTER TWENTY

THE GLITCH

I went back to Patawalla. The reincarnation thing seemed plausible to me.

"I remember every detail of her death, Walla. It's not somebody else's memory. It's mine. You don't remember something like that second hand."

"We believe that sometimes the reincarnation process has glitches."

"Glitches again?"

"You die and then the deliberation begins as to your reincarnation."

"Sort of like The Last Judgment for Christians? Somebody decides where you're going to go."

"We return. We don't do last. Very few reach Atman which is something like last stage beyond which there is no greater awareness and perfection."

"Sounds like entropy without the greater awareness and perfection."

"Think of the universal self, identical with the eternal core of the personality that after death either transmigrates to a new life or attains release from the bonds of existence. Moksha, also called mukti is a liberation from the cycle of death and rebirth. Samsara. The term moksha literally means freedom from samsara. "

"So, where's the glitch?"

"Perhaps in the release or perhaps in the cycling from death to life. You remember every detail of her death because you were there or because an earlier incarnation of you was there and the details did not dissolve. Like a post-traumatic stress experience that you inherit. Could be she is still in process or being released."

"And that means I can find her? I have this panic drive to find her because she's not dead."

"If she's been liberated, you won't see her. You won't find her."

"But if she's processed into another life form?"

"Then it seems your attachment to her is so strong that you may recognize her in her new incarnation. She may recognize you. Have you met any women who you are drawn to and seem drawn to you?'

"Not lately. But you mean they could be her? Or one of them could?"

"Unless of course she's devolved into some life not human. She could be a frog."

"I don't think so. She was celestial is what she was. Becoming a frog wasn't her destiny in any religion."

"Well, she should not be hard to find. A woman of celestial qualities."

"Really?"

"Europe might be a place to look. Though I don't think so. Or India is very celestial in places. And then in other places the plumbing is very bad."

I didn't exactly go to a defrocked whiskey priest for answers. It was just that I was sitting at the bar at *The New Pompey* and Father Balsio was there. Balls is what they called him now, *sans pere*.

"May her soul and all the souls of the faithfully departed rest in peace. May perpetual light shine upon them."

"Perpetual light. I like that. But thing is she's not dead."

"Coma? Didn't have a DNR?"

"She may be. In a coma. But I've got no reason to think she is. I'd have to find her."

"Well, wherever she is, we certainly want perpetual light to be shining upon her. Good words, nonetheless, my son. How do you like sleeping in the hope of eternal resurrection? I mean if it turns out she is dead."

"Sleeping? You know what Shakespeare said. Perchance to dream for in that dream who knows what shit may get stirred up. I'm paraphrasing, Father."

"Let's tell ourselves that she's alive and in the light of day. How's that? Is there something you wish to confess?"

"I thought you were defrocked. That's what Dirk told me."

"Dirk? Dirk Bratter?"

"My twin brother."

"I don't see how he can be saved. That woman he's living with is leading him to perdition."

"Eve Solly? I thought she was dead. Blown up. That's what Dirk told me. A bomb under her ass."

"Sympathy, my son. May perpetual light shine upon her. On every conjoined piece of her."

"But you're thinking perdition is more like where she went?"

"Darkness visible, I'm afraid."

"You kind of scare them into belief, don't you?"

"Not anymore I'm defrocked. But I still look forward to the resurrection of the dead, and the life of the world to come."

"I'm summing up here, Father. She's sleeping and also looking forward to resurrection. Right? If she's dead."

"Of course, you can be alive and looking forward to resurrection. No one wants to look forward to the void."

"What if she was simply lovely heart and soul and her spirit was as pure as Jesus's but her life here was enough for her? She wasn't aiming for Heaven. She was just good without hope of reward. Not incentivized."

"Her life with you? She has no belief?"

"In what? You mean belief in whatever you believed before you were defrocked?"

"You misjudge me. I didn't give up belief. I just got thrown out of the church for moral turpitude reasons. I got #MeTooed by the Ladies of St Antony. I remain a sinner with belief. The sinner is loaded with belief otherwise he'd have no appreciation of sin. A sinful act couldn't be distinguished among all other acts. Sinners confess because of their belief. Every sinner is a believer. Those who don't believe, never worry about sin. The Void doesn't distinguish sinners from saints, those who confess and those who don't."

"You confessed to moral turpitude?"

"I did but only after I was accused."

"Didn't you fight the accusation?"

"Why bother? I'm a Jesuit. I know the world. I got pilloried on social media. Accused now means convicted. Besides. What evidence could I present in my own defense when all real evidence is washed away by alternative evidence?"

That made me feel very uneasy. Listen, if you're beginning to doubt your own sanity wouldn't you like to believe that you could distinguish fact from bullshit? Or you had a shot at doing that?

"Did your girlfriend have a personal relationship with Jesus?"

"She wasn't promiscuous. I was the only one in her life."

"I mean did she have faith in Jesus as a participant in God's triune nature?"

"More like Nature was where god was. All life is holy. Squirrels, birds, babbling brook, floating clouds, sun, moon and all the stars. Tell me, Father, if we found life on, say, Mars, do you think Mars was created in seven days like it says in Genesis? Garden of Eden, The Fall, Jesus, and so forth? Jesus was immaculately conceived on Mars or elsewhere in the cosmos?"

"It would be hard to say how the Holy Spirit plays out in the cosmos but I'm certain it's there. Perhaps not the Father and the Son but the Holy Spirit is pandemic. Your girlfriend then was a heretic?"

"Far more just sweetness itself. 'So passing lovely, Beatrice show'd,/Mind cannot follow, nor words express/Her infinite sweetness.' Lines from Dante's *Paradisio*. She wasn't infinite sweetness because she feared the pains of hell or the loss of heaven. It came natural to her."

"Perhaps she was good because she knew being bad offended God. I have sinned against you whom I should love above all things."

"She didn't offend. Quite the opposite."

"That would work, resurrection wise. If the love was directed at God in his triune nature. There's a lot of focus on Jesus as the one who could save you and The Father who will judge you but if I were you, I'd put my money on The Holy Spirit. He's a pantheist, like your girlfriend."

"You know, Father, this may be a confession, but I feel the guilt of slavery seems more like something I should accept than original sin guilt. It's clear to me how fucked up slavery was. I can't say I see clearly what went on in the Garden of Even. Eating a forbidden apple isn't in the same league as a whole lot of human history. Of course, I throw that out there as a guy without belief so I'm not waiting to be struck down."

"I wouldn't worry. I've got my wonders. Like I wonder if humans were around for some six thousand years why did it take so long for the curtain to go up on the resurrection plot? But I think such thought have come to me since I was defrocked. Previously, the timing of salvation didn't come to mind. 'His ways past finding out.' Romans."

"You know I have to say she never mentioned Jesus all the time I knew her."

"But then again, you say you're not sure you ever heard her say anything?"

"In the sense of you never really hear what anybody has to say. In the you never know anybody sense. But I must admit also in the sense that I'm not sure I knew her like you say. Since she died, my mind has been going hay wire. For instance, a lot of what you're telling me is kind of deja vue, stuff I told myself that I'm repeating. I'm not even sure we're here talking and having a beer."

"She died?"

"I'm not sure of that. It's kind of like how I'm not sure she ever lived. With me at least."

"Given all that, we can extend to her the widest range of belief. God the Father for instance. She might have read the Old Testament each night before going to bed."

"I have this clear picture of how she would go to bed. You know, the routine everyone has and so on. Then again, I'm not sure I ever saw her go to bed. But I'm firmly convinced she was more mother oriented than father oriented."

"As I say, this is where the Holy Ghost comes in to save the day. If she believed all life was holy, then we must admit that's the work of the Holy Ghost inserted in all things. Belief in all things visible and invisible. The Nicene Creed."

"Yeah, I think that might work. She always said there an invisible life in the trees and the sky and the rocks and the birds and the babbling brook and so on. The fish. It feels like I'm repeating myself here."

"You know, my son, the more I think about what you're telling me the more I think her pantheist beliefs won't save her. Although of course, as Gerhardie has said, in the end Mother Nature puts us all to bed. Perhaps though her only hope is still being alive so she can confess.

"I hope to find her alive for sure, but I'm haunted by the suspicion that she died. I was there in fact. I see it all. I was by her side. By the side of the bed. We were at home."

"That was a blessing. She would have wanted that."

"Why do you think I think we were at home? Doesn't that mean I know we had a life together?"

"Do you remember an address? Something about the bed?"

"Oh, she existed alright. It all existed. She still exists. I mean she exists for me; I see her."

"You have faith, my son. You see through and not with the eye as that madman, William Blake advised."

"That doesn't sound good."

"He died singing. Of couse, he led a hard, tortured, unrewarding life so he had no reason to be singing. Reason might have prompted him to curse. Tell me, my son, have you seen a psychiatrist?"

CHAPTER TWENTY-ONE

THE GROUP

I found out about The Group online. *Crank's List*. It was the *She/He/They Died, You Lived Group*. They met every first Friday.

"I write such detailed memories; they must be mine."

"May we assume they were madeleine moments?"

I looked at the questioner, a pasty face bloated guy sitting next to the pasty-faced woman, also bloated, Mx Facilitator. He had introduced himself as Adenoid. "I'm called Ad by my friends." Everyone was dressed in shades of black. As I looked around, I saw not an ounce of joy in the room. They looked like they belonged to a group called 'Everybody died, and we did too."

I hadn't said anything, still pondering the madeleine comment.

"Involuntary, as in Proust," Adenoid said, pompously, "who took a bite of a madeleine biscotti and remembered several thousand pages of his life."

"I read *In Search of Lost Time* in French. *La Recherche. The Search*," I shot back. "Yeah, my memories come mostly in dreams so I guess you could say they were involuntary, madeleine moments."

"Do you want to share them with the group?" Mx F asked me.

"Sure. I've got them written down. I can read them."

"Go ahead. Everyone pay attention. Our Theodorus is hurting, and we need to help him."

"Will he take comments at the end?" Adenoid asked.

"Yes, Ad, but not the sort you make on *Twatter*," Mx F told him.

"The Constitution prohibits prior restraint," he told her angrily.

"Fine. Just don't tell Theodorus to suck on a bullet. You may begin, Theodorus."

"It's kind of a poem."

"What kind?" someone shouted out. "Haiku?"

"Idyll," I mumbled, and I began to read:

"I have no defense, no remedy, no solution, no counterpunch,
No answer, no way out, beyond, or through
Her dying
Except a narrow path on a treacherous cliff
Above the void
The oblivion that faith attempts to deny
The awaiting absence of life
An eternity that does not end
With a bright new beginning
I have only my feeble path of words
Shaky, deficient, forgetting
Even the enchantment of her smile
But it is all I have
This sad sweetness of momentary stay
In my writing
I send my sentences out like emissaries
To plead my case
I see her when an orange is peeled
Carving small animal figures out of the peel
I see her walking briskly ahead of me on Boldwood Court
I see her looking at me wearing a jacket like mine
"We look like twins," she says, smiling
I see her across from me at the table
Saying "Please" in such a way
I cannot urge her to eat just a bit more
We are so sad just then
I forever fall apart in the sadness of that 'Please"
I see her ruddy faced in the driveway
So determined to do her share of the snow shoveling
I see her dancing alongside me
Her mouth held tight her elbows bent
Her hands closed
Her feet moving in that inimitable pattern
So true to the music
The music I hear only in the way she dances
I see her sitting waiting for the weekly blood draw
Asking the phlebotomist how everything is going with her?

I see and hear her concern for others
Even as she is just hanging in there
"I hope you're okay" she messages on the phone
I hear the pause of all eternity
And then
"I'm hanging in there."
"I'm going," she calls out to me from the deck
As I work in the garden
On her way to meet friends for coffee
"I'm going for a walk" she calls up to me
"Hurry up if you want to come"
I scramble for my shoes and rush out
Shoes untied
She is already halfway up the hill
"She doesn't wait for you, does she?" Phil says
"You better run to catch up."
And I do
She calls me while I am on campus
"Joe, I fell down the cellar stairs.
I don't know if I've broken anything.
Can you come home?"
I rush like Mercury to her
My bike my winged heels
But she's alright
I hear her calling me to supper
"I know. You need to finish a paragraph."
"Would you get the paper for me?"
"The birds don't have any seed."
"You're behind schedule!"
"Right now, you're doing this!"
"I'm waiting for you to say `Nice fire'
"Einar sent us something!"
"I don't think I'm going to talk to you anymore!"
"You should go to Europe if that's where you want to be"
"Joe! There's two bunnies out here!"
"When is the last time you called your sister?"
"You will cry and grieve forever
If anything happens to her
I see her standing with her friends
In front of Rico's Luncheonette
Transistor radio in one hand
Cigarette in the other

Singing softly
"Come see about me"
I see her walking toward me my first day of class
"I thought I would meet you"
"Let's finish watching this tomorrow. Bedtime"
And I never hear her again after that
Except on the cassette tapes she recorded
Reading stories to her daughters
Except when I'm asleep and I hear
"Joe'" or when I look into the darkness
And I see a light and, in that light,
I see Elaine.
Or in the garden when I'm working hard
'Come sit with me, Joe.'

I looked up. I know my out loud reading voice sounds like William Borrows reading Spare Ass Annie. I mean I sound like a guy who nobody could love and who couldn't love anybody.

No sounds. I looked around at The Group. Kind of comatose. And then Mx Facilitator:

"She died. You lived. Excellent. Let's pause in the reading now for comments."

"That was it. That's all I've got. I'm finished."

"What you've got, dude, are implanted memories. Where's Rico's Luncheonette, for instance? What's a transistor radio? Where's Boldwood Court? What's a sentence emetics? What's a phlegmologist? What year Mercury did you have? What songs did she have on her playlist? Who the hell is Joe? You're Theothomas or something. Did you ever think that light you saw when you woke up in the darkness was a flashlight the house invader had in his hand? And that that guy was probably Joe?"

"Maybe Joe was a neighbor with dementia who was wandering around in the middle of the night looking for his late wife."

"That would be Elaine, for sure."

"Thank you, gentlemen. Might I remind you that this is an idyll. There is no need for verifiable accuracy. Nor is it helpful to Theodorus if we all drift off into our own personal histories. But I do wonder, Theodorus, what your own thoughts might be on who Joe is?"

"I think he might be the guy who writes this poem and sends it to me. He's another life. Of mine."

That kind of shut up everybody for a while. And then:

"So, you feel some connection to the name Joe because he's who you were in a previous existence?"

"Yeah, he lived with her. I didn't. His memories kind of slipped through to me."

"Adenoid, you have a comment?"

"All I can offer is the observation that it's not at all a good sign if one person begins to talk of himself as two persons."

"Any other comments?"

"I believe I can clear up the name confusion. Names are changed in the spirit world. They get spiritual numb de plums."

"And you know that, why. Crayola?," Adenoid asked her, aggressively."

"I think it's obvious. And my name is Carola, not Crayola. You can't keep your earthly identity in a dimension that has no connection whatever with our earthly life."

"So, you die and become somebody in a spiritual world who is not you?"

"Yes. You are totally cleansed. You can't take you with you into the spiritual world."

"You can't take you with you?" Adenoid shouted. "You know something, Crayola? You are an idiot. How did you get in Group?"

"I'm a regular. You, sir, are nothing more than a bullying interload. What loved one now dead would you have had as it is clear no one living could have tolerated you."

"An important question, however, arises," a little, frightened looking guy to my left said.

"Let's not stray," Mx Facilitator interrupted. "Has any of this helped, Theodomus?"

"No. Frankly, no. I've got more idyll though if anyone wants to hear."

"How does this other guy who's you send it to you?"

I don't know who called that out, but it got a lot of laughs.

"Go right ahead, Theodomus. Ignore The Group. They've had too much caffeine."

"Get closer to the conflict," the same Unknown shouted. "Augment the suspense. Give us a voice we can identify with. Make someone goddamn likeable. Keep the dialogue/description ratio to one in five. Keep in mind the fourth-grade vocabulary algorithm requirement. Say 'enter' and not 'fuck.'"

I gave Mx Facilitator a puzzled look.

"Don't mind her. She's a parolee."

I don't know why I didn't walk out of this hornet's nest, but I didn't. I held on to the hope that someone would throw me a preserver.

So, I once again did my "Spare Ass Annie" voice.

"I see her in the Fall of 1970 coming to meet me on my way home
Seeing her coming toward me elates me
I am coming home to her
I see her in Amherst Summer 1970 enter the parlor
She is wearing a kind of dressy lounging robe
I don't know what to call it
But it goes down to her feet
She is golden lovely the gentlest brown eyes
And I think I have not lived before I met her
And I cannot ever possibly live without her
I cannot say how I lived before her
When she was not with me by my side
It cannot be that we are gone from each other
For as long as the Earth turns, and rain falls
That what we were together is over
I see her sitting there five months ago to this day
In a year that has passed
Trying to rise not able to speak
The will to live and show courage
At the time of her dying overwhelms me
And like an epiphany a eureka moment
I realize I have been with her more than fifty years
That she is leaving me now
That she is truly going and never to return
That I will never lose my love for her
That no different spots of time
Will erase my memories of her
Visions of loveliness, of such fine dignity
The precious fellow passenger of my soul
The heart of a world in which I circle
Such a remarkable recognition
That all life is holy and is to be cherished
Though I am a crudity at the bottom
A crack in any glass full or half full
But I would at any moment have given
My life for her
Done in a heartbeat without a word
I reckon somehow, she found me holdable
Not always or rarely worthy

Seldom coming up to the mark
I see that the greatest mystery of her
Was her long life with me
I've never been to Heaven
But I've known someone
Who comes from there.

I looked up from my words.

The actual Dead are ready to attack. I can see it in their dead eyes.

"I'm sorry but I don't hear this as an idyll but as a fragmented confession. So unfortunate. I'm a real poet, by the way."

I looked at the speaker. He looked to be a child. He was. Maybe 6 or 7 years old.

"Please ignore, Clematis, Theodorus. Our nanny quit."

"She had her reasons," Clematis gurgled, smiling.

"Shut up and listen, Clematis. You want to be informed, don't you? Mr. Bratter has experienced the numinous and is seeking the support of The Group."

Actually, I didn't feel as if I experienced the numinous or was seeking the support of The Group, but it was too late to cancel the idea that I was doing both.

"Sister Joan, did you have something?"

"She's a nun?" I whispered to Mx Facilitator.

"Oh, God no. She's my sister. She's an After Life Denier."

"I think the answer to the question," her sister began " of whether you ever lived in Amherst will settle once and for all whether you made this stuff up, or someone implanted it in your memory bank when you were sleeping, or whether it's the real deal and you should be grieving her or searching for her."

"Before we answer that," someone cried out, "we need to once again refer to Proust."

"Fuck Poost!" someone muttered. Clematis, I think.

"You all recall that Swine's tendency to idealize Odetta leads him to fall blinding in love with her. Even though they are not at all compatible. He is unable to see her as she really is because he is more focused on how deeply romantic and perfect his own tragic love for her is. In short, he doesn't love her. She's just an extension of his own self-love. What Theodomus is telling us is that he isn't some reincarnated former self but just himself. A vain, self-loving man, who now has woken up to see he never took the time to know the woman he said he loved."

He hesitated, looking at me.

"Of course, I say all this as your friend, or, at very least, an acquaintance."

"Thermodophilus?"

"What?"

"Amherst? Did you ever live there?"

"I visited Emily Dickinsad's house once. I could imagine her throwing a poem out an upstairs window."

"An important question, however, arises," the meek little guy once again began but he was cut off.

"Excuse me but I can't believe that is the question that comes to mind when it's clear the fraud comes in when he says they've lived together for 50 years. How old are you, sir?"

"Thirty-four."

"So, you realize you couldn't have been married for 50 years to this woman. I was and you get to look it."

"Stop right there. The phrase 'this woman' reeks of harassment. So, I caution you, to be wary of taking The Group below its Woke state."

"May I continue, Mother? Now, he's thirty-four but he thinks he's lived with whoever for fifty years which means she's a figment of his imagination. Maybe she's someone he loved but lost when he was a teenager. Maybe she broke up with him at The Hop or the School Dance or The Prom and he couldn't accept that, so he deluded himself into thinking all this malarkey he's giving us here. You know, Mr. Bratter, we're here for each other, but I think you are going way beyond imposing on us."

"Isn't it nap time for this kid," I said.

"He was mensa at age five," his mother, Mx. Facilitator moaned.

That hurt. I looked at the kid. Had I been that bad? He was a little shit just as I had been a little shit.

"You got the wrong group, mister.," someone said. "This is the *She Died, You Lived Group* not the *She Never Existed, You're Crazy Group.*"

"May I say something while the whole group is still here? Thank you. Thermopylae, you say you cannot live now that she is gone but the fact is that you're living right now, and you've been coming to Group for almost two years, never missing a session. Egomaniacals do not die of grief. They can only be shot or hung."

"Stake through the heart," was a suggestion from The Group.

"I think the person who wrote what you just read did die of grief. I think therefore that it's horrible and disgusting that you take that poor dead man's words sent to his departed beloved and try to convince us that his life was yours and his beloved is your beloved. You are an impostor imposing upon the good will of The Group."

"Theo?"

"What?"

"I think you should apologize to Group and consider yourself ejected this day, never to return."

"Nobody ever returns in the end," someone said.

I turned and saw the little meek guy who had been telling us that an important question had arisen. I wonder if what he said now was the answer to that question.

"Anyone up for a drink?" I asked.

Almost all of them indicated they were more than ready.

They're not a bad bunch, The Group, given the circumstances. She died, and you lived. No joy in that.

CHAPTER TWENTY-TWO

A TRUE HEAVEN

After The Group, I sought comfort in The Mater's arms.

"Perhaps you think so badly of men, Mater, because you've married two gangsters."

"Farnsworth and Richard Port are not gangsters. They are successful in every way. I have a low opinion of men based on your father, that idiot in a lab coat."

"Was it my fault my marriage didn't work?"

"Don't be silly, Theodorus. You were never married. You weren't, were you? Not inviting your Mater?"

"Let's just say hypothetically, I was married. Do you think it would work, or would my wife walk out on me?"

"Well, if she had any brains, she would but so few have them nowadays. Tell me, Theo, is a Smart Phone really that smart? I forget to charge mine and it goes dead whereas I wake up every morning, without being charged. What young woman are we talking about?"

"Do you remember the woman Dickel divorced?"

"You married her? Why, she's my age."

"Not her. Her daughter. Bettina. Bettina Parisi."

"The one you spent a summer hiding in the sand with down by the Beach House? You think you married her? I don't think so. She loathed you. Or was that your brother she loathed? Probably both of you. Such a loathsome pair. Your father genetically engineered you two. It disgusts me to think I had enough fertility to give birth to twins. I delivered in a public hospital to make matters worse.

Where is Bathsheba now?"

"I don't know where Bathsheba is, but Bettina I fear might have died. At least, I can't stop crying thinking about how she died. Half the time I think she's alive and waiting for me somewhere."

"Only the Public think they'll see each other when they die. They see Heaven as a big public space like a football stadium parking lot. It's disgusting. A true heaven is by invitation only. You should see my therapist. Dr. Groan. Very private sessions tailored to your income."

"Dr. Goran? I think I did. I thought I made him up and was talking to myself. You know I even joined The Group."

"The Group?"

"We sit in a circle and one person babbles and the rest of us just stare in this person's face and that person finally comes to the end of the rope and is thanked for sharing. It's therapy through social interaction."

"It sounds dreadful. Why would you publicly expose your private obsessions? Anyway, Dr. Groan says that all relationships between men and women are unjust and it's the woman who suffers the consequences of that injustice. I have it recorded on my phone. Listen:

"*Were it true as Plato said that the soul of man is immortal and imperishable, it implies that the soul of women is mortal and perishable, if indeed he gives women a soul. I see now that women bear the brunt of the difficulties of relationship with men and that is so because a foundational inequity exists. Perhaps this inequity is due to millennia of male physical dominance. The greater success they had in survival indelibly imprinted a dominating sense in the male. Perhaps its due to the Genesis account of Eve in which the woman is molded out of a man's rib, not out of Celestial created mud but derivative like a byproduct, like dross or chaff. Perhaps this inequity stems from the fact that every founding law, every account of humanity has relegated women to subservience. Much has been required of women to amend the damaging results of this corrupting condition. The damages of relationship with men are for women to repair. The give required is what they must give. So, I see then that the soul of women is in truth closer to imperishability and immortality itself because of the trials they go through with such quiet courage. And I believe there is a form of consciousness in that state of courageous resistance that has no fear of the void that may follow death, that feels and thinks and knows so removed from the blank absence of Oblivion that such oblivion remains something laughable that only men fear.*"

"Don't you think that was brilliant, Theodorus? He firmly

advises me not to marry."

"You mean a fourth time?"

"No time. He doesn't know I'm married. Or was ever married."

"That's kind of his thing, Mater, not wanting to know anything about you but charging you five hundred dollars a session? What then do you find brilliant in what he says?"

"Oh, I love the way Dr. Groan and Playdough give women a soul. I have been courageous in all my marriages."

"And your divorces."

"Don't be so cynical, Theodorus. Is there something else you wanted to ask me?"

"I'm sure that in her imperishable immortal state Bettina's soul knows I hunger for her and that with all my heart I want to know and feel that I was worthy of her, partaking of so many years of her life, and I know that I bear now within me traces of what she was and my own awareness that she is every minute with me, taking me to where she is, my raft to ride the seas of what life I have left."

"That was so nice. So poetic. You've always had that taint of a poet in you since you were a small child. But I would use the expression 'my guide' instead of 'my raft.' Is your brother still going about with that little tramp? My friends tell me they have a radio show that's absolutely disgusting. Public radio station. I get sick thinking about my son's voice on the public air waves."

"He speaks through his hand puppets. He has one of you. He calls it The Mater."

"How humiliating."

"She's a favorite of what Dirk calls The Pubic."

"I listened to one of their dreadful shows demanding that The Public had the right to be free. Some kind of public option for the people to choose this right and that right, everything now being a right The Public demands. Don't they realize that this country was built on the rights of privacy and privatization, and that nobody has any rights unless the man paying your wages gives them to you. And Mr. Farnsworth told me owners don't make a policy of giving anyone but themselves anything."

"I didn't know Dirk had any thoughts about all that."

"He didn't. He doesn't. It was a dreadful first-time caller. He spoke the way people speak on public transportation. Is that some kind of terrorist group? First Time Callers?"

"What was Eve Solly's response?"

"Oh, she tore into this First Time Brawler in such a dreadful way that I doubt he'll call again. She asked him if he was a paler shade of white, and he said he wasn't any part white, and she told him to run whenever he was told to halt and put up his hands and the only right he had was to shut up and bend over if he didn't get away. She said the right to run was inviolable and he should always be ready to run because white people were out to fuck him over. Could you imagine such language on the radio?"

"Public air waves, Mater."

"I wish you would stop using that word. Why do you come here to aggravate me?"

"So, you don't think I was ever married?"

"I haven't thought about it. There's something disgusting, almost loathsome about it. Don't you think? You and that poor, lovely girl. Perhaps she ran? What color was she?"

CHAPTER TWENTY-THREE

NOT ENOUGH TIME IN THE LAB

Suddenly it dawned on me that The Pater and The Mathematics would give me all the answers I needed.

"I'm not sure I ever met this girl you speak of. I might have but I'm sure I wasn't interested. Your brother and you are terrible distractions, you know. Did you ever bring her into The Lab?"

"Thing is, Pater, I don't think I ever met her. I mean not in the old-fashioned face to face way. Except maybe for a brief summer interlude near the Beach House."

"Perhaps you met her on one of those online dating services?"

"No, I guess I could look for her there. And in the obituaries."

"You don't know if she's alive?"

"Actually, or ever was. She could be a dream love. One I don't wake up from. I have a terribly deep yearning for her. I'm totally devoted to her. But I may be dreaming."

"Do you dream you're a butterfly?"

"A butterfly? No, I don't think so."

"The other side of the equation then is that you could be a butterfly dreaming he's a man. Nevertheless, unproven. I told your mother, you, and your brother . . . How is your brother by the way?

"He's happy, I guess. He's taken up with a woman."

"Real or virtual? Alive or dead?"

"Very real. Very tiny. Little Person. Vicious temperament. But he's devoted to her. I think she's one of those S&M dominatrices. You must have met her."

"What gives you that idea? That's not the type we have in The Lab."

"Dirk told me he had brought her around."

"Old fashioned face to face? I don't think so. You and your brother spent too much time with those head doctors. You were both too young for that nonsense."

"Dr. Fraud?"

"Good name for him."

"We also had Dr. Wrong later. She said Dirk was bi-polar. She was wrong about that."

"Hence the name."

"Exactly. Dirk doesn't have a two-pole mind. He barely has one. Dr. Fraud said he had border line personality disorder."

"What the hell is that?'

"Your mind walks a thin line between different moods. Dirk's not that complicated. He has one emotional state. Troglodyte."

"The fault is mine. You boys didn't reach far and deeper enough into The Higher Mathematics. You both fell into the pit of words. There's no precision there. Just faith. Mathematics has no faith. Just perfect elegance. For instance, to what do we refer determinately when we say 'faith' when compared to the precise referentiality of the number 2?"

"You got me there, Pater. I went to see Fr. Balsio. He's defrocked but he knows eschatology. I wanted to know where Bettina is if she's dead."

"Who's Bettina? The girl you never met face to face? What did this defrocked priest say?"

"I quote: *'But I do not want you to be ignorant, brethren, concerning those who have fallen asleep, lest you sorrow as others who have no hope. For if we believe that Jesus died and rose again, even so God will bring with Him those who sleep in Jesus. For this we say to you by the word of the Lord, that we who are alive and remain until the coming of the Lord will by no means precede those who are asleep.* Thessalonians 4:13-15."

"So, you think she's sleeping in Jesus?"

"Until the coming of the Lord. Bettina never ever mentioned Jesus though."

"Phone conversation? Text? Zoom? Or she's talking to you in this dream you're in?"

"No. It was during the time we lived together. Or I think we lived together. From a scientist's point of view, can I feel that I surely did live with her for many years and that I missed the experience and for me, now that she's gone, either dead or somewhere I haven't been able to find her, I'm not sure she was ever in my life, or I was in hers?"

"As a scientist, I would say first that you need to delineate your hypotheses in a clear, empirically verifiable sequential line of examination, elimination and retention. And secondly, that you've either drifted away mentally from solving the equation or you cross parallel universes without knowing it."

"Do you think some earlier incarnated me is messing with the new reincarnation of me?"

"What pile of dumb shite did you pull that out of?"

"Swami Patawalla. Remember him? You hired him to teach us cosmogony and theogony at the prekindergarten level. You fired him but he lived in the woods for years and me and Dirk would go visit him and listen to him. I thought he was dead, but I found him. Behind a bush. He didn't mention a parallel universe. How do I cross into a parallel universe?"

"Well, say, you make a choice here and you live with the consequences. In a parallel universe you make a different choice and everything subsequent is different. You can get wildly separated so that your life in this universe isn't anything like what it is in your other self's universe. You could already be dead in one, you know. Of course, one plus one still equals two. And you can still prove that 1.99 is equal to 2."

"I'm confused because I'm going back and forth?"

"From what you tell me you are experiencing some of the choices this other You made. You don't know this woman here, but you also know her because your other You knows her over there. You haven't lived with her for a long time, but he has. Meaning the parallel universe. He there. You here. Both You but not you. He loves her and yearns for her because he knows her. You have the same feelings but she's really nothing to you. You're yearning for what you don't know, never knew and will never know."

"She's nothing to me?"

"She's only something to you in the parallel universe. He has her. Or had her. You don't. Never did. Not in this universe. It's a theory. Can't be proven mathematically but my advice is to stop looking for her and get yourself a woman in this universe. Someone real. Someone on the number line. Remember, the absolute value of a number is its distance to 0 on the number line."

"Could she be dead over there? In this other universe?"

"Undecidable. You are thinking she's dead in this universe because you can't find her. But that doesn't mean she's dead over there. You can't find a person doesn't mean they're dead. I couldn't find where your mother was most of the time. I was in The Lab. Didn't mean she was dead. She was in the bathroom."

"I dream vividly of Bettina."

"You can thank your parallel universe self for all that. We cannot reject the possibility of some drifting from one universe to another. There's no Mathematics disproving that possibility."

"There's a lot of sex."

"Well, I guess you can claim it as your own but it's not real. Your sex is an imaginary number, like the square root of -1 is not a real number."

"Can I hypothesize something, Dad? What if I will never see her again but somehow when we are both dead and returned to the star stuff we come from, we cross paths? We come by sheer accident to touch each other and know each other? She may be the flower I light upon. Say, I'm a pollinator."

"Mathematically there's a less than infinitesimal chance you two would cross paths as you say. And less chance that your differing atomic structures would recognize each other. The Mathematics doesn't calculate consciousness."

"So, you don't think I have a better chance of finding her being where she is? I mean dead

"There is absolutely no After Life Mathematics. But if you think she's going to be under your boot soles in the grass as that mad poet believed, you're a greater disappointment to me than I ever thought you would be."

"I'm sorry about that."

"You know what you're really sorry about? You're sorry she's dead when others, the ones who could combust and the whole equation not change, are still alive."

The whole equation? That didn't make sense, but it did.

"I see it all going on as if her being kind didn't matter. As if she never meant anything."

"I saw my own life end forty years ago while I was still alive. It all went on anyway."

I started to tear up. I think it was for him but probably it was for me.

"Not enough time in The Lab is what's done it for you," he told me angrily. "The knowledge of which The Mathematics aims is the knowledge of the eternal."

<h1 style="text-align:center">CHAPTER TWENTY-FOUR</h1>

<h2 style="text-align:center">DAN</h2>

"Of Mans First Disobedience, and the Fruit
Of that Forbidden Tree, whose mortal taste
Brought Death into the World, and all our woe,
With loss of Eden, till one greater Man
Restore us, and regain the blissful Seat,
Sing Heav'nly Muse."
"Does the woe include dying? Death?"

"Well, let's say death is a kind of gate or barrier you have to go through after The Fall so you can get to Paradise. There were no such gates in The Garden. As it goes."

"You sound skeptical?" I asked, at the same time wondering why I was sitting on this Prospect Park bench talking to a guy with holes in his shoes clutching a brown paper bag. He had the kind of bronzed purplish outdoor face the Homeless get, bronzed by the sun, purpled by whatever alcoholic elixir he had in that bag. I'm sure the gentrified meritocracy elite who had turned most of Brooklyn into their garden of chat radical but complacent politics loved having this guy still around.

Why the fuck was he still around? Why the fuck was I talking to him?

"I was born skeptical.," this fuck up told me. "I suppose it's what destined me to my present lot in life. I didn't get your name, young man."

"Dan," I lied.

"That's my name too. What a coincidence."

He gave me a wink as if we were brother under the skin. Still, I thought he would pull a shiv on me, and he probably thought I was just a meritocratic elite gentrifier out for a stroll in old Brooklyn Authenticity.

"I've heard you reciting stuff here before," I told him. "Pushkin. Leopardi."

In between the lines: Why do all the bums stinking to the heavens have more erudition than the President of the United States?

"I'm a busker of the poetic line. And you?"

I was about to give my usual litany of patent leather creds but instead I said:

"I think I lost the woman I love."

"Lost as can be found? Or lost eternally?"

"I'm not sure. Tell me, you really think the disobedient man Milton wrote about includes me and you?"

"A Christian would say yes. If you say, no, that you personally weren't in on that Biblical felony, then you're probably not a Christian."

"If I'm not, does that mean I have to give up all hope that she passed through a gate to the other side?"

Dan laughed.

"She might have despite your lack of faith. She might be there right now and forgotten all about you. I doubt if one enters Paradise with all one's mortal baggage."

"Like a memory of our love?"

"Did you both engage in the nasty sex of mortal voluptuaries?"

That took me back. I thought about getting up and getting away from this guy. What the hell was I doing talking to him in the first place?

Instead, I said:

"Probably. I don't have a clear picture. Only some of the time."

"Well, all that would have to be vacated upon entrance to a perfect Afterlife. You see the need?"

"The need to be someplace where everything about you is …vacated? That doesn't sound like a perfect place. It's sounds like a lobotomizing."

"Think of it as a brand-new tabular rasa to be filled with the accoutrements of a perfect Afterlife."

"I thought you said you were a skeptic?"

"I'm not a skeptic about the inner workings and processes of the Afterlife. I am only skeptical about matters I can entertain with reason, not those beyond reason. That would be like being disparaging of a food I never ate. I assume and presume, however, that a Celestial Perfection would arrange a pleasing segue from mortality to immortality."

Now that made me laugh.

"You're more charitable than I am, Dan. I think the workings and processes of mortality are totally fucked. Maybe they must be, so we yearn to get out of here. But maybe all our shit has nothing to do with your Celestial Perfection. I mean how could it be? It makes more sense to think that some evil force rules down here and some of us break out and some don't. I don't know how they break out. Maybe they don't turn mean and angry, kill, rob, cheat, rape, pillage, exploit and fuck over. They stay clean of all that."

"I'm not skeptical about the Celestial Plan. It comes up blank, zero and a big nothing in my brain pan. Like the Entity itself. What some whatever totally different than me thinks and plans, I have not the slightest. I come up zero on all of that. That's not a denial of all that. It simply means I can only be occupied with what I'm able to think and feel about. Comprenez-vous?"

"You speak French?"

"I speak all the Romance languages," Dan said, in an egotistical, repugnant way.

"You don't ever think who or what might be behind all this?"

I did a sweeping gesture with one arm, capturing the gentrified and meritocratic elite strolling about, enjoying their holdings, the rewards of their money-making money as they walk their anointed heirs in strollers that cost more than the rent of thousands.

"No, I don't reach out. I leave that to mystics. I'm not much of a visionary either. You know why people think heaven is in the sky? Because when you look up all you see are wisps of clouds moving on a gesso canvas. Ambiguous vacancy. Nebulosity. Unclear. Uncertain. No definition. Like Heaven. Anyhow, in celestial matters I don't go further than some quasi-humanoid shown on *Star Trek: the Next Generation*. When I think Celestial Entity, the closest I come is Q. You recall that chap. Or the Traveler."

"Well, I don't see how taking the woman I love from me forever fits any plan I would accept."

"Maybe the plan is that you suffer for a while, as you clearly are, review and revise and then you find her and it's all so much better between the both of you. Perhaps you're like Dimitry Karamazov who realizes that a man such as he, one who fails time and again to mend his ways, requires a blow, a blow of fate to get his attention."

"Killing her off just to get my attention is a fucked-up scheme.

Why would I be worth the price of her life?"

"Well, Dan, maybe you'll find her. I mean if she's alive. I'd say it's time for a nip."

He held the rumbled bag out to me, and I took it. I took a long pull at the pint and gave it back. Zubrowka.

"I remember the God is dead fad," Dan told me, after he had taken a long pull on the bottle. "We either lost interest. Like when Tony Soprano says of his Mom ''she's dead to me.' Or the Celestial lived and then died and somehow, we mortals found out about it. Angelic Fed-Ex. Or, as we created such ourselves, we decided it was in our best present entrepreneurial interests to announce the death. I mean terrorists set out to destroy capitalism were doing it in the name of their god. A fully present Celestial kept the world together for centuries. No longer needed in the digital age. Think of the Celestial as analog scheduled for extinction like pen and paper."

He sighed deeply.

"Of course, it could be that creation was a botched job and we're left with it. Like a painter walking away from a canvas he's fucked up."

I shook my head. This guy Dan was very unstable mentally.

"Who could kill a Celestial Perfection? And why would such a perfection find any fault in himself or they self that had to be killed?"

Dan nodded.

"I agree with you but only if I thought the CP was a presence. But what if the CP is some sort of emerging something, not quite formed yet, on its way. In process. Pre-presence never to be present."

"So vulnerable it could be killed?"

"Forget about the God is dead crap. It's for idiots. It assumes something exists when that assumption cannot be made."

"And how does killing my girlfriend forever fit into that processing? I mean besides being a wake-up call to me."

"I sometimes envision that we mortals are part of that Celestial processing. We're sort of working off each other. We're needed in the Celestial dialogue. We're the Celestine's companions on a journey. 'You complete me' sort of Rom-Com script. Your lover, Bettina, was on that journey. Alive or dead she still is."

It stunned me that Dan knew her name. I mentioned that.

"I took a wild guess," he said, flippantly and took another slug. He passed to me. I did likewise.

"I still think this sucks. She's being used. Who agreed to help this presence reach maturity? I never signed up to be a babysitter."

"Did I say presence? Forget that. What if there's a certain light that came out of the Big Bang and it radiates in all of us?"

"Like radioactivity?"

"More like a photosynthetic process but one not confined to time or space. Or plants. Or the sun. Or air. It doesn't break off when you die. It's a wave of memory, particles of endless transformation. Is the light on us now in this park the light of yesterday? Or last year? Or a hundred years ago?"

I threw myself at this like a drowning man grabs the head of his rescuer.

"She's in the light?"

"Maybe. And in what one place is the light? Am I wrong in saying that you see Bettina everywhere?"

"Yeah, I do. You know, her death is the first real experience in my life. I was a kind of slob of the ego before."

"I can see that. Too bad you're looking for her presence. That's very anthropomorphic. Like a hammer destined to see only nails."

"Yeah, right. I see that it's more of a light traveling through."

"That's also a shit way of looking. Physics won't help you with death."

"I think I'm just hooking up with what you said about light and all that."

"Did I say all that? Look, Dan, you are all alone here on this park bench talking to yourself. You didn't share that bottle. You drank it all yourself."

"And that's how it ended?" Dr. Wrong-Wong-Nutley asked me. "You were alone on that bench talking to yourself?"

"Is that very bad?"

"I would say it's not good at this point. Did you find some relief in what you told yourself?"

"You mean what Dan told me?"

"Clearly, you grasp that you were Dan, and he was Dan and there was just one Dan, you."

"But I'm not Dan. Why didn't I say I was Theo?"

"The schizophrenic does not give his own name to his alternate identities. That's textbook."

"So, I'm textbook?"

"Perhaps if you didn't drink so much you wouldn't talk to yourself."

"I spend a lot of time talking to Bettina."

"At this point in your therapy we haven't established a real existence for Bettina so it might be best to say as little as possible to her until her presence is verified empirically."

"I talk to her even though she might have died."

"My professional opinion is that talking to the dead does neither you nor the dead any good. "

"Why is that? In your professional opinion?"

"You wind up revisiting all quarrels, old injuries, trespasses against each other which cannot be resolved, one of you being dead. In this case, Bettina."

"Maybe she's not."

"Maybe you know very well she's gone, and you just can't accept it. At any rate, we will wait for empirical verification. Meanwhile, stay out of Prospect Park. It's lost its gritty, scummy authenticity anyway. Travel elsewhere. But don't go back there. You don't want to run into Dan again."

Book Three

CHAPTER TWENTY-FIVE

WHAT IS THE BOND?

"So, she is with you now?" Madame La Babeuf asked me, as we sat in front of the dryers watching the clothes jostle around. She handed the photo back to me.

"You mean physical presence?"

She gave me a baffled look.

Madame La Babeuf was a very dignified old lady with her silver hair combed back tight and into a bun. She wore the palest of coral lipstick. At any age, French women are sexy. They don't leave their apartments without looking sexy.

I hung around my laundromat near the Louis Pasteur Institute just to see and talk to such lovely ladies. I had this idea that Bettina would be old now, dignified, lovely mature with shining silver hair.

"Elle est principalement avec moi dans l'esprit maintenant," I told her.

"Elle est morte?"

"We lived together *cinquante ans* and then she died. A cancer that came and went and then finally came and killed her."

She didn't seem to accept that story because her eyes narrowed, and her nose wrinkled.

"Cinquante ans? Je pense you are not forty?"

"Twenty-eight actually," I said. *"Vingt-huit."*

She laughed.

"Vous etes fou toujours."

"Maybe. It's just that I tell different stories of our life together. She is here. Back at Rue Mouffetard. She called me up here in Paris

one night. Must have been early morning in the U.S. and Bettina--
that's her name -- said if I wanted to have her for her whole life, I
could."

I had to translate that. What Bettina had really said was that she
agreed to come to Paris, but I wasn't to take this as any kind of long-
term commitment. She'd expect to pay all her own expenses.

I went on to tell Madame La Babeuf how happy the last ten years
of marriage had been with Bettina. We had two daughters who
already possessed the strengths and loveliness of their mother.

I went on and on, embellishing, detailing, laying down all the
events of Nonie and Sylvie's growing up, and not neglecting to
disclose the great bond between Bettina and myself.

"Quel est ce lien?" she asked, dubiously, either at the one word or
the whole story.

"Our bond? Eh bien, we had all three pieces of amour. Affection
of course. Each time we came together again, we would kiss. Not
just in the French double cheek kiss but full on the lips. *Forte étreinte.*
And beyond that we had a deep sharing so that apart we yearned
for each other. An existential shared being in the world."

I paused.

"Like Sartre says. Ontologique."

"That man!" Madame La Babeuf dismissed with a wave of her
hand. "He loved a woman who loved every man more than he. *Un
cocu.* She. *La scandaleuse.*"

I pedaled hard to get her off poor Jean-Paul and Simone.

"We had that. Bettina and myself. Sex. Coït. Private. Not
scandaleuse."

She gave me a skeptical look.

"Tu as l'air trop gros pour autant de coït."

"Elle m'a monté. C'était une selle confortable."

She laughed and slapped my shoulder.

"Where are your daughters now?"

"They go to school. They want to be artists."

"Tu as des photos?"

"Photos? Of them? Not on me. "

"That is a disaster, n'est-ce pas?"

Yes, she was right. No photos. Even worse. I didn't know if they
were real. Of course, they existed.

"Do you not think if you had two daughters, they would come to
look for you?"

"I don't know."

I wanted to say maybe I only knew them when I went looking

for water. The time that wasn't in time. And if I knew them at that time that wasn't in time. They would be unreal. Illusion.

None of this did I express to Madame La Babeuf. She might think I was just another crazy hanging out at the laverie.

"A great deal seems unreal to me these days," I told her.

She put a hand on top of mine.

For a second, I wondered if she was a reincarnated Bettina, but Bettina would never get that old.

"Le temps sont irréel. I believe that we live at a moment when the unreal seems most real to us."

"Un autre catastrophe?"

She shrugged. She didn't know.

"Perhaps it saves us. *Le reel non.* It is the invisible that all believers believe. *N'est-ce pas? L'invisible est le lien.*"

"It's the most real?"

She nodded.

"Et votre femme?"

"A photo wouldn't do her justice. I have her clear in my mind. Her face, her hair, her hands, her neck, her bosom, her thighs, her legs, her ankles, her feet. "

"Alors, elle est très jolie?"

"Comme les cieux," I told her, looking from the linoleum floor, in poor shape, to ceiling glass to the rain outside and a dark grey ceiling blocking out the heavens.

She gave me then the kind of look mothers give a child destined to fail, a look of such sadness that you thought I had told her I was going to kill myself, a look you give someone bowed down in grief because they have lost the woman they've loved their whole life.

"Le temps est l'école dans laquelle nous apprenons," she told me, putting her aged hand on my big paw. *"Le temps est le feu dans lequel nous brûlons."*

I muddled over that for the rest of my life, never sure what it had to do with me.

Funny how that stayed with me.

CHAPTER TWENTY-SIX

CHEZ CAROLIEN

By the time I was thirty, I began to find Bettina in every place I travelled to. If she wasn't there, I fit her in.

The truth was I couldn't be any place without her. If I saw a beautiful woman, she was Bettina. If I saw young lovers, it was Bettina and me. We went everywhere together, met all challenges, overcame all obstacles, dreamed together, held ourselves together in a oneness that could not be divided. Death was intimidated, stayed away, like the snow cannot hold ground in the shimmering sun of early Spring. We were bound stronger than the tides to the moon, the grass to the sun, the dreamer to the dream.

It was so that I sold the laundromat, left Paris, and moved to Utrecht, The Netherlands. I don't know why there. I didn't want to live in the World's Fair/Times Square circus of Amsterdam. I told people I was a European tour guide and perhaps I was, touring only two people, Bettina, and myself.

I wound up at Carolien's, not quite a pensione, not quite a two-star hotel, not quite a hostel, not quite a flop house or a boarding house. It would in time be knocked out of business by the *AirBEDS* and *VBROS*, but they were not in existence then. So much digital tech was yet on the horizon.

Carolien's was a world scheduled for extinction, ways of living declared obsolete, but no one knew it. I mean I didn't. There was no "back in the day" dismissals because the past had not been so abruptly dismissed as old and analog.

No, the past still flowed into time present and on into time future without a technological review or proof of graduation required. I felt I could reach out to whoever I wished to reach out to and that I was reachable. I didn't imagine that a smart-ass phone would conclude I had never reached anyone, and no one had ever reached me, that I had been out of touch with all the marvelous stuff that was going on in cyberspace, a dimension of a new reality inconceivable in those dark analog days I was now living in.

It seems we were all solipsists before the advent of a handheld widget that could make us all sociable, just as we were all doomed before the advent of Christ who amended the doom his Father had plotted. I became a permanent boarder at Carolien's retreat from those dark confusions.

What is a permanent boarder you ask in a world in which each one of us right now has not been promised tomorrow, or even another second of life? What is a permanent boarder when all boarders are mortal?

And why would I now seek permanence of a life which pains me terribly because I have lost someone who was the essential part of my existence?

Nothing for me either lives or dies, remains forever, or disappears totally because this one person who is more myself than what remains now of me is gone. I am now tortured by a sense that when we loved I was not there, that I was fully aware of what I had only after she was gone, gone permanently.

Why then would I be now so magnetized by this promise of permanence, by permanently boarding in a world in which the lasting center of my life was gone?

I suppose I thought: What if I could find her here, or only just a window to her, to what doesn't die, what lives though believed dead? I believe I felt that I could find her here among those who couldn't be evicted, who would stay as they were, in these digs, forever. And if anyone went looking for them, they would be found here because they would always be here, timeless.

In short, I decided I needed to immerse myself into the craziest disorder of life, so full of aberrant energy and mindless living that death would leave me alone. I went into a world where as Carolien put it "The rule here is that there is no rule."

Not even Death's.

One characteristic all the Permanent Boarders at Carolien's had in common was an alcohol or soft drug connection, alone or combined. We smoked and drank, rolled joints, sliced hash, swallowed magic shrooms, passed bongs, slugged beer, decorked wine, talked incessantly, laughed, cried, fought at all hours of the night, slept in the day, and woke up mid-day to enjoy the 24-hour breakfast Carolien's offered.

We were all like roosted birds whiling away the time in so many ways that made us always unaware of what day it was, or more, importantly, where yesterday had gone or what inevitable darkness lay at the end of everyone's road.

We slept late, bayed at the moon at night, eyed the working world passing by as if it were an insult to us that would never mean anything to us. I wore the same shirt and ripped shorts for weeks on end. Nothing we could wear, or hold meant anything to us. We bought cheap beer by the case and wine cheaper still. We pooled dole money to roll wicked thin joints. I said I had a pot trust and was living on that.

It was a place where I could live without feeling I had lost my reason, my lovely, sweet reason to live. Or thought I could. It was a world without a center.

Strangely and quite insanely, in Carolien's eyes, we all had promise of one sort or another and though we were each our own worst enemy, she saw some faint embers in our souls that someday and somehow could be brought to life.

The one rule this marvel of a lady had, as I say, was that there were no rules. The unruled could change their lives without choosing to or planning to. There was no rule that could keep us in any one place. We couldn't die because death demanded eternal obedience. And we would not give that. We were bad subjects of Death's Rule.

On another level I simply asked myself what had all the rules and plans in the world done for anyone but lead them to the grave? Why wouldn't misrule detour us from that? The bottom of it all, Carolien told me, was not order but chaos. La Commedia she called it.

Did I still ask myself: Was this wonderful woman crazy? I think, yes, she was mad, but it was a harmless, generous madness. She was loved.

I think Carolien suspected in my case that a lost love haunted my soul, although I never mentioned Bettina. If I did while talking late at night out in the garden, I don't remember. Although it is commonplace to tell the grieving that they have their memories, the truth is that such memories are a torture and more torturous still when we think they may be false.

Carolien might have gone the extra mile with a great many lost souls but her sister, called simply, *de Keurmeester*, "the judge," frog walked and ejected from the boarding house those who she pronounced as worthless, burnt out, thieves or moral miscreants. So, one sister was generous, forgiving, and compassionate and quite grandly mad and the other was deaf to all excuses, a veritable hanging judge, mean in her heart and narrow of focus.

This judge of the soul of others asked us to follow the rules or get out. But because love and madness interrupt all lesser orders, no expulsion held. It is quite true that the place went from sunlight to darkness depending on which sister walked in.

What it came down to was that while Carolien lived in an anarchy of fantasy within a fantasy of total anarchy, a topsy turvy world where the Losers were noble dreamers, her sister lived in the real harsh world of business and had a 24-hour job keeping anarchy and fantasy from ruining their business. Her sense of order was defined by profit making as if the way to know thyself was to know what your income after taxes was. She was in short, a rigid bookkeeper of The Order of Profit.

Such an Order of Profit, this order of *de Cheermaster*, was not one the Permanent Boarders could recognize or appreciate. Of course, I realized that if any of them lived back in the U.S., they would have been living in cardboard boxes under bridges and Interstate overpasses.

We Permanent Boarders had all the basics provided at Chez Carolien gratis.

This morning, Carolien tells me she has four thousand sausages of unknown origin and unknown composition and twenty-five hundred *pizze* in miniature. Along with variables such as these, there were always eggs, yogurt, bread, baked and unbaked, jams, pasta, milk, and cheese. The "on the black market" cheese of the week was Raclette.

I travelled but always came back to Carolien's. Over the years, I had come back to Carolien's the way so many of the creatures we call "lesser" periodically journeyed back to one place. For me, the place was something like a human nature depository, a most curious natural history museum, where an endless variety of the human species could be found, a kind of aviary where strange birds perched and flew, slept, and screamed. I observed as if I were a

Charles Darwin and Carolien's was the Galápagos islands. I got to know the individual species very well. And I learned a lot from them.

I had this feeling that Bettina would admire what I was becoming. I was looking for her in everyone I met and so I had the zeal of the panicked. Among so much life, there would be her.

I could tell you I returned the way a man wandering without water in a desert returns to an oasis he knows. But then when I left I did so because Bettina wasn't there and I had to go and find her and when I returned to Carolien's, I returned with hope in my heart that in this strange world of The Permanent Boarders she was there too, permanent.

It was a sad circling, but it was what my life had become.

The Pater could have set up a Lab here, bringing all his Post-Docs with him. I wrote to Dirk every so often telling him to drop that dirty radio show and come to Carolien's. He said he couldn't because he might marry Evangeline Solly and she wouldn't want to live in a country where the average height of the women was 5'10."

He wrote and told me that he ran into Bettina at *The New Pompey* every once and awhile and she asked after me. I know he was lying. He was trying to make me feel good. Anyway, I couldn't imagine her anywhere but with me.

I don't know when I started seeing her here, travelling with me but I was so happy just to see her. Even if she wasn't there. *Maladie imaginaire* Madame La Babeuf called it. I don't know what Dr. Fraud would have said to this, but I'd rather see Bettina than not see her and that was that.

Tonight, most of the short-term tourists had gone out for the evening. Simone, who had worked in Milano before he decided he could no longer live in a country ruled by Silvio Farabutto and had emigrated to The Netherlands, was making spaghetti alla carbonara in a kitchen that was open to all. However, it was Simone who easily commandeered the stove, with everyone's blessing, when he was inspired to cook. His talents in the kitchen were breathtaking.

Sadly though, he said politics had destroyed his will to cook. He could not begin an elaborate preparation without seeing Farabutto's face in an onion or a potato, could not chop and dice without going into a fury of chopping and dicing that face. He was inspired to cook mostly in the middle of the night or about midday when he usually woke up.

Simone occasionally went out to pursue his Dutch citizenship or rail to Amsterdam in search of a variety of pot with magical, mythical mind-blowing properties -- il Grand Kronik -- or work, when his funds ran low, *"sotto il tavolo"* he would whisper, in this or that restaurants in Utrecht, mostly those on the Oudegracht, the Old Canal, where the higher price tourist restaurants were.

Reinout, who was a sort of part time postman/drug dealer, on call squatter, and full-time anarchist, showed up just as Simone and I were about to begin twirling with fork and spoon a first portion of the one kilo of carbonara Simone had made. Reinout's trademarks were the sported palestino scarf he wore around his neck and the tear in the backside of his pants out of which colorful briefs showed.

Wouter, who sat at the other end of the table, had been instructed by Carolien to bring up from the cavernous cellars of this early 18th century *herenhuis* a few cases of wine, mercifully dry and red.

I found Wouter interesting because he had a style that engaged you on multiple levels. Talking to him was like going up and down on an elevator accompanied by a man using a jackhammer. His eyes teared incessantly making it hard to look straight at him.

The easy key to Wouter's volatile chatter and his watery ducts was in the drugs. These drugs, mostly uppers or a smorgasbord of what Wouter could get his hands on, mellowed out with pot and beer, went to work to produce a hi-speed, souped up alertness. His reddened eyes went wide, watered, blinked as his words tumbled out. Drugs didn't put his brain to sleep but kicked it up to hyper speed. When his mind was rolling faster than the Eurostar, Wouter presented like one electrified, sparking nerve end.

I found the lethargy of Simone a relief from Wouter. For sure, it was interspersed with violent outbursts against Italian oligarchs, but I paid little attention. Simone went around in a perpetual hash cloud which, I observed on numerous occasions, did in no way affect the sharpness of his mind but perhaps mellowed him into a steady state of lethargy. He could sit on the veranda smoking pot, chugging vino, and gabbing hour after hour.

He never tired of berating Farabutto whom he referred to as *"Quel maiale scandaloso,"* a disgraceful pig, and bewailing the fate of his country in the hands of this pig. But then again, he always added as a codicil, his countrymen deserved what they got. They had learned to wallow in the filth thrown at them by the super wealthy, *i Magnati,* by the global thieves who trampled on all that was of quality: *"Essi calpestano tutto ciò che è di ottima qualità nella vita e sostituire tutto con merda."*

This evening, all the Permanent Boarders were seated under the tent canopy in the courtyard below drinking up the wine and listening to Ferdinand Corbeau, the crow, although strangely he called himself "Le Loup," the Wolf, speak of his amorous adventures in Sweden.

Le Loup had been a gendarme in Marseille, but that policing life became too dangerous as the hashish gangs comprised mostly of North African immigrants armed with assault weapons brought in from Eastern Europe had made policing the streets a tour in a war zone.

After gang members driving a vehicle customized with a heavy battering ram had rammed into Le Loup's police car and sent him to hospital with multiple fractures, he had resigned and left Marseille. He went to Sweden as private security where, according to him, he spent most of his time wooing the Swedish ladies whom he described with a very French gesture of kissing two fingers and closing his eyes. According to Le Loup, the Swedish women looked upon a Frenchmen as an enticement they couldn't resist. And, according to him, he was especially irresistible.

I had observed the harmless Le Loup sitting in front of a computer, studying the home page of a business he was attempting to launch while glancing furtively at any attractive woman who entered the reception. Le Loup had been launching that business for all the years I knew him and thus far it existed only as an incomplete website.

I remained curious of this behavior. Le Loup could be very amusing. I concluded that he was a self-deceived, collapsing man in his forties facing some sort of *crise de quarante*. However, in his own imagination, Le Loup fired up images of himself as a reincarnated Don Juan, a man who women could not resist. He lived in a deep delusion of himself, a wolf to all women.

Why Le Loup had left such a glorious life among all those admiring women in Sweden, he never told anyone, and no one asked but suspected one or the other of those women had brought harassment charges against him.

There were few questions of that sort among the Permanent Boarders. Also, no one questioned what Le Loup said because they all knew that among a house full of inveterate liars, Le Loup was merely a standout. Among those who daily lived in illusion and delusion, Le Loup was just the easiest to identify.

Hamlet saw an illusion on the parapet of Elsinore Castle; Hamlet's delusion was that he was capable of avenging his father.

The Permanent Boarders wanted their own pasts kept private

and had made an unspoken pact not to question others regarding theirs. But I knew from what Carolien had told me that Monsieur Corbeau was more of a stalker and voyeur than a romantic figure women found irresistible. He was tall and his hair dark, but his face was long and his look hangdog, *un coup d'oeil de chien battu*, or in Corbeau's case *le loup battu*. The wolf was more the cowering jackal that observed from the shadows, afraid to come forward was the way Carolien phrased it.

Carolien referred to Corbeau as a man seeking to both find and forget a truth he already knew, an irony he failed to appreciate because he lacked a sense of irony. He was both hopeless in her view and yet worth saving; he was simultaneously already finished and at the end of his rope and yet always within sight of beginning a wonderful voyage.

Carolien was a Sigmund Freud in her grasp of the subtextual life of every one of her Permanent Boarders. She did not refrain from turning an examining eye on me. I feared it because while I knew in my clearest, sanest moments that Bettina Parisi was not really with me but somewhere, probably in love, in Brooklyn, she very much nevertheless existed for me there at Carolien's.

Did I talk to Bettina? Yes, I did. I couldn't help it. For me, she existed everywhere I was.

I feared Carolien telling me straight out that Bettina was an illusion and that my delusion was in thinking I could find her.

I had reason to fear. Carolien gradually surmised the existence of a woman in my life, perhaps because she heard me talking to someone I called Bettina? She did indeed pull the name Bettina out of me. I proceeded to tell her the whole long story of my life with Bettina, from the young love we shared at The Beach House to the last time we spoke.

From that moment on, Carolien's advice was for me to return to Bettina and tell her I was a hopeless wreck without her. It didn't matter that I told her repeatedly that Bettina had her own life now.

And then sometimes, I told Carolien that I preferred to think Bettina had died than think I had lived with her for so long and yet not fully grasped the wonder of each moment, that I had somehow not been there with her. And yet, I admitted to Carolien, my hope that I could find Bettina. Re-find her.

To all this, Carolien did not respond, and in that, that response of silence, of a look I could not understand, of yet patience and pity,

I remembered Bettina.

Carolien's acute observations left out no one. She had M. Corbeau, Le Loup, on a one more complaint status and he would be thrown out of the pensione. He was, Carolien told me, easy to read but Iuliana was not.

Iuliana was not quite so simple. Iuliana, the only female Permanent Boarder and as such, treated as a queen. She was quite a tease always in a dishabille state, moving about the pensione like royalty. She had already told me that I was fun, sad, *inconscient*, the world's biggest dupe, *très cynique*, *un idéaliste*, a worthless liar, and the only man she would ever love.

"She tells all of them that," Carolien warned me.

"You know, Carolien, the first time Bettina saw me she said to her friends "That's the one I want.""

"I didn't know that. How would I know that?"

"Truth is, I'm not sure I know that. It's kind of just in my head. But I like to think it's real."

"Some things need to be shoveled out of the head."

CHAPTER TWENTY-SEVEN

IN THE MIDDLE OF IT

Iuliana, I discovered, spun stories as readily as a spider spun thread.

She spun them for a purpose. A different story for each victim. What her purpose was in the case of Le Loup, for instance, I don't think she knew except to know that he was a faithful dog to her, tongue hanging out like a dog following a bitch in heat.

Iuliana had that effect on men. In fact, the Permanent Boarders called her Circe, the one who could turn men into swine and then devour them. They all, in their turn, waiting anxiously for her to do so.

I was already under a spell, enchanted with Bettina. What I saw in every woman's face was the face that I had lost, and a jolt of deep longing held me, and I felt so profoundly alone without her. My enchantment coupled with my sense that all was lost, that I was now forever to be alone swept over me like the tsunami that had cast me into the sea. And yet persistent was a panic to find her. That was all real to me.

Dante showed us that one can suffer greatly in the Inferno but on any ring of that Hell was there simply a lover such as myself, one who had loved and lost his love, or one who felt he had had an angel by his side for a very long time but had failed to recognize her, or one whose only salvation was to find once again this great love but was tortured with the thought she was beyond rediscovery, that she was dead.?

I don't see those sorry suckers in any ring of Hell. I mean those whose loss was unrecorded by any poet but were plunged into a fire of torment while still alive.

I couldn't dwell on feeling I had lost Bettina, that she had died, that I had missed a life with her, that, at the same time, I had had a life with her, and I had been always unaware of it and of ever realizing that without her, I would be a lost emptiness. I was realizing that even what Bettina had repeatedly called my oversized, ridiculous sense of grandiosity could not find a path through this unbearable feeling of having lost her.

I tried to distract myself with the lives of my fellow Permanent Boarders, lives which did nothing, accomplished nothing, declared no purpose or ambition yet seem so energetically alive, so mired in every present moment, going on from hour to hour, day to day without any review, without any summation. They had no beginning and no end. They were always in their own screwed up ways always in the middle of it, of the passing moment, never ahead of it or behind it.

And this is where I no longer was. Regardless of our age, we always imagine ourselves right smack in the middle of the vibrancy of the moment when in fact we are everywhere in our minds but in that moment. We imagine all the moments to come when in fact we can be seconds away from an everlasting end regardless of what our age may be.

What a mockery "Be present!" and all the mindfulness claptrap is to a man who knows he was never present, could never be present but whose nature would endlessly rewind to what was and what was lost. My mind was full of loss, of a presence now absent.

I sought life as it moved in the present through the lives of The Permanent Boarders. Certainly, they had no Celestial Permanence, but they were here to be seen and heard. I yearned for that presence.

It was in Paris that Iuliana first heard of Carolien's pension in The Netherlands where meals were gratis and lodging possible for those willing to work. She and Carolien were at once compatible. Carolien admired the young lady's ambition to succeed in one day owning her own business. Iuliana was fervent in studying Dutch so that she could become a Dutch citizen and most helpful as a staff member who could speak French, German, Italian, Russian, English and each day more and more Dutch.

Iuliana was a vivacious spirit at the pensione. *Une étincelle merveilleuse de la vie* Carolien called her. A wonderful spark of life. For me, she was at times a noise, a glare, a kind of rude visitor into the privacy of my quest. At other times, the way she brought us all to life, brought each of us out of whatever demons suddenly visited us, sparked the *Élan vital* in my own soul.

No Beatrice or Dulcinea, she, however. In her way, Iuliana sized up all the Permanent Boarders as she did everyone else: either something of use to her, possibly of some limited use, or not of any use at all. And on this scale, they were all some limited use to her but at bottom nothing that she yearned for could come of knowing them, being with them, talking to them, making love to them.

Iuliana had obviously noticed immediately that Carolien and I were old friends. She complained to Simone that I had brought an arrogant and pissy flock of Americans into <u>her </u>home, as she now thought of Carolien's pensione. What I had done was simply find digs for the sad bunch of American tourists I once in a rare while had corralled.

I was indeed the world's worst tour guide for so many reasons. I didn't look to the ease and comfort of the travelers. I didn't care what was on their bucket list of the day. We moved on when I said so. I mocked their attempts at speaking French or Italian and told them to shut up. I couldn't bear to eat with them and go through the madness of listening to them order, divide the bill, and push their noise into the ears of quiet diners.

The Germans may be demanding travelers, but they do it *sotto voce*, poisoned darts of speech precisely targeted. The Brits, in their arrogance, made more of a fuss over not finding the joy in everything that was foreign and should have been British. Americans, though, took the prize, in my opinion, their heads didn't even enter a foreign country though their mouths boomed full volume everywhere. They were always mind wise and temperamentally back in Indiana or some other coronary arrest of the American heartland. They could dream of eating a Big Mac back home while walking through the culinary capitals of Europe.

I went full out nasty on all of them over almost everything.

So, I tortured those who paid me to guide them. Word got around. I was shunned. No one wanted to be guided around Europe by an unlikable tour guide. No one wanted to pay the price of seeing a world not already in their heads. Of course, I was unlikable for other reasons. Loss hurts but it also gives a dark cast to the eye.

I was running out of the money from the *laverie* sale and staying cheaply at Carolien's was a necessity. These Permanent Boarders, masterless men and one woman really, were for all their madness deeply in the flow of life. They were confused and confusing but not as I was. They pulled me back into a place where grief and confusion got lost in the crowd.

Dr. Groan wanted to charge me $500 for 40 minutes of therapy for 19 years, none of which added up to what I found as a Permanent Boarder.

The story Iuliana best loved to tell was her own. It was the thread she was skilled in spinning and while I didn't believe a word she said, I remained spellbound by every word she said.

I think this was so because what I felt was that she had seen more death and dying from the very start of her life, felt threatened and endangered, ran from it but couldn't find the safe spot.

She was, in short, experienced in seeing and knowing death, and I found genius in that perhaps because Bettina's death, if she had died, had ambushed me, blind sighted me, gone so far and outside what was in my head that grandiosity changed to pitiable in an instant.

I may never be likeable, but I loved one person with all my heart and am humbled and awed by death in ways never marketed.

Carolien's was a temporary refuge for Iuliana, and I knew this because Iuliana told me. I was a confidant only because she thought I could be her passage to the U.S. There was no death there, only frenetic life. For her, the After Life was already going on in southern California, the Hamptons, Miami Beach, Las Vegas, the Big Easy! the Big Apple!

I found it so sad. She didn't listen to my sad story.

She only laughed.

"You are like a baby who has a life full of toys and is still a whiny baby. You loved someone and then lost her. So what? There are other women in the world! And you didn't even know if she loved you. Such a baby!"

So what? So, everything I told her.

Of course, she laughed at that.

The arrangement Carolien had with Iuliana was different than the one she had with all the other Permanent Boarders. She would let Iuliana stay if she didn't break the hearts of every worker in the place and have them at each other's throats for her sake.

I thought Iuliana was just full of all kinds of ambitions.

"Maybe something else," Carolien replied. "Bad family. Bad government. Bad everything. Lots of courage she has to come this far. Maybe she can calm down now. I don't know. She may be ruined. Here."

She pointed to her temple.

Carolien studied my face.

"She is young, but she has lived already so many lives. All no good. Hard. You know? Hard. But real."

She punched me on the arm.

I know Carolien thought I spent too much time in my own head where my thoughts became less and less real, more and more exhausted in discovering what may never have existed in the first place. But in that place, Carolien's, we, the Permanent Boarders, were all equally caught in a blind, mindless attraction; we were all digging holes distant from the real. Perhaps we were all too frightened to look up and see that we had wasted our lives on trying to escape it. Life. Our fallen lives. And now death.

But Iuliana was different. Her life had brought her into close contact with death and yet she believed that she could find so much life that death wouldn't touch her. She thought that for her there would be no death.

So very strange. Even though she had been surrounded by death, the fear of it, the recklessness of it, she didn't know that death shadowed her, that people who went to Dizzyland, U.S.A. died too, that mortality wins at the roulette wheel of our lives, that someone who is more a part of you than yourself can die and send you into a vacuum where you spin but never move.

I knew too, on the good days, that Bettina was positioned inside me, neither one of us apart from the other. On bad days, I think we separated but on all the good days I know even death couldn't do that.

I dreamed that I was on my knees digging a hole in the mud, looking down into it for it was dark and deep and then I saw Bettina down there, no, I saw her alongside me looking down, unaware of my presence.

"I miss you," I told her.

'You don't miss me," she said. "I don't miss you because you're going away. I must think of something else while you're gone. Why would I miss you if you're going away?"

And then I realized I'm not on my knees looking into a hole but standing. I'm on a road with Bettina and I'm crying.

"Put your big boy pants on," she tells me. "You don't' have long to go. See, the road ahead is not long but this is where I stop."

Yes, it is, I see for she heads down a side road and fades into the distance, and I look ahead.

I'm alone but the road ahead is not long as she said. I can't see where it ends but I have the feeling it can't be long. The kind of sweep of wind that empties you heart, mind, and soul wrapped itself around me.

I was so dreadfully alone that it frightened me into waking.

I heard loud voices and laughter coming from the garden below.

The Permanent Boarders enjoying their permanence.

CHAPTER TWENTY-EIGHT

THE Q TRAIN

It was the habit of Wouter and Adrianus to make their appearance by midday, puffy faced and sleepy, unprimed to say much before the sun set for it was their habit to stay up late under the garden pavilion drinking and smoking a variety of pot. They would join Simone and Iuliana on the patio, enjoying the first drink of the day, the four of them making it clear to the transient guests that theirs was a sacred ritual of the pensione, one that the Fly Throughs, the Tourist Wide Eyes, the Booked Tour Sucker Class -- all such impermanent intruders could not hope to share.

Adrianus, the dean of us all, called them Mortalism Refugees, a diaspora scattering everyday lives into a ten-day world of hospitality predators.

In the eyes of we Permanent Boarders, the Fly Throughs were no more than fools who overpaid for their comforts, their pleasures, their future memories of traipsing throughout Europe as dupes. The more they were duped, the more they loved the place and the people.

Italy was much loved, the one place that had three hundred years of learning how to scam, fleece, suck dry and bamboozle tourists, especially Americans. The French found it hard to bend to the buffoons they considered their cultural inferiors. They would not stoop to putting up with Americans, regardless of the money to be made. I thought the Italians, though, found their satisfaction in the con, in drawing Americans and Brits especially into a glass bead game in which the Italians knew that they were the master, that reality so cleverly played and so richly enjoyed.

Although each of the Permanent Boarders targeted all tourists as transient fools and inveigled them in various cons, the midday boozing was not an occasion to pursue those interests. This was one of the times during the day that we bonded as a family, an unusual family with odd bonds, but a family nonetheless and I found myself part of it, found some rest and peace to be part of it, found something once again amid exile and La Commedia and the angst of my own mourning and confusion.

It was better than being exiled in my laundromat, chatting with les grandes dames all day, though I did find them all so much more decent than The Mater. I never thought that Madame La Babeuf would stoop to marry a low-life, criminal degenerate like Fartsworth, or after he croaked, marry an even greater degenerate, Jabba.

Each of us as Permanent Boarders needed this consortium because we had each in our own way already lost, shattered, or been ejected from all normal forms of societal connections. Being Permanent Boarders, although this idea was itself illusionary, gave us a last refuge of solidarity.

I recognized both the connection and the illusion. We all suffered from the same malaise. We wanted to live in a world that didn't exist or couldn't exist. We wanted to live within the enchantments that possessed us. We wanted to find a true love and live with her all the days of our lives. I couldn't find Bettina but somehow here among this lot, yearning for what was illusionary, or worse, dead and gone, kept me alive because their lives without purpose made so much sense to me.

Everything that had been predicted as my fate by so many, from my own distracted parents to my ridiculous tutors, to my demented mental health care professionals, as well as my own twin brother's ill-tempered, distasteful girlfriend, a fierce Maenad, had come true.

The thorns I had fallen upon which had me bleeding were a fate to be without the woman I loved, who I could not find because she had died, or, a deeper misery, that we had been happy together for a very long time and I had failed to relish each moment. I had been absent during the finest, sweetest moments of my own life, my time with her. Time now left to me made ashes of my soul.

I had a dream that Bettina was just up ahead, pulling a roller pack and another bag in her other hand. She was moving very fast. I was behind her trying to keep up. We were heading for the Q train and there were people all around us moving in the same direction.

I caught up with her.

"Let me carry that one," I said reaching out for what she was carrying in that hand, and she held it out and I took it and we kept on walking quickly.

I guess we were worried we wouldn't get to the Q train before it left. She never looked at me. I don't know if she made it to the train because the last thing I remembered before I woke up was that the Q train's last car was leaving the station, the throng of people were gone, and I was alone on a very silent, empty platform.

I told that dream to Carolien and asked her why the Q train? What was with that? Why was it so prominent? I never heard of a Q train, never had been on one.

"It's a mystery, no?" Carolien said to me, nodding.

"Really," I replied.

I told her it did make me feel good that Bettina in the dream had handed what she was carrying to me.

"It was like she trusted me."

But for what?

CHAPTER TWENTY-NINE

SQUATTERS

In Carolien's wise words, we Permanent Boarders were "outliers," liminal souls and outcast rebels, failures and malcontents, incorrigible by any standards, on a final precarious edge, barely functional in any productive way and yet we felt a need and a mutual benefit in being together, to see ourselves as a band of brothers and one sister.

To me, they were indeed the family I had never had. They made my tutors, Spinalzo and Patawalla and all the Lab Post-Docs and my shrinks, Wrong and Fraud, and my Mater and my Pater -- all of them -- blockages that I had managed to flush.

I did, however, miss my twin. Dirk wasn't worth much on re-sale, but I didn't measure worth the way Jabba did. Dirk had a good heart. In fact, he got the heart, and I got the brains. Unless of course you're a Romantic and think it was my heart that bound me to Bettina's. Or you think no one of intellect would be in such a state of confusion as I was.

You can be unlikeable and still have a heart. You think only those you like have a heart, as if you're liking gave it to them? The "others" you are to "do unto" are other to you because there is nothing about them you can identify as likeable. You don't have the heart for them, these others, and so you can never see the heart in them.

I saw and heard the heart of my fellow Permanent Boarders.

"The burden of horrific memories has a way of dissolving very quickly in the American psyche," Bram Adrianus told us one evening as we sat under the tent awning at the end of Carolien's garden.

He had a soft, mesmerizing voice, so attracting that when he spoke, we all listened. As always, I could hear the drink in his voice, but it never clouded his mind.

"They feel no shackles of class and family," he went on, "nor do they fear the power of religions and political ideologies to make them distrustful of their neighbors. The fear of a wealth divide igniting a bloody revolution is a non-existent fear in America because the poor are branded to think they are always one step away from fortune and fame. The Great American Delusion. Endless delusions feeding on delusions, conspiracies, paranoia and illusions of self-empowerment."

"In America, " New York said, loudly, "a hot lady from Slovenian who can hardly read or write could marry a hedge fund mogul or the president. "

"He's talking about you, Iuliana," Simone teased.

"He's talking about the president's trophy wife, idiot."

I had heard Adrianus go on about Americans many times before. I knew his take. Americans were not burdened by the darkness of their own congenital defects because they simply had no ingrained awareness and slight consideration of the past, especially a past that happened to others, elsewhere, the foreigners.

What they didn't experience within their own minds did not exist for them, nor, as they were, in market and military value, the premiere country in the world, were they motivated to learn the lessons of elsewhere.

As Adrianus expressed it, the Americans were incurious, ignorant of all but cost effectiveness, rash, violent and bloody, in a rush to despoil the world for quick returns on investment. More and more wealth in fewer and fewer hands did not frighten the Americans. What social class your family had been in for centuries did not matter. Dividends, the moment, and ego were all that mattered.

"In the U.S., everyone is brand new because otherwise they would have to study the old, by which I mean Europe," Adrianus told us one night as we sat under the tent in the far corner of the garden, "So, they need to make up their own religions. Photoshop Jesus within ludicrous home-grown religions to fit the American rural psyche. They need to ignore the superiority of the British parliament, the Dutch acceptance of sex, drugs, and death. If they had a past, they ignored it. Every new birth is filled with possibilities untainted by the past. Innovation is their god because they are too arrogant to study what already exists. They rush to Italy to show the Italians how to make coffee, or to France, to show the French how to eat hamburgers, or to Islamic countries to show them how to render to Wall Street and throw away their religion. They fuse the poisons of their own productions into timeless classics the way street punks graffiti Notre Dame. Unbearable lot, really."

These were harsh words and, as the only American present, smoking and drinking under that awning that night, I could feel eyes upon me.

"What Adrianus says are reasons as to why you left that country?" Reinout asked me.

"They make pepperoni pizza," Simone said, shaking his head. "What is a pepperoni? They make it up. The word. Peperoni is a green pepper, not a sausage. They eat spaghetti and meatballs in all their ristorante. What Italian ever eats that?"

Eyes were still on me.

"I had personal, not political reasons," I said, sadly.

"There are no personal reasons," Reinout said, angrily. "Americans are at each other's throats not for personal reasons. The structure of their predatory economics has chewed up and spit out all the pretentions of their farting founding fathers."

Le Loup laughed at that.

I knew the heat would die down as the drink and pot settled in. But Reinout was still on a roll.

"White skin losers are gonna crush the dark-skinned losers because the white skinned winners tell them to. Even the French sans-culottes gutter wretch knew who was sucking his blood and it wasn't anybody laying in the gutter with him. But the Americans? The exploited think it's the exploited who are making them poor. I mean it's clever. The rich winners get the people they've fucked over to kill each other."

"It takes a lot of stupido to pull that off," Simone said.

"Well, the Americans have been working on priming that pump for a long time," Adrianus told us. "Shrewd beasts who innovate widgets and devour each other."

"They rally to Jesus," Reinout said and spit on the floor.

"You are all jealous," Iuliana cried out. "It's sour pits. You were nothing and became something in America, didn't you, Theodorus?"

"Sour grapes, I think," I told her. "Not sour pits. And, no, I thought I was something, a big something right from the start. Now,

I'm nothing. What I loved died. Where you are doesn't matter if the one you loved isn't with you. That's not political or structural. There's no economics to it. I loved and I lost who I loved."

"I hope there is profit in love," Iuliana said gayly and we all laughed.

She went on to express the view that this America was a country in which she knew she could do well.

"You are so much a man *dirige vers une mauvaise fin* that you make for yourself. I think you have a fatal *crise de nerfs*. That's not American. I've seen men like you in my own country. They are dead because they mourn for the dead and want to be with them. It is so stupid. They are alive. So stupid to go after what can never be returned to you when in front of you is everything. I think you will probably die in prison. Here is a man running to something he can never reach. She died to make room for another. That's the way the world goes on."

"I congratulate you on explaining death to us," Simone said, gallantly.

"I'm going to die in prison?" I asked, my voice weak.

"Of course. You are in there now."

"Hey, mio amore," Simone called out to Iuliana. "Where is your own country?"

Everyone laughed but I was still thinking about what she had said. I would probably die in prison?

At around midnight, we all went off, more than half in the bag, as they say, to an abandoned building some squatter friends of Reinout the postman were holding down squatter rights style.

Reinout knocked at a door with a glass pane painted black.

The door was opened a crack, Reinout was observed, he said a few words and we all followed him into a large empty room that looked as if it had once been public space. The walls were also painted black. We could hear music now and followed Reinout through a curtain and entered what looked like a large garage. The music was low volume techno and there were about forty or so people, some milling around, some standing watching the dancers who were the center of attraction.

Wouter immediately went in search of drink; Le Loup had already eyed his prey and was walking stealthily around the dancers and toward those standing on the other side of the dance floor.

Simone was the only one who at once got on the dance floor solo and though his body remained inert his oversized head moved in between the beat.

Later, when Iuliana showed up, wearing what looked like layers of gauzy veils which yet hid nothing of belly button and nipples, she sidled up to Simone, who remained in a Kronik daze, and gyrated while Iuliana had her arms over her head and eyes closed, moving to some rhythms far slower than what was playing.

Simone quit his dancing, such as it was, and came over to stand beside me.

"I told her I could take her to America. But she says she would have to be desperate."

"She's looking for bigger game."

"I bet she will throw a net over someone's head and all she has to do is bring him into the boat."

Simone returned to the dance floor and made his way to where Iuliana was doing her thing. Simone did his head shake alongside her.

"Hey, look who it is? The guy from New York."

I turned to see a tall man in his thirties with a big smile on his face and his arms wide open. New York. One of The Permanent Boarders, more occasional really than permanent.

New York had not been at Carolien's on my last two visits. He looked different, worn out. We spoke like old friends, fellow Permanent Boarders. It was clear that things were tough with him, as if his permanence had rusted.

"You over at Carolien's again?" I asked and New York nodded. He had arrived that evening. He was still a travelling salesman, selling what I never knew because New York never wanted to talk about his present life but only the plans he had for his future. He disparaged what he was doing and didn't what to talk about it.

"And you? You have another bunch of crazy American tourists with you?"

"I only had that one," I told him. "It was a bust. I've never liked people, especially the needy ones. And the rich, spoiled ones. Bettina once told me that to have a friend, you must be a friend. I guess I never worked at it."

"Look at Le Loup. He likes everybody."

I looked over and saw Le Loup talking to a young woman. She looked like a frightened bird mesmerized by a snake.

"He likes the ladies, eh?" New York said, elbowing me.

New York would tell me about the last country he had travelled through but would never tell where his home was. In his heart, he lived in New York, a place he had never been. He and his family lived in Slovakia. He had a wife and three young children, the youngest only a year, the oldest seven. Two girls and a boy. But New York had always represented himself as a free ranging rooster, open to all opportunities to get to New York where he would fulfill his potential. He seemed intent now on maintaining that pose, although his voice was losing its former exuberance in each succeeding year.

Carolien had told me what the case with New York was really and told me that the man had so much debt incurred by his stupid get to New York schemes that his wife had arranged with his employer to send his wages directly to her. New York would have to leave his family, his country, his job to achieve his dream of living like an ex-pat in New York.

I concluded that New York was an ex-pat of desire never to be fulfilled. When I expressed that thought to Carolien, she laughed. She told me that there was no certainty in what myself in particular imagined regarding the life of others. In Carolien's view, I was having enough difficulty detaching myself from my own delusions.

"There is a man running to something he can never reach," Carolien had said about New York. "And you are living in your head with a woman who is not living with you."

"She is. She's just not here right now."

"She's just not here?" Carolien mocked. "Look, you can go back to something some time ago in your head. But you can't change it. You're not here now, you keep trying to do that. And you know, for you now, I look at you. The future is dead. It's very sad. You need to snap out of it. You see the Boarders? They are shiftless and I think I'm done with them. But you know what?"

"What?"

"I'm going to throw all of them out. Watch."

She didn't. She said it a lot, but she didn't. She had hope that each one of us would resurrect ourselves.

The music suddenly went from tolerable to maddening and New York and I went outside. New York pulled out his wallet and showed me a card in Dutch.

"You see that?" he said. *"Ondernemer van de eerste orde.* Entrepreneur of the First Magnitude. Seven-week course and I passed with high honors."

"Congratulations," I said, beginning to look for an escape.

The last thing I wanted to return to was tragic sadness, glories never experienced, dreams never fulfilled.

"You don't think that's good being an entrepreneur? Start your own business. Financial services? There are three great things you can be in New York. Private equity partner. Hedge fund manager. Asset Management manager. Everybody in New York is busting for the future. Follow the money, my friend. I have an interview with Gore and Slash coming up."

There was a crack midway in New York's voice. That crack branded him more truthfully than his words.

"You know I think you're crazy," New York said, taking hold and trying to regain his full salesman confidence. "You come from New York, and you live here? With all these losers? Man, you should just give me your passport. Let me be you. I'd be out of here so quick."

He made a flyaway jet plane swoop with one arm.

"You have a woman waiting for you back home?" I asked.

His face flushed.

"Yes, my wife."

"Miss her?"

"To go fast you need to go alone," he told me, trying a smile.

Once again, my eyes rested on the shoes.

They looked like shoes that he had been wearing for a long, long time and they had survived because he had taken very, very good care of them. Polishing the leather every night before going to bed. But that hadn't saved them. They were finished. They had seen the farm.

And then when I force myself to meet New York's eyes, I notice that he had on an open collared cotton shirt with a frayed collar. His pants were rumpled, and the crease had vanished. His belt was black with some leather worn spots. He was a young man, but he seemed prematurely worn out. Rusting is what I had thought. Maybe New York knew it, and, in his fear, he used the word "entrepreneur" repeatedly as if the word could change things or protect him from a sad ending that was the common lot.

Our reunion lost its luster and after a while New York went back inside and I walked back to Carolien's alone.

I had wanted to tell the poor fool that he could survive, though close to the bone, if he gave up his ludicrous dreams. Traveling with dreams and visions of what could be was like traveling with memories of what was lost.

I was halfway back to Carolien's when Bettina joined me. Her cheeks were rosy, and her eyes sparkled. Her smile displayed the most perfect white teeth, except for one incisor that leaned a bit in the front, ready to bite you with a smile.

She glowed in a shaft of moonlight.

"Where have you been?" I asked.

"Well, unlike you, I have two daughters I'm taking care of. I guess if I had testicles I could wander around Europe, carefree, no responsibilities. As if I didn't have a wife and a family."

I started to say how sorry I was but only said,

"I have a wife and a family?"

CHAPTER THIRTY

"WE ALL KNOW WHAT YOU KNOW"

Afterward, I felt as if someone had slipped the latch on the front gate and the dead had walked through.

In this dream, I was standing at the bar Dirk and Eve frequented, *The New Pompey*, looking down at a shot of whiskey that the bartender, Sal had just poured.

People were three deep at the bar, most of the barstools taken by the ladies, the men standing around them like escorts. Sinatra was on the jukebox, the jukebox supplied by the same management that brought fuel oil to your home and sent your family life insurance representative to your home every three months to pick up the premium. You were insured for another three months that the guys this guy represented would not harm, injure, or maim you or your family.

This was the kind of place Dirk and his chosen little lady, Eve Solly, spent most of their waking, drinking hours when they weren't doing what they called their radio show, *Shut Up*.

I had expected to be there, having gone to bed with the question that poor fool New York had put on my mind: What was I doing there when I could be back home?

But *The New Pompey* wasn't my home. Somehow my dream had crossed Dirk's swill world. I could only figure that Dirk had a clearer sense of home -- this dump -- than I did. My laundromat wasn't home. The Beach House? Last time I was there, bullets were flying. The Fartsworth castle and compound? Where The Mater was? That was just a place I'd set a torch to. The Pater's Lab? That was his womb and tomb; it wasn't my home.

I noticed that Iuliana was one of the ladies seated at the bar. She seemed to be having a good time. She either hadn't noticed me come in or I hadn't come in. In dreams you never come in or go out. You just appear out of the blue. You're just there. I knew that. I was just there. It could be she hadn't seen me or didn't want to see me, or she was in an altogether different dream.

Or maybe nobody could see me. It was my dream. I turned and, in the darkness, where the tables were and some booths against the wall, I saw Bram Adrianus at a table all by himself, his model city covering the entire table, Bram intent with a headlight on and a small tool in his hand. No one seemed to be paying him any attention. I like the way totally incongruous events and people turn up in a dream, as if you shouldn't question that they belonged.

"Who's the sweet Lolita you come in with?" someone said and when I turned, I saw this guy, primped to pimp, at my elbow.

I recognized him as one of Dirk's low life associates. Curious name I recalled, although there is never anything real to recall in a dream. Coco. Or Niko. Pilo. Something asinine.

"She's on her own," I told him, looking over at Iuliana. "She's looking for somebody to take her to the U.S."

"I can see that," Jocko said, nodding, and I wondered how he could see that.

"Somebody paid to bring her over," Jerko went on. "Now alls she's gotta do is pay it off."

"I thought you didn't know her?"

Rico laughed.

"I know what you know. We all know what you know. Everybody here. We're here for you, Dirk."

"I'm not Dirk," I told him.

"See. I knew that."

When I looked back at the bar, I saw Bettina Parisi sitting there and Iuliana was gone. I started toward her, but she turned and spotted me.

I got over to her as fast as I could. There's no slow or fast in a dream. You either are there or you're not. There's no sense of speed. There's no pedal to the metal. You are both observing yourself moving while you are standing still. Dreams are quantum.

But I got up to her close. She smelled like Marseilles sapon and vanilla extract. I think it came off her hair which was in a mass of warm browns falling to her shoulders. Her eyebrows formed a perfect arch over soft brown eyes that always reminded me that heaven must exist. She was looking straight into my eyes.

"I've been looking for you," I said, my voice sounding strange, tight, weak. It was hard to speak.

"I'm not going to talk to you anymore," she told me, taking hold of my hand, and squeezing it. "I don't think I'm ever going to talk to you again."

And then I was standing there alone. I mean the place was still full and noisy, but no one was there. Maybe they were there. But Bettina wasn't.

I became aware at a particular moment in this my most recent return to Carolien's, that Iuliana, who shifted to whatever room was vacant that night, unlike the Permanent Boarders who shared a dorm in the basement all the time, was sleeping in the storage room next to a new arrival's room, a man named Nick Rise.

I was leaving my own room when I saw Iuliana with a towel wrapped around her and a towel wrapped around her head knock on Rise's door. The door opened and she went inside. I concluded that this Nick Rise had been netted. It was like her to break that cardinal rule of the Permanent Boarders and take up with a tour wanker, a fool with an itinerary, a weekend fly in and fly out sucker. An American with a U.S. passport looking for a hot, young trophy to take back home.

I don't know how someone as clever as Iuliana believed in that scenario. I can only conclude that our cleverness, our smarts go on inside our illusions and are never outside them.

This Nick Rise had a complexion not dark but rather his face seemed darkened as if he were standing by a bonfire at midnight and his face was fluid in both shadow and firelight. In fact, when you got close to him, you could feel a cold draft that somehow swept over you.

I tell you right off that I don't know whether I dreamed him up or not. If I did, I didn't know why. He just showed up. After all, I may have dreamed up Bettina also, but I had reasons that went further back and deeper than any religion.

I tell you right off he wouldn't be the hero with whom you would identify. I suppose none of the Permanent Boarders would be, not so much unlikable as not your thing, their illusions not your own.

Carolien called Mr. Rise, Méphisto and said she wasn't sure what his business was, but she was inclined to throw him out anyway. I found the man's talk more than interesting, spellbinding in almost the literal sense. Nick would settle himself in a corner of the couch, a bottle of Old Overholt rye at his feet, glass in hand, sip and talk and gesture, smile and laugh, his eyes seemed like black marbles, shining, unblinking. He had the kind of voice that made you think there was something additional in his vocal cords, a resonator, as if his throat was an echo chamber, an amplified voice, not loud but capturing your attention regardless of how far you strayed or whether you were too tired to listen. He never disappointed.

He had a lot of self-confidence. Bravado. Like a guy who had been and seen everything, been around to all the rodeos and been around every block.

The cold front that the Permanent Boarders offered every intruder into their permanent wallow didn't intimidate him. He ignored us. I mean, he ignored our obvious dominion in this place. It was antagonizing. He had a mocking way of speaking, even if it was just about the weather.

I began to think that Méphisto was a good name for him. I remembered the line: *"I am part of the part that once was everything, part of the darkness which gave birth to light."* I had a sense that Nick was a slow burning fire, a plume of smoke rising from the top of his head.

That surely was dreamwork.

And where had he gotten hold of a bottle of Old Overholt rye in The Netherlands? Devil's work.

Nick was gone most of the day, returning at dusk and settling in on the sofa with his drink. We sat around him and listened to him against our will. I mean that. Very strange. We Permanent Boarders didn't like him at all.

There was a lot of dreamwork in this but if it was, it was a dream set up by a craftsman. Maybe Nick was.

He was certainly a man of many thoughts, and all, when uttered, seemed to have been in the world forever but never said. At the same time, it all seemed banal and cliché. At least to me. He ridiculed much with wit and that drew me.

Conscience was a thing that moneylenders had implanted. It was a purely profit entity and somehow it had become attached to good and evil. The victim had to feel that it was a matter of conscience to repay the predator. The idea of goodness was a sop to those who lived in fear of doing what they wanted in the short span of a human life. Cowards were goodness fools. Such fools lived with a shield of conscience and hid behind it and called it their inner life, their moral sense, their sacred integrity.

"The man of conscience pays all his bills on time," Nick said, a mocking look in his eye. "Conscience serves the shop keeper."

"Sure," Reinout snapped, "but religion shoved a conscience up our asses at birth. You can't be free if religion's got your head tied up in all those good and bad heaven and hell knots. It's the world's biggest prison. You're not telling us anything we don't already know."

"Don't you think a good conscience will guide you to a sweet seat in the After Life?" Nick asked him, smiling. "No, I guess you don't. But you seem like a man who knows how to be free. I wish you'd tell me because I don't know. I get distracted and tied up with stuff that won't mean anything to me on my death bed."

"When the clowns leave me alone, I feel free," Reinout looking Nick straight in the eye. "All kinds of clowns."

I cleared my throat and spoke.

"The freest I've ever felt in my life was when I was chained heart and soul to a woman. I was lost if I were away from her. There's no freedom when you feel like that."

"Find another woman," Iuliana said then and we all laughed.

"It's difficult for a woman to feel free, having started out as just a rib," Nick told Iuliana as he reached down for his bottle of rye. "She has so much further to go than a man."

"The rib developed nicely I think," Simone said. More laughing.

"Has anybody ever been known to go down to hell to take someone else's place?" Nick now asked a grey haired couple who had wandered into Carolien's, little realizing they were now halfway between an asylum and rings of the Inferno, lured I guess by the "free 24-hour breakfast" online bait.

"Pardon?"

"NO!" Nick Rise thundered in their faces. "What they do is send other people down."

"Who are you talking to and what are you talking about?" the old but burly man asked Nick who returned the man's angry look with a smile.

"Absence made the heart grow fonder in love," Nick said, looking now at Iuliana. "How many idiots tie themselves to somebody they know very little about. And in religion, absence created faith. You love Jesus because you know almost nothing about him."

"He did rise from the dead," the woman said, in a very weak voice, a very timid and frightened voice.

"And you will too," Nick said, eyes fixed on the poor lady like lasers. "If you get that last minute death bed confession. You know the one where you tell Father Pedophile that you fucked only a few of the neighbors and lied in the confessional only a few times. But you know, as I look at you, I think there's a good chance you'll lie at your deathbed. You'll be afraid to tell the truth and so lose your soul."

Hell of a surprise just then when this guy rushed at Nick, pulled him off the couch and sucker punched him in the face. Nick dropped back into the sofa like a soft pillow.

"I'm waiting," the guy, looming over Nick, said.

Nick was wiping the blood from his chin.

"I apologize. Your wife didn't fuck the neighbors."

"That ain't it, asshole. We don't do confessions. Got it?"

Nick nodded.

"You don't do confessions. I apologize."

I heard Iuliana giggling as the couple made their exit. You would think Nick would have been less attractive to her after that, but you would be wrong.

One morning, Nick was settled into his sofa pulpit earlier than usual, a small leather bag at his feet. No one knew what was in it but when he was up early, as he was now, the bag was there, and he would be gone all day and then return in the evening.

Nick and his satchel, which the Permanent Boarders opined was a bag full of euros, a bag full of cocaine, a bag with a head in it, a bag full of dirty laundry, a bag full of handguns, a salesman's bag full of samples. But what might he be selling? A bag full of stolen souls, Simone told me.

Curious, Wouter followed Nick one day and came back to tell us that Nick pulled a chess set out of the bag as well as a fat cushion he sat on and played chess with the locals at a café near the oudegracht.

Simone surmised that the chess pieces were made of platinum and that was the way Nick laundered Farabutto's ill-gotten gains. New York said that the chess pieces were just chess pieces but that there was cocaine in the pillow, cocaine that Nick would take with him when he went to New York. You get the highest prices for cocaine in New York and LA.

Reinout found all these words laughable because it was clear to him that Nick belonged to a terrorist group and they communicated to each other on the chessboard. If for instance, Nick used the Ruy Lopez opening, it indicated where a bomb would be placed. A Sicilian Defense, very complex and annoying in Reinhout's view, might mean a bank holdup. And so on.

Le Loup was certain that the chess game meant nothing and was merely Nick's excuse for sitting there and looking at *die mooie dames*, the lovely ladies that strolled along the *oudegracht*. Adrianus had no opinion but when pressed by the others, as his opinion was respected and would settle the matter, Adrianus told them that Nick was clearly playing out on that chessboard the lives of a world he had fabricated in his own mind. He was arranging destinies.

I generally sat there sipping my coffee listening to Nick. He had been humiliated by that old guy with a Mike Dyson punch, but the humiliation hadn't touched him. We felt it for him, but he didn't seem to, like you couldn't shame the Devil.

If you were bold enough, Nick told us, you would see that everything about life could be seen in the flight of a bird who enters an open window, flies through the room, and exits through another open window. Where the bird came from and where she was going was impossible to know. An entrance out of mystery and then a return to mystery. The flight was short and arranged by Chance. We could have all been any of the countless billions of sperm that lost their way.

We were all there at that moment in the room by Chance, Nick told us in his mocking way as if a trick had been played and he was enjoying it.

Celestial Entity was a favorite topic. Or, Entities, in respect to the Greeks who Nick told us were no fools. According to him if such an Entity was giving us a chance to prove ourselves worthy by throwing a lot of shit in our faces in the course of our short lives, he wouldn't play along in that game. If you weighed all the lives born fucked or fucked by accident alongside those who by their own actions deserved punishment and then put all those next to the lot that proved themselves worthy of being saved, it amounted to a really shitty Celestial plan.

"And," Nick went on, "you must consider the lot who are a mixed good and bad bag, which is most people. Most people ain't Jesus and most people ain't Satan. What do you do? Bring the good part back to life and burn the rest? Or do you come up with a plan where they spend six months in Flint and six months in Vegas? Or whatever exceptional American cities strikes you as a living heaven or hell."

He laughed.

"It's all amusing. The Celestials are amused."

"You should have your own radio show," Bram told him, dryly. "Nobody in this country believes in Biblican stories any longer so I think you should save your breath. Besides, you assume God, or the gods are personally invested in us. We don't care about them, and they don't care about us. They're not amused by us. So much repetition. Same sins, different lot. Very boring, especially if you have a Celestial mind."

Nick gave Bram a long, unblinking look.

"You are going to die in the streets, my friend," he told Bram in a whisper we all heard.

"I misjudged you," Bram told him, smiling. "When you say god or the gods you meant you."

"I love the role," Nick said and we all laughed.

I couldn't help asking Nick at that point how he got along with the idea of oblivion.

"I don't mind forgetting people. It troubles me that I will be forgotten."

He did indeed seem troubled. His spritely offense dropped.

"It's like sleep," Simone said. "Oblivion is. But you don't wake up. Why would you be troubled if you're forgotten? A hundred years. Probably not so long. Forgotten. No trouble for you."

He seemed happy with that dark and dismal religion. Simone was by nature a happy man. He didn't let lying in the ground for an eternity make him less happy. Only Farabutto did that.

"You're dead, you're not asleep," Bram told him. "We humans know the difference. Troubled sleep? We understand it. We talk about it in the morning. I had a tough night we say. Troubled death? There's no review you make the next morning. Next morning? There is no next morning."

"So, time doesn't pass when you're dead?" I said, wondering why I said such a stupid thing. I guess it was because Bettina and I needed more time.

"Time passes away when you pass away," Bram told me. "It can't be in eternity either otherwise you'd be watching the clock."

"You'd get bored," Nick quipped.

"You're aware of everything but nothing is temporal, so you don't appreciate this moment or fantasize a future moment or rekindle past moments. An awareness without any awareness.

That's eternity."

"You know," Nick said, pointing a finger at me, "it was a man who had lived with a woman for fifty years and then she died suddenly in his arms who called his subsequent life without her a burning, a torment. Thus, Hell was created and picked up and popularized by Dante in the 14th century."

I heard Simone giggle. I saw also that Iuliana was once again in Nick's audience with the look of a student so anxious to learn. Of course, she was more like the spider watching the fly move into her web.

Carolien at this moment passed through, listened, and then shook her head. *La Commedia* was her pronouncement on all that she witnessed. According to her, what Nick had in that bag was our brains.

And then one day, Nick Rise was gone. No farewells, no notes left. Nothing. I think we Permanent Boarders were glad to see him go.

Whether Iuliana went with him, we didn't know. But she was gone too.

"She'll come back," Simone said to me, nodding his head like Yoda. "Beautiful women always come back. They never die."

CHAPTER THIRTY-ONE

THE PERFECT CITY

Bram Adrianus was indeed the unelected, unofficial, de facto leader of the Permanent Boarders, not that he acted in any way like a leader or like someone who assumed he was in charge.

Bram was a tall Dutch man with chiseled features, wavy brown hair, and tortoise shell glasses. He wore buttoned down shirts, creased slacks, and expensive shoes. He had been propelled from an elite lifestyle, one his wife's wealth had provided until she found that Bram was, like Lord Byruin, mad, bad, and dangerous to know.

How this might be, I at first could not see through the distinguished look, the magnetic charisma of the man. It was certainly the case that Bram had charisma, not the Devil's own kind like Nick Rise but one trailing clouds of glory as Wordworthy put it.

I guess it was the way he sat quietly at his table working on his miniature city in such a medieval artisan way. He spoke and when he did, we all listened. He often would say nothing the whole night as we Permanent Boarders sat under the tent pitched in the corner of the backyard, beyond the life-size chess figures standing in the moonlight on their chessboard, our most noble avatars. Like the life size Dizzney characters Carolien had posted throughout the place, these Kings and Queens and their royal court tickled Carolien's fancy, were part of her world of La Commedia.

Bram was unapproachable in a kind of way no American is, regardless of how much a gated Wall Street player and kleptocrat he may be. I felt awe in his presence and wondered how this man had been ejected from his own marriage. Of what had he been guilty? Was it possible that he was now full of regret for failing to appreciate the fineness of the woman he had married? How had he sinned? I look for regret in him but saw none. It might have been there, but I couldn't see it.

There were nights, such as the one when he had held forth on America, where he did speak, and we dutifully listened to him.

I found Bram endlessly interesting even though he might just sit there smoking joints slowly passed, beer cans popped opened. We all sat, listening to Wouter give us the latest count of black-market goods being sold locally, posting the changes in the stock of this or that, speculating how much this or that's resale value was on the street and providing us with news flashes of what he called *"la vie souterraine."* His eyes never stopped watering, his feet never stopped moving and his hands conducted the symphony of his drugged brain.

As the night worn on and drink and pot flooded Wouter's brain pan his language collapsed into drivel, the babble of a three-year-old. On those extreme occasions when he made no sense at all, Bram, like a good father, would tell him to go to bed. Wouter would nod, get up and zigzag his way to bed. Almost always, Wouter would turn to Bram for confirmation of this or that calculation and Bram, who smoked a pipe in between hits on a passed joint, would nod knowingly, in some way comforting the nervous, always jacked up Wouter.

"Please, go to bed," Iuliana ordered, disgust in her voice.

"They were a couple one time," Simone whispered to me. "Wouter and the Princess."

Right now, Bram was listening, eyes half closed, to Reinout go over the latest plans of his sparse membership Anarchist Club to assert squatters' right in this or that abandoned government building or derelict structure discharged from the bowels of free enterprise. Reinout saw revolution as a slow occupation of the space now owned by the rich.

Le Loup was snickering.

"His politics is women," Simone whispered to me. "If it was his economics, he'd have died of starvation."

Bram always had great patience with Le Loup's lies and fabulations regarding his latest conquests at the *Cubana,* a salsa bar Le Loup frequented and, if you believed him, was a treasure house of hot women just waiting for Le Loup to show up.

Simone kept his contributions to whispers, drinking and smoking without pause, the dark rings under his eyes further darkened by the enormous dark glasses he wore. Sometimes he would speak of his culinary next day brunch plans, noting prep time, availability at that moment of this or that, the delicate art of confining the fried egg within two sliced of fried bread, the trick to beating egg yolks and sugar to just the right point, of introducing the right amount of white wine vinegar and the best Irish or Danish butter to prepare a proper eggs benedict.

When New York was with us, he would speak into the darkness of the early morning hours of what were the first items on his New York City list to be accomplished as he designed his way to a fortune. First, he would observe the Wall Street financiers, how they dressed and walked and spoke. Then he would spend whatever money he had on buying the same clothes. He would imitate everything the moguls did. Follow them to the places where they ate, to their golf clubs, to their spas, to their homes. He would in this way become like them. The secret of being a millionaire in his view was to mingle with them, rub elbows, blend his life with theirs.

To all this, Bram would listen and then always advise him to be himself which was far better than being a copy of someone else.

"The dead do not mix with the living," he said quietly to New York.

"Who's dead?" New York shot back, confused.

I felt that New York was so fixated on being what he was not and would never be, that he could not listen. It was sad to see him living in a dream world that was so very different than the world we are in. He was very much like the man who had gone to find water, thought that he lived a whole life with the woman he loved between the time he went out and came back, and then when asked if he found the water was traumatized forever after.

Until Iuliana disappeared without even leaving a note for any of us, she was in the habit of bringing with her this or that tourist staying then at Carolien's for a night or two.

We Permanent Boarders did not welcome these strangers but neither did we do or say anything that got in the way of Iuliana's plans for them, whom Simone called her victims, *vittime*, Wouter called local idiots, although none were local, and New York referred to as phonies and frauds, pretending to have money when they were just poor salesmen.

We all found it amusing to watch the Spider Lady's entrapping methods. She was the one who had introduced Nick Rise to us. We all immediately felt sorry for this fly caught in the web. We needn't have worried as it turned out. We should have been worrying about her. I feel a deep sadness when I think about her now.

I never could quite make out Iuliana's face in the darkness on any of the many nights we sat there. Darkness was what we preferred. But I could catch her fragrance, a gamin, playful fragrance that she owned. Simone said it was nothing more than Savon de Marseille. I laughed at that. That was Bettina's fragrance, celestial and at the same time, earthy. There were other scents, odors really, in the night air but nevertheless, this particular one broke through and encircled us all, overwhelmed all else. It seemed as if pot smoke was in a battle with an enchantment only I knew its source.

I don't know when I became aware of it, but it was always Bettina sitting there beside me in the darkness. I was deep into the flux of life, and it had brought her to me. There was no chance she was dead. Death had no place there in the darkness with us. Our chatter was immortal. That death could be overwhelmed with so much life, even life that was hanging on the very edges of subsistence and sanity, was what I believed then.

I remember the last night Nick Rise spent with us. On that night, Bram spoke at length about the city he was building in the corner of the room Carolien called The Big Room, the lounge/parlor with a long antique oak table running down the middle and small sofas and assorted easy chairs around it.

In the corner of that room was Bram's worktable with his miniature, finely carved wooden city laid upon it, a city of the future, he was painstakingly putting together, most of it carved by his own hand. He had been some sort of engineer designer architect and he had a talent for working small, aided by a large magnifying glass mounted in front of where he sat on a high stool. There was always a large, illustrated book nearby.

Iuliana was asking Bram now where women fit in his city of the future.

"I have three types of dwelling for women," Bram told her, after a very long silence, making me wonder if the question had been heard. Maybe she had just whispered it in his ear?

"One for impregnation," Bram told the darkness.

"I'll stay out of that one," Iuliana told us, and we all laughed.

"One for sexual release without impregnation."

"I won't go in there without some compensation," she said, and we all laughed again.

"One for lactating mothers and child rearing. Every neighborhood in the city has each of these."

"I like this one," Simone said, pointing. *"Fecondazione. Cazzo con la speranza di fare un bambino."*

"I don't want to hurt your feelings, Chef," New York told him, "but you'd make a lousy father."

"Raw dog fucking," Le Loup said. "Where's that?"

"What if women want to go into business and make a bundle?" New York asked. "Do you have a dwelling for them?"

Bram didn't answer this but after a joint had made the rounds twice, Wouter told them that there probably would be no business in Bram's city.

"But what if a woman just wanted to be free," Iuliana cried out and then laughed, maniacally like Dostoevsky's Nastasya Filippovna. "Free to do what she wanted."

"There's a separate dwelling I've made in my city," Bram said, surprising everyone that he was answering. "It's a dwelling where men and women go to talk about conundrums and paradoxes, such as why things go on when they shouldn't, or why anything ever emerged from nothing, or why we presume we can separate ourselves from what we see, or why we need to live in fear of punishment in the After Life when we are willing to pay the price for what we've done right here in this life."

"I do," I said to no one but myself.

"I hope they can smoke some Kronik in this place," Simone shot out and then once again whispered in my ear that Bram was probably crazy.

"E 'folle. Carbonara?"

No, I didn't want to eat spaghetti. I wanted to listen to Bram, especially what place death and the After Life had in his city.

Simone smoked his Kronik pot but also chugged from a five-liter carboy of red wine that was by his chair.

"Everyone is free to grow what they wish," Bram said, as if someone had asked him if everyone was free to grow what they wished. "I have designed growing fields in every neighborhood of dwellings."

"Cut out the dealers," Wouter said. "Smart."

"No one deals," Bram told him, sternly. "No one buys or sells. There is no money."

Iuliana laughed and New York just cried out "You just lost me, man. I will definitely not be living in your city. How would you know who's rich and who's poor?"

"Why?" Iuliana said, giggling now. "I mean what could you do without money? I mean it's fun to have. Think of all the things you could buy with it. The places you could go."

"Money is too small to make," Bram said matter of factly. "Too small for me to make out of wood. Dwellings are easier and can be made of wood. So, I make dwellings. I paint houses. For a long time, I painted boats. But boats do not make a city. So, I make houses. Measured exactly."

"Truly pazzo," Simone whispered to me.

That was indeed the mad part of Bram is what I calculated. We had yet to see the bad and the dangerous, which Bram's ex-wife had obviously seen. Carolien said that the ex-wife had an injunction in effect that kept Bram from being closer than a kilometer of her. She also had hired security to keep tabs on Bram 24/7. They came through the pensione occasionally looking for Bram.

According to Carolien, the ex-wife was a woman of inherited fabulous wealth plus all Bram's savings that the Courts had given her. She remained deathly afraid of what Bram was capable of doing, what she feared that he one day would do.

"She thinks he is going to kill her," Carolien told me. "What do I think? There's no rule saying he can't."

I did feel that under Bram's calm, sophisticated, professorial demeanor, there was a powder keg with a short fuse. I saw him play life size chess with Wouter and suddenly pick up and fling a White Knight at Wouter in a rage.

"I like it!" Reinout suddenly cried out, as he pulled a tab from a can of cheap but good beer that was stacked in 48 can cases within easy reach under the tent. "No fucking government!"

"He's pazzo too," Simone whispered, passing a joint to me.

"You are wrong, Reinout," Bram corrected him. "And you are right, Reinout. There is no government because there are no laws. No taxes. No regulations. But there are government dwellings in every neighborhood."

"What the fuck for?" Reinout, as totally committed to his anarchism as a Celiac was to eating gluten-free.

"So, this is a dwelling where men and women can go as they feel the need to talk about laws and government. The talk is all. The talk governs and restrains. Words preempt dangerous actions. Thus, there are no police. Talking stations, if you will, and not police stations."

After a long silence in which I could hear brains working and beer cans popping, Wouter exclaimed,

"So fucking crazy, man!"

And then, as on almost every evening, a long time passed in which we sat in a stupor of pot, wine, and beer. It wasn't oblivion but it was close. But tonight, that stupor was challenged by visions of Bram's future city.

I was getting interested in the future for the first time in a long while. When you are looking for someone, you are not thinking this looking is my future. It all has so much more to do with the past.

Le Loup broke the silence.

"The dwelling that I go to," he said with his Marseille accent, "how do I pay if there is no money?"

"He wants the dwelling where he can fuck," Simone said and then whispered to me about Le Loup being truly pazzo.

"I thought you said, Corbeau, that you don't pay for your sex," Iuliana interjected. "I thought you romance your ladies. But maybe all you do is talk. Put him in that talking room."

A very indignant Le Loup told her that women paid him for sex.

"Very ancient women do that I think," Iuliana said. "With a very young man. That's not you, is it?"

They could hear Le Loup sputtering.

Then Iuliana laughed and told him she apologized.

"I'm so sorry, Corbeau. I know drunken women let you take them home."

"Is there a God in this city?" I sheepishly asked.

"Is there a Pope? And a Church?" Simone called out. "I don't mind his god your god her god no god as long as there are no churches and no gestapo popes."

"I can't build the Celestial out of wood. Even small."

"I don't think the gods have treated me right," Iuliana told us.

"There is a dwelling where men and women can work out their Celestial difficulties, but I can't make out of wood whatever is invisible."

"E cosa dire il Papa?"

"Everyone is free to call themselves whatever they wish," Bram replied. "There is no wood behind words, so they don't matter."

"So, there is no authority. Is there?"

"I can't make that out of wood," Bram said, not to my surprise. I was getting into the logic here. If it could be cut, planed, chiseled, turned on a router and so on, it could exist in Bram's perfect city.

He was the ultimate materialist. To be was to be of wood. If an idea could be made in wood, it existed.

"Ah! But, mio amico, they make saints out of wood, no?" Simone said.

"Sometimes I put a tiny medal on someone's chest," Bram told us. "Or a crown. Some are in uniform. I have generals too. I had a queen once also. It doesn't signify. Whatever anyone appears to be, means nothing. A spot of red could be a medal, or it could be a birth mark. No one has more prestige than anyone else in the city. All figures are carved to the same size."

"I like that," Simone shouted. *"Alla fine, il re e il pedone vanno nella stessa scatola."*

"What's he saying?" New York demanded.

"He says that in the end, the king and the pawn go into the same box."

"Even so," Reinout shot out. "What's to stop any slob from taking over? Crush your whole city under his thumb. Shove shit laws down your throat, make you fall in line, stop at the red, go at the green. Throw you in a fucking prison because you fought back? Or what's to stop a guy who only cares about himself from winning the hearts and minds of the forty per cent of the population who are idiots? I'm talking about the U.S. Yours is a U.S. City?"

No response. I thought Bram was setting himself to speak. Setting himself to say that there was a dwelling where men and women could bitch about whatever they chose to bitch about, and country didn't matter. And there were prison dwellings in each neighborhood where. . . What? People could talk? If there were no laws because Bram couldn't make them out of wood, there were no crimes. You couldn't make crime or authority out of wood. And yet there would be crimes, even in Bram's city of the future. He couldn't carve human nature out of wood but that didn't mean that it wouldn't kick in. Things could get dark, fast. All the bad stuff was invisible. Wood resistant.

Then I thought: You couldn't make love, but you could make a room where you could have sex. But love endured; it didn't need a room in Bram's city.

And then like a lightning bolt it hit me.

Bram's city was his own wrecked brain where all the dark stuff could be nullified because he couldn't carve any of it out of wood. Therefore, in Bram's logic, it didn't exist. The best defense was to make all attack, writs of malfeasance, injunctions from his wife -- all of it would become a material impossibility. Every room carved out of wood was made of protective walls, every building isolated from every other. A compartmentalized psyche, superior protection.

Reinout started to laugh and very quickly, he was laughing so hard he began to cough.

"This one is the craziest of all," Simone whispered to me.

"What's to stop me from crushing your fucking city?" Reinout screamed.

Bram didn't respond in his usual tempered manner. What he did was show his bad and dangerous side.

He jumped up, knocking his chair over and throwing his beer against the wall behind the tent.

"I will kill anyone who crushes my city! I will fucking destroy them! I will rip their hearts out!"

"Okay, there you go," Simone said to me as he jumped off his chair and backed out of the tent. *"Totalmente pazzo. Affamato?"*

Hunger wasn't on my mind just then.

It was too dark to see Bram clearly but a man so tall and a voice so commanding, like Moses, was a presence, visible or not.

Iuliana was repressing her giggles, Simone was chattering in Italian, Wouter was probably shaking more than ever though I couldn't be sure, New York was repeating "Fuck me, fuck me, no money" and Reinout who had a knee jerk reaction to any loud authority utterance had stopped laughing. He stood up in the darkness, a head shorter than Bram.

"So now I understand," he said calmly, "you're the Gruppenführer in your city. The self-proclaimed god. Where's the dwelling where we talk about that?"

"I will protect the city I've built," Bram said, now calm.

"And what if I decide to burn it down?" Reinout said, his speech slurred. The empty beer cans were rolling underfoot now. "And what about squatters' rights?"

"Here we go," Simone whispered. "He's going to burn his city down and this one is going to kill him when he says he will burn his city down. *Pazzi assoluti.*"

"Relax, bitches," Iuliana said, and yawned. I saw that.

"If you burn his city down," Simone said, "where is the building in which you will squat?"

The two men stood confronting each other in the darkness and then Bram said in a low voice:

"Outside the city there will be a cemetery. With wooden gravestones. It's Death's medium, wood is. When we die, we will be buried there in a forest of Death."

I couldn't see their faces, but I could see that neither man had moved and then Reinout said, "Okay, as long as we get squatters' rights," and sat down.

"If I ask what just happened, kill me," Simone whispered to me. *"Uccidimi, ti prego."*

"Evil will break out," I said when it seemed as if they had all chilled after a round of passing the smoke. "You can't just think you can talk evil out of doing what evil does."

"This American bastard is right," Wouter said, his voice shaking. "What's to stop someone from going up there right now and stealing stuff out of that little city of wood you've been working on for a long, long time. Why burn what you can steal?"

"It makes sense to me," Simone said, and then whispered to me, his breath reeking with the Kronik and the red wine:

"Cosa c'è di meglio che essere un ladro? What's better than being a thief? "

I was sure Simone and myself weren't alone in thinking that Wouter, whom Carolien's sister was convinced was the thief who was drinking up the wine stored in the basement, had already foreseen how Bram's city of the future would be a thief's paradise.

"You build a city, Wouter," Bram said, his voice back to its charismatic calmness, "of the future to not be like the cities you live in now. Otherwise, what is the sense of it? If you see no need for laws or prisons, you don't build dwellings for them. And when you don't build a dwelling for gods, there are no gods. And when you don't build a dwelling for evil hearts, there are no evil hearts. Who would recognize them? There would be no place for evil. It would have to build dwellings for itself in a city that has no place for it. No one will build those dwellings because no one will know how to build them. Do you understand, Wouter?"

Wouter, as Bram's loyal drinking buddy, his sidekick, his man Friday, his disciple, his advocate, his fool, his partner in lunacy and crime, and always a thief, agreed.

"Ye…yes, I do," Wouter responded, giggling nervously. "As long as, you know, someone doesn't accuse me of stealing something. And I didn't steal it. I might have seen it. But I didn't steal it. Seeing is not stealing."

"Evil is transparent," Bram's voice penetrated the darkness. "Words cannot conceal. Not in my city."

"Oh, shit," someone said, and it sounded like Wouter.

"That is out there, man," New York said. "Way, way out there. I wish you luck. The city for me is right here and now. New York,

New York."

"New York, New York," Simone sang out, taking another slug out of his red wine 5-liter carboy. *"Accogliamo con favore asini testate come lei, signor Jackass."*

"Lots of evil there, my brother, in that city," Le Loup told New York.

"Bring it on!" New York shouted. "I will feed on it. I will suck it dry! You know how you make your fortune in New York City? You take whatever totally fucks people up and you turn it around. You sell short. You double down. You leverage. You bundle. You soak the lenders. Fast ball the banks. You hedge. You take a crisis and make it your chance to make millions. You turn everything public, from air, water, and dirt to private equity! You go full-tilt Warfield Fuckit!"

"Will you take with you to New York your wife and fifteen kids back in Bratislavia?" Iuliana asked him. "Or is it going to be just you and Mr. Fuckit?"

"Minchia!" Simone exclaimed. "He has fifteen bambini?"

"Well, I'm not taking you that's for sure," New York shot back. "I don't have eyes in back of my head."

Somebody threw a bottle at somebody. It was New York who screamed.

"Don't ever put her in your city, Bram," New York said. "She'll have everyone killing each other over her."

"I don't put people in my city," Bram replied.

The aftershock to this statement was palpable.

"So, who do you put the uniforms on?" Simone asked.

"I am not responsible, Simone for who lives in the city or for what they may do. There is no gestation in wood."

Bram's words were déjà vue for me. I had heard them all before. In a nightmare, a dream that went way beyond the shores of dream and into the dark mare, the Black Sea. This moment had been foretold in those dark waters. I felt a chill go through my whole body.

"I'm going to drink to that point, which I see clearly," Simone replied, picking up the carboy and head back chugging at it the way a drowning man gasps for oxygen.

When he put the carboy down, he whispered to me:

"Assolutamente e senza dubbio pazzo."

"What good would that do?" Bram said, standing up in the grey light of dawn, towering over us, his head touching the top of the tent. "Seeing my point? The city has no point. The city just is."

Iuliana laughed.

"I don't go anywhere unless I'm in love," she told us all. "And we're not in love are we, Mr. Rise?"

Nick who had been strangely silent up till this point told her it was a possibility.

"You should be in love with Nick Rise," Simone told her. "I'll bet he is a very important man in America. He talks like one."

"Is this true, Nick?" Iuliana cooed.

Nick ignored the question and addressed himself to Bram.

"I like the way you eliminate a lot of inefficiency, Mr. Adrianus."

"Dank je."

"You get real efficiency when you get rid of people," Nick said. "No mess, no fuss. And no one around to be unhappy about the fucking fuss real life makes."

It seemed to me that Nick was here adopting a very cut and dry way of talking, an efficiency with words, obviously now a man who didn't chit chat.

"Take the word `wood' out of it and put "technology" and your city makes a lot of sense. I'd invest in it."

"You are an American investor?" Simone asked him. "Maybe you want to invest in my restaurant. Two dining rooms. In one, the aroma of *pomodori, aglio e olio d'oliva* and in the other, *cucina bianco*, without a *profumo* of the Mezzogiorno. *Un milione e mezzo euro.* Is it a deal? *È un patto, fratello?*"

"Waiters and cooks," Nick said. "Cashiers and truck drivers. Clerks, secretaries, travel agents. Wage slaves. Robotic. We're at the end of the line with those jobs done by people."

There was a long silence as the Permanent Boarders mulled over those words.

"Fuck robots," Reinout finally said.

"What do you do for a living?"

"I deliver the mail."

We all heard Nick laugh, a short, dry laugh with a sneer to it.

"Extinct in one generation," Nick told him. "There's probably no one sitting here right now whose job won't be extinct or done by robots."

"Fuck robots I said!" Reinout shouted.

"We don't work," Wouter said, slurring his words and then laughing. "We don't have jobs."

"I'm investing in that," Nick replied, no indication that he was kidding. "Both male and female. Programmed for sustained orgasm. Fuck Robots is a good name. I'll use it."

"What do people do in your future when they no longer have jobs?" I asked.

"You mean the people who remain? Extinction means disappearance. Those who are on the profitable side of technology will require recreational therapists, emergency management directors , masseuses. ."

"And you're investing in all of this?" New York asked.

"What do you do for a living?"

"I'm an entrepreneurial investment advisor," New York told him.

"He peddles Chinese shit in shit holes," Iuliana clarified.

"Hold on," Nick said. "Do you think that anyone in the future will need a person to help them buy something or a person to deliver their communications or a person to cook and serve their meals? Robotics. Not people. Think about it. I invest in the future."

"And right now, you're smoking dope and drinking beer with us because?"

Le Loup had asked this, and they all laughed.

"Because this place and you people are also the future. For a time. And then you will vanish. But for a time, people scheduled for extinction will live like rats, without hope but only a great need to forget how miserable they are. Your pot, your wine, your beer, and technology will keep you sedated until it's all over. I thank you gentlemen for allowing me to witness it all firsthand."

When Nick Rise stood up, they could see his face, the dawn approached.

"You know you're a prick, man," Reinout told him.

"I'll be out of here before you all sober up," Nick told them and walked quickly across the yard toward the stairs leading up the veranda balcony. I think he was feeling that sucker punch delivered to his face the day before.

"Nicky!" Iuliana called after him, getting up.

"Maybe he'll take you into this future," Bram told her.

"At least until the orgasm robot comes on the market," Simone quipped and we all laughed. I couldn't help it. The orgasm robot.

"It's not a problem," Iuliana said, sitting down, a cooing yet in her voice. "I like bold men who think of the future and don't just sit around talking about wooden cities."

"Why don't you and Nick go and talk about fucking in one of Bram's houses," Reinout said and there was some laughter as the first rays of sun started to turn darkness into a visible greyness.

"Eve whispers to the snake," Simone said, whispering to me, "and then she whispers to Nick."

"I heard you Simone," Iuliana said. "Whispering."

"I only say that you are like Eve in the garden," Simone replied. *"Incantevole. Seducente. Meraviglioso."*

"Sono male, Simone?" Iuliana teased. "Not even a little bit evil?"

"You are wonderful to look at, mio caro," Simone responded. "Like a bracciola all tied up nice and plump in a wonderful sauce."

"I would be very fearful of that man," Bram advised Iuliana. "You would be better off living in my city than in the world he believes in."

And then Bram got up and walked away, none too steadily toward the steep metal stairs that led from the yard to the deck. We watched him make the slow climb.

"Pazzi," Simone said out loud. "Totalmente pazzi."

I went to my room and slept a bit and then wrote and told Bettina what had gone on that night. I wasn't sure where to send the letter and then decided to send it to The Beach House, Farnworth Estate, East Hampton, Long Island, New York.

I dreamt about the cemetery in Bram's city and what filled them if there were never any people allowed. It was a way of beating death and the death in life heartache of missing Bettina; I mean not ever to be born. I couldn't go for that. I had loved her; I still loved her. Why would I have given that up?

CHAPTER THIRTY-TWO

"GONE"

About a year later when I returned to Carolien's, none of the Permanent Boarders were there.

There would no longer be Permanent Boarders at her hotel. Whatever had encouraged Carolien to think she could stop the downhill trajectory of those she had seen as worth saving had worn away. That faint gleam of what they once were or what they could someday be had vanished.

I mourned their absence.

It was a great loss in my life. It was as if a center of permanent existence had blown away, as if the frenzied, dissembled energy of all we Permanent Boarders could be brought to the grave. We made no sense and made no effort to make an order of sense and in this we were at one with what the whole world was, what human existence was. We should have gone unobserved, our disorder no challenge at all, as that of every deluded declaration and dogma. We had erected no center but spun already in a space with no place. And yet we vanished.

I thought death only comes to those who establish an order against it or mindless to it. Ours hadn't upheld the binary of life and death. We had observed no distinction, lived within both.

And yet we vanished. I tried to think this had nothing to do with Bettina.

None of this was so great as the loss that somehow was attached to my love for Bettina, a feeling that she was gone when I knew very well that she and I were spending our lives together at this very moment. Death could never have her as long as I lived. We would never vanish but together. I know of no better place than to be with her. I seek no better place.

Sometimes I thought my wandering was a search for her but that made me laugh. I knew where she was. I didn't have to search. She wasn't missing. We were wandering together.

Carolien sadly told me that Bram Adrianus had been the center, the magnet that kept the others together, but his mind melted down and so the Permanent Boarders lost their center.

"But he was mad," Carolien said calmly. "A beautiful, kind, intelligent man. A gentleman, here. In his heart. But here in his head? Not so good."

She paused. "But you know, Theo, when something is like a healthy plant, but you see just a little speck of something not right on a leaf. And there is no stopping this, I think. Something in his brain was always there and not right."

"He drank and doped a lot," I said, stupidly, wondering if having a center at all had done us in.

"After many, many times," Caroline went on, wisely not paying any attention to me. "I didn't want to call the police but then they came. He was no longer Bram. They put him in an asylum. And after that, Wouter. I had to throw him out. He stole wine, drank, was drunk then he stole money from the reception. He lied. I threw him out."

"What became of the city Bram was building?"

"It went to the basement and then I don't know. It fell apart. Someone threw it away, I think. I think maybe Wouter stole it."

"And the postman?"

"The anarchist. Reinout? He's squatting someplace in the city. It's all he knows. What a shame. He has only one thing he thinks in his mind and it's not good."

She didn't know where he was squatting.

Simone had gone back to Milan, to Farabutto and to cooking. Love of country, he said, drove him back to slavery.

"He doesn't like this man. Farabutto. I don't understand. What has this man to do with him? Does he know Simone? Everything is too personal with these Italians is what I think."

Le Loup was living on the streets, riding around on his bicycle. She had to throw him out. He was making all the women guests very nervous and after a few arrests, Carolien had decided he was hopeless. Behind what he called his keen observations and eye for women was nothing more than a stalker and a voyeur.

New York had not gone to New York but had lost his job as a travelling salesman and had returned to Slovakia to find that his wife had died.

That turned me pale.

"She died? Is he sure?"

She gave me a pitying look.

"Even in Slovakia they can tell if someone is dead."

"He had a lot of kids now to take care of, right?"

"Lots of kids but they don't have him. He tried to kill himself. They had to put him away also."

I turned a pale shade of pale.

"He tried to kill himself?"

"He only says one thing now."

"He wants to go to New York?"

She shook her head.

"She was ...his wife was his whole world. He never knew. A stupid man."

'He'll get better?"

"Better? Better than what? No, he's at the end. Finito."

"Finito?"

"He had the only good thing in his life, this woman and he wanted something else. This I don't understand. So much stupidity."

"And Iuliana. I think she went with that one. Nick?"

"Mephisto?"

Carolien shook her head and sighed.

"I think he took her to sell her someplace. Or he killed her."

"You…You think she's dead too? Really?"

"The mosquito comes back to your face. Unless it's killed. A dark hole she fell into. Stupid girl."

I shook my head.

"I don't think she's dead. She had so many plans to be alive. She was very, very alive."

"Now, I think she's very, very dead."

I had a hard time imagining a young, beautiful woman, especially one so tanned on a high bank of sand dune behind the Beach House, very, very dead.

I looked around and imagined I saw them all. The Permanent Boarders. Their permanence had been like that slope of sand Bettina and I had found one day, different the next, what had been, impossible to resurrect.

Bram at his worktable building his city, Simone at the stove making his carbonara, Rideout coming in, loud with new squatting plans; Le Loup sitting at his computer shifting his gaze to women's ankles, Wouter coming up from the cellar, eyes red and tearing, Iuliana half-dressed repeating her Dutch lessons.

"Do you think, Carolien, the greatest tragedy in the world is the fading beauty of a lovely young woman?

She gave me one of her *La Commedia* looks.

"You didn't see it fade, did you?"

I shook my head.

"No, I didn't. "

"You know that one, Iuliana. She was in love with everyone. And no one. Only herself. You know what? That's the worst it can be."

"It's all too bad," I replied, saddened not only by the fate of we Permanent Boarders but also for Carolien who had lost what she had for so long been able to do, to make a family of those long adrift from family and from any sense of belonging anywhere.

We had been Permanent Boarders, that ironic title, at Chez Carolien's for a mortal moment. That had always been for me the allure as of a dark mystery I had neither solved nor ever been a real part. Somehow, I had started out on the outside of everything, had a chance, a moment to come inside. And now. What did Carolien call it? *L'exile*.

In truth, my exile was very different. I had someone and then she was gone. And though I felt at night that I didn't know she was my center until she was gone, I felt in the day that she wasn't gone, that she and I both knew we had found a center together, and that I was both searching for her now but traveling with her in that search.

I felt my mind was melting. I am sure I am convincing you.

I was circling in the same few, dark thoughts. I was circling in the same waters of drivel, writing the same sentences, orbiting without GPS. Dead Reckoning. That's when you can't see her dead. Dead Reckoning is when you can't provide a happy, uplifting ending, or a plot, or a suspenseful movement. Death has no beginning. Beginnings come with a story. I have not been able to find Death's story. It has the silence of wood, a medium other than words.

Okay, I was quickly following Bram down that path to madness. Bram in an asylum; New York holding a razor to his throat; Iuliana into an unmarked hole in the ground; Reinout squatting in some derelict house hoping to create a revolution.

When I left Carolien's that time, half convincing myself I wasn't going on searching for what was lost, Carolien held both my arms and looked up at me.

"Hey, you find her, you don't find her. You lived together; you didn't live together. She's alive, she's dead. You pick the one that makes you live."

"You think everything will just go on now that she's gone?"

"Iuliana? Nobody does anything in memory of her."

"No, I meant Bettina."

"Oh, I think she is not gone. Not for you. As long as there is you, there is her."

I kept on traveling.

Don't you see? I couldn't stand still. So much of her captured me, burst my heart to tears, so many memories of things, words, gestures, looks -- all that was and would never be again -- besieged my soul and crumbled me. The present couldn't breathe. There was no space for it. And so, I rushed away.

When you travel, unless it is an everyday, repetitious deal, you need to pay attention. The present comes alive and is in motion. Your reality is chameleon, and you need to see what each new surround is clearly. You can't sit and brood. All is flux and you are in motion with it. How to get there? Where to stay? What will this cost? Is there a train and when will it arrive? Where to eat? What does this or that mean? What is being said to me? What threat or danger is there? When to leave? Who is watching me? What weather is this? *Cómo se dice? Comment dites-vous? Come se dice?*

It wears you out. But guess what? You are in the midst of all this, distracted from the hard coal of loss that burns deep inside you. You are in the midst, a place I never thought her death would allow me.

No, you are not totally distracted. That is not possible. But it helps. You gypsy about as a therapy, a bum on the off road of your own thoughts.

I took the path the Buddha didn't advise taking. I dove into the flux of the moment, so skeptical of meditating beyond or through or outside my love and loss of Bettina. I wasn't up to that. I couldn't see how it could be done. I traveled into the flow and flux of life hoping that it would take me.

When I lie back and close my eyes, just allowing a glimmer of moonlight to slip in, I see Bettina, glowing, shimmering above me, an apparition I welcome. And at once I feel that she and I have loved through the ages, from generation to generation, that this now is only the most recent affair. It comes over me that we were Adam and Eve, that the original romance never died but was reborn in every couple who have ever spent their whole lives loving each other.

This is a perpetuation and continuum that keeps the world of base humanity from devouring each other. It is the place where all notions of spirit are grounded in a love between two that never dies. Whatever immortality might be, it is this.

For me there was never a better place that I could be than with Bettina. For me, Heaven was not a riddle.

BOOK FOUR

CHAPTER THIRTY-THREE

CRAFT COCKTAILS

Of all the gin mills in the world, she came into *The New Pompey,* and I was there.

These days I was only there when I was called to come and get my brother.

I say "these days" only to establish some order of time in my life but in truth time had no order in my life. I circle in and out of moments. Even when I am not traveling, I am in motion. And when I am in motion, I am fixed, unmoving, sometimes seeing the face I seek, sometimes desperately in search of it.

These days I was only at this bar on New Utrecht Avenue to gather my brother. They called me first, gave me a half hour or so to get over there and drag him out. Otherwise, Sal, the bartender, said Gee, the owner, said they'd call the cops.

Gee didn't like to call the cops because cops rushing in and dragging a guy out of his bar did not upscale the joint. Ever since he had remodeled his back room into a new Brooklyn style bistro serving an artisanal menu, Gee thought he would draw the young gentrifiers. He had as much chance of doing that as I had of sorting out my memories, the fake ones from the good ones. I was haunted by the feeling that love for me now was housed in memory and was as eternal as that memory allowed.

I show up.

"He's in the back," Sal tells me.

"With his little person?"

"She threatened to shoot him. We stopped her. Gee threw her in a cab."

I found Dirk slumped over a chair, passed out. I went back to the bar.

"I need a forklift to get him out of here," I told Sal. "Why don't you leave him back there to sleep it off?"

Sal's response was to call over to Angelo Bari, a guy as big as Dirk and me.

"Ang. Can you help Theo lug his brother out of here? Drinks are on him."

We got Dirk into a cab. I gave the *pied a terre* address.

"If he doesn't wake up," I told the driver, "leave him at the curb."

Ang and I kicked it a bit. He was in love with a screwy debutante he thought was mixed up in some shady stuff he couldn't figure out but nevertheless he couldn't get her out of his head. It sounded like something from Rayman Chandelier. I told him nothing about Bettina in return. If you want to know more about him, he anti-stars in *Get Ready to Run*.

When I went back inside to pay for the round, she was there.

She was at a table, near the juke box. It was dark as always in that place and it was hard to see who was sitting in the booths against the wall, but I saw her, together with three others.

They were laughing. I wondered what had brought them into the place. I hadn't seen her since our summer of love at the Beach House. I hadn't seen her since that time I almost drowned and Dirk had brought me to shore. He had saved me. Left the boat to its fate on that lee shore and jumped in and rescued me. If I were the grateful type, I would have been grateful. Maybe I was. I had come to rescue him in this dump. We were even, according to The Mathematics.

"What brings those ladies in?" I asked Sal when I went back to the bar. And my drink.

"My good looks. They wrote about me in *The Parisian Brooklynite*. They said I had a genuine old school Brooklyn accent, served shots in shot glasses, and was the only bartender in Brooklyn wasn't #Metooed and didn't insist on a gender."

"Good," I told him. "So, you've seen those ladies before?"

"No, but the good looking one came in, about a week ago, and asked for you. Now she come in again. And you're here. It's destiny."

I looked over at their booth. No one was looking my way. But she probably had seen me come in.

"Is that special lady your brother says you can't get over since she dumped your ass?"

I felt like throwing a punch, but I didn't say anything. I went over to the booth. I came up so close I could have bent my knees and pushed the table up.

"Hello, Theo."

"Bettina. Sal said you had been in here looking for me."

"I don't know Sal."

"Who was that guy you were dragging out when we came in?" one of her friends asked me.

Before I could answer Bettina told them it was my twin brother.

"His better half," she added.

I smiled. Teasing was good. It was a better start than I was making.

"He looks whole. We can squeeze in, and you can sit."

I did.

"Mercy, Jill, and Sally," Bettina pointed out.

I nodded.

"Theo."

Sal came over and put a shot in front of me.

"Ladies, ready for another round?"

"What are you giving them?" I asked.

"Craft cocktails," Sal told me. "I went to school for the craft."

"And they are so very, very good."

"Pouring liquid from a bottle into a glass is a craft?" I asked.

"It's so much more than that," Mercy said.

"But if Theo doesn't think it's anything," Bettina said sharply, looking at me. "Then it's nothing. Or something or someone to make fun of. This is the twin who knows everything."

"I think I prefer a guy who knows nothing to a guy who knows everything," Sally said.

"Her ex-husband knew everything," Mercy told me.

"Okay," Sal said. "Here's what it is. This is what puts the craft into the operation. They must be made with great care and with fresh ingredients. All I put into these creations are fresh-squeezed juices and handmade syrups. No drinks will be made from mixes. Not in this bar. I don't have a mix behind the bar. No perfumes and preservatives either. No gluten, dairy, eggs, peanuts, fish oil or meat. One hundred per cent artisanal."

"Thank you for the explanation, Sal," Sally told him.

"Okay, Sal. There's a drunk at the bar wants you to pour him something artisanal."

Sal turned and looked.

"Oh, Picoline? He can wait. Ladies, more craft cocktails coming up."

"He's very authentic," Sally said, indicating Sal.

"Authentic what?" I asked, enough snap in my voice to put a frown on Bettina's face.

"Authentic, old-school Brooklyn," Sally informed me. "Neighbors sitting on stoops, uncovered garbage cans, old newspapers fluttering in the gutters, muscle bound guys leaning against walls smoking. You know, that kind of thing."

"Also, everybody says fuck this and fuck that," Mercy added.

"So much great architecture left to crumble. Our generation is all about urban revitalization. Bring the good old stuff back to life."

She hesitated. Jill.

"As it was," she added.

I had to laugh.

"I don't think any of you could survive here back then."

"Too fragile?" Sally asked.

"He wouldn't know," Bettina told them. "He grew up in the Hamptons. On a compound. He doesn't come from Brooklyn. New or old."

"My brother lives here. He's got a *pied a terre*."

"Ooh! A *pied a terre*."

"You sound English."

"He went to Oxford. They brought Oxford to him. He had tutors."

"I bet you had a nanny. Or a maid. A housekeeper. A ton of retainers."

I detected some bitterness in Sally's voice.

"No, but he was having sex with one of the maids when he was eight."

"*Droit de seigneur*," Jill said.

"I was nine," I said. "We didn't have sex. We played gin rummy. I was well behaved."

"So, you are very rich, well behaved and very tall and …now I know why we're here."

"He's not very rich. His family disowned him."

I didn't know who was talking now. I was pissed. I wanted to speak to Bettina alone, without the chorus.

"That sounds so interesting. I mean when a scion gets disowned.

Did you have to do your own laundry?"

"What's with you?" I said, turning to the speaker. One of them. I felt like I was all of a sudden under attack.

"Don't mind me. I'm drinking to forget."

"Forget what? That you don't know shite about me, but you think you do."

"Why did you get disowned?"

"Aberrant behavior," I told them, just as Sal came over with a tray full of crap cocktails. He put another shot in front of me.

"I'm not my brother," I told him, taking the shot, and knocking it back.

"Eve called. She's looking for Dirk."

"Who's Eve?"

"She's a circus performer," I told them. "Think short clown. Did you tell her he should be back at his place?"

"I didn't get the chance. Ladies."

Sal nodded, smiled, and went back to the bar.

"We should talk," I told Bettina.

"Why? Aren't we talking?"

"You were looking for me."

She pressed her lips together as if she had just applied lipstick.

"I wasn't. I was. Then."

"And now?"

"Anyone want to hear my mother's poem?" Sally sang out.

"No," I said.

"Not a poem then. A note she left."

She pulled a very wrinkled piece of paper out of a jacket pocket.

"She died today of crumbs and dirt. Her friends were not surprised. Her husband, shocked, as he had seen neither crumbs or dust. It's a gift! She longed for years to have a pair of testicles to render her sightless to such things. They never appeared. Body parts come and go, but alas, no testicles."

There were tear in her eyes as she gently refolded the paper.

"What happened to her?" I asked. "She sounds very depressed. And angry."

Sally gave me a look that chilled my bones.

"She's dead. She suffered, died and was buried."

"Sally's father was a liability. Her mother's health couldn't afford him."

I was mystified. I think my face was registering that. Bettina was staring at me.

"Can we talk in private," I whispered to her. "I've missed you."

"When?"

"Every minute of every day. Right now."

Dead air, as Eve would say on her show, mostly after some caller had been speaking. But now this was total silence. And then the Choir:

"I wish my partner would say that. He calls himself a financifier. They just don't talk …They talk differently. For instance, they invest in something with financing from lenders that they persuade to lend. And then they take that fortune and do it again. Of course, they do a grand amount of consumption on the high end all along. Among themselves. Others, they consume. I think you're right, Sally. It's a testicles thing."

"I think I want to marry you," I heard someone in the next booth say.

Sal came with another round. He put a double in front of me.

"I'm not my brother," I told him, knocking it back.

"I don't think loving someone is a thinking thing," Bettina told me and I realized the voice from the next booth had been mine right here in this booth.

"Ladies," Sal said, smiling. "I'm here. As needed. Beck and Call, as the lawyers say."

He walked back to the bar.

The line of regulars that were in there any time day or night had turned on their stools and were rubber necking the craft cocktail table.

"We're not in that kind of relationship anymore," someone said.

"What kind? Marriage? What kind are you in?"

"I'd say it's more ironic than real."

"Great," I said, dismissing the voices "Look, I'm not thinking. I love you and want to marry you. I've loved you since you were …"

"Adolescent. I'm not that anymore. And as such, I can't take your offer seriously. Not if you're not thinking. What if tomorrow you wake up and you think and you think I should never have asked her to marry me. And, besides, you are drunk."

"I won't wake up like that," I promised. "And I'm not drunk."

"I guess you should believe him, Betts. I mean you said he knows everything. So therefore, he knows the future too."

"I don't know what your problem is but just stay out of this."

"Don't snap at Sally like that," Bettina said, angrily.

I was about to scream when out of the corner of my eye I saw Eve Solly come in. For a woman closer to four feet tall than five feet she barged in like an Irish brawler looking for an Englishman.

She couldn't miss me.

"He's not in his cave," she said to me angrily. "Where the fuck is he?"

I was about to say I didn't know.

"Hi, Eve," Bettina said. She was smiling as if it was a great delight to welcome Eve.

Eve returned the smile, but when she looked at the others, the smile turned to puzzled.

"I hope you haven't gotten back together with this fool," Eve said to Bettina, gesturing toward me but not looking at me.

She sat down squeezing two to the right. I was standing now.

"I'm not," Bettina told her, still smiling. "Ladies, this is Evangeline Solly. Eve this is Jill, Mercy, and Sally."

"You do that radio show with a parrot and another guy?"

"This jerk wad's brother. Jack Wad. I'm looking for him."

"The parrot is on loan," I said. "He's mine. I taught him several languages. I speak all the Romance languages."

I saw the pitying look Bettina and her friends gave me and I regretted touting my language facility.

"We lose listeners when the bird speaks French. My listeners don't like the Frogs. They don't like the high jab gab, pompous ass, or the ball breaker. They're also anti-Semitic. They like black people if they're singing. They generally like colored featured people if they're on death row."

"It does sound like you're having a lover's quarrel with his brother."

"The opposite. I need to kick him in the balls."

"What did he do?"

"Enough to want me to kick him in the balls. I can't sleep until I do that. I'm in behavioral therapy. Most of our listeners walk around on their knuckles. Sal said you put Dirk's fat ass in a cab and sent him back to the peed."

"What's the peed?"

"She means *pied a terre*. I rent it and my brother lives there. With her."

"Shut up. I don't live there. I go there to fuck. There's a difference."

That produced a great deal of laughter.

I wasn't amused with all this. I had been a foot away from getting Bettina back into my life. Or so I thought.

"The cab driver left him on the curb," I told Eve. "Check the police station."

"The 66th?" Eve just about snarled. "They have a poster with my face on it."

"Are you wanted for something?"

"We're all wanted for something and then we get it. It's called death. Once again, what the hell are you doing in this man cave?"

She was looking at Bettina, who seemed disconcerted by the question.

"She came looking for me," I said.

"What's wrong with this place? It's so authentic. There's no plastic."

"That's true," Eve said, "just a bunch of Neanderthals hustling their balls."

We all looked over at the bar where everyone there was looking at us. Eve Solly entering was to them like Brunhilda coming on stage. They expected drama every time.

"Sure. That's how they think women are attracted to them."

"You hang out here with Dirk," I said. "His game seems to work on you."

"It's a business arrangement, Big Brother."

"Not the sex?"

I could see they had taken to Eve. Don't ask me why.

"I said we fuck," Eve told her. "If I called fucking sex on my show, I wouldn't have a show. I'd confuse my audience. Men 'enter' women. They don't fuck them."

"We understand. The politeness, I mean."

"I know you didn't come in here with your support group looking for Doris here. I always thought you had more control of your life than that."

"I don't think I do," Bettina said in a low voice.

"We have a lot of shared memories," I told Eve. "We grew up together."

Eve laughed.

"You and your brother grew tall. That's it. Protozoa also grow tall. Babe, whatever low point you're at now, don't go lower with this guy. Erase the memories. Join the cancel culture. You can't grow into anything but an object in this guy's life. I know. I'm experiencing it. And his twin? Dirk? He's the better one of the two and he's an amoeba."

"I know," Bettina said, tears in her eyes.

She stood up.

"I think we're leaving."

All three of the support group got up the way the half loaded with craft cocktails get up.

"I'll see you again," I called to Bettina

Eve sat down. Sal came over with the check.

"I don't have a hundred and whatever. I will never have it. Put it on Dirk's bill."

"Don't, Sal, or I'll shoot you."

The .25 caliber she always carried was in her hand. Sal nodded. The gun disappeared.

"I thought you were looking for Dirk?"

"He's in a gutter somewhere. Dirty. Slobbering drunk. Or in a cell. Whatever. He's at home."

"I'm going to bed," I said, getting up.

"You should just do that beautiful lady a favor and leave her alone."

I nodded. Eve was a fierce figure from an Anonymous Botch painting, but she didn't delude herself or feed illusions. She saw them.

"Yeah.," I mumbled. "I should leave off with her."

But I couldn't.

CHAPTER THIRTY-FOUR

"GO AND BE HUMBLE"

"How did I wind up with you?" she said, looking at me, bewildered, angry, genuinely troubled in trying to see what had ever brought us together.

"We couldn't stay away from each other," I said, as if it had been a cross word puzzle clue to answer. "It started with that."

"I was a child. I was in a daze. I should have let you go. You should have let me go. We have absolutely nothing in common. There's so much about you that I don't like."

"Not at first," I said. "I think you more than liked me at first."

"How would you know? By the time I realized how everything you did and said was so different than what I felt, it was too late. I also stupidly thought you'd change. But you never did. People don't change if they don't see the need. And you never did. You were too deep into your own self to see what was right in front of you. And you presume I know what's going on in your head. You get annoyed that I don't know where your mind is going."

It was one of those very few times that Bettina said what was on her mind, or, perhaps more truly, I heard and remembered what she said.

"This is strange," I told her. "When I look at you, I feel happy. You make everything come alive for me. I don't think I could find anything in you that I didn't like."

"You live in a fantasy world. I don't know who or what you see that makes you happy but sometimes what I see in you makes me want to just hit you. Wake you up."

I shook my head.

"I don't know how I'd live if you weren't with me."

"You'd live. Your ego wouldn't let you down."

"I can change."

"Come and find me when you do. Meanwhile, leave me alone. I have my friends."

"I could be your friend."

"You're not my friend. I laugh and enjoy with my friends. Why do you think I never ask you along? I avoid introducing you to them. Why would I want to expose them to you telling them you speak all the Romance languages, or you went to Foxford? Or your twin brother is an idiot and you're brilliant?"

"He's more autistic maybe. The Sorebones. I was there also."

"Don't you see I'm escaping from you every chance I get? I forgot. You don't see. Maybe you will someday when I'm gone but it will be too late."

"Damn! I didn't see that coming. I thought I'd be the one to make life interesting for you."

"I don't even want to take a walk with you. What you say can turn a beautiful day into whatever is twisting you the wrong way. You don't know joy."

"I don't. I had some bad psychiatric advice when I was growing up. I mean I had joy, but it got knocked out of me."

"Don't make me laugh. You come out of the school of soft taps."

"I had my knocks. They were just analyzed incorrectly."

"Don't blame…what was his name? Faust?"

"Fraud. Dirk and I called him that. And then Dr. Wong-Wrong-Nutley. I had a session with my mother's shrink, Dr. Groan. He was on family retainer, so he tried to put me on the lifetime plan. Fraud wasn't a psychiatrist. He had no professionalism. What professionalism is there in telling an analysand that he's a sociopathic scumbag?"

"I'm sure he had his reasons."

"That's just it. The irrationals have their reasons. There's the problem right there. Everyone has their reasons. And now they post them every second in ego media. And Dr. Wrong? She said Dirk was borderline between borderline and bi-polar. Does that make any fucking sense I ask you? Dirk's moods don't fluctuate, and he has no personality Eve Solly hasn't given him."

"Dirk didn't give people nasty names. You did. Your brother is certainly strange but he's not annoying and disgusting."

"You haven't been in his *pied a terre*. He lives with hand puppets and a devil of a dwarf. His frig is a cess pool."

"You don't like Eve Solly because she doesn't let you interrupt her, and you can't match her wit. She's better at putting you down than anyone I've met."

"I don't know how I found you, but I did. I think I could find you now or die trying."

I saw some hope for me in her eyes.

"Well, I don't know why but you haven't lost me. Yet."

Honestly, I don't know if I dreamed that conversation or it happened. When she talks, sometimes I hear my voice when I should be hearing hers. And there's a clue right there.

I couldn't believe that I felt, minute by minute, such a yearning for this girl who had just celebrated her sweet sixteen without inviting me to the party, who would hardly speak to me, who would walk off while I was making my pitch. Nothing worked with her. She was a kid really, but she mocked my game.

"Don't trifle with me" is what she'd say, and I'd be left standing there with the word trifle nowhere in my personality.

"You like her, don't you?"

I looked at Dirk. He was full of sand from head to toe because he was playing some stupid ball game where he and his idiot friends had to knock down whoever had the misfortune to wind up with this ball in their hands.

"Why don't you jump in the water and get that sand off of you and leave me alone."

"Okay, but she doesn't talk to you, right? I never saw her talk to you."

"I don't talk to her. Blow."

He started to giggle; he was nineteen but not my nineteen. More like nine.

"I saw you talk to her. You told her something stupid."

I turned to face this defective brother of mine.

"I don't ever say anything stupid. You got the stupid part of the egg."

"I'm just saying it's what she said."

"And what did she say that you say she said which is inadmissible in court because it's hearsay. But go ahead. What did she say?"

"She said what you said was very stupid and you should learn how to talk in a decent way to girls, that you have a nasty way of talking like you think you're better than everybody."

"Is that what she said? Really? Because I didn't hear that."

"Yeah, she said that too."

"She said what too?"

"That you never listened to what she said so she wasn't going to bother talking to you."

"I didn't hear any of that."

My brother had a way of angering me that probably had something to do with the fact that he had some kind of short cut into my brainpan. An identical twin thing. A lot of what he said had come into my mind, but I rejected it as, well, stupid.

"That's what I mean," he said, giggling and before I could land a punch on his fat face, he ran to the water. I watched him do his stupid praying hands headfirst jump into the surf. Perfect bellywop.

I looked over at Bettina Parisi to see if she was looking at me. She wasn't. But I knew she was or had been. She had a quiet allure is what I concluded. But I think her atoms and probably her sub-atomic particles were reaching out to mine. My words annoyed her, and she didn't have any words for me. But I knew there were atoms working, interconnecting, bringing us together. It was magical. It was deep.

Bu I understood it.

Pay attention: The reason why I have no life beyond trying to find Bettina traces back to our first kiss when she was sixteen. That kiss proved to be a minor perturbation affecting the course of my whole life.

I had a master plan for my life which I extrapolated from my early accomplishments: Caesar's Garlic Wars and the Plutonic Diatribes at the age of five; all the Troubaboor Poets by the age of thirteen; groundbreaking algorhythm creation at the age of 5; Bridge meister at the age of 10; virtuoso on the Satyr; pants fly record holder at LaGoona Gated Spa, and so much more.

But being with Bettina proved catastrophic, like the flapping of a butterfly's wing a decade ago affecting the path of a tornado today. She was a sweet butterfly flapping my well-designed future into a storm of unpredictability.

When you bond on that sub-atomic particle level you fuse for life. You also can't fight wanting to be as close to each other as possible. We were getting into that cycle, whether I was an egotistical disbeliever, and she was already aware of that and disgusted by it, didn't matter.

Everything lower and less admired than words and thoughts had us bound. Our love had nothing to do with language or mind. My heart resonated to her voice.

An admission like that, a sentence like that disgusted me. I had such more profound ambitions.

And yet between us it was love and yearning all the way down.

"I like your bikini," I said, really liking it.

I had walked over to the blanket Bettina Parisi and a couple of her friends were lying on. They all wore sunglasses, which each of them lowered to look up at me. Bettina didn't. I guess she knew my voice.

"It's a two piece," she said, crossing one tanned leg over the other. We could hear music coming from the Beach House.

You know when she said that I had a feeling we had done this scene before, the same words. I want to advance the plot. You want to advance the plot right after you find it. But this is a search in which we never advance. I can't because the plot was her. And I lost her. There is no advance beyond death. All you do in the face of a loved one's death is circle backward.

"You're blocking the sun," one of the girls says.

"It's his privilege. His family owns this beach."

"They don't own it," I said, as I sat down cross legged in the sand. "If you mean Jabba. And he's not my family. My mother just married him."

"Nobody just marries anyone. It's love or money."

"Pregnancy," another said.

"I know I wouldn't marry for lust. It would be unnecessary."

"A lot do, though. The stupid ones. They get so horny they think marriage is the answer."

"And it isn't?"

"No. They should just wait it out until the lust goes. It always does."

I followed the brilliance of this conversation of Bettina's sixteen-year-old sagacious friends without saying a word and then I asked:

"What do you think, Ms. Parisi?"

She lowered her glasses.

"I'm waiting to hear what you think. Your brother says you tell people what to think all the time. And don't call me Ms. Parisi. You sound like an old man lusting. Very creepy."

That made all her friends laugh.

"Who's his brother?" one asked.

"Dirk Bratter."

"You mean that big, goofy guy acts like he's twelve? Talks through hand puppets?"

"This is Theodorus. His twin. The serious one. He doesn't have a goofy bone in his body. He knows umpteen languages."

"You do? Give me one."

"Sono desideroso e innamorato del tuo amico qui."

"What did he say? It sounds lovely."

"It's not French. I took three years of French. Say something in French. That's the romantic language."

"Je suis dans la luxure et amoureuse de votre ami ici."

"Qu'est-ce que la luxure?" the third-year French student asked.

"Desir séxuel," I told her.

"I think he wants sex with you."

"No," Ms. Parisi said, "he's much too intelligent to believe he'll get that."

"You know Bettina is underage, don't you? You'd go to jail if you had sex with her. Statutory rape."

"Right now, I'd settle for a kiss."

"That's how it starts. You want a kiss. Then you want some tongue. And then you want to feel her breasts and then ..."

"Hey! Quit with the play by play. Look, I'll give you one kiss if you promise me one thing."

"What's that?"

"Acquire some humility. Your ego is ruining our beach day."

All four of them laughed.

"Yeah, okay. But how do I prove to you I've acquired humility?"

"Work with the poor in Africa and then come back."

"No. Don't tell him that. What you need to do is simple. Convince yourself that you and I are not going to be lovers and stick with that. No contact. You. Me. No contact. You'll never be worthy of me."

"Forever?"

"No. Maybe. Until I contact you."

"Do I get the kiss now or when and if you contact me?"

"It's a trial by fire. You have to prove you can control your appetites."

"All of them or just for you?"

I got a laugh out of her then.

"Kiss him and put him out of his misery."

Before I could move, Bettina sprang to a sitting position and grabbing my shoulder pulled me toward her and kissed me on the lips. It wasn't a long kiss. She sat back.

"Now go and be humble."

I didn't do that.

By the middle of the summer Bettina and I kind of got used to each other. I had been spending most of my time at The Beach House and had somehow got hooked up with a wild, ditzy kind of girl who wasn't shy about grabbing me and yelling "Come on. Last one in is a rotten egg!" Me: "Really?" was all I could say. Or "Let's grind to this one!." Me: "I don't think so." Or, "I'll show you some real fireworks tonight." Me: "Were you talking to me?"

She wasn't Bettina but still there wasn't anything unattractive about her. I mean the physical, body thing. She had allure is what Dirk told me, quoting me, but not knowing what the word meant. I don't think Ditsy had much going on up in the wheelhouse besides knowing every pop tune, how to keep her toenails pink, and how to poke fun at me. I was kind of like a big teddy bear toy to her. I never had time to respond to anything she said or did. She rolled and roiled me along.

I got to say it was amusing except when it was annoying. And she was legal. She made it clear she didn't go all the way, as she put it, but guys thought she did anyway. She seemed to be waiting for me to say something, so I told her when I was around 9, an upstairs maid had abused me. I don't know why I said abuse because the fact is all I ever did with Juanita and then Anna was play gin rummy. I had no precocious sex relations although I went along with everyone thinking I did. Dirk and I both went along with the lie. He because he wanted to keep up with me, his superior twin, and me because my self-image demanded a sexual precocity.

"I guess you can learn a lot from that kind of abuse anyway," Sandra -- that was Ditsy's name -- told me. "I mean besides getting dramatized. I mean if those maids were very good at what they did. To you."

"You meant traumatized. But yes, I think they were very good at what they did but still it all has affected my sexual maturity."

"I don't think so," she said, laughing jumping up and punching me on the shoulder. "You're like a big unmade bed."

"You're thinking of my twin."

"The guy who looks like you? He's your twin?"

It was strange but my dalliance with Ditsy, or, more precisely, her dalliance with me, brought me and Bettina together. I don't know when but all at once the atoms had reached fusion point, the water had come to a boil, the tide had come in. And so on.

It happened at one of those Beach House wild parties in which the guys have beer chugging choking speed contests, testosterone fights break out every fifteen minutes by the short boys, drunk girls run naked into the surf wild about drowning, sea turtles lumber up the beach to lay eggs, rockets are set off to Mars from the Beach House roof by loners, couples dance close enough to gene splice, nerds and future CEO's talk about their AI or Waldo Street ambitions, fathers who have run off with nubiles are cursed by suicidal sons; nubiles whisper of drunken uncles who show up in bedrooms late at night; some attention is paid to a music teacher who is hot or a wood working teacher who's a pervert; and some bodies pale in the moonlight wander off, hand in hand, up the beach, following the turtles, seeking dark, secret bowers.

That's what Bettina and I did. I have no recollection as to how the trek began, or who started it, or who first held out a hand to be held. But find our bower we did.

From that night on, when we weren't going to see each other for a whole day and night, we spent all that time anticipating when we would be together again. There weren't long time outs. We didn't see each other on Monday and Tuesday but we did on Wednesday, when we usually went to the Bridgehampton Drive In, and then of course at the Beach House Friday and Saturday night. We reserved Sundays for long walks on the beach. It didn't matter from where or to where. We didn't seem to notice any surround. The thing about walking together is that you're together. You could be walking together in a grocery bag or inside a chimney flue. It didn't matter.

Bettina had grown her auburn hair to her shoulders, her face and body tanned by the summer long beach sun, her eyes such a light, shining brown that could never be caught in oil paint. Her smile revealed pearly white teeth, an incisor slightly askew which made her smile unique. She was lovely then and in all the years ahead lovelier yet. She was Blake's Woman Clothed in the Sun.

I wish I could say what I remembered of her wasn't filtered falsely, fictively, self-protectively through memory, that on all those occasions when she shone in the sun, whether it was sunny or not, that I saw her as she was, that I had a full awareness of what she was.

I wish I could say that. I so wish my words were true, but they float beyond my meaning, attach themselves in your minds to what they mean there. They lead us astray. A "certain slant of light where the meanings are." And so, as graspable as light itself.

Why repeat and re-see as if I couldn't move forward simply because I hadn't gotten all of it right? Perhaps there are no steps beyond the moment she died. Not for me. We are taking them anyway, n'est-ce pas? Not forward. Not backward. The forward/backward of dream.

Or madness.

Isn't The Void the place where both the Dead and the Mad go?

CHAPTER THIRTY-FIVE

THE NORTH STAR

I dream many dreams, which I've learned to recall by retrieving them before I get out of bed.

Dr. Fraud taught me a great deal about this when I was a precocious thirteen.

He said people in a postmodern, postindustrial, post-truth, semio-globalized, financialized capitalist world are programmed not to pay attention to their dreams. It's not productive to be a dreamer. There's no profit in it unless you're paid $500 an hour to interpret the professional meritocracy's dreams.

That doesn't happen much anymore because Freud, as Dr. Fraud told Dirk and I, is now recalled as a laughable fictionalist, a kind of kinky sex freak. A very creepy old guy who would have been #Metooed by everybody from Annie O. to Little Hans. He's been superseded by fantastic neuroscience which had already taken the mystique out of consciousness and replaced it with a $100 a day pill.

"We can easily make androids dream of electric sheep, the new androids of algorithms tell us," Dr. Fraud told Dirk and me. "Or Mickey Mouse or a well-endowed woman. If something humans do is repeatable by artificial life forms, then it's not special to humans."

Dr. Fraud dismissed all that as horseshit. "Humans can relate their experiences, including dreams, to their overall awareness of their existence. You, for instance, Mr. Theo, are a classic SS, a young, narcissistic, arrogant, sociopathic polysnot."

"That's a YNASP, I think," I interrupted. "And you meant to say polyglot I think."

"Shut the fuck up. You are the closest entity to a sociopath I've ever encountered. You flinch but nevertheless you know what I say is true. You know that because you have a gestalt view of yourself, not simply an aggregate of implanted memories. You don't need algorithms to reach into what you know you are. You possess a self-aware wholeness. And that, as I say, makes my assessment of you correspondent with your own."

"I wonder if assessments are better using 0 and 1s instead of words?"

That comment intrigued him.

"Interesting. Steve Gobs would have come along a lot sooner. But that might have retarded the discovery of the Alphabet. I'll have to think about that."

"Maybe it will come to you in a dream. Tell me, Doctor, what about Dirk?"

As I asked this, I gave Dr. Fraud and then Dirk a dirty look. I didn't particularly care for the polysnot diagnosis. Was that in the new DSM?

"Does Dirk possess a self-aware wholeness, the kind that makes him aware he's polysnot?"

"Dirk? Dirk seems to be aware of himself through the ways other people are aware of themselves. He thinks YOU first and I second."

"He's a 0 and you're a 1?" I asked, still biting that lemon.

"Not at all. He's a kind of idiot Dostoevsky composition. He's likeable, though. While you are not. Likeable. No doubt you think yourself a very interesting person, but the truth is that you are too unlikeable for anyone to ever develop an interest in you. For instance, if you were, unfortunately, to write a personal memoir, you would irk, confuse and disgust the reader because you'd be circling over and over again in the flywheel of your own selfish fixations."

"Angel ne mozhet nenavidet', ne mozhet ne lyubit'," I recited. "You didn't know I knew Russian, did you Fraud."

"An angel cannot hate, cannot help loving," Fraud translated. "I love those words. Not much chance of you running into an angel, is there, Mister Theo?"

"You're something of a show-off, aren't you, Doc? The smirking kind. Truth is, as you like to say, I have loved and have lived with an angel."

"And what was her fate?"

"She died. Or maybe she's someplace."

"Hiding from you?"

I realized then that I was no longer thirteen, that this was Fraud and I years later. I was circling. It was Now.

I didn't know I would have someone to love forever but she would die.

"So, what explains why I dream so much?"

"It's obvious, isn't it? You fall asleep thinking the very best of yourself, as all narcissistic, arrogant, sociopathic polysnots do . . ."

"Don't let me threaten you, Fraud," I said, puffing up the way one of those desert toads do.

"Go right ahead. Or have you done it and I've missed it? To continue. You fall asleep thinking very highly of yourself and then what you know but keep hidden from yourself, namely that you are really a . . ."

"I got it. Go on."

"Comes knocking at the door of consciousness and you can only admit it as a dream that you can discount as just a dream. It's all nonsense you say and after all you're the captain of your consciousness."

"I'm after the White Whale," I jested.

"When you don't come to accept what is disclosed in the dream, it will be repeated. You protectively ridicule dreams as nonsense. The more you ridicule them, the more intensely do they return. You can't accept what you are although on some level you know who you are. You don't like you. It's all messaging from that place your dreams come. I'm conscious of what you are, and you could be too. You'd be cured if you could accept what I know about you. Nothing is hidden in your unconscious. It's all very, very visible. To me. You're a …"

"No, I don't accept that," I told him angrily." Anyway, I'm young. I'm thirteen. I'm a precocious child. I could change. I've got time."

I had suddenly circled back. It was the need. I used time the way a drowning man reaches out for what the next wave brings closest to hand.

"Death does not heed time," Faust told me coldly. "Thus, your being young doesn't try you in Death's juvenile court. Death doesn't have a young person's court. We think it's always sunrise; the day is young. But it's always for us mortals the last breath. Besides, precocity is a bad start."

"Good thing you're the only one looks at things that way. This is not a country of fatalists."

"A country that values everything in the way the stock market would value everything, has neither time nor patience for dreams. Besides, we imagine in dreams and the whole world can turn on what we imagine. You can brainwash people into wanting only money, but dreams aren't so easily mastered."

I remember all this in several different timescapes because everything I need in order to continue living hinges on a dream.

What I'm going to tell you is not exactly as I dreamed because a dream is itself not exactly anything and recalling it when you wake is another level of inexactness. Dream never supplements reality with any exactness. It layers it.

I am recalling this now in Dirk's *pied a terre*, the one I pay for, listening to him snore sprawled on his overstuffed chair. I am lying in the bed, a bespoke bed for giants.

Now I am in a car. I am driving. I am alone. I am going someplace but I don't know how to get there. I am following the car in front of me. In that car is my brother, Dirk, and The Pater. I don't wonder why he is not in The Lab. I just know the two of them are in that car. I have my eyes fixed on it. We are driving through a place unknown to me. I don't recognize any landmarks. I am not anxious though but full of confidence because I know I can rely on Dirk and The Pater to take us to where we want to go.

At some point, I lose sight of them. Then I become anxious. I speed up. Suddenly, I am in the busy part of some place I don't recognize. I have to stop for a red light. A feeling of being lost, a fear as if I were a child and had lost sight of my parents.

When the light changes, I see that up ahead there are two road signs and two roads going different directions. I don't move. I expect to see their car parked waiting for me. But they aren't there. They've kept on going. They probably weren't aware that I had lost them. A horn blows behind me. I don't know what road to take.

And suddenly I am overwhelmed by the feeling that I am lost for the rest of my life, that I will be alone, that I must rely on myself to know where to go but I can't do that. It's too sad. I will be alone on a road I don't know, going to where I don't know.

You see for my entire life, a life which began when I first saw Bettina on the eve of her 16th birthday, a party held at the Beach

House and to which I wasn't invited, though a spectator at a distance, Bettina has been my North Star, a light I have followed.

I see in the steady gaze she sometimes focuses on me that I have gone off course, yet I don't know it. As often as that, she would sit quietly and look at me, trying to draw me out of myself and toward her. Given how I was and still am, it was a hard task for her, but she never gave up. I think she hoped that one day I would see her.

Now, that she is no longer sitting across from me, silently looking into my eyes, I know that I never did see her, that saying to her that she was a mystery to me was no more than an admission that I had failed to go from myself to her.

These words come to me: *"She longest lives, who most to others gives, herself forgetting."*

I was the one to whom she gave.

I feel now that wherever she has gone, she is done with me. She knows she has done all she can for me. She has left me with the rest of my days to try and find the mark she set which I never seemed able to reach. Why should I not be happy for her, her lifelong trials with me at an end?

"I don't miss our life together the way you do," she tells me, voicelessly, "because you are full of regret, sorrow and self-reproach for what you failed to do, and I look back differently. I did all that I knew should be done, I cut no corners, I gave in no half-measures but gave all that I could with all my heart and all the energy and talents I had. I never sought to escape the difficult challenges, sidle passed the hurdles that had to be faced. I met others with concern and compassion, and putting myself aside, I felt for them and let them know I was a friend they could rely on."

She never said all of that to me. Never "said." It wasn't her way to share so much of what she thought and felt. But I hear her now. I hear the words her looks were expressing.

There is no more poignant and heart wrenching communication than what my Bettina now says to me. I hear it all now. I can wait for a time when time does not move but I will never see her nod, smile, and say, "You finally got it."

For me now, time is a fire in which I burn.

"Every woman's face becomes yours," I tell her.

"That's not my fault," I hear her say.

And her smile is real.

At the end of that dream, I knew that she, Bettina, was dead, that without her I could travel anyplace in the world and not know or care where I was, that I was doomed to wander without her guidance and therefore I would never have direction again in my life. That she had been there and given me that and yet I had objected, or rebelled, or just didn't see is the darkness I carry in my travel pack.

CHAPTER THIRTY-SIX

"SECRETS OF THE CONFESSIONAL"

At some point in my yearning for Bettina, the deepest yearning of my life that I was feeling after she had died, I drifted to Rome.

Not for spiritual solace or some encouragement that I would see her again but because I knew I hadn't lost her. She existed but she was no longer a presence in this world.

Besides, I had lost her countless times when she was alive. I mean I had lost so many chances to say what would have made her happy, act in ways that brought me close to her as we who had faced so much together should have been.

I'd like to blame all that on a father who never came out of The Lab and to a mother who left my brother and my upbringing in the hands of Commendatore Spinalzo, who had us memorize *The Communist Manifesto*, and Mr. Patawalla who had us memorize the thousand or so unhealthy mental factors, and our shrinks, Fraud and Wrong, who delved into our unconscious minds looking for what they knew would be there.

Dr. Fraud found that our relationship with our mother was exactly like his relationship with his mother. *Quel supris!* And Dr. Wrong warned us that if we grew up to be like her ex-husband, she'd find us and cut off our balls. As always, she told us she was speaking metaphorically. She did years later shoot and maim her ex. I read that on *Facetweet*, the double-ply roll edition.

That's it. I'd like to blame all that on what I've just written, but the factoid of truthiness is that I've been certifiable since birth.

Your life is yours to make, as the "Just Will It and It Will Come" and the "Personal Choice Solipsists" believe, but if you start out with jagged, twisted parts what you are led to is the State of Confusion, uncharted territory, not knowing who's alive and who's dead, seeing what never was but maybe was, and just walking further and further into the fire.

You're like that damn bird who flies in an open window, wings it across the banquet hall of life, flies out another open window. Where you flew in from, you don't know. Where you fly into, you don't know. Who you first heard this tale from you don't know. Why you repeat it over and over again, you don't know.

But for me the banquet hall was on fire, and it was a fucking burning hell of a flight I was on.

So, I didn't go to Rome to find Bettina. I took her with me. It would be yet another journey, another world she and I would enter together.

I hadn't lost her. She was just up ahead, there at the open window with the Exit sign above.

There was a time when Dirk and I were growing up that the Mater turned to Roman Catholicism.

She liked the ornament of church, the sound of Gargantuan chant, the forehead dusting of Lent, Caesar's Latin churchified, Christ's Passion on plaques on the walls, below graffiti, epistles of Paul the Promoter to conquered provinces read from the pulpit by neighbors.

She didn't know what belief came along with all this. She could recite the Credo the way kids who memorize it recite it. Without understanding how way out it is. Most people outside asylums don't believe in "the visible and the invisible." But she did feel that if Dirk and I confessed monthly we'd be more manageable, like giving saltpeter to troops or a Gameboy to a two-year-old.

Fr. Balsio was our confessor. He subsequently was defrocked for political reasons he told everyone. Liberation theology had gotten him into trouble, a dissident movement not to render to Caesar, doomed by its defiance of transnational corporate plundering south of the border.

In his view, he should have been made a saint. I didn't buy it. First of all, I don't like the meritocracy of holiness or the branding of celebrities as life models. Influencers with thirty million devotees. Secondly, there was more drink than politics in Balsio's life. He drank all the booze Dirk and I brought to him on confession days. We also gave him our room so he could hear Juanita's sins. The privacy of the confessional boudoir.

I think Dirk told him truthful things while I had much fun telling all sorts of wild lies. I was very descriptive about my imaginary trysts with Juanita and that was the beginning of his hearing her confession in the privacy of our room.

Over many rounds of drinks, I told Balsio not my sins but only a mad rush of thoughts.

As long as I was buying, he was listening.

Foundationally, I don't like the idea that you say words and your fuckups are expunged. I mean what are you if the shit you've done doesn't haunt you? I think even when a snake sheds its skin, it keeps what it did in that old skin in mind.

Did you ever think how boring it must be for a Celestial Entity to listen to you lie knowing that you are going to lie?

Such an Entity has no need of a Spoiler Alert because such an Entity is always already alerted. Everything for this Entity is Always Already. Our lives may have drama, but they have no drama for the Celestial Creator. The CC isn't curious about the ending because the CC already knows the ending. The show isn't missed because it is for this Entity "always already."

It's difficult to say what's in it for the CC in regard to creation.

Really, part of my wondering why Bettina is dead, if she is, is what's in all this for the CC? The adoration, the faithfulness, the loyalty, the love received from some is scripted. Always Already. Heresy, blasphemy, atheism and even the proud profundity of the agnostic is all just Always Already for the CC.

And death? What dramatic plot, even Creation, Fall, Redemption, can justify what death is? I mean is this the compassionate ending to our compassionate drama of our existence?

It's possible that the kick in all this for a CC may be that the celestial-ness is somehow tied to mortalism. To us. Somehow our deaths are nourishing to the CC, or enable the CC to remain the CC. We are growing together, in a dynamic relationship of fulfillment, making us accomplices in the divine plan

Lost as my own being is in Bettina's, I understand this symbiosis.

Nevertheless, if that's the case, we mortals are the ones paying the price. We could be spared the drama of our lives and the loss of our loved ones. I mean close that window that bird of Anglo-Saxon legend flies through. The whole thing isn't worth the price of the ticket, death being the price. Given a choice, I would not go into such a partnership. I would be an unwilling Founder of this world. Is this a way to implicate me in my own punishment, bring me into a drama that in no way can justify death as salvation?

"Oh, that would burn you alongside Giordano Bruno, my son," Balsio said and laughed.

I kept on.

I hear the words: Better to have loved and lost the beloved than never to have known and loved her at all. Better to have lived than not lived at all. The sweetness of life does not lie in a celestial plan but in the sweetness and brightness of love, those who give it and draw us to it. It is the living sap of our mortalism. It is here. Not transcendent.

"Well, you're quite a pagan," Balsio said to me, pointing to his empty glass. "Death never dies but love is forever?""

"I seriously don't know if death is a dark, terrible thief or the yang to the ying of life. But I do know that Bettina being gone from me forever is in no way ever something even conceivable to me, no less "better." There is no "better than" because I cannot imagine anything in the same world equal to her being gone forever."

"What can a defrocked priest say?" Balsio said, smiling. "Deep grief kills. Madness too but differently."

When I got to Rome, I looked up a friend of Fr. Balsio, Fr. Cardenale, a priest with seriously bad connections in the Vatican who would be happy to show me around.

He was a Liberation Marxist. Just as he thought India should have done waste management, plumbing and an efficient flush mechanism first and democracy second, he thought religion should do poverty first and heaven afterward.

He reasoned that poverty was like the bird in the hand while in heaven there were neither birds nor hands to end a poverty that miraculously ended once you got to Heaven.

He was tough on the concept of Heaven. He couldn't help seeing it in terms of what he had seen in Guatemala, Honduras and so on. He couldn't help seeing Jesus as passing the buck to Caesar when it came to mortal life on planet Earth.

In short, he felt Jesus should have left us with a politics of liberation, as the Marx brothers and Sacchelli & Rigoletti had done.

"Heaven is like oblivion," he told me. "Oblivion is like a good long sleep except it's not long because there is no time in oblivion. It's the void anesthesia sends you to. You don't know where you are because there is no consciousness in oblivion."

"But if someone is thinking of you…" I began.

"In oblivion?"

"No. You're here. Not in oblivion. And you're thinking of someone . . ."

"In oblivion?"

"There or wherever."

"It can't be there or whatever," he said, shaking his head.

He did look kind of like Frederic Kneejee, but he had Walt Whiteman's luminous blue eyes.

"Consciousness is always connected with the world. You can't think of someone no place. He has to be some place."

"She. It's a she. I think of her a lot. I think she knows that. I think as long as I think about her, she exists."

"Your thinking brings her to life? Okay. We'll let that go. You think of her at some time when she was alive?"

"Yeah. A lot of different times but the thing is I don't know if those times were real or not. I think they're real and then since she's gone, I think I was never really with her. Not totally. I mean I kind of missed her when she was there. I mean here. Alive. And now I think I'm trying to make up for it. Fill it all in. But you can't fill it in now. I mean she's gone. It doesn't count."

Fr. Cardenale looked at me intently and then nodded.

"*Ego te absolve*. Say ten Our Fathers and ten Hail Mary's."

I nodded.

"There's no hearing in Oblivion," he said. "I just wanted to let you know."

Capital stuff I thought. We hit it off right from the start.

He didn't come at me with "After Life" when I said "Death." He went right at the event.

He told me that Balsio was destined to be defrocked. He was a drunk, a womanizer, a thief, and a liar. But the worst was the fact that Balsio didn't believe in Karl Mox and Oblivion. He believed only in perpetually recombinant atoms and thought heaven was free single malt Macallan and Midleton very rare. Each of us had our heavenly menu order.

Cardenale himself wasn't sure that the Greeks weren't right about many gods because in his view it clarified the confusion of the world. Gods disagreed among themselves. It was the way they were. The confusion and tribalism of Mankind was the by product. The Greeks personified Oblivion and her name was Lethe, daughter of Eris, or Strife.

He did venerate the passion of young women wanting to be nuns. Vestal virgins he called them. That held him in thrall. It was mesmerizing the way he was devoted to the concept of female beauty, so close to my devotion to Bettina. Such beauty was what we demanded of heaven but if she were already deep inside me, what need had I of heaven?

I told him within a few days of how I was myself enthralled with Bettina Parisi and that she would be joining me at the nunnery any day. He told me that Beatrice was Dante's Bettina. Not quite real either. Very hot was how he described her. Like Eve.

"It was Paradise," he said. "Eve had to be a perfect ten."

"It's Eros and not Heaven that puts Death out of your mind," he told me, winking. "The one has a wonderful body. The other has no body."

I admired how a man like him had survived in the Vatican. I was to discover that he was indeed hanging on by his fingertips.

This Cardenale arranged for me to stay at the Villa Amata, a nunnery that had been in existence since the Renaissance and where Cardenale served as a spiritual advisor to the young novitiates. I saw this rather like putting the fox in with the chickens, or a Marxist in the secret bowers of private equity.

I had a small cell like cell with a horsehair mattress bed and I ate in the Commissary with other secular guests. The top floor of the palatial nunnery was reserved for important visitors to Rome, both clergy and laity, as there were no longer enough nuns to occupy the entire premises. The constraints of cloistered life now seemed both socialistic and bureaucratic in an age of personal and private determination. In this age, believing a woman would want to become a nun was like believing the uninformed wouldn't go inside their own heads to get informed.

The nunnery rules for visitors were simple:

You could take the birdcage lift with your gender only, which was held at two;

All meals were to be taken in the visitor *sala da pranzo*;

Communication with the serving nuns was to be kept to a

minimum;

Villa gates would be closed at 22 hrs. and not opened until 6;

Walks in the gardens, orchard and vineyard were allowed visitors only from 13 to 16 hour and then from 20 to 22 hour.

I had a room next to Cardenale's and soon the two of us got into our own routine:

Cardenale would go off in the mornings and do his genealogical research at the Papal library, return at noon for lunch, afterward we would play pinochle under the grape arbor, at 16 hours, Cardenale would attend to any matter of what he called spiritual counseling of the novitiates, at 20 hours the two of us would leave the nunnery and explore the neighborhood, returning at any hour as Cardenale had both a gate key and a key to the front door.

We used the Tiber as our guide, departing from it and into the neighborhoods Cardenale knew so well and then returning to it on our way back to the villa. Cardenale could stand the noon day meals at the nunnery, but he insisted upon exercising his complete palette by taking *cena* at one or the other of his favorite ristoranti.

He had a special passion for *spiedini a la siciliano*, which he was now admiring on the plate before him, a skewer of veal, flattened, stuffed, rolled, dressed with a bay leaf, tooth-picked and then laid across a pan cut to allow the flames to rotate a wheel of punctured blades which sent the heat upward cooking the spiedini to a perfection that could not be duplicated by any other arrangement.

"Your cousin Ettore introduced me to this delight," Cardenale said, as he slowly turned a morsel on the end of his fork.

I didn't have a cousin named Ettore, at least as far as I knew, but I kept my mouth shut.

"Let's talk of the future and then the past," he said, pouring us both wine. "And drink the present. Only Barolo is fit to accompany the spiedini."

He then began a long and knowledgeable discourse on the wonders of Barolo. It was a very clever way of "being present," a meme of the young gentrified.

I had wondered how Cardenale ate and drank in so costly a fashion to which Cardenale replied that it was good for business to see a fat monk eating alongside the sinners. They would think that the food must be good to make a glutton out of a monk. It was a temptation that even a monk couldn't resist.

For this sly advertisement, Cardenale's meals were gratis in many places. In those places, he ate well.

"I have today heard the confession of a novice nun, a young

woman who is contemplating taking final vows who admits she has doubts. I speak here generically and archetypically of course."

"Of course," I said, savoring the words and the wine.

"Our Eve feels that she can avoid being tempted by becoming a nun. It was my duty to say that a snake can find its way into any garden. They are very attracted to beautiful young women."

"She's beautiful?" I asked, taking out my wallet which was filled with photos of Bettina.

"Yes, that's her exactly," Cardenale said, handing the wallet back.

I began to wonder who the young nun was. I had only seen the short, old nun who served us prima colazione and pranza. She was attended by a taller nun who kept her head down. I suspected then that this was a transmigrated Bettina.

Yes, this beautiful young novice was my reincarnated Bettina. She had doubts because she didn't want to leave me, whom she loved. I figured all that out on only a half-bottle of Barolo.

"At the present occupancy of the holy third floor," Cardenale went on, "there is me, yourself, and a Cranditch."

I interrupted him to ask what a Cranditch was.

"An aging Wall St. Goldmine and Sackit, who seeks heaven at the last minute after arrogating what is rightfully another's into his own pockets for perhaps sixty years. He believed he was doing God's work but now, as most of his organs, his legs, his arms and his brain have withered, he believes he may have been doing the Devil's work."

Cardenale paused and his face and every grizzled hair on his full beard now expanded as if inflated to the popping point.

"In other words, a snake in the hallway. Then further down the hall, we have The Bastard."

He waited with a sly smile for me to ask about The Bastard, but I didn't. What more was there to know?

Cardenale went on as if I told him to tell me all he knew about The Bastard.

"The Bastard is a high prelate's illegitimate son who has been living here for, let's see, he was here on my first holy visit some few years ago. He also has keys, coming and going as he pleases. He's in the garden when he shouldn't be. He roams the stairwells. He's brought women back to his room. A good-looking young man. A perfect snake. Our young nun is already attracted to him. She told me in the confession, as if admiring the young man was a sin."

"You mean Alphonso?" I said. "I've met him. He's a Spanish expat."

Cardenale nodded and repeated the word "expat."

"Let's say a man who is living in one country discovers that his blood ties are to another country. Secondly, his blood ties are those of a bastard, but the bastard son of a prominent person. Remember, you cannot prosecute a man for being a bastard. And he's most likely promised to reveal to the usual enemies of such eminent persons the provenance of his bastardy. And then, lastly, the bastard returns to his genetic home, Italy, purely to blackmail his eminent father, who, we know, has taken a vow of celibacy. God bless his soul."

"And this bastard son winds up living in a nunnery?" I asked, pouring both of us more of the Barolo.

Cardenale considered Alphonso's residency.

"As our good guide in life Rabelais tells us `Friends, you will notice that in this world there are many more ballocks than men.' Remember this."

"And that means?"

"That your expat Alphonso has the balls to pursue his greed. And his eminent father is keeping him on the down low here. The Bastard is going along with it as long as he gets everything he wants."

"So, you think your young nun is pining for Alphonso?"

"Or it could be that she's pining for you."

"She mentioned me in the confessional?"

"Not in so many words but she described you."

"How did she describe me? I'm curious."

"As a young man wandering like Odysseus looking to return to his true homeland but not sure where it is and what it might look like. In this true homeland there is a woman, his soul mate, but he doesn't know whether she still lives. And if she has died, perhaps she has transmigrated into someone else, someone our wanderer, whom she believes is you, is still able to recognize."

"That young nun told you all this? Kind of incredible. She believes in reincarnation. I was thinking she was a reincarnated Bettina."

Cardenale shrugged.

"She's just a novice. She wanders in her beliefs. In your case, she sees your faith that your love will be reincarnated and that you will find your love as both very romantic pursuits. You are therefore very appealing to a young, cloistered nun who has not yet taken her vows, can't leave the place and reads romance novels under the sheets."

"You know all this from what she confesses?"

"That. And her dreams. She has many Eros dreams."

I felt like I was blushing. The thought of Bettina dreaming about me in that way overwhelmed me. But then it was most likely the wine.

"So, you really think she's interested in me?"

"I would not take it personally. Both you and The Bastard and the one who delivers the bread, and two or three altar boys are part of her dreams. She's very young and has no worldly experience so her romantic nature has no particular focus. She also dreams of herself as a postmodern Jeanne D'Arc as well as an American very popular Influencer. I have no idea what any of that means. But I think she sees in you the freedom to wander that will soon be taken from her."

"She likes wandering, eh?"

"Anyone who can wander anywhere anytime they want is the true ambition of all men and every woman's fatal attraction to men who wander. I call this a post-truth world, a world in which the truth of anything doesn't matter and performance, like a journey, is all that matters. You are a foreshadowing of the new millennium to her. If you are sedentary, as in a Nunnery, you might as well be dead."

"And how would she be thinking all this about me? I've never spoken to her. I don't think I've seen her."

"Well, I of course have told her. Isn't this the woman you've lost? Nina?"

"You think this is Bettina?"

I was elated. Such confirmation from a monk as to what I myself was thinking.

"I told her all about your grief. As part of my spiritual counseling, I need to tell her about everything she's walking away from. Or in her case, walking into. I tell her not to hide away from a world she doesn't even know. Give Eros a chance. Thanatos comes too quickly There's sin in the world but if you're not a sinner, you don't indulge. You live in a world you'll never know and go to a Heaven that can't be known, at least in any way you know anything. My son, if it's not you who goes to Heaven but one who is cleansed of all that is you, who is it that is in Heaven? A total stranger. Celestial but a total stranger. How can you connect? It's sad. Very sad."

"You're a strange kind of spiritual adviser," I said, more than amused by this guy. He was a trip without moving from one point to another.

"Only the ones who I don't reach belong here. I give them the test."

"So, what exactly did you tell her about me? I mean besides my loss, my grief, my wandering ways."

"She didn't ask much after that. She seemed more interested in your rival, The Bastard."

"You told her he was a snake?"

"My young friend, I cannot reveal the secrets of the confessional."

CHAPTER THIRTY-SEVEN

"NOTHING IS GONE THAT STILL EXISTS"

Midway in our life together, Bettina phoned me and in a tearful, frightened voice cried for me to come to her.

"Oh, Theo, I've fallen down the basement steps. I think my ankle is broken."

I hear her voice now and forever and it makes me weep.

She was hurt and crying out to me, and I went to her not seeing anything but only her lying on the bottom of the steps. That she was hurt and called to me as the one who felt for her life in such a way that I would come to her wherever or however I was, that I would come to her and she to me, true to the deepest and most profound affinities possible in life, beyond affinities of the seas to the moon, the winter to spring, the end to the beginning.

All this illuminated my soul forever.

I wake before dawn, my first thought is not a thought but a feeling of absence, but when I look up, I see her in the doorway.

"Come here, please," I say, holding one hand out to her.

And she does and I reach up and put my arms around her and she lets me kiss her and I know this is the way I should have kissed her on every morning of every day of our lives together.

I thank her because I know she has done this for me, come to me to tell me that though I cannot find her now, that she is not to be standing there in any doorway ever again, she loves me and can be found wherever I look.

I am so grateful for this, this kindness in her that cannot be diminished, existing as she, eternally. The whole world is an omen of her presence in my life.

I re-read what I have written.

I should write for Hallmarx Cards. My expression mocks what I imagine. Or it could be that my imagination is false and what I write is then artificial. I am like then the lying politician who always begins his lies with "Let me make this perfectly clear," or even worse, "The truth is " and then nothing but lies follow.

The truth is it's a big leap from the unlikeable to a soul illuminated forever. The truth is Dr. Fraud had analyzed me as slightly more offensive than just unlikeable.

Maybe I was in this Nunnery for a purpose, a cleansing purpose.

At breakfast the next morning, I couldn't help trying to get a good look at the face of the old nun's companion.

This companion moved young, agile, and the more I looked, the more I thought she moved so you wanted to watch her. As she extended forward to place a platter of Roman rolls on the table, I could see a well-shaped hand of a young person. I made a motion to retrieve something underfoot and tilted my head to look up at her face.

It was Bettina, Bettina in the way a bud promises to be a rose.

Cardenale noticed the move, smiled, and shook his head.

Surprisingly, Alfonso the Bastard joined us this morning. It was not his usual practice to be up at 8 for collazione.

"*Buongiorno a tutti,*" Alphonso said sitting down. He seemed not only very awake but full of good spirits. Cardenale commented on this.

"*Penso che forse la fortuna è venuto il vostro senso, signor Alfonso.*"

Alphonso laughed, not paying the least bit of attention to my Bettina who stood with a platter of eggs by the side of his chair.

"Good fortune, yes, Padre. I believe what has been promised me will finally occur."

Cardenale nodded.

"As our wise guide in life Rabelais tells us "*Tout vient à temps pour ceux qui attendent.*

"I'll take my eggs hot, not cold," snapped old man Cranditch at my Bettina.

"Speak English," he then ordered Cardenale.

This was the American magnate who sat at the head of the table.

I remember that pig Jabba telling The Mater that his philanthropy would buy him a spot in Heaven after spending a lifetime sucking the blood of laborers, he'd spend his last years gifting stoats and goats to the needy.

Here was a wanker, Cranditch, trying in his twilight years to pay back his leveraged debt owed to a Celestial Being he didn't believe in.

I guess the wanker had a selling short kind of relationship with The CB. He had a savvy profiteer's view: if no such Celestial Being existed and there was then no debt owed, a dead Cranditch would not be awakening after death to take note. Insentient dust faced no punishment.

On the other hand, if such a Celestial Being existed and the debt was unpaid, Cranditch would be awakening to the Fate of Celestial Debt Default.

Cloistering himself in The Nunnery was his backup leverage.

I had wondered if it was now a thing for old predators to retreat to holy places in their last years, hoping maybe that some of the purity of the spiritually devoted would rub off on them before they croaked. It was like John D. Rockeflotter hanging around his gardeners when they were at lunch so he could vicariously eat a sandwich forbidden his failing digestion.

"Good things happen to those who wait," Cardenale told Cranditch, "but in certain circumstances one can wait too long and bad things are sure to happen. The rich can get screwed in their final hour. God reads intentions."

I almost choked on the roll I had been dipping in my coffee to bring some life into it. The Roman roll was a terrible representation of Italian bread.

Cranditch, who had been confessing to Cardenale every morning, stopped stirring his own coffee.

"It was my understanding that even a death bed confession would exonerate a man's soul? That it was an airtight contract to be honored everywhere. Like letters of credit."

"It would be a nice trick to play on a Supreme Being, eh?" Cardenale said, winking. "A difficult one for we in the lower orders to pull off. But my humble experience with winning is not as great as with a man such as yourself who has achieved such prominence. The distance from yourself to the Supreme must be infinitesimal. You can therefore expect with good odds to trick your way into heaven. A Supreme Intelligence won't notice."

Cranditch turned the color of a prune plum.

Alphonso lit a cigarette and leaned back in his chair.

The squat nun pointed to him and shook a finger. Alphonso ignored her.

My Bettina had stopped and was listening, no effort now to hide her face which was beautiful and perhaps more beautiful framed as it was by the pure white wimple.

In a film, her part would be played by Juliette Binoki. She was a young Deborah Cur as Sister Clodagh in *Black Hibiscus*. She was Bettina standing at the doorway.

"We could spend our lives fulfilling all our lusts and greed," Cardenale went on, leaning across the table, the sleeves of his robe pulled up and his huge forearms stretched out on either side of his plate. "Scrunching the lives of our inferiors under our feet. Eating the world and everything in it, the people too. Greedy for more of everything. Our appetites, our gods."

As he said this, Cardenale took a huge bite of a Roman roll. He sat there chewing slowly, not taking his eyes off Cranditch. He reminded me of Spinalzo when he tortured-tutored my brother.

"And then in our old age retreat to a nunnery, say our prayers, confess our sins to a fat monk who wouldn't be fat if he thought his gluttony was a sin and at our death find ourselves in even more luxurious surroundings, the surroundings of heaven. I say that any man who can pull this off deserves everyone's respect. *Dio vi Theoedica.*"

With every word, every phase dramatically expressed, hanging in the air, long pauses like picture frames between, Cranditch visibly cringed, twisted in his chair, pulled at his face.

Cardenale raised a glass of water and held it high. This fat monk, as he called himself, was a barrel full of monkeys' fun.

I looked over at the young nun to see if she was getting a kick out of this. She gave me the kind of disappointed look Bettina gives me when she sees me hate and enjoy its fruits. I was setting the old man up to hate for no reason beyond the fact he was rich and sought to continue making profits in the After Life.

"Saluto ai maiali audaci di questo mondo, ovunque essi siano."

"I truly repent all my sins," Cranditch screamed then croaked something, a curse upon Cardenale. He was standing up, almost apoplectic in his fury.

"Bravo!" Cardenale shouted, but Cranditch was already rushing out of the room.

Cardenale asked for another serving of poached eggs, but the squat nun shook her head as she glared at Alphonso.

"Un prete deve essere un esempio di moderazione, anche un prete grasso."

Cardenale laid his knife and fork down and nodded.

"We can't win all our battles, *mia buona sorella*."

She gave him a look of great disappointment and, motioning to my Bettina to go on ahead of her, they both left us to ourselves.

"She's a tough old bird, that one," Alphonso said, blowing smoke rings.

"She doesn't like the commotion that the third-floor visitors create," Cardenale told him.

"She seems to like you," Alphonso said to me. "And you're a third floor transient."

He had a sneer on his face.

Maybe I was angry because I had disappointed Bettina once again with my meanness, but it flared up now.

"Next time you talk to me," I told him, "tell yourself this guy is six feet five, weighs close to 20 stone and you yourself are just a skinny wanker. You'd want to watch your mouth. I'm not a Roaming Catholic. I sin."

"This guy has anger issues, Father," Alphonso said to Cardenale.

"Theo is an expat, Cardenale told him. "A totally different category than transient. Not a visitor, not a tourist, not a nomad, not a bum. But someone who is in a permanent state of exiting from someplace else. He's in search of his sweetheart. Bathsheba. She may be dead. If so, God rest her soul."

Alphonso didn't admire this condition and said so.

"I don't get attached to any place or any women," he told us, cheerfully. "I don't hate or love where I've been. I mean not enough to think about it when I leave it."

"Ah, the sentiments of the true bastard," Cardenale told him. "Your father undoubtedly felt that way when he left you. But you're incorrect in that expression. We humans all live in the deep remembrance of Eden and of our unfortunate exit. We are truly unwilling expatriates of a country to which we cannot find our way back."

"I believe Satan made a home of Hell," Alphonso replied, crushing his cigarette out in a saucer, and smiling at the Padre.

"And so he did," Cardenale agreed. "And was very welcomed but I think I'm more certainly to be an expat of that country than any other. I'd rather yearn for a Heaven I've lost than rule in Hell, to quote a Puritan."

Cardenale stood up, nodded to us.

When he had gone, Alphonso remarked that if it wasn't for Cardenale, the dump would be dull.

"He's witty," I told him. "He thinks Karl Mocks could make heaven out of the United States if it weren't for Walt Dizzy and the ubiquity of leisure and consumption. They kind of detour the masses from revolt."

Alphonso didn't seem interested in these ideas. Actually, I was quoting Eve Solly, believe it or not.

"Firing off a tweet is like firing a gun now," I continued. "Money is now virtual digital. They're trying to make war not real. At least in everybody but a dead soldier's mind.""

"Could you pass the cream, brother?"

I did.

"So, you're leaving us?"

Alphonso made a Who knows? shrug.

"This is a sweet niche. I've got a place as the permanent thorn in everybody's ass. But I've got sanctuary here if you know what I mean."

"I don't. You probably have a swell back story, but I don't care. No offense."

"I mean that there are a lot of reasons I can't go anyplace else," Alphonso said, lighting another cigarette. "I don't think I'm safe here anymore. I overplayed my hand."

He laughed.

I remembered what Cardenale said about this bastard being the Pope's bastard. Blackmailing the Pope? Too much drama for me. I'd have to get Bettina out of here.

Fr. Cardenale and I were sitting in the garden. It was a permissible time. Some nuns were hoeing rows nearby.

Sister Valerie, my Bettina, had come closer and was now just below us, head down, moving her hoe deftly and swiftly.

"How does she know she won't regret signing away her life?"

"Who? Oh, she is very beautiful in the sun, isn't she? Think of it as a marriage but no divorce possible."

"She can run away. What will they do? Send the Nunnery police after her? I just think she can't know in any certain way that giving up her life...for Heaven is...I mean why would she give up her life? Hide herself away in a place like this. It's got to be a whole lot of ignorance that does it. I mean she's giving up everything she can't possibly know anything about. She's probably travelled from some small village in the *mazagran* to here and that's it. If she knew what she was giving up, she wouldn't give it up. It's life. If she spent just ten minutes dead, she'd know what life is. She wouldn't be here. I think she's exploited by the church, a large and very profitable institution too large to fail."

I was getting angrier and angrier. I was sounding like a political activist. I was losing touch with the real me.

To those two words I could hear Bettina telling me I should have lost touch with that long ago. Not real and not good. The real me.

Cardenale seemed amused by my agitation over the young nun. He didn't understand that I knew who she really was.

I didn't like that.

"She's down there working in the field. She's a serf without freedom. Maybe someone who deeply loves her is searching for her and the poor bastard can't find her and gets to thinking she's dead? You know what I think? I think when she was just a teenager she fell in love with a guy and because this guy was too into what he thought was real, but wasn't, he didn't cherish her the way he should have Because, you know, she was the only real. He could know."

I clanged to a stop, like a steam engine at the station. I was out of breath. A rush of words. I also realized I was losing it.

"Well, it comes down to faith," Cardenale said, clearing his throat. "One side or the other. It is for her God's garden she gladly works in. If it turns out she's wrong and she's just another one in a long line exploited by the oldest transnational corporation on the planet. Well, she won't know. And those after her won't know that she's in a place of Eternal Unknowing. Dust that never rises."

Back to the Void again. I didn't like to think that's where Bettina was when I knew she was right in front of me hoeing a row of cabbages.

"I don't think she thinks about heaven or oblivion," I said, as Sister Valerie paused and looked up, as if she felt someone was looking at her.

"No, she does it for love," Cardenale said. "It's in her. She feels it. It's a great gift. This love you can't reason with. Jesus is always a handsome young man. Six feet tall, golden, shoulder length hair and golden beard. Every religion needs a celebrity front man. Of course, I personally think a woman like Joan Get or Urethra would have been wonderful in the role. But religion was patriarchal back then. And white and blonde was the preferred color scheme."

'Yeah," I said, not paying attention to this sarcasm but nodding to Sister Valerie whose eyes met mine and then quickly looked again at the ground. "He's a luminous personality alright. A celebrity."

"Necessary to put a face on the product," Cardenale said, continuing his line of blasphemy. "Although Judaism and Islam do alright with supporting actors. Is it not ironic that a religion irrationally believing in the invisible yet grounds itself in a presence? Two in fact. An Old Testament Father and a New Testament Son."

I didn't see the irony probably because I wanted Bettina present not invisible. I yearn for her presence. Absence is nothing. It's shit.

"I do a lot of dreaming," I admitted. "A jumble of the real and unreal. Even the real is fucked up."

"You must focus on the externalities. Like death and the weather and spaghetti carbonara. Hold on to your plate and your mind won't spin away."

I guess that was funny.

"I think too much. Or not enough."

"I understand. The Cabbala and all that. Most of my Catholicism is Judaic. The Unthought."

"The unthought?"

"Of course. It's at the wheel of your thinking. The way the unreal sharpens the image of the real. Dream is a carrier, like grapeseed oil as a hair tonic."

The guy annoyed and abused my deepest thoughts.

"You know I thought faith was a matter of belief in God or the gods. Not in all the screwy shit. My dreams are about to carry me to the nut house. I tell you this quite frankly."

"And yet what we dream goes on every day. Call it everyday life. It's our real estate. Settle in and make yourself comfortable."

"You know, forgive me, but I don't think I'm going to find her there. She's someplace real. A place. She's outside my mind. Outside the crazy dreams. She's in a real place."

"Tell me. Is she beautiful? This Carmela?"

"Heart, body, mind and soul. Beautiful. Bettina."

"Well then, that's where she is. That's where you'll find her. By the way, I told the Mother Superior I was counselling you for the priesthood."

Then he was dropping his cigarette butt and stamping it out with one supersized black, military boot.

"Why did you tell her that? I'm looking for my woman. Why would I want to go celibate?"

"Not to worry. She's not buying that line anymore. She wants you out. She thinks you are irredeemable."

"Exact words?"

"Irrecoverable fantasist."

"Did she use the word polysnot? Did you tell her I read Latin and Greek?"

"No, I didn't. And if you do, don't mention the Greek. The Church spent a fortune on expunging Greek thought."

"Well, when I leave, I'm taking Bettina with me."

Cardenale was lighting another cigarette.

"Good. Who's Bettina?"

I told him that I was fascinated with what I imagined about the young nun. Her loveliness in my mind possessed a magical attractiveness that only what we cannot know for sure or ever know always possesses.

There was not even a shred of fact or proof in how she could be my Bettina. I had never spoken to her. I didn't know if her voice was Bettina's. But an exterminating war had begun without a shred of fact of proof as to why it should begin so why would I be more demanding?

Cardenale heard me out and then said:

"Think of her as one whose path you cannot obstruct. Also, I believe you need to talk to a therapist. The place to go for that is Newark or Santa Cruz. A talking cure. But I recommend you say very little. In this way, you compel the therapist to reveal the dogma of sanity to which they subscribe. Here in Rome, those in a state of grace must always be sane. The sinners are the ones who are crazy. It's a clear, simple, easy to follow dogma."

"I'm not crazy," I snapped. "Besides, I've spoken to a whole bunch. They say I'm not crazy."

"Of course you're not. But still, you're in a bad spot when everyone you encounter thinks you are. It's unfair, judging a young man of superior intellect crazy because of how he acts and what he says. And then there is the fear of what he might do. But we do not define who we are by the opinions of others, do we? Isn't it the quality of this superiority to be not understood by inferior minds?"

"Yeah, well, amuse yourself, Padre, but I'm taking Bettina out of this hive."

Sister Valerie didn't serve at the next meal nor did Cardenale or Alphonso appear.

I didn't see the Rabelais priest until later that night. He stood in the doorway, a huge, lumbering figure in his robes which he seemed always to wear regardless of the heat.

I stepped aside as the good father solemnly entered his room.

"I must preface what I am about to say with the last words of Rabelais: "I have nothing, I owe a great deal, and the rest I leave to the poor" by which I mean I have nothing to gain nor am I protecting my own ass, as the American CEO's say, in what I tell you Theodorus."

"Sister Valerie?"

Cardenale sighed deeply and sat himself down slowly in the only comfortable chair in the room.

"Sadly, she is distraught and in the presence of an inquiring Mother Superior -- a woman of extraordinary focus but limited depth and breadth -- she repeats your name. And as I am here associated with your name, the good Mother Superior summoned me. What are the young man's intentions? Does he know he is guest in this sacred nunnery? Does he know that Sister Valerie is not available to the outside world? And so on."

"Cut to the chase, s'il vous plait."

"The good Mother Superior -- who as I say has excellent hearing but no understanding -- wishes me to tell you that your welcome here has ended."

"And what about The Bastard?"

"Alphonso? As I say, his worldly corruption will be pursued to its own end. He will probably plead at the gate that he has done nothing wrong. No admittance. The ones who feel they are not worthy to pass through, who feel that they deserve to burn in the fires of Perdition, they go through. There is a certain irony to salvation, my son."

"But The Bastard will be allowed to remain here?"

"What can I say? If he's only the bastard son of a bishop, his trespasses will one day overwhelm a bishop's protection, a protection guaranteed by love or perhaps blackmail. But if he's the bastard son of a cardinal or a pope, his offenses will always seem preferable to a bestseller which tells all."

I started to say something but then figured what's the use.

"I'm ready to leave."

"I have some last words then for you. I suppose an imagined past is better than none at all. But it has no roots. What you dream cannot flower."

"Either does oblivion. It's a dead end. Literally. Bettina is not just a dream. She exists. Has existed. Exists now. Will always exist. I see her reincarnated in others. I just lose track of her every so often That's not my fault."

"Every guy's seen you before somewhere. The trick is to find you."

"What's that?"

"A line from an old, hard-boiled movie."

"I find her more than I lose her."

Cardenale watched me in silence then closed his eyes and seemed to have fallen asleep.

"Our friend Cranditch has taken his departure," he said, suddenly opening his eyes. "I see it as a sign of his possible redemption and ascension into Heaven for he now realizes he has no faith and cannot bullshit St Peter at the pearly gates."

"And that will save him? That he has no faith?"

"God loves an honest man, my son."

I swung my backpack over one shoulder, embraced Cardenale, or tried to get my arms around the fat priest. I got to the back of his shoulders.

"You're sad to leave her? The young nun?"

"I'm full of sadness. It's what I've got. Promise me you'll keep Alphonso away from her?"

"For the brief time I myself remain here," Cardenale said. "But I don't think we will have to worry about the young nun."

He said this as we made our way down the narrow staircase, the birdcage elevator too small to accommodate me and my backpack as well as the ample Cardenale.

At the outside gates Cardenale gave me another hug.

"I have a feeling that our Sister Valerie will not take her final vows."

"Why do you say that?"

Cardenale laughed.

"It's not because she's seen you and has thrown off her vocation. But it may be that she now thinks she is rejecting a world that puzzles her, a world she does not know at all. Intelligence does not permit this. You must know what you are saying no to. You have to know also what you are leaving behind."

"What if you know what you had is gone?"

I walked off at a brisk pace.

"Nothing is gone when it still exists," he shouted after me.

I turned and saw him striking his heart.

In my heart? Sure. But my mind? I was losing it.

Sister Valerie bushwhacked me at the gate.

"Please, come here," was what I heard and when I looked, I saw her. She was hiding in the cedar grove not more than ten feet away.

She had a finger held across her lips.

I looked around and then made what probably looked like a very suspicious amble from the gate to the grove.

"I must tell you something," she whispered, taking both my hands.

Her calling out to me like that reminded me of a dream I had the night before.

I was in a rail terminal. I don't know where. It was very busy, and I was rushing along through the throng. I had a destination. The train would be leaving, and I didn't want to miss it. I thought I heard a voice call to me from my left, but I just kept walking. Then clearly:

"Theo!"

I turned and saw Bettina standing there with our two daughters, ten and seven; I recall that instantly. They were standing on either side of her, looking at me.

"I was calling to you," Bettina said, smiling.

"I didn't hear you. You surprised me."

"Why?"

"I mean it wasn't conceivable to me that you would be here. That the three of you would be here. That I would see you like this."

She gave me that look which always meant "You are such a fool."

"Of course, we're conceivable. We are here, aren't we?"

"I still feel I'm imagining you being here," I said, shaking my head.

I don't know why but I felt like such a fool.

"You imagined us here, didn't you? I think you had a reason."

I was stunned.

"I always imagine you."

"You are such a fool. Let's go home."

"Yeah, of course. Certainly."

I woke up at the Nunnery.

And now several hours later I was hiding with Sister Valerie in the cedar grove.

"You are leaving, Padre tells me. But I have to tell you something before you go."

I couldn't conceive what she was going to tell me, but I knew it was connected with my dream, that this young novitiate was really somehow Bettina, channeling her.

"Okay," I told her.

She led me to a spot where we couldn't be observed from any direction, from the garden or the house. There was a small bench she went to and sat, motioning for me to sit beside her. When I did, I saw directly in front of the bench was a small statue of Our Lady of Fatima. I knew the story.

"Padre tells me that you believe very much in your dreams, and you hold them to be true, no matter how strange they seem to you. Like mysteries."

"Sometimes. Other times I feel like I'm being hit over the head?"

"Scusi?"

"I mean something obvious that I shouldn't have needed a dream to show me."

She gave me the kind of puzzled look that I was used to. I puzzled myself.

"You had a dream that mystifies you?" I asked her. "Ti mistifica?"

She nodded and her eyes lit up.

"I dream that I was once in love with a young man who went far away and after a time, I couldn't live without him, and I went in search of him."

"Fascinating," I mumbled to myself.

"I know it's a silly dream because there was no young man in my life. That was last year."

"Last year?"

"Now I dream we were married for a very long time, and we had children and then he died. Of this I'm not sure. Sometimes he has just gone away and forgotten us or married someone else. Sometimes in some dreams I see that he is trying to find me, and I want to tell him I am here, but he doesn't come. I think it's because I am here soon to take my final vows and this man never existed and the time, I dreamed of us together never happened."

She paused and looked at me.

"Totalmente pazzo, no?"

I didn't know what to say. If I say, yeah she was totally nuts, I was admitting what I didn't want to admit about myself.

"My dilemma is one in which if I remain here, I will never have the life I dreamed. But if I leave, I go to my illusions, for certainly these dreams show me illusions. Non la pensi cosi?"

She waited for me to say something, but I didn't know what.

"You don't think your dreams are wrong? Vero?"

"Vero."

No, I didn't think my dreams were wrong.

Months after this, I heard that Sister Valerie had left the Nunnery.

I didn't know how to feel about that except I wished her good fortune on her journey. Better than I was having.

CHAPTER THIRTY-EIGHT

"THERE IS NO HERE OR THERE"

"You want to be someplace wandering around Europe," Bettina told me, pointedly.

"You don't want to be here. That's obvious. And I don't want to keep you from finding whatever happiness you think you can find someplace else. I don't know what you're looking for, but I do know you haven't found it anyplace we've been. But I'm staying here."

When she stands there looking straight at me, not angry, not in any way emotional, I want to stand up, go to her and hold her, look in her eyes and tell her there's no place I want to go to if she's not there, that both time and place only matter because for me she alone gives them meaning

But I don't do that.

It's a dream. One that never leaves me. And she's died and so I can never move to her as quickly as I once did, never speak to her as deeply from my heart as I would now that she's dead. I cannot feel when I am in this dream and when I am not that I did at that time reveal to her how everything in my soul is forever bound to her.

It is not within the compass of time as it flows in the present second by second to minute by minute to hour by hour to day by day to week by week to month by month to year by year, from birth to death to give you all that is needed, to allow you to say all that should be said, to convey all that is in your heart and to do so in such a way that in the years ahead, the years after she can no longer be reached and spoken to, you will not be driven to the madness of regret, of feeling that she does not know that no place mattered compared to her, that no desire ever matched a desire for her alone.

I have so many words and we had so much time together, but I am oppressed with the feeling that I failed with both time and words.

I went looking for Bettina in Spain, in the Basque region. Donostia.

If she were in Oblivion as Cardenale thought was where the dead went, I wouldn't find her in Donostia. I wouldn't find her anyplace. Nor would I find her after I were dead, waiting in some celestial form to welcome me. Over millennia our atoms might run into each other but that wasn't exactly all that I was hoping for. Sub-atomic particle recognition?

The question in my mind was whether there is consciousness in our cremains. Plato said that even after death the soul exists and can think. The soul is imperishable and thinks but thinks about what? I mean does it have a memory of mortal life? Why would any vestige of our mortal natures, corrupt as they are, find a celestial home?

I had these bad dreams in which I saw Bettina, but she didn't recognize me. She had forgotten me. The Greek spirit, Lethe, had gotten to her at her death and filled her with forgetfulness and left her in Oblivion.

For eternity? I didn't think so. An immortal soul is full of life, not oblivious to life. I looked for Bettina in others because I believe though her soul might be reborn in others it wouldn't forget me. Her spirit didn't just lie fallow in some cave of forgetfulness. What kind of destiny is that for an imperishable, immortal soul? That's death.

Lousy crumbs, the worse shards of humanity may waste away forever. They're dead. That's death. They don't go on to live forever. Bettina, the lovely Bettina, had a goodness that replenished the goodness of the world, and I knew her sweet soul would never die.

For sure. My old, cynical, nihilist, ridiculing self found endless amusement in my pitiful gushing. Part of me didn't understand how my life had gone full blown soap opera tearjerker. I could have made a living keening at Irish wakes. When it came to what I felt about Bettina, my love for her, all I had was the vocabulary of schmaltz.

Is that a likeable type? Does a reader gush tears and hang in there, full of sympathy and pity, straining for empathy?

I didn't care. None of it was likeable to me. I didn't want to be tormented with what was and never grasped, or what I never had but think I did.

Dreams, my friends, are not tear jerkers. They dig deep and hurt. You cry out in pain.

Histrionics and schmaltz. None of it fit what I felt for her. "Terrestrial love is not for ever -- perhaps once for all eternity." William Gerhardie wrote that. When we talked about such love, we'd talk crap like "How prettily she laughs," and when we talked about war we'd talk happily "You're all shot to pieces." Whatever touched the eternal deteriorated on the ground. We talked crap. About love. About death.

We gush it.

I didn't pick Donostia because I had a better chance of running into her there than anyplace else. Or because a spiritual world lingered there, among these pre-Indo-European people. Or, because I could fall apart among strangers with impunity.

No, I picked Donostia because a huckster named Frohberg had sent me there. Carolien had recommended me to Frohberg as a multi-lingual tour guide. A polyglot. So here I was working for him, so to speak.

On my way out of the cybercafé and heading toward the *Astelena,* I ran into that very guy, my boss, Frohberg.

Over the years, Frohberg had gone bankrupt, had fled the U.S to escape the IRS, had returned and re-started the business after returning from Romania with what he called "stimulus" money, had gotten married and then taken to the cleaners in a divorce suit by a woman he called simply "Nemesis" and consequently had gone bankrupt yet again, gone off to places unknown and returned to the States for health reasons, remarried "Renemesis" with the same sad result, gotten a job as a European agent for a tour company and was living far below his own self-estimate now in Spain. Before all that, he breezed through the Ivy League and graduated *some come loudly.*

In short, he was pitiable.

He could easily have risen in American meritocracy, but like so many of the most brilliant, he saw through the nonsense of all that and went on the piss. Less nobly, he was a hedonist who liked booze and women.

Recurrent divorces, illness and alcoholism had stripped Frohberg of houses, cars, mutts -- Getum and Bitum and their offspring Chasem and Chewem-- most of his savings, and one kidney.

Despite his own difficulties with women, romance, and marriage, Frohberg tried to pass a lot of life advice on to me from the get-go regarding love, marriage, career, and family life, in none of which had he succeeded.

So, I listened but I also considered the source. What this guy knew about life would get you what it had gotten him. And he was a wreck of a man.

For instance, Frohberg's claim that he understands the psychology of women.

Men didn't have a psychology. They didn't need one. They had beer, guns, and the game, whatever the game was. They only responded to the psychology of women. First, women were a ball and chain, if not now then later. They wanted their men sedentary, not nomadic. Tribes became nation states on this foundation. In response, men, like prisoners, tried to escape. If they didn't try, women would treat them like house pets, mock their macho. At the same time, women would be attracted to the "bad boys" who somehow had escaped ball and chain, rode Harleys, ran out on paternity suits, played drums in dives, and showed every sign of treating women like shit.

According to Frohberg, every woman had a secret desire to escape the cage of home-loving and uxoriousness she herself had created, not by personal choice but driven by the need to procreate and preserve the species. If personal choice really existed, most would choose not to preserve the species. Frohberg said he was perfectly willing to see the human race end after his death.

Every man had the same desire to escape. Men and women, Frohberg told me, would meet up in a bar and have the illicit tryst they both desired.

I didn't know who the devil was here in his view, men or women, but it seemed Frohberg had little respect for the ways they entangled, neither ever as wonderfully and romantically entangled as Hallmarx, Dizzyny, and Bollywood portrayed. There was no long-term relationship, certainly not one that survived death. If you stayed together, the man would become a prisoner and the woman a jailer. Increasingly unsatisfactory lust fests followed gooey young love which itself didn't last long. He called this his High Romantic view.

I took great exception to this miserable view of romance Frohberg told, disgusted by his perverted and demented story of men and women in love. Devoted as I was to my love for Bettina and deep as I was in my tearjerker self-moaning on and on about lost love, I had to stand up to Frohberg and defend my love.

I mentioned Bettina, which I was always compelled to do. He conceded that I was the kind of self destroyed bastard that a woman escaping the nest might mistake for a romantic rebel.

"You probably drove her into her grave," he told me one night when we were drinking hard at the *Astelena*.

I tried to land a punch but fell out of my chair. I was helped to my seat. He was still sitting there, eyes out of focus, dead drunk but still yapping.

"I jes said that," he said, waving one arm. "It wasn't personal. That's what somebody told my father, and somebody told his father. And so on as far back as you can find a cockroach. Not personal. To you."

I was now too tired to hit him.

"But look. Why would she be looking for you? Do her a favor and don't look for her."

"Because I killed her?"

"Not history…hysterically but just think if you weren't good for her, give her break. Leave her alone."

"She's dead."

He waved that arm again in my face.

"Well, there you go. Problem solved."

After that scene I tried not ever to mention Bettina again. And he didn't either.

When this sad life tumbled into the office of a Millennial Life Support Coach, he was diagnosed with "bi-polarity," what he considered a step up from a past "paranoid schizophrenia" diagnosis.

The diagnosis created no fear in the man. The President of the United States was a narcissistic paranoid schizophrenic, and he was the fucking President of the United States was the way Frohberg looked at it. It was a noble illness.

He was in good company. I told him I had been diagnosed as a Sociopathic Polysnot, which he seemed to think after knowing me all of six seconds was accurate.

In time, Frohberg would earn the diagnosis of "Asperger syndrome" with a limited range of empathy. A second opinion which he sought for laughs said labeling him autistic insulted the autistic. He was just an ordinary run, analog, back in the day, paper and pen, brick and mortar psychopath.

Whatever, he concluded. He was in a fast speed orbit that had him escaping into one of his own "travel packages" as well as into voluminous fifths of Jameson.

Somehow this wreck of a man had recently convinced a new travel abroad consortium modeled on Shamazon.com -- in this case you saw your travel deal online, clicked on it and the agency would then contact its local agents "on the ground" to make it all Offline REAL -- that he was their "man in Pays Basque," the "agent of accommodation," "the catalyst of the Caribbean," although they never did tours of the Caribbean.

He was the Genie of Dream Tours Come True, the Matador of Colossal Bullshit.

Frohberg could set up bedbug free digs, artisanal cheese tours, Red Light district crawls, field triage, craft cocktail river voyages, sudden bowel collapse prevention, front pocket boosting, hotel skip and run, Irish pub decorum 101 and street vomiting, 24/7 on the piss tours, reckless and polite eyeballing 101 on topless beaches, leverage with surly bartenders, advanced jackassing the locals, and sucker punching smarmy Parisian waiters 101.

This lunatic had what he called a meritocrat's resume.

In the curse. . . I mean course of his life, he went to sea, taught English as a default language, washed pots, distributed late night bar flyers, unloaded trucks, swept, painted, picked, clerked, salvaged, safeguarded, carried, washed, drove, escorted, delivered, exchanged currencies, and dealt with random madness. And he had an EU private investigator license issued by Interpol. Wherever he took a tour group, a dead body was sure to show up. Frohberg said he was in good with the police because he had led them to the lair of the Icepick serial killer.

You could see it clearly in his eyes that derangement was working on him the way fungus runs through brie, and I should have run the first time I saw him, but I didn't for all the reasons already given.

When you're on a crazy mission yourself, you are drawn to any kind of derangement in other people. It fascinates. You feel a kinship. You could go on *Fotchbook* and run into all kinds of crazies who in another age ranted their craziness alone in dark basements but that cyberescape now ran on podgurgles of twelve year old Influencers.

As I was fascinated by death, I asked Frohberg at one time whether he feared death, he being kind of close to it given his many ailments.

"Death? If you look quick, kid, it's always over your right shoulder. Carlo Castaknockers said that."

I did a quick look over my shoulder.

There was a lovely women with auburn hair glistening in the sun seated at a table with some wankers.

"I see her," I mumbled. "She's not dead."

"Yeah, you didn't look fast enough. Death is too nimble for you."

"It's Bettina" was all I said.

As Frohberg put it he brought the travelers into local color contact with no cyber screen residue, no religious restraints, and no local police involvement, no STDs, and no guilty consciences. Whatever happened anywhere never happened anywhere.

He considered me right off as one of his "subcontractees," an important part of the local color. I wasn't a local, but I did speak Euskara, the Basque language. Only a local could speak that. Commendatore Spinalzo had taught me, hoping that when I grew up, I would join ETA, the Basque homeland and liberty organization and get myself blown up. Dirk took to that idea enthusiastically but the language, like all languages, including English, proved beyond his grasp.

I was at first reluctant to join up with Frohberg because it seemed clear to me that any association with this guy would produce nothing good, nothing of use, and nothing sacred. I didn't want to accumulate more scars on the brain pan of my memory.

But then I saw what drew me to him. What was that attraction?

I saw in him life going on after the wreckage.

It was as simple as that. Everything had been taken from him, but he continued to live in the aftermath. And he was visibly haunted by mad dreams he couldn't handle. They set off an angry defiance he couldn't control. So, yeah, he was mad.

I was drawn to that the way Dr. Jackal was drawn to Mr. Hide.

Being interested in his story was like discovering the coordinates to my own collapsing life.

"Who do we tour around?"

"We escort," Frohberg corrected me. "The wealthy, the retired, the newlyweds, the gentrified, the meritocratic elite, the dividend recipients, the 50th wedding anniversary celebrants, the chauvinists and bigots, the micro aggressors and the apologists, the legacy brats, the hopeless romantics, the pharmacologically depressed, the aging voluptuaries, the potheads, the lunatics, the genealogists, the Woke and the Cancelled, and the dying and the dead."

Today, I was flush after having taken forty-five euros in poker the night before from a local clown named Freddie Martos who had appointed himself my aide de camp follower. Patawalla had taught both Dirk and I how to cheat at poker.

"This is what you need to understand, Virgil," Frohberg said as we leaned over our wine at the *Astelena*.

It was midday and the sun beat down on the Plaza Constitucion so fiercely that the plaza was deserted. The *Astelena* which would be packed with tourists by 19 hours was now empty.

Also, Frohberg called anyone who worked for him as a tour guide, Virgil.

I watched the new barman practice a cidre pour, bottle extended over his head, eyes looking straight ahead. I saw he was pouring too much of it on his hand.

"This is a Yale group," Frohberg was saying. "Skull and Bones types."

"I went to Oxford and Cambridge," I told him.

"Is that my fault?" Frohberg snapped. "These guys have euros coming out of their holes. I'm just asking you to take them around the dives in the old town, introduce them to some of your colorful friends. Talk the lingo. Make them feel like they're hanging with the homeboys, giv'em the full ETA way over on the dark revolutionary side. Dark side tour. Basque'm up. You know the script. Make them think their lives are in danger wherever you take them. Nothing excites tourists more than thinking they're in the real world and nothing convinces them more of that than telling them danger surrounds them. But you'll keep them safe. You know all these dangerous scumbags. You're their John Drain. It's all in the script I gave you."

"That's the problem. What you call the script. Papal bull. The tour guide shalt not do this and the tour guide shalt not do that. Tell me truthfully, Frohberg, what has that script ever done for anybody who ever worked for you?"

Frohberg smiled, exposing teeth needing some care. As an excuse, Frohberg said the teeth went perfect with his Brit, when he put that on. He sounded like a guy from *The New Pompey* putting on an Oxford accent.

"The Commandments?" he said. "Okay. Forget about them. When the hell did anybody ever follow them anyway? Oh, yeah, and get Bombal. He'd do. He's local color."

"I thought you said he was a fat thief."

"He's fat and jolly. The clients love to listen to a fat and jolly local. They want to smile for selfies and laugh their asses off."

"I thought you wanted me to make them feel their lives were in danger?"

He ignored me.

"Fat Bombal is perfect. I just wish the suckers would pay up in advance."

Frohberg knocked back his shot of Polish vodka. He had given up Jameson after reading Ian Fleming's advice to drink clean and purified vodka. It was easier on the one remaining, overworked kidney. Of course, giving up drink totally would not enter Frohberg's mind. Still, he looked bad and sad.

"What no Yalie advance?"

"They'll pay when they get here," Frohberg said, pulling out a handkerchief, removing his hat and revealing thin, wispy grey hair hennaed to an orange. He wiped the forehead and ran his handkerchief over his head.

I could see he was nervous about the venture.

The man fit a pattern, a template but also was one unique bird. An amalgam Finn, Pole, German, Irishman, dash of Ojibway from someplace in the Midwest, Frohberg disarmed his fellow heart landers by responding to his nationality with the question "What's a Jew to say?" which was a funny line because Frohberg wasn't Jewish. He had adopted the name for reasons only a mind like Frohberg's could comprehend but he had a way of making you believe lunacy was perfectly rational and that aberrant thinking was normal. But, as I say, who am I to judge?

Frohberg had asked everyone to drop his nickname which was "Buddy" and call him "Frohberg." As Frohberg put it, a Jewish name wasn't useful in joining the country club, or a Brooklyn Italian social club, but it did mean he knew how to run a business. And to be fully useful, the name had to be used. He robbed it from a tombstone.

In his view, there was something comforting and reassuring to Americans in meeting a New York Jew in Europe. He wasn't from New York but pretending to be from there was now good business. Americans encountering foreign looking people speaking a foreign language would rely on a New York Jew to keep them safe and get them the best deal, whatever the deal might be.

It was a security thing. If a Jew is your guide, Frohberg told me, the limeys, frogs, wops, krauts, spics, towelheads, square heads and so on couldn't cheat you, couldn't rape you, couldn't rake you over the coals, stiff you, spin you, and toss you in a lime pit.

"You don't sound very woke," I told him. "The younger ones are all woke now."

"I'm publicly woke," he responded. "I was a student of Roy Corn, a guy meaner than Joseph "The Animal" Barboozala, and young Donnie Rump's mentor."

When Frohberg opened his mouth, the Indiana Security Moms knew they were in good hands. Even though they would sweetly tell you they've never seen a Jew but were fully aware of their "difference," Frohberg had a way of not frightening them. He was an empowering link, a reminder that wherever you went, the American dollar talked, and who could talk the American dollar better than a New York Jew named Frohberg?

He was, tout court, not a guy a reader or a viewer would be encouraged to identify with on page or screen. And yet, he was so unlikeable that he seemed to fit in with a type that in crisis of any sort would get the vote sooner than the Good Samaritan. Corporeal Wheelers and Dealers didn't get their killer instinct from the Beatitudes. Everyday Americans didn't put winning in the hands of Jesus but in the good hands of Oil State and E.F. Button.

But Frohberg really didn't fit in here. He was just a charlatan, broken in every way, failed, jailed and un-hailed. A kind of cockroach who could talk. Heaven wasn't where he came from, and Hell didn't want him.

But I didn't judge.

All in all, I hesitated to introduce him to Bettina. She didn't like pretenders, people who prefaced everything they said with "To tell the truth," or "The truth is," or "Truthfully speaking" and worst of all: "Let me be perfectly clear." All such announcements only proved in her view that I was reaching for something I didn't have and didn't know.

I'm talking about me, not Frohberg.

"You are such a liar," she would tell me and "Do you ever tell the truth?" But you know, she knew, despite what I might say, I was only always speaking metaphorically or for comic effect. I didn't trust words and, as I told her, I was always trying to communicate on the deepest, most profound level with her.

"You can't help yourself, can you?" was her response.

No, I didn't think she would take to Frohberg and for the life of me I don't know why I did, despite all the reasons I've given you. He was a crumb of a man, but he was still breathing. If she were dead, there was no reason for me to be alive. Only the vile go on living.

I couldn't be happy anyplace but here I was. I wasn't any kind of guide for anybody, but here I was. A lost Virgil. The awful thing about wanting to be with someone who is no longer here is that you are still here. When emptiness is both here and there, there is no here or there.

And no place for a guide.

CHAPTER THIRTY-NINE

"KK"

I crossed the plaza and headed toward the beach.

I passed a line of men leaning against the wall on Calle Aldamar waiting for a seat in Senora Garbi's restaurant. She had a one dish daily menu and if you liked it, it was a bargain. You just had to extract the implant of choice equals freedom from your mind. Of course, in the U.S. you had all of consumer Kapitalismo working against you. Freedom was wrapped up in consumption the way your order from Shamazon! was wrapped in plastic and oceans were wrapped in the same.

Unlikeable thoughts; maybe I had them because I was living in the lower depths and the elite were walking above me, on my face. I had the unlikeable thought that Death was an inconvenience to the economic order, more of an obstacle than unions, taxes, regulations, class action suits, and the prepositional phrase "promote the general Welfare" in the U.S. Constitution.

In short, we got face slammed out of the blue with Death because we were molded not to know it. Blabbing about an After Life was just a branding distraction. Death wasn't bad; it was an eternal leisure and shopping paradise.

That's the most admired and profitable flimflam of the economics of Eat Up the Whole World and the After Life Too! Campaign.

I sound like a hard-fisted revolutionary for The Cause. That ain't me, as I said the first time I saw Dirk fall on his face. I am angry because Death took Bettina and nobody, not one damn soul, can tell me anything but empty jabber and prattle like The Void, or Oblivion. The After Life. Heaven and Hell. You become somebody else in another life, but you don't remember who you were. Or maybe you do, and you go nuts. You go back to being a plant, or maybe you never left. You were always inside everything on the planet. Even the stones. If you're the ocean now, you're choking in plastic.

I had a closet sized, cheap room in Andoni's pensione with no balcony view of the Plaza, but it was what suited my mood.

I walked beneath the shady arcade until I came to the heavy double doors of no. 21.

The foyer was dark and cool. There was no lift, an absence that would have turned away many a tourist dragging tonnage on wheels.

The old man, Juan, was standing by the door as I entered, his shirt dirty and rumbled, his white wiry hair crowning him like a madman, which he was.

"Que pasa amigo?"

His eyes red, his breath stinking of wine.

"Nada."

"*Ah, Senor Nada. Con usted, señor Theo, siempre es nada. Todo es nada con usted, señor Nada.*"

"*Pensé que me llamó el hombre que vaga, viejo,*" I told him, pushing past Juan's belly which he had the habit of sticking out like a weapon.

"*Es brutalmente caliente por ahí, pero los hombres no nos importa el calor, no Senor gitano?*

So, the old man was on the right side of sanity today I thought as I turned the key to my room.

Juan took a pleasure in bullying the young innocent tourists who www.Hotel dot Bullshit led to the *Pensione Maialen* for a "half price special" which was always the same sucker's price with a la carte add ons like a room key, hot water, toilet paper, towels, room cleaning, shower, lights, a pillow and sheets, a fan. The bed was gratis as was the share-all bathroom down the hall

Juan's real pleasure was to fuck with the Brits who trouped in with nannies in tow. His glee boosted also when young Americans stumbling over high school Spanish stood before him. He showed them no mercy. He told them all about how superior the Latin American novelists were to the North Americans who were in decline.

And Juan drooled over the sweet young things who bounced around the tiny passageways of the *Maialen* in their tiny swimsuits, long legged underwear which their asses rippled in, or exposed thongs and tramp stamps.

He mocked their young escorts by denouncing their tiny penises in speed freak Spanish that made the tourists laugh though they didn't understand a word he was saying.

Many assumed Juan was a retired professor of history or philosophy or literature because he never tired of quoting the memorable thoughts of genius, but I knew from Juan's old lady, a true lady in every way, Signora Maialen, for the pensione had been named for her, that Juan had been a banker and that dollars and cents and not words were what he knew.

Juan had gotten into trouble on several risky loans, or because of a too close collaboration with an American hedge fund, or because he foreclosed on properties he later made a profit on, or because he was a dirty, corrupt prick and had gotten away with everything right up until he would have gone to prison.

In short, he was the Basque version of Jabba, just another fat predator. Or Fartsworth in the compound Greed had built. He was the Spanish Cranditch too.

Yeah, I stereotype my villains. I should render to Caesar. But I don't want to, and I don't like the Caesars. Life Coaches say that if I got to know each of them personally, I'd get to like them. The U.S. Department of Justice can't get to them personally even with subpoenas, so I don't figure I've got a chance.

And I don't want to.

Someone or some turn of the wheel had pulled Juan out of his troubles and dropped him in the pensione business, a business that his son, Andoni, ran. He was the old thief's front.

This old thief was the resident gestapo, the always present concierge, the gatekeeper, the guy minding the store, the floor walker, the inflated bag of bullshit, the night watchman who stalked the digs with a bottle of wine close by. The first time, Juan stupidly tried to pull his gestapo shit on me, I slammed him against the wall and put a fist the size of his head in his face. Even drunk, he got the message.

The son, Andoni, was a decent guy who wore the old man around his neck like an albatross. I didn't understand it but then again, I didn't understand Basque families either and the way blood was an all-purpose pass that would never fail.

I never thought I was bound to The Pater or Mater in that way. Dirk was another story. We shared an egg. As far back as you can go, there's no closer tie than living in an egg together.

Unless of course your life is blessed with your own Dulcinea, as I have been, though I have a very spotty memory and what I remember pains me for I have this feeling that I scarcely lived in a Don Quixote lifelong service to Bettina.

There was a small center court where Juan hung up the laundered sheets -- one of his duties --and there was a window in my room which looked out on this court. That courtyard was kind of the old man's lab, his retreat, his man cave. The Senora kept him monitored with good reason and so there was really no escape from the wanker. I rooted for her.

What woke me up now was Juan out there making as much noise as he could and muttering under his breath. His wife had most likely berated him for any of the million reasons that could be summoned. I finally got back to my nap.

At about 17 hours I was seated at the *Sendoa.*

It was the time for *pintxos y vino,* and the tourists were filling up the place.

The Anglos' eyes were on the locals dropping the thin papers which served as serviettes onto the floor without guilt, hearing the heated political conversations they could not understand, eyeing the array of pintxos on the bar, naked, uncovered, un-curated, unprotected by plastic, unrefrigerated and handled in a manner that produced the great tourist paranoic fear: Foreign Fecal Fingers which they knew gave you the travelling shits.

"I am amazed this place doesn't have a viral multi-platform presence. Why is that?"

I realized this wanker in golfing pastels sitting behind me was talking to me.

"Maybe it's because the streets smell of piss, vomit, and salted cod fried in olive oil," I told him.

The woman sitting next to him, sun bleached blonde hair, halter top, sandals, was amused. Trophy I thought. She looked splendid and he looked like what the tide washes up. Money doesn't have to look good, Sal had once told me.

This wealth bag was struggling with my response when a kid I knew passed by and seeing me laid down some Euskara. I responded and he laughed, pointed a finger at me like he was scolding me.

"You're a native?" the blonde asked me. "Basque?"

"Don't talk to this fellow," Tidal Washup told her.

"No, but I teach the language if you want to learn. Five lessons. Five hundred euro."

She laughed.

"We are leaving, my dear," Tidal Washup ordered.

"No. I think I want lessons. But can I ask you why they don't clean the streets and so on. More attractive, no? I mean if they want to attract tourists."

"They don't," I told her. "They try to dissuade tourists, but it doesn't work. Tourists are like lemmings. You have to drown them. I say welcome the flush. Just beat a tourist over the head and take his money. Or talk her into fluency lessons in Euskara."

"Oh, you're very funny, you know," she said, laughing but I could see she was nervous. She needed Tidal Washup to rescue her from me.

"I say they should keep pissing in the alleys and frying their cod at five in the morning for tourist control. Donostia doesn't want to go where Venice has gone. The local Venetians can't live in their own city. Prices are too high, and lemmings overrun the streets."

"Oh, that's so much like Brooklyn," she moaned in deep sympathy with the old school Brooklyn evicted. "It disappeared and we had just bought."

"Brooklyn? Never heard of it."

"We've evicted all the local authenticity. I just hate that."

Tears were coming to her eyes. She had the kind of accessorized face that cost more than a month's nut.

"No, we haven't," Tidal Waste snarled. "They were using the streets like urinals. Like this fellow says they do here. Is that what you call authenticity?"

I handed him one of Frohberg's tour guide cards:

"Authentic Crawl"

He looked at it and threw it on the table. Then he got up quickly, grabbing her arm.

"I don't want to see your face again," he told me.

"You won't. We don't swim in the same waters."

No, I didn't think she was Bettina re-incarnated. When I think about it, I don't know why anybody is worth re-incarnating. When you've lived a shining life, you can't be cloned. No algorithm would lead you to Bettina.

I got up and found a place at the bar, eying the delectables arrayed on it.

The place was jammed with tourists.

I saw the con man, Freddy Martos come in.

He was con artist, a card cheat, but not as good as me, a drug dealer, a fence, and the town gossip but at least he was a witty rascal and I thought better company than most.

But, yeah, he wasn't the kind of guy who you would welcome as protagonist for say 300 pages or two hours of movie. He was a side pit at best.

But he was ridiculous, not that he was unaware of this, and he made me laugh. When you spend your whole life looking for someone without success, life becomes deadly serious, which meant, there were times when it all cracked open into carnival and farce. More *La Commedia*. Say hello to Freddy.

"I tracked you down," Freddy said, holding up his cell phone. "It has *Foursquawk* so I can track where everyone is."

"For what purpose?" I asked. "I try not to know where everybody is. I don't like everybody. To be honest, I think I only like one person. Can I use it to find a particular person I'm looking for?"

"Of course, but with this device it tells you where everybody is and then. You don't go there!"

He laughed.

"I'll just use my eyeballs, thanks."

"But you are here and almost everyone is here."

"I was here first."

"There is now a tour guide app you can purchase. Let us consider that you are only several meters away from a viral influencer. Your app will inform you of this."

"What the fuck is a viral influencer?"

I said this loudly enough for several of the yacht set to turn and give me a censorious look.

"A twelve-year-old Life Coach who each hour of the day tells you how to live your life. If you get in her circle, you are made. In cyberspace. Immortal."

"I'm not much interested in listening to twelve-year-olds. And where's your end in this? How do you get paid?"

"Attention! We are minutes away from the best French restaurant within fifty kilometers and going in there right now is Salvador

Dollie."

"Isn't he dead?"

"It's encrypted. Anywho, the on-line life is immoral."

"Immortal?"

"That also. I tell you my friend, Tod, with this device you won't be able to walk past anything of significance. Only listen to the voice of your phone. It's a wonderful new world, amigo. Just join the hash tags. Do you know your American president, Senor Cardoza, tweets in the morning before he takes a shit?"

As he said this, he was occupied with his own handheld device which he called "Mona." I was wondering who she might be and also whether or not I had missed an election back home.

"You should be more of a follower," Freddy said, without looking up. "You know, to see what's happening in the lives of the most successful. You can live your life through the life of a celebrity."

"Any chance this could help me find a woman I've lost track of. Here's a photo. My wallet is full of them. Look."

He took my wallet of Bettina photos, taken at every age, from three to the last time I saw her, which was in a dream.

He handed the wallet back to me.

"She looks like Mona. But she's dead. But maybe not so. If this Mona is alive and if she is in San Sebastian, I will find her for you, Ted, my brother."

"Yeah, well, she might be dead. Not to me but it's kind of the way I feel she's here is a very personal thing."

Freddy gave me a WTF look but then said:

"I understand *totalmente completamente*. What is her name?"

"Mona," I told him, deciding that a correct name might impede his success. "So how do you profit on this thing?"

I pointed to his phone.

"It's called social grooming," Freddy said. "You groom the social network and then you suddenly observe a window you can insert yourself in a profitable manner. "

"I'm lost."

"Ask me what's happening,"

"Even if I don't care?"

"Felon Must goes to Mars. Jeff Jezus sells the Russkies a space station. Men become women. Women become men. A candidate has artificial intelligence. What do you get?

"Confusion? A dying planet? Lots of dead innocent people? The loss of language, history, science, penmanship? A candidate for what?"

"You get slippage is what you get."

"Slippage?"

"Is where Freddy Martos appears. In the slippage. And what slips in the slippage? *Tanto dinero que usted piensa que está en otro soviético bonanza de libre mercado!*"

The word slippage reminded me of what Patawalla had said about a reincarnation gone wrong, namely mine. I didn't like the process.

"Until then, what do you have that you can sell me cheap in the way of underwear? Mine are developing holes."

"I have shirts of a wonderful fabric from Egypt sewn by skillful 13 cents an hour Bangladeshi hands. Socks and pants of the same magnitude and generosity."

"You're not much of a human being are you Freddy?"

"Who is?' Freddy replied smiling his infectious smile which lit his eyes up like sparkling jade. "Who wants to be human when you can be a cyborg?"

Freddy leaned over and whispered in my ear. His breath smelled awful.

"*Yo tenemos algo para insertar en relación con su amigo de allí que no es de uno a acercarse demasiado a.*"

"What?"

"I say don't get too close to our friend Frohberg."

"Is that an insertion or a slippage?"

"That one is now a dangerous trending topic for what reason I don't know," Freddy said "There are even hash marks on the Tweaker. The nuts and bolts are now loose in his head. Slippage."

Slippage. The final slippage.

"Tell me, Freddy, do you ever think about death?"

Freddy shrugged.

"I don't think it pays me anything to think about that. When the show is going on, I don't jump to the end."

"Send the shirts around," I said, heading for the door which was not a door but an open wall where now the sun was going down and you could walk where you wished. I could take just so much of Freddy at one time.

"KK," Freddy said.

Phillips turned.

"KK? What the hell?"

"It means OK," Freddy said, smiling. "It's easier to type than OK. Just K is even better."

"What's that? Language slippage? Don't answer. Just send the shirts around, OK?"

"With such a shirt with such a price the especial ladies will be crying to meet you!" Freddy called after me "I have the photo on my phone. It will go viral. All legal photos."

I waved back. I was confident. He had a fallacious name and a dream photo. He had as much chance of finding her as I did.

Of course, it would be funny if he found Mona and she turned out to be Bettina.

CHAPTER FORTY

DEATH IS A HARD BLOW

I was packed and ready to go for a long walk on the Santiago Camino, but I was postponing it and instead I was sitting under an umbrella in the Plaza Constitucion with Freddy Martos drinking beer.

I had this feeling that the best place to find Bettina, or the new body her soul was in, was on the Camino de Santiago de Compostella. Why? Goodness of soul goes on such a pilgrimage; she was most likely right now a *peregrino*.

Bon Peregrino!

But I was having many such launch days like this in which I didn't launch but just sat and drank with other launch disabled souls.

Maybe my thought was, if there was a thought, that I would be as likely to see Bettina walk by as find her by wandering around on a thousand-year-old trail. I mean the sun just stayed in the center and it saw everything. It didn't move around. All life is holy so she could be any place.

I was wearing one of the shirts Freddy had acquired for me "on the black." It was a black shirt with black figures wearing black shirts.

Freddy, meanwhile, had his thin body pressure wrapped in a cheap suit of powder blue. He kept his size down to the size of a thirteen-year-old because, as he expressed it, it was cheaper, stylish in a heroin chic way, and a magnet drawing wealthy, older women.

According to Freddy. wealthy, older women were drawn to slim, young matador types.

I thought he looked like a shady marionette. I was certain that Dirk would have made a hand puppet Freddy.

"*Foursquawk* shows me they are close," Freddy reported.

"They?"

"This is more the Monster behind the Monster," Freddy explained. "The unknown Monster so far removed from anyone's view…"

"Except Freddy Martos."

"*Si, El es el hombre detras del hombre que esta detras de la persona que esta detras del chico. El unico que los tweets.*"

"The guy behind the guy behind the guy. And the guy up front in the queue is?"

"A big hodge fund which runs like a secret cabal. If you ask how much it is to join, you don't belong. *Hijo de puta!*"

Freddy jumped up and started to run across the Plaza.

Strange dude. He'd be a star in Dirk's puppet show.

I was hoping to spot Bettina that morning, you know, tanned and hair shining in the early morning sun. and instead, I got this lunatic.

Some hours later Freddy returned

He was overheated and collapsed in a chair. His powder blue suit was sweat soaked, and pants and cuffs were pulled up. He took hold of my beer and swigged it.

"What became of the Monster behind the Monster. Did you run into him?"

Freddy shook his head.

"They all went out to a yacht. Thirty meters at least. Eight to ten million. His phone is a Ulysse Nardin at fifty thousand dollars. He owns the house in Nice of some archaic dead celebrity of the name David Nimbus."

"You're really up on this guy, this Monster."

"I have the Apps that reveal the photos and the chat and the twitters. I have pimped my twitter to the highest level in order to survive. "

Before I could wrap my head around that statement, Freddy mumbled "Attendez!" and brought his phone close to his face.

"The target is approaching."

"The target?"

"American dowagers with money."

At that moment, the dowagers in question, six of them, emerged from the arcade and took a table close to where Freddy and I were seated.

"The Spanish tutor," Freddy whispered to me and then said loudly, "Repeat after me. *Es un día hermoso.*"

"What the hell are you talking about?"

"Pretend you are a student to whom I am teaching Spanish," Freddy whispered. "It's the Spanish tutor scam."

"*Que bella dama!*"

"*Qué hermoso reloj.*"

"*San Sebastián es una ciudad hermosa con gente bella.*"

"*Y he oído que hablan español. ¿Cuál es la palabra? Bellamente.*"

I figured what the hell and joined in.

We went on like this until one of the dowagers begged our pardon, but she would like to know if it was easy to learn Spanish?

Freddy unreeled his scripted response, a response that would hopefully lead to a request to tutor the dowagers and that would then, in no time, lead to Freddy sticking to them like a mosquito and like a mosquito suck their blood in every way such affinity would allow him.

He would wind up selling them everything from Basque underwear from China to Basque jewelry from Antwerp and genuine Basque footwear from Walmarx.

I suddenly felt I had sunk very low and that if Bettina was somewhere looking at me, she would be heartily disappointed in what had become of me. I too was disappointed in what had become of me. My early blossoming genius had withered, and I had the disturbing thought that maybe Dirk had all along been the twin in the yolk.

"Be better," is what she had once told me, sweetly, sadly.

That night at the *Astelena* I found Freddy with his party of dowagers.

They greeted me like a long-lost brother. We shared as Americans the experience of learning a travel-ready Spanish under the tutelage of the affable Senor Martos, whose pedagogical method left everyone satisfied.

Freddy had exchanged his powder blue ensemble for shorts and a striped French sailor's hoodie. Why he wore shorts in the evening and a suit in the morning I have no idea. Could you be bat shit crazy and yet clever enough to fleece these dowagers? Yeah, it seemed so.

"How's your Spanish coming along?" a young woman who had

also attached herself to the dowager tour asked me.

She had a mass of lustrous, amber gold hair, Hollywood hair, a splendid tan and a smile that showed the whitest most perfect teeth. And she was a head shorter than me. In fact, she was exactly Bettina's height.

I had found her. She didn't recognize me, but I recognized her.

Now she was suddenly here at my side as I bit into *pintxos* and sipped wine. She didn't belong with this troupe. What was she doing with these dupes? Had Bettina's soul been corrupted in passage? A slippage?

"I'm Rebekkah," she said. "And I've been to San Sebastian before. Many times. I've seen your friend many times but never you. He's a con man, isn't he? Are you with him?"

"What? Me. No."

She was giving me the sort of smile that told him "I know you're lying and that you guys are con men and I think it's funny because you're so bad at it."

She laughed.

"I don't care if you are. I ran into these ladies on the train from Pamplona. We've already fallen out. I'm tax the rich, hug the trees, get woke type. These ladies are right to pillage. They think the lives of poor people are an infringement on their personal freedom. They think public libraries are an attack on the capitalism they love. They would privatize air for a profit if they could. They cringe when they hear the word 'public.'"

She paused. Maybe she saw me cringing at the word 'public' but I hadn't said a word.

She was Bettina alright but then again Bettina would never share all that with a stranger. And to tell the truth, I'm not sure what Bettina's views were on all that. She wasn't that removed from conditions on the ground, sometimes literally, never ready to share her thoughts and feelings with anyone, least of all a stranger.

More concrete particular than abstract universal. More like feed the birds, please, Did you ever think of cleaning the bathroom when it's your turn? Did you ever think that sometimes it should be your turn to do the chores? Did you ever notice dust and crumbs on the floor and do something about it? Try hard not to interrupt and please try to listen so much more than you talk. Did you ever answer the question asked? Funerals are about the dead person and not about you. Please don't presume people prefer what you think to what they themselves think. Why do you presume anyone is interested in your thoughts when they've got their own.? Just having testicles is such a gift in this world. Apparently. And unfortunately.

Stuff like that, which she didn't bullhorn all over the place.

I thought of running all this by the reincarnated Bettina, but I didn't want to presume an interest.

"Y he oído que hablan español. ¿Cuál es la palabra? Bellamente."

I liked the way she said that word "bellamente." Beautifully.

"I speak all the Romance languages. But you know that already."

She laughed.

"Why would I know that? Are you one of those people who presumes other people are inside their heads? More people than you could imagine believe their own thinking and feeling are universally shared. It's a form of narcissism. It makes real communication impossible. For instance, I don't even know your name. I said I'm Rebekkah and you say?"

"Theodorus," I said, feeling my face flush. "You look so much like someone I know. I got confused."

"She was inside your head? Her identity was a stolen rib of your own?"

She laughed.

I was more than confused. I was losing it, as Bettina prophesied. She wasn't dead because she was here looking at me. Calling herself Rebekkah.

So, this was the transformation we could expect after death?

I never for a moment believed that someone who when alive had distilled in themselves the better angels of human nature would simply blow away like dust when dead. There had to be a way in which such fineness went on forever, in whatever way or form, material or immaterial.

Still, would that recaptured fineness show up here and mock me?

But then again, the Freddy Martoses, Frohbergs, Bastards, Jabbas, and Juans and Nick Rises of the world would have long ago eaten all of us alive if the world was not permeated with the pure essence of souls like my Bettina. They had to linger. Persevere. Be in the grass just below our feet.

But why here?

Maybe I needed her to be here. Maybe I just presumed Bettina wouldn't just obliterate because I didn't want that destiny for myself?

It's a hard blow for an egoist. Death. Probably harder for a narcissist. Was I self-loving regardless of conditions? Egoist? Think of the world through my own eyes? Kind of inevitable, that. Egotist? Let other people know I think of myself first? Or don't bother to wonder what others think and feel?

Death is a hard blow for that whole lot.

"Are you okay?" she said, and I realized I must have drifted off someplace.

"I'm not with Freddy," I stuttered. "He was helping me find someone."

"The someone I look like?"

I nodded.

"I'm not her. I'll tell you that right off."

"Okay."

"This place gets very noisy," she said after a long pause. "I'm gone. See you some place."

She walked away.

See you some place? What did she mean? What place?

I followed her but lost sight of her in a sudden tidal wave of millennials on display.

Yeah, I went looking for her.

But you were prepared for that.

I found her the next day, early morning, listening to Fat Bombal over coffee in front of the *Astelana*.

"Ah, my friend here can help explain what it is I mean," Bombal told Rebekkah.

"By all means," she said. "Join us."

I did.

"Senor Bombal is expressing some hope in both English and Spanish that I can convince his son to return to school. Someone told him I'm a teacher."

"Are you?"

"Not at this moment, no."

"I know the kid," I said. ""I think he doesn't want to go to school. Which is all good. The kid is doorknob dumb."

She frowned.

"Walter is a good knob of a door," Bombal said, shaking his head. "but he doesn't know what he wants. He has much to learn. *Él desea viajar como lo hace el señor Butt.*"

This comment about how I travelled interested Rebekkah.

"And how does Senor Butt travel?" she asked Bombal but was looking at me.

I could see she didn't like me.

"Walter has a lot of potential, though," I mumbled. "What do I know? I don't really know the kid that well."

Bombal shrugged.

"I'm waiting, Senor," she said to Bombal.

"Tell her everything, Bombal. She'll find out anyway."

"Senor Butt moves with the pull of something in his mind that he has lost. It is like he is the magnet but nothing he is looking for pulls to him."

"That again?" she asked me. "The woman you lost?"

"He doesn't know what he's talking about because I haven't spoken to the guy more than once or twice. And this is the twice."

"But he tells everyone all the time," Bombal said, disagreeing with me.

"What does he tell them?"

"I'm right here. Ask me. I don't tell anyone anything."

"He tells them the story of a man who meets another man who tells him he is dying for need of water and will this man go and find some for him? So, this man . . ."

"The first man or the second man?" she interrupted. She seemed to be enjoying all this now. I had always been a source of humor to Bettina, as if being me was just comical. It was unnerving. I couldn't impress her enough with my patent leather Oxbridge credentials and my erudition.

"The first man. He goes to find water and what he finds is a woman whom he loves *tan pronto como la vie* and she is also dazed by this man because he appears so different than anyone in her life. But he is a reckless man in this real world, and he follows romantic dreams, and she follows with him until she realizes that he is a *un hombre que sabe menos del mundo real que ella* and she is no longer *aturdido*. In a daze. They have a long life together even after she will no longer follow his dreams. A family with two children. A very long marriage. When he sees her, he tells her it makes him happy to see her. It is after so many years that she becomes sick and in the middle of the night she is close to dying which is what she does as he cries and tries to do the GPS, but she closes her eyes, and she dies."

I saw Rebekkah looking at me. I was tearing up. How the hell did this fat bastard know this story? I was hoping it wasn't mine, but it sounded familiar.

"And then what happened? She died?"

Bombal shrugged.

"In this story that Senor Butt tells he awakens as if in a dream and she is no longer there, but he sees the man who needed water. . ."

"The second man in the story?"

"Si. And this man says to Senor Butt "Where is the water I sent you for?"

"That's the end of the story?"

Bombal nodded.

"It is very sad."

"But what does it mean?" she asked, looking at me.

"I've never heard that story. Don't ask me. This guy doesn't know me. First clue. Who's Senor Butt? The whole deal is a false narrative."

Bombal shook his head.

"Ask anyone here right now in this place who knows Senor Butt and they will tell you he has told them this story. He tells everyone. It is a story he must tell. We forgive him that he knocks out our brains telling this story so, so, so many times because after all, the woman he loves is now dead forever and it is too sad a story. But I think he thinks of a life with her that never happened."

"Or maybe not," I told the fat bastard angrily. "Maybe it's all real."

Bombal thought about that, giving me a close inspection.

"Could be maybe so *acaso*. If she is dead, why does he look for her? I don't believe he believes this woman is dead. And I don't think he had such a long life with her. Maybe a romance of the young that goes hot like fire and then dies. Could be a weekend or a long holiday. He says Marlena was very lovely."

"Marlena? She's the woman in the story?"

"Bettina," I mumbled. "She was magical at every age."

"I can see that," she told me, sympathetically.

I didn't know what she saw.

"Look, I've got to go. Some place."

I stood up.

"Okay," she said. "I'm not surprised. Have a good day."

"Sure. You too."

"Some place," she called after me.

CHAPTER FORTY-ONE

"COME HERE AND SIT WITH ME"

The afternoon of the next day as I walked along the beach with Frohberg, Rebekkah called out to me from where she was sitting on a blanket about ten yards from the water's edge.

I had on a bathing suit, but Frohberg had on his customary afternoon garb: tight black Mexican suit, rumpled white shirt, necktie hanging like a noose, black shoes, and white socks. He held a black umbrella over his head although he had a Panama hat on.

We made our way over to her.

"Hey, kid," Frohberg greeted Rebekkah, and at once dropped down on the sand and moaned.

"You know Rebekkah?"

"We've seen each other around. Cheese and crackers! What is this sand? Lava? Hot lava on the boil in a hot sun?"

"Surely you're not feeling it through your shoes?" Rebekkah, who was in a bikini said, pointing to Frohberg's shoes splayed out on the sand like two loaves of bread. White socks reached beyond the jacked up trouser legs.

"I feel through my eyes, kid," Frohberg said, leaning on an elbow and looking up at Rebekkah. "Then it goes to my brain and because I have thoughts and feelings, I am aware that it's fucking hot. In short, I am a sentient old motherfucker."

I squatted down and tapped Frohberg on the knee.

"How come you've seen her around and I only saw her for the first time a couple of days ago and I'm the one looking for her?"

"I guess she's been lucky," Frohberg said, squinting up at me

"Until now."

"So, you're still looking for someone you insanely think is me?"

I nodded.

"He thinks I'm Gina." Rebekkah told Frohberg.

"Bettina."

"And she's dead. Or half the time he thinks she is."

"Yeah, he's a cockeyed kid," Frohberg said.

"Maybe she's just a dream," Rebekkah said, still enjoying the wind up.

"Ignore him," Frohberg told her. "He thinks every beautiful young lady is this Bettina. He's nuts but he speaks the local lingo and I need him. I've had some bad news. I'm not getting any upfront money for a tour I'm expecting. Forgive me if I sound like an old motherfucker but I am trying to convince my friend here to at least give me one good piece of goddamn news for the day and take the local color job I'm offering him."

"Oh, I didn't know you were local color?" Rebekkah remarked, shading her eyes to look at me. I was sitting in the sand across from her.

"I'm not. I haven't been here long enough to qualify. Not for the languages. I speak all the Romance language. Euskara is pre-Indo-European. I speak that as well. I just don't qualify in the local color department. I don't see color. Everything is dark black to me. Like a dark tunnel focus on one person."

"Bettina?"

I nodded.

"I myself enjoy the local color. I've decided to stay longer but I need a place to stay other than the tourist hive I'm in."

"You can find a room for her at your place, can't you, Bratter?"

"You wouldn't like it. The floor walker is an old mean drunk who will try to get into your life and you'll smell fish frying at all hours, and everybody spies on everybody else, and the staircase has no lights."

"No plus side?"

"On the plus side it's right on the Plaza Constitucion and you can probably get a room with a balcony."

"Sounds charming."

"I'm warning you," I told her, "the old guy will try to get into your pants."

"Get him to stay," Frohberg said, standing up. "Pretend you're Wheatena. This is hell heat. I'm out a here."

I helped him stand and he did a creaky walk back toward the

shore.

"Are you going to help him with his tour?"

I shook my head.

"I'm not staying here much longer. I know you're not her, by the way."

"Sorry. I'm just me. You are haunted by that story Bombal told, aren't you? What do you think it means? Or don't you? That might be the reason it stays with you."

"I know what it means. It means while your whole life is happening, you're not there and when the end comes, you know you've missed it. It all happened in the time it takes to go somewhere and come back."

"Like looking for water?"

I nodded.

"And that's painful?"

"There's a kind of time flow you can't be into as it flows. It's like you can't grab a hold of it and look at it. You can't stop the flow and pause it and say come here and you hold her, and you see her there and then in that moment for what she means to you. You hold her and she holds you in that moment that doesn't move. Then there's a kind of time flow that runs backward and makes clear to you all you've missed, that you didn't seize the moment or even the day. Your whole life doesn't flash before you when you die. Just all the pieces you missed. It hurts."

I stopped. I didn't want to be talking so much.

"I was intent on finding water. I had ambition. Purpose. I was always leaving the moments as they happened behind because they didn't matter compared to where I was going. And in this other time, I'm in pain because you see I wasn't going anyplace that compared to just being there with her. Minute by minute. This is the only time I live in now. I travel. All I do now is travel but I don't go anywhere. My journey is over."

She didn't say anything. She was probably knocked back by my outpouring. I know I was. Where did all that come from? I'm so heavily damaged I can't shut up.

I laughed.

"I think I'm experiencing a kind of archetype."

"You have a lot of regret," she finally said. "I mean, timewise, more than one person in one lifetime. I'm sorry. I shouldn't presume."

"Go ahead. Fire away. I know I'm crazy."

"You're too young to have gone through all that. You realize that, don't you? Somehow, you've taken on a whole lot of dark issues that can't be yours. I think you just fear that all what you say may happen to you. I mean don't we all fear dying without knowing why we lived or dying with the feeling we didn't live at all, that we made the wrong choices or missed what was right in front of us? Forgive me. I don't mean to laugh."

"Not at all. It seems appropriate after what I've told you."

"I just think it's very adolescent. Your fear of the future, of loss, of death."

"I don't fear death. I mean personally. I fear it for her. I fear she's gone someplace and needs my help like the time she fell down the cellar steps and telephoned me. Can you come home quick? I fell and it hurts too much to try and stand.'"

"Did you go home and help her?"

I shook my head.

"The dream ended before it got to that part. You know, when I look at anyone now, I wonder how close to dying are they and will they be missed and will their lives be totally forgotten, like she never lived?"

"And what do you see when you look at me?"

I stared at her. The question made me uncomfortable.

"You see Bettina?"

I nodded.

"But I see her very amused by that and I know you're not her."

"Maybe you're waking up."

"You know, I didn't have an adolescence. My brother and I had nannies and tutors. And shrinks. Also, I fell out of a boat on a lee shore and hit my head on the rocks. Dirk saved me. My twin. I think it all began with that head injury. Or maybe not. Bettina was real. And lovely. What I felt for her wasn't because my head slammed into rocks off Montauk Point. I had a concussion. I was in Montauk General for over a year."

"That was a long time," she said, almost in a whisper.

Then she said:

"Those days are over."

That whisper sounded familiar. Eerie.

I looked at her. I mean into her eyes.

"Where did you go?"

"When?"

That sly smile on her lips.

"You were sitting there. On the edge of the bed. I didn't see how you got there. Sitting there. I asked you if you wanted help standing up? You didn't say anything, so I got up and went around the bed and stood in front of you. You looked up at me and raised both arms over your head, very slowly. 'You want me to help you up?' I said. No response. I stretched my arms out and without grabbing you with my hands, I lifted you up so you could stand but I saw at once that your legs were like rubber and you couldn't stand so I gently lay you back down on the bed, never a word or a moan or any sound from you and your eyes didn't stay open but they weren't closed either but I knew against all odds and all expectations that I was looking at you dying. And you did, silently, as I called your name over and over, gently stroking your face, calling to you but you never spoke a word or made a sound. Aren't dying people supposed to make a sound? And I thought later that it was so much like you to not make a sound, to not speak, to share with me what you were feeling or thinking or wanting. But your eyes said `Let me go.'"

I think it was the touch of Rebekkah's hand that woke me.

I saw her. She wasn't Bettina.

"Where did she go?" I persisted in asking.

"Heaven, some would say," she said, still that whisper. "I hear in your voice how you loved her. I'm sorry. Forget what I said. You were fortunate to have her in your life."

I didn't say anything. I didn't want to be rude. I didn't want to tell her that she was young, and I was young at that moment because it's the way I dreamed it had to be. I never went in search of Bettina as an old man. I was always young because when I found her, she too would be young, young as we both had been when we first met at The Beach House, when we went with the tides together as they came in and went out.

It's been a cold winter and the snow is thrown into mountains that can't be touched except by the Spring sun.

I am outside now splitting wood. The sun has come out and it feels good. It lasts here in mid-Winter for an unchartered time, sometimes an hour, sometimes minutes. I am busy going back and forth for everything my eye falls upon reminds me of something to be done.

I am in the middle of that when my eye takes me to a new demand, and I go to that. I stop at the entrance of the garage, turn, and look up at the sun, which is a hazy winter sun, but its rays are warm if you stand in the right spot, one that will change before too long. I am looking up at the sky and then downward to the trees, the oak that has been there for almost three hundred years. I pan lower and to the right and see the birds swooping on and off the feeder, an old wooden feeder I have repaired more than once. I scan the winter bushes, bare, spindly with no memory of how green and lush they were months before.

I am looking for her, her spirit now interfused, dwelling in that winter sun, in the air I am breathing, in the sky above my mind and in my mind. I see her spirit rolling through all things. A motion and spirit that impels all things. I believe in these lines of Wordsworth now more than a resurrection of my own self achieved if I die more virtuous than not. I look for no eternal reward or fear any eternal damnation. Losing Bettina has been a defeat I feel now and have no way to conquer. There is no sin here to confess; no ambition to be saved. Bettina was my incentive to live in a way she would respect.

I am standing there in a spot that the sun has already left and moved on.

And then I hear her:

"Come here. and sit with me in the sun."

I don't know why I turn and look into the garage, into its shadows as if she were there, but my eyes fall upon a green and white ribboned folding chair. Hers. She asked me to buy it for her to use when she went to a park to sit with friends. Every Friday. She only used it twice.

I go over to it and pull it down from the nail I've hung it on, and I bring it out of the garage. I see where the sun is now, and I open it there and I sit. I remove my glasses and let the sun's rays shine on my eyes. I feel I have entered that moment in time Blake tells us which Satan cannot find, that no worry or fear or grief can find.

I don't know how long I sit there but I know she is beside me. That we are together for this time in which I no longer burn but am happy with her. It is as it always was: she made me happy just to be with her.

When I wake up from this dream I know at once that someone in deep sadness over the loss of a love shared for eons and eons has somehow reached into me. I feel that they are both long dead and yet this pair is not dead. They are living in me.

I've never lived in the mountains or split wood or fed birds or had a garage or bought a green and white folding chair or knew she sat in a park with friends. And yet when she says "Come here and sit with me. in the sun," I go to her.

The last time I saw Rebekkah she told me she was a poet.

"I didn't know that," I said.

"You never asked anything about me. I know it's hard to be you right now, but I feel it's hard to be me."

I realized then that what she said was true. I hadn't tried to find out anything about her. That was a pattern. It hit me like a brick to the face. If this woman was Bettina in some mysterious way, I was committing the same sin, the perpetual one with me. Crying and moaning about having lost her when it was clear to me now that something like that, so much what I was feeling, thinking, ranting, had blocked my view of her.

And I was doing the same thing now with Rebekkah.

I tried to express that to her, as if Bettina too was somehow listening.

It amused Rebekkah.

"Not to worry. I've seen it before. It's a kind of pandemic among Americans. Self-absorption on the edge of solipsism. It does get boring. I mean no amount of unbalanced appetites or daily furiousness or operatic weeping really justifies boring the hell out of those we meet. Don't you think?"

Don't I think?

Yes.

"I'm so sorry. Forgive me. Oh, please forgive me."

She laughed again.

"I'm sure she found you funny. That's a path to forgiveness. Laughter."

After a time, we talked again about her.

"You see things clearly? I mean as a poet. I know. I have in mind me. You were very good. What you said. It's a gift."

"It's not easy to put the soul of things and people back into things and people when the soul is everywhere being taken out of them. It's very hard is all I can say."

She went silent for a few minutes, eyes closed and then opened them and smiled at me.

"Maybe it was easier for the Romantic poets like Keats and Shelley. But it's silly now to write 'I fall upon the thorns of life, I bleed.'"

She laughed again. I told her I get that, about thorns and bleeding.

"The dead don't bleed. You do. It's not something that can be done. Making the death of someone you loved all your life somehow a poem, somehow lyrical."

"Did you ever do that? I mean try to be lyrical about love and death?"

"Not in any satisfactory way. That's probably why I'm just an adjunct in creative writing. You see, I'm not a writing school poet with a master's degree. I came from nothing. But I think it's best to start out that way. Rather than from knowing."

"Or money?"

"Oh, you need just the right amount of money. But I don't think I'll have that gig either next Fall. Anyway, to get back to your question. Nothing any one can write about love dying is better than what a 25-year-old two hundred years ago wrote."

"Keats," I said. "I studied British Romantic poets at Magdalen College, Oxford."

"You know them, then? Then you know the lines *'She cannot fade, though thou hast not they bliss, Forever wilt thou love, and she be fair!'*"

I didn't feel relieved. She saw it in my eyes. And I didn't miss the mockery in her saying I knew the poets. Knowing meant nothing here.

"You'll want to give up looking for her someplace. Or thinking of where or when you loved her. Or thinking about all that being gone. I think what this young man fated to die young is saying is that it was all always on a different plane, just as life and death are. If we're doing anything, we poets are trying to get through the mask of things to the mystery underneath. We'd like to live there. It's the real place, pardon the use of real. But as I say, it's hard."

She paused.

"To do that."

CHAPTER FORTY-TWO

"OLD OVERHOLT"

"I am in a waiting room. I hear a clock ticking. I don't know if it will be a long time. I don't know if I have been there a long time or if I just arrived. I don't know what or who I'm waiting for because you see, she is dead. No matter if I wait for eons, she will still be dead. But I'm waiting for her nonetheless for you see I don't know where I end and she begins and I will never feel I begin when she ends."

"Deeply fucked up dream, clinically so deeply troubled I don't believe I can help you," Dr. Fraud told me after I stopped talking.

I had tracked him down to this seedy apartment in Brownsville, the one place in Brooklyn immune to gentrification. He looked seedy too. He had some wisps of hair coming out the top of his head and more growing on and out of his ears. Time and chance had not treated him well.

But appearances and reality aside, I had the feeling that he was the only one who could help me.

"I haven't given you the full picture."

"I wouldn't have listened to the partial picture if you hadn't given me a hundred up front. Besides, I'm not practicing. My license was taking away. Your mother arranged that."

"The Mater?"

"After you told her I said she should be euthanized for her own good."

"I don't remember that. I said a lot of crazy things growing up."

"You told your father I was touching your brother improperly."

"Damn! I said that?"

"You told both of them you had caught Patawalla and me having sex in your mother's boudoir."

I laughed nervously. I kind of remembered that. I mean the telling, not the seeing. I don't think Bettina would have respected me for that.

Maybe I'm not the hero of my own life. Bradley Stooper won't play me in the movie.

"So, that got you fired?"

"That and thrown out of the profession. I've been a WorldMarx Greeter for the past twenty years. It's not so bad. I've got a name badge. You face nothingness which is essential to authenticity in life."

He stared at me.

I squirmed in the torn overstuff chair I was in. It was the color of stains, all kinds.

"In fact, you should become a WorldMarx Greeter and brighten the lives of Everyday American shoppers. Or better yet deliver packages in gentrified neighborhoods and bask momentarily in the perfection of the winners. They are so grateful for the delivery. You'll be thanked for your service, like you won the Silver Star."

"You…You reach authenticity doing that?"

"Nothingness. You'd be delivering the existential authenticity of that."

I knew he'd gone crazy. Well, he was crazy way back then, but you know there's a limited number of resources and networking you have if death is your topic.

"I don't believe that French horseshit by the way. Nothing isn't liberating. It's nothing."

"I'll give you a thousand if you hear me out."

I didn't have a thousand, but I said it any way.

He was seated by the only window in the room, a bottle of Old Overholt on a lamp table next to him. It was almost empty. He had the kind of worn carpet slippers that Dickens wrote about. I wondered where he got them. It wasn't the first time I felt I was time travelling.

"You don't have a thousand dollars."

"I got enough for another bottle of Old Overholt."

"Six bottles," he said, gargling and spitting into a handkerchief he pulled from somewhere.

"Tomorrow? This time?"

"I gotta greet. I don't want to disappoint the consumers. Make it around seven. You can buy me a WorldMarx dinner. Plastic meat in a Styrofoam dish wrapped in plastic."

A month later and several cases of Old Overholt:

"Your mind is deeply troubled. So deeply troubled I don't think I can help you."

"That's what you told me sixty-four bottles ago."

"What are you gonna do? Run to your mother and father and have me fired and thrown out of the greet profession?"

He laughed. A kind of laugh that would have made a small child scream and run kind of laugh.

"Can you tell me how my mind is deeply troubled?"

"I have notes," he said, showing me the composition book, he wrote in while we talked over the last month.

"Good."

"You were born with a mind permanently encased within itself, potted like a plant whose roots twist back into itself. Your thinking tends to go up its own ass, assuming mind has an ass."

"You told me a long time ago I was a sociopathic polysnot. Nothing's changed?"

"Maybe you've had a moral epiphany. You may have had that. That would be a change."

"What exactly is that? A moral epiphany?"

"That's when an arrogant, narcissistic prick realizes some person in the world is more precious to him than himself and then that person dies and the reformed prick realizes he had not shown that person while she was alive that she was more precious to him than anything in the world, including himself."

He paused.

"It's all in my notes."

"Thing is I'm not sure she died. Or, that I was the guy who spent a whole lifetime with her. I've been looking for her nonetheless."

"That's what you say. You see her in almost every woman you meet. It all comes down to *cherchez les femmes*."

"You don't think I'm honestly looking for her?"

"You weren't an honest kid. You were rotten. Now you're still that but confused. Up to this point, you are treatable. I don't mean pharmacology. That's not treatment. That's erasure, replacement, coverup. I am a psychiatrist of mind, not a drug merchant. Although presently I am a WallMarx greeter. Welcome. How are you today? Good. Okay. Fuck along."

"I'm treatable? So, how do you treat me?"

"We find the launch point. The genesis. Consider. You first met Regina when you both were teenagers?"

I nodded.

"You must have met her or seen her back then. And you believe you've been married to her for almost fifty years, lived with her all over the country, had children with her and, in short, enjoyed so many years with the most precious person in your life."

"I'm solid with that. Her name is Bettina. Not Regina."

"Not very solid at all. Because you also believe you didn't have that lifetime with her, and you only think you did to propel you on a search to find her. And this time, you will be fully aware that you need to cherish every moment you have with her. In short, you are looking for a second chance. You are looking for a do over. She asked you to be better and you failed. Now, you want to be better but she's not here so you can't dance around and tell her you did it."

"And that's not treatable? I mean, what if I find her? I mean that's possible, isn't it?"

"Within your crazed mind it is. Consider. How old are you?"

"Thirty-two."

"Don't you think you'd have to be a lot older if you had that long life with her you think you had?"

"I remember a lot of very specific stuff about those years. They may not have been fifty. I mean for me. I think I did some time with her in another lifetime. And when I reincarnated into me now, I got a memory of those years. Patawalla called it a glitch in the transmigration processing."

"Patawalla? His head was half-way in a sand bucket. Eyes and ears covered. Besides, didn't he wear your mother's under garments? Or was that another false story you told?"

"Maybe so, maybe so, but I'm clearly sharing a previous existence."

"What you clearly are is tortured by the belief that you had many, many years with someone and you can't remember them. You don't feel you lived them with her in a way that showed how precious she was to you. Your mind is haunted by that failure."

"Yeah, I know. Sometimes . . ."

"But as none of that life together actually is real and true because you are a young man not an old man, then you are tortured by delusions, not reality. My telling you this is not a cure. My telling you this does not mean you will leave here and stop living in mental figments and rejoin reality, which you were never part of in the first place. No. The only reality you know is delusional."

"That's not true, Doc. Sometimes I think, yeah, I didn't have all those years with Bettina and then she died. I'm too young for all that like you say. And if we didn't have all that time together maybe she didn't get sick and die. Maybe she's alive someplace. She'd be about 28 or so now. That's facing reality, isn't it?"

"Is that what you've been doing? If that's the case, why come to see me? I'm a WallMarx Greeter."

I got up and went over to the lamp table and poured myself some of the whiskey I had been supplying the old guy with.

"Yeah, I haven't been doing that."

"No, you haven't. You've been looking for her in the faces of other women. And you feel as if you had the most precious love of your life and didn't realize it."

"I feel that way all the time. All the time."

"Good. You were an obnoxious little prick. I like to see just rewards. As a WallMarx Greeter."

I saw a sly smile on his face as if my burning pleased him. It was his revenge. I had taken his professional life from him. If that was the case, then everything he had been telling me over the last month or so might have been just made up, fabricated by him to give me the maximum pain. If that was so, it would just be another marker on the crazy path I was already on.

That was our final session. Before I left, he recommended I give myself fully to the attention economy.

"I've never heard of it. Is it U.S.?"

"Here, there and everywhere. What you do is give yourself fully to some bullshit and then you get distracted, and distraction is what you want. The whole global economy is designed to help you with this."

"It is?"

"Working 24/7 to get your attention, push the product, then distract you to another sales frontier."

"And this is going to help me how?"

"You know how I got paid for pulling the nuts out of patient's heads?"

"You distracted them, and they weren't nuts anymore?"

"They were nuts differently, let's say. Of course, the drugs helped. You combine drugs with distracted focus, and they start off the day like they were brand new. Always smiling."

"I don't think I want that," I said, wondering if I wanted that.

"Everything you told me about, what's her name?"

"Bettina."

"That would be just a distraction among distractions that never stop distracting you. Think about that. I think it's what a prick like you needs. An eternity of distraction."

I shook my head.

"No, I'm totally possessed by her. Heart, mind, and soul. I could never be distracted."

He laughed.

"You're a bag of distractions in that head of yours. She's alive, no, she's dead. You lived with her, no, you didn't. She's real, no she's not. You can find her, no you can't. But don't take it personal, prick. You're a pure product of the attention economy."

Those were the last words I had with Dr. Fraud. I heard he died soon after but I'm not sure. I mean whether I heard it or whether he died or whether both were true.

Anyway, none of it helped.

CHAPTER FORTY-THREE

SHARDS

Believe it or not, I now sought the advice of my brother's girlfriend Eve Solly.

It was strange. Eve Solly had once told me that narcissists like me had to be avoided like used toilet tissue.

"You know," she said, pointing her steak knife at me in a very fine artisanal restaurant in Nolita. "Jerks like you don't let other people get in the way of seeing yourself in the mirror. I think your girlfriend played it smart and just got out of the way of such self-love and admiration. It's vomit making. What are you doing with that menu, Dirk? You look like you're in shock."

"What is it mean when they say a very grammable crispy rice cake lasagna?" Dirk asked her, looking up from the menu.

She told him to keep looking at it, that truth would be revealed.

"You know narcissists who have a twin are the very worse," Eve said, turning back to me. "They're like a double dose of narcissism right in the face."

"Order the spaghetti casserole," I told Dirk so as to put him out of his menu misery.

"Does that come with noodles?"

"If that's on the menu, I'm out of here," Eve snapped. "Grammable means a person, place, event, or contextual situation that is worthy of being posted on *Instagram*."

That was another of a thousand things I didn't like about Eve Solly. She always had to prove she knew more than I did, there of course being no noodles in a spaghetti casserole or, to put too fine a point on it, no such thing as a spaghetti casserole, though a favorite dish served throughout the Midwest and in the border states. But why demand authenticity at this tragic point in my life? Everything was faux except the love I had for Bettina. Or have. That thought led me to say:

"I've changed. I don't look for me. I look for her. I've become a better person."

"He means Bettina," Dirk said, head still in the menu.

"I'm Emerson and I'll be your server this evening.

I looked up.

Emerson was tall, had a hushed voice and a very prominent Adam's apple with a bird tattoo perched on it. I thought the ink might have penetrated his vocal cords.

"I'll have the steak," Eve told Emerson. "Very rare."

"Tofu or lentil or leaf?"

"Hereford. I don't need to know its name."

"You mean ...beef?"

He said it like the word was an expletive.

Eve gave him a scowling review, head to toe.

"Very rare. I need to see it bleeding in the dish."

"I'll see if we have that," he said, as instructed.

"Better yet. See if you can give it to me still alive."

The bird went up and down on his neck.

"We have a bolster for that chair," he said to Eve, clearing his throat.

"Do you see a baby at this table?"

"I'm not ready to order," I said, coming to the kid's aid before Eve took out her .25 ACP and shot him.

"I'll have what he has," Dirk said.

"This twin," Eve said, pointing to me, "thinks this twin over here is just himself in another body and this twin over here goes along with it because he's an idiot. Bring him a steak, very, very rare. Repeat that."

"Two steaks very, very rare."

"Don't be nervous. That's good. What's the matter?"

"Is a steak beef because we don't have beef. Or anything dead. This is a Carcass-Free Fine Dining Bistro."

"Okay. Can I have a steak burger and fries?" Dirk asked Eberhart.

"I'll have the house specialty," I said.

"For four?"

I nodded.

"Double Zubrowka for me," Eve ordered. "I want the bottle froze.

Not the glass."

"Also," Dirk said.

"Also," I said. "Double down on that for me. I think I'm going to need it. That's four shots for me and four shots total for them."

"I'll be right back," the kid said, making his escape.

"By the way, bro, the love of your life just called you an idiot."

"She calls you a monster," Dirk responded.

"So, you meet this little tramp, and she tells you that I'm a monster and that's it? Maybe you are an idiot."

"I'll stab you if you say little again," Eve said, pointing her butter knife at me.

"Maybe she didn't say monster," Dirk said, coming to my rescue. "She said you have a lot on her plate."

"Her plate?"

"Speaking of plates," Eve interrupted. "What is the house specialty?"

"I don't know, and I don't care. But I have to tell you every time I'm in a restaurant, it all goes bad. Every time. I'm like Sissypus rolling a rock up and it ends at the bottom. I destroyed my chances with Bettina in a restaurant."

"Who?"

"Sissypus."

"No, I mean the other one."

I went blank and then pulled out of it.

"Look, Dirk, she's right. I have so much on my plate that I can't see if any of it is real or not."

"Tom Hayfield said that we are free to the extent that we know what you're about."

Dirk told me that very seriously.

"Go back and study the menu," Eve told him. "Look, Doris, you're disassociating from reality."

The drinks came and before the bar server was a step away from the table, Eve ordered another round.

"I think I did that a long time ago but I'm not sure. Disassociate."

"What's the last thing you remember that's clear?" Dirk asked me.

"Bettina died and I went into a tailspin."

"Who's Bettina again?" Eve asked, full of sarcasm as usual.

"You met her. Bettina Parisi. I called her Bettina."

"Clever calling her by her first name."

"Other people called her different names."

"When she die? She was young."

"I don't know," I said, rubbing my forehead. "I'm not sure she died."

Eve kept her beams focused on me for an uncomfortably long time.

"Okay. Sure. The clearest thing you remember is that a young woman called differently by different people died but you're unclear about whether whatever her name was did die. Okay. So, how is that clear?"

"I guess it isn't," I admitted, as a new server wheeled a cart toward us.

"Emerson is off shift. I'm your new server. River."

"What's that?" Eve asked as a huge platter was hoisted to the middle of the table and the cover removed displaying a profusion of colors, shapes, and sizes.

"It's the House Specialty Leaf and Fungi Presentation. It has an installation quality."

"Is there a T-bone steak in there?" she asked.

River did a half smile. River looked like River could play football. River recited a slew of identifiers, none of which identified a steak, or anything Eve could identify.

"Another vodka. You got bread sticks?"

"We have gluten free artichoke sticks."

"Okay. Hold those sticks or compost them. Whichever. And bring me two more vodka doubles."

I could see River found Eve very amusing.

"Your voice sounds very familiar," he said.

"It's a radio voice."

"Wait! Evangeline Sullivan!"

He looked at my brother.

"And this is Dick! They are my favorite!"

"That's right," Eve told him. "Sullivan and Dick. Can you do me a big favor, Flood? I'm gonna get really drunk if I don't eat something. Got any chips back there?"

He winked.

"At the bar. I'll get them."

"And bury this special thing back under the tree you found it," she told him.

She looked at me. I was crying.

"I'd give up every day of whatever life I have left just to be with her just one more time."

"I don't think the dead are on loan," Eve said. "And stop crying. I get enough of that from your brother."

"You do?" I said, looking at Dirk, who nodded.

"Every time one of his hand puppets is injured."

"Injured?"

"He thinks I get up in the middle of the night and cut holes in them. Getting back to you. I say if she's dead, you'll get over it because you don't seem sure you and she were a thing. Two, only soul mates and octopods mourn the death of a loved one. You're not an octopod and your soul is barely breathing. And three, if she's dead, she doesn't know it and you don't seem to know it either. Okay, I'm ready to get out of here. Not enough gluten in this place. And the only blood will be the one I spill."

We went to McSorley's and drank double mugs of old but good. We had the cheese sandwiches.

Eve heard me out without interruption.

"Did anybody ever call up on the show sounding crazier than me?" I asked at a point when we were all very mellow and I had warmed to this small, charming lady's style.

I even began to see that I had found the person Bettina had become. Yes, you can get that loaded.

"All the questions I should have asked. And didn't ask. That haunts me. All the times I should have just wrapped my arms around her and told her that I loved her beyond what I could ever say. All the times I could have made her life easier, been the help she needed, been at her knees begging her to forgive me for being blind, for being stupid in not seeing what was going on with her, for not ever thinking she was most precious in my life and not then making what was precious to her precious to me."

I stopped. I was crying. Dirk had put a hand on my shoulder. It was heavy.

"Is that it?" Eve said. "Hold the rest. Suspense full. Truly. I can't wait to see how it turns out. I'm going out for a smoke."

"Okay," she said, coming back ten minutes later to our table. "Continue. You killed her, right?"

"Where was I?"

"You were regretting things you did and didn't do in a life you may or may not have with a woman who may or may not still be alive who may or may not have known you but if she did, I'm sure she didn't like you and regretted ever having known you."

I thought about all that.

"That a lot," I said.

"Yeah. A lot of loss. Absence is the only presence in your life now. You were made for it. Just you, yourself, and you. Nothing I like better than a truly unlikeable guy filling me with absence and loss. It's riveting."

She was harsh. There was no Bettina in her.

"I'm tortured."

"Maybe. My money would be on just plain old crazy. Did you ever think…Wait. What am I saying? You're thinking yourself into a strait jacket. You've weaponized your own mind against you. Bravo. Anyway. As Dorus Daylight sang what will be won't be if you want it to be. But if you were a call in and you went on and on like you just did?"

"What would your advice be?"

"If you called up on my show? I would have cut you off before the Begats. My advice? You're not gonna find this dream lady in the present or in the future. You haven't found her in the present, have you? Travelling all over. What did you find? Nada. Then chances are what doesn't exist in the present is not gonna be around in the future. Pick a time in the past and go back to that. Pick some time when there's no doubt she's there and you're there. And live in that."

"I'll have to look at photographs."

"Do you have any?"

"No."

She looked at Dirk.

"Your brother could help."

"I could? Yeah. I could. How?"

"When was the last time you saw nutcase here with this Bathsheba?"

"Ba who?"

"Bettina," I corrected.

"Any of those names," Eve shot back at us. "You know, one is too much and two of you is too much squared. So, when?"

Dirk studied me, a kind of scowl on his face, which he got when he had to reflect.

"Nothing passes through the palace of your mind?" Eve said to him.

I don't know how Dirk put up with her nonstop sarcasm. But he did. He was hopelessly devoted to her. He was a strange brother. It was hard to understand that kind of devotion to someone who you could see was plainly nasty. I mean she was right in front of him, and she was as far from the flawless, Biblical Eve as a woman could get.

"Wait. I've got it."

Dirk had his eyes closed and now he opened them.

He looked at me and his face flushed.

"Okay, so what, when, where, who?"

He looked at Eve.

"It faded away."

"Bullshit," I told him. "You remembered something that embarrassed you."

That got Eve interested.

"You saw them in flagrante delicto?" she asked him, winking.

"No, not that," he replied nervously.

"No, not what?"

"Whatever you said."

"I bet it was at the Beach House," I conjectured, trying to save the poor fool from more Eve attack.

"Yes, it was!" he said, eyes lighting up. "Not in there exactly."

"If they weren't inside," Eve said, "then they're outside it. Where?"

"Up the beach."

I remembered. Our private alcove.

"Yeah, I remember. She was there."

"Good. Finally. Okay. Stay there. Don't go looking for anywhere else. Just go back to that spot in your mind and stay there."

"That's it?"

"Sure. Why not? You know she was there. She wasn't dead. She was real not just in your head. Just don't go wandering. The kind of mind you have will spin you like a flywheel. Last stop. The looney bin."

"It works," Dirk told me, compassionately. "I focus on my pillow when my mind starts to jump all over the place. When I'm sleeping."

"You mean dreams?"

"Maybe," he said. "But I'm not awake but things are still going on in my head. Sometimes I can fly, low off the ground. Sometimes I'm swimming up the Hudson or climbing a rock face wall."

I had been away from my brother for some time, all the time I was in Europe and before that I tried to stay away from him as a health measure. Dirk could fuck up the sanest minds on the planet in one sitting. Would he go looking for Eve if he lost her? Probably.

I looked at Eve. She seemed impervious to all of Dirk's life-threatening dreams, as if she had built up antibodies.

I understood that. When lovers don't build up antibodies to

immunize themselves from each other, their love falls apart. Or one dies or disappears. Separation. I got that dark view out of my head.

"Sometimes I'm fighting an alligator in a swamp."

Despite long experience with Dirk's way of thinking, I pursued the thinking.

"So, how does your pillow come into this?"

"I just keep saying `pillow' every time I think of something not pillow."

I looked at Eve. She shrugged.

"I'm going out for some relief. I've heard it. I'd rather smoke my lungs into Stage One than listen to it again."

She got up and left us.

"Not pillow? Exactly what is that? The whole world exclusive of your pillow?"

"Let's say I wonder whether Eve is screwing our sound engineer."

"You wonder that?"

"Well, not really because I say `pillow' and I stop wondering."

"Too bad Othello didn't know about that particular pillow."

"Yeah, it's easy enough to learn."

"Sounds like it. So, if I start wondering whether Bettina and I had a life together which maybe I didn't have but maybe I did but I kind of missed it. All of which makes my life miserable now. I should just say pillow?"

Dirk thought it over.

"You'd have to be in bed. And you'd have to have your head on a pillow."

"Of course," I said. "I'd have to be in bed, and I'd need a pillow."

"That's what works for me."

"Tell me, bro, what if you start flipping out when you're not in bed and there's no pillow around? Saying pillow wouldn't help much then, would it?"

"I don't think so. That's never happened."

"You don't feel anxious, fearful and like that. Like you're losing it in the daytime?"

He laughed as if what I had just said was the most ridiculous thing in the world. Very many times I wondered if I could only see and hear my brother as an idiot and that in reality, he was always just being kind to me, that from day one out of the womb, he looked at me and felt he had to protect me.

Before I could get to the bottom here or find out what he was laughing about Eve came back into the bar.

"What's my jocular co-host laughing about?"

I filled her in on what Dirk and I had been talking about.

"Sure. Dirk here is no match for reality day or night. He doesn't need to say pillow when I'm around. He just looks at me."

Upon hearing her say that, Dirk got a lovey dove smile on his face and reached out for her. She smacked him on the side of the head, and he sat back.

This was a brand of human companionship that nobody had ever thought, read, or experienced until now.

"So, at night, he says pillow, and, in the daytime, you smack him in the head?"

"Not always. Sometimes, I just lightly squeeze his balls. You know you use the coordinating conjunction *so* a lot. Narcissists do that. They don't hear or really answer the other person. They just say 'so' whatever you said doesn't matter and I don't give a fuck about it but now listen to me. When a caller does that, I know they'd didn't call to hear me talk but just to get their voice on the radio. It's all about them."

"And you cut them off?"

"Their balls? Oh, on the air? Yeah. We cut them off. They can talk to their hand or the bathroom mirror or a partner they're abusing."

That thing about narcissists got me thinking.

"Can a narcissist die?" I asked her. "I mean if they see their own face everywhere, do they see it dead?"

"That would destroy the self-love image they're into, wouldn't it?" Eve said to me very slowly as if I were in the third grade.

"So. I mean, therefore, narcissists don't worry about dying?"

"You die. They don't. No worries as they say."

"But what if they love someone so deeply that they fear they might die? I mean what if they would give their own life so that the person they love would live?"

"I would do that for Eve," my brother said.

"I'll remember to ask," Eve snapped. "Look, for the narcissist to love deeply they'd have to actually see the other person and not just themselves. Doing that would be like the zebra changing his stripes."

"So, they can't love? Somebody not themselves?"

"They wouldn't be alone. Most of us can't love anybody or won't ever love anybody or if they run into someone who loves them, they are a big pain in the ass and they regret running into them."

She looked at Dirk who just said 'pillow.'

"The price of love is loss and for the narcissist loss of themselves is too big a price."

I thought about that.

"Love is an illusion too?" I asked her.

She laughed. I regretted asking.

"My father says everything is illusion."

"He's a Buddhist scientist?"

"Mathematics is his huckleberry. He won The Fields Medal."

"Probably an illusion," she said, smiling, waiting for me to light her cigarette.

"You can't smoke in here."

"Let's say everything is illusion. All you have is illusion. Nothing is real. So, what good does it do to say everything is illusion? It's all we've got, the real being absent. You can't find it. What's the sense of looking for it? Illusions will do fine."

She was fucking with me as always. I saw it in the gleam in her eyes. They sparkled with mischief, like Rumpleskinfull.

"She's fucking with you, bro," Dirk mumbled, not opening his eyes. "The Great Tormentor."

"Are you saying I shouldn't have to worry about whether Bettina was ever real to me or not? I should just accept the fact that I think she was?"

"Yeah, okay with me, but the thing is you can't accept what the deeply deluded call a fact."

"And that's me? The deeply deluded?"

"She's a soul tormentor," my brother whispered in his sleep.

"Sure. You delude yourself into thinking some goddess, some princess Snow Bright and White loved you, married you, bore your kids and lived with you into the sunset."

"Bettina," I said, nodding.

"And I ask why the fuck would that loveliness wind up with you? Delusion. And you know what drags ass after delusion? A whole world of illusion."

"She's twisting my balls in the wind," Dirk moaned, still sleeping.

We both looked at him.

"Yeah, you're right. That's a bit of the real. I stand corrected."

"I've got delusions and illusions but what the fuck does it matter. You said that's all we could ever have."

"Philosophically the case. Sure. Therefore, merely academic. Not injurious. We share the same illusions. Consensual validation. Society. We have that. You? Pathological case. Your illusions follow through on your delusion. You need to think you had this great love, but it can't be confirmed. You fear you can't find her and of course you can't so you don't. You keep searching to oblige the delusion. You search inside your illusions."

I had to laugh.

"Is that it?"

"You mean something more than you circling and going up the ass of your own mind? Sure. Within the illusions there's the possibility that you did have this love and you wore it out. Your narcissism sucked the life out of her. Thus, guilt. The guilty are always in search of forgiveness. You can confess to her when you find her. Of course, at the same time, you're haunted by the illusion that you never had her, and she can never be found despite your delusion that you were both into a deep romance early on."

"Oh, torment me and make me live!" my brother moaned so loudly that everyone but the regulars in the place looked over at our table.

"Why the hell does he put up with you?"

"Well, I'd say, brother of his, that I make him feel that he's the yolk in his life and in mine."

"What?"

"Not just the runny white."

After that, though there never turned out to be a real after, the three of us relapsed into an alcohol heavy thought stupor.

I mean me. Dirk remained asleep, magically, and Eve was just quiet. Finally, she spoke.

"I don't know shite about illusions. Forget what I said. But you like to say you got all the brains and sleeping beauty here got the husks."

"The twin who got the yolk and he got the runny white."

"Yeah, he loves you. And I figure if that's true you're worth something. I listen to a lot of fucked up stuff on the show. I've got a background dealing with hurt. I do think your brains are capsizing your mind. It's like a stinger stinging the guy who owns it."

Dirk was snoring softly now. He'd build up tempo, like that bassoon piece by Villa-Lobos.

"You think you had a life with a woman you loved but one, you can't be sure of any of that, and two, you think you had all that but you kind of missed it, like your mind wandered off just at the point of orgasm. And you did that for lots of years, enough years for her to get old, sick and die."

She elbowed Dirk just as the snore was in crescendo.

"Of course, you're about thirty years old. That's what I call on my show the *estocada*, the killing stroke that deflates the bag of bullshit a caller is throwing at me. There was a girl, and Dirk says there was, and I remember her too. She was too good for you was what I thought. Sparkling eyes, beautiful smile. So, she's real. Probably mid-twenties now. Not old. Probably not dead."

"I didn't find her."

"Did you search on social media? She's probably on *Facebotch*."

"She would?"

"Look, if she's not there, then you go back to point A."

"Point A?"

"Yeah, she got married and her name changed."

I hadn't thought of that.

"I never felt she got married."

"Except those hundred years she was married to you. You know, what fascinates me about a best and brightest guy like you is that your mind is turning you inside out, open revolt and storming the Bastille. And at the same time, it's barely working. You got the kind of mind that preempts lived experience. You're around when things happen, and you see what's happening but at the same time you're not around at all and you don't see shit."

"It feels like that now."

"Then one day you wake up and you're living in a whole bunch of fantastical fears, and you just know you got to recuperate, redeem, relive. None of that is possible. Or put it another way. Everything is possible. Like in a work of fiction. You could spin in a billion directions while you're looking for a place to land."

"And do I? I mean if I got back to that one place I know was real?"

"The spot on the beach? Girl in a bikini?"

"Two piece."

"That's good. That specificity. Shard of reality I tell my callers. That's what we're all looking for. In fact, most horny guys that call up, attracted by the kind of throaty sexy voice I've got, have girls on beaches in bikinis as part of their shards. You're part of the norm right there. Of course, it could be a fixation. Psychotics have them."

She gave me a light slap in the face and at the same time elbowed Dirk.

"Wake up and let's get out of here."

When I was getting into a cab, Eve invited me on their radio show, *Shut Up!*

"Give the first-time listeners a real treat," she told me, winking. "You're not any place other people haven't been. Although I admit you'd be lesson. I mean they'd all feel they weren't as nuts as they thought they were."

I should go on that show I thought. Make all the nuts living in illusions feel better.

I didn't do that. I went back to The Beach House, where she was. Bathsheba.

CHAPTER FORTY-FOUR

STAR PARTICLES

Did you ever think that everything precious in your life will blow away and turn to dust literally and in the minds of all those who, say, are born the day you die?

A lot of it will be repeated in different ways by others in the future or maybe not at all. But all your personal devotions, all your deep relationships will just vanish. You and she will be as if you never were.

"That's one way of looking at it. Then again, you said maybe you and she really never were you and she."

"What?"

I looked up from my drink. I hadn't realized I was speaking out loud.

To Sal, the bartender at *The New Pompey*. The fount of wisdom at the fount of booze.

"Like it says in the Bible. There's a reason to sew and a reason to bring it to *Good Will*. You gotta make room."

I stared at this fount. Dirk went to this guy for life coaching.

"For what?"

"What?"

"Room for what?"

"Ah, that's the question we're all asking. We're all heading for the exit."

"Sal, may I ask you a question? Why do I and the woman I've loved all my life. . ."

"Bettina?"

My eyes opened for the second time in my life. It was like Heaven walked on earth the first time I saw her.

"You know her?"

"She used to come in. Her and her girlfriends. I made them Woke Cocktails. Then I heard you mention her couple three hundred times."

"A couple three hundred times? Do I come in here a lot?"

"We got your slippers under the bar."

"Those are my brother's. You have us confused."

"It's a confusing world, especially since Cardoza got elected."

I let that pass. I must have missed that election. I couldn't get beyond thinking that she and I and our love for each other would be pushed aside and disappear. It made no sense. Who Cardoza was would have to wait.

"Why would she have to make room for anyone? Why would our love just be shoveled into the ground or turned to ashes in an urn after we had a bond that nothing could break?"

Sal shrugged.

"Life's a one-if, like they say. But you know what I think? People become MIA way before they're dead. They just fade from the scene. They lose the situations that made them."

"You mean context? That changes and without that . . ."

"My nephew can't sign his own name. It's cursory and they don't learn that no more.

"What?"

"Buggy whips. Global Maritime Distress and Safety System. Phone booths. Totally forgotten. Splats. Dead wrecking. Totally forgotten."

"I don't forget Bettina. I can't. She's always with me."

"Sure, you got a place for her in your heart. On the house. To her memory."

He had poured a shot for himself and now knocked it back.

I looked at mine and picked it up.

"She's not dead," I said. "What's dead wrecking?"

"That's when you think somebody's dead but they ain't. You know why?"

"Because the soul endures, age is an illusion and there is no death?"

"Naw. You feel her here."

He thumped his breast with his fist.

I drank the shot.

"I miss her body. Her physical presence."

"Sure, you do. Wherever she is, she feels you. That's part of the package."

"The package?"

"Nobody parts with anybody at death."

I nodded. So wise, and I wasn't paying by the hour. I could sit at this bar all day and hear this gratis.

"No, they don't."

"They can't take themselves out of you. They can only take off with themselves. It's physics. Fourth law of thermal underwear. At least that's what Padre Balls says. I think it was before he was defrocked. I don't know what he says now. Oh, yeah, the other night, he and Piccolino got into a psychotic and Balls says let the dead bury the dead."

"What did Micalino say?"

"Yeah, they do if they leave money for funeral expenses in their will. Otherwise, somebody living has to fork up."

I fell into a thought review.

"You don't think he meant that, right?" Sal asked. "Let the dead bury the dead? Let's say you're dead and you're in the Good Place. Why the hell would you have a job burying the dead? Of course, if you were in the Bad Place, the Devil might give you a job like that. Am I right here?"

I pointed to my empty shot glass. True, you needed to fortify to stand at this bar and listen. If you listen to the voice of The People, you can go nuts. If you listen to yourself, it's worse. Two fucked up situations, as Sal would say.

"So, what do you think about that?" Sal pushed after a several minutes of silence. "Sounds to me like Balls lost his faith in the spiritual world. I'm quoting Gee on that."

"Gee? Jesus?"

"Giordano. He owns the place."

"Some say that," I told him, half smiling. "Look, I think it's hopeful if the dead bury the dead. I think it means there's another world filled with people who have died, and they welcome those who have just died. They assume all responsibilities for a warm transportation to another realm. Don't you like to think the dead care for each other in the way the living never did?"

Sal's mouth was open. He was kind of young for that slack jaw response to what pinged his brain.

"They bury them in the other realm?"

"They are all buried from our sight."

"But the old dead take care of the new ones, right?"

"I think there's no old or new dead. The dead are all equal. There's no seniority. No elitism among the dead."

Sal liked that thought. He nodded, given it his approval.

"That's the one good thing about being dead," he told me. "They're all equally dead. But where do you think they are?"

"If I could see it, I'd tell you. But I'm alive and I'm looking for her, not to bury her, and I'm alive and so is she."

"Gotcha. You want me to call you a Huey?"

I wanted to go back in time in my mind to Bettina at her secret spot on the beach, but I wasn't ready for it. I went to see The Pater in The Lab.

I circle.

If you think life narratives are linear, I remind you of these words "Dust thou are and to dust you will circle back."

Of course, Biblically speaking, Genesis is a beginning: "In the beginning was the Word and the Word was with God." Then we get a bible of words, old and new. You could say every word in there started a new religion with a new reading of words or at the very least a new weekend tent revival.

Adam sat on a rock and attached words to whatever passed in front of him but then what happed after The Fall, words didn't carry things with them, and things didn't have words attached to them. God was a Word that floated free of any certain connection. It was the first totally floating free signifier.

But it is convenient to have a beginning so you can calculate when you're at the middle but once you're in the middle, the end looms. If you're smart, you'll stay in the middle. The end -- Death --is a fearsome sight. You want to circle back to a place where Death doesn't loom. *Revelations* helps you with that. Linearity continues beyond Death in a totally different place with a totally different you.

As I don't want to be any place she never was and as I don't want her different, I orbit, returning repeatedly to the same places hearing the same words, saying, and writing the same words.

If she's dead, showing me an Afterlife doesn't help. My dreams show me that time and space are parts of dreams, that excusing Death by offering a new beginning, maybe a new linearity in an Afterlife, is a carnival barker's trick. I mean we kick the pins out from under a beginning and an end if now we hold to a false flag beginning and a deathless Death.

The only beginning and end I will know is how Bettina and I

began, and the only ending will be when we end. What begins and ends elsewhere I can't get into, even for the sake of giving you a map of where we are right now. In short, I can't help you if you're mystified. Mystery is Death's URL.

The Lab was now not what it was before.

It was now my father's living quarters. He hadn't had Post-Docs in a long time. His grant proposals had not won. He was living on a small settlement, some patent royalties, and Social Security.

"You're not Dirk," was the first thing he said to me. "It's Dirk who comes by."

"I've been out of the country, Da," I told him. "No new Post-Docs?"

He looked around, surprised.

"Not here," he said. "They're probably at lunch. You know I met the diversity requirement years ago. You know what I got out of that?"

I said I didn't know.

"I got fucking hash tag me towed. I got more microaggression charges against me than you've got air in your head. You know what a micro-influencer is?"

I said I didn't know.

"That's a newborn with 800,000 followers who tells me The Mathematics is just my fucking opinion. Can you believe that?"

I said I couldn't.

'I didn't know any of that. I'm sorry you had to go through so much of the New Millenium.. You look like you haven't been out in a while. That's a kind of requirement too."

He gave me an annoyed look and waved me away, although I was still standing in the doorway.

"It's too late for that now. You know when I should have gone outside?"

I took a wild guess.

"The formative years Dirk and I were growing up?"

If he heard what I said, he didn't respond to it.

"I got some patents out of it," he said, waving one arm back and forth as if he were swiping at invisible flies. Or patents.

"Not as profitable as Page Rank, right?" I said, wondering why I was needling the old wreck. It seemed that he didn't need any help in tearing into himself.

"I should have concentrated on Mars," he told me, going over to a rocking chair and staggering down into it. He was a relatively small man. I mean relative to Dirk and me. We got our size from the Mater. He had the brains, and she had the height. From a worldly view, she had married two billionaires while he was here sitting in that old rocker ranting against everything his Mathematics couldn't equate.

"Drink?" I said, pulling out a flask I had filled with Midleton Irish

"No," he said, waving me over. "There's no drinking allowed in The Lab."

I walked over to him and held the flask out and he pulled it out of my hand.

He took a long swig.

"My funding dried up," he said, angrily, placing the flask between his legs. "My research went out of fashion."

You know, I never knew what kind of research he and his Post-Docs did. I swear to God. I don't know if it was chemistry, biology, a mix of the two, physics, botany, mycology. I was never much interested. Dirk wasn't either, or if he was, he showed no signs of it. For all I knew the Pater might have been working on a fusion bomb.

"What was your last pitch?" I asked.

"Why would you care?" he said, giving me a mean look. "How did you get in here anyway?"

"I delivered the whiskey."

He looked down at the flask.

"Okay. Alright."

He helped himself to another long pull.

I wanted to mellow him out. I didn't want him sloshed.

"You were working on subatomic particles, weren't you?"

"Where's that?" he shouted.

"In flora," I said but he got angrier. "Didn't I say fauna? Fungi?

"Pathogens!" he screamed. "Bloody, goddamn pathogens! What I did was isolate a pathogen destroying the planet."

"Wow! I bet that got you some big investors."

"You are the idiot one, aren't you?" he said, squinting at me.

"I jumped levels. I was destined to do elite level in the meritocracy. Being qua being."

"What the hell does that mean?" he shouted. "Humans have no essential nature. Or it's shit. You're a good example. You and your brother. The lethal pathogen in this world is homo sapien sapien. They didn't like that. They didn't want to hear that. Science reveals the truth, and they don't like it. Give me an octopod any day."

He started to laugh the way I guess no one should laugh.

"You had a cure proposed?" I asked, meekly.

"Yes, I did. Annihilate humans! End the abominable Anthropocene!"

"No vaccine? Just annihilation?"

"And hope that a new species, a mutation will arise."

I was leaning on one of the old, dusty lab tables. Rusty Bunsen burners and glass tubing scattered.

"I'm surprised they didn't commit you."

"They tried to. My sons came forward in court and spoke on my behalf."

"They did, eh? That was nice of them."

"Yes, it was. The judge understood when I said that once we were all dead, the whole human race, then the good things could start to happen again. We need to re-boot."

That kind of interested me. I was at the point of really wondering why I came to see The Pater. He was making me realize that I was in the state of mind I was in for genetic reasons. But what he said about death piqued my curiosity.

"There's good things in death?"

"What? Of course, there is. Did you spend any time learning anything in your life."?

"Mr. Patawalla taught us about how dirt was piled on a sea turtle's back and then he walked away with it and that was the world."

Da thought about that.

"Interesting. Was he the one who wore your mother's undies?"

I nodded.

"Well, he was dead wrong. The real story is this. Great burning bright stars filled with amazing luminosity, burn down, blow apart and send their subatomic particles all over the universe. When we are born, we are born with the particles of dead stars and when we die, they return to the universe and gather to make new stars."

"What about someone who, say, just died, or maybe didn't die?"

"What about them?"

He was back to the snarl.

"Well, are they somewhere becoming stars too or are they still here? And are they conscious of where they are? Or what they are?"

"Doing what?"

The question threw me.

"I don't know. Watching us."

"Why would dead people be watching us?"

"Well, the star part of them. Give us comfort. Let us know that they're not really gone."

He sighed deeply.

"You are the idiot one, aren't you?"

"Well, I'm just guessing regarding the process."

He took another long swig at the flask and then closed his eyes.

"I was hoping you'd tell me what The Mathematics made of death," I said, nervously.

He opened his eyes.

"You know that Leibnitz does not allow death in the sense that a substance is destroyed. There's a pre-existing harmony that would be disturbed or destroyed if substances were eliminated."

"Substances? Like bodies?"

"You know it's stupid to fear death, don't you? What did Epicurus say? `Death, the most awful of evils, is nothing to us, seeing that, when we are, death is not come, and when death is come, we are not.'"

"I don't have fears. I have regrets. But I wouldn't have that if I could apologize and explain. I mean I could make amendments. Or I could live with her in such a way that I'd have no regrets. I also have a lot of memories, but I don't know which ones to trust."

"She's dead I'm thinking. And you don't care where she went or what happened to her but you want her to be here alive so she can hear you groan and moan for her to forgive you for being a selfish bastard? Do you see any of that as precisely what a selfish bastard would want?"

"Da, do you think that if there was nothing but ashes ahead for us that there would be someone so fine, so sweet so full of light as Bettina here with us? At all. Why would anything destined to be ash ever achieve such fineness? I mean isn't she an emissary from a better world, a spiritual, kinder world? Otherwise, her presence would be unnatural. And it isn't. Her beauty in body and soul is something as natural to all that is or will ever be. It's like a spark in a dark tunnel but it shows us that there is light in darkness. I mean she's the substance that can't be eliminated because it's part of the harmony. She never left off being a star."

"Sounds like a lot of claptrap. The one good thing about everything is that there is no permanence. You, her and all that crap in your head will be no more."

"There is no permanence?"

"Not to atomic assemblages. You looking for her face? Well, that's gone."

I knew it wasn't because right then I saw Bettina's face. She was standing behind his chair. Smiling. She had a beautiful smile. I could see she thought the old man was funny.

"But isn't it so that regardless of how many lives you are reincarnated into, it's always just you. Just your own unique identity. And each new you remembers the others and in the new face, you can see the old face."

"You got a beaker full of bullshit in your head, don't you, Dirk? Micro-atomic re-assemblage isn't reincarnation. Physics isn't ruled by identity preservation. When the lights go out, you're not conscious of anything. There's no permanence to consciousness. It's a feeble thing. Hit somebody over the head hard enough and they wake up with a new consciousness and a new identity. So, who cares about the fucking opinions that come out of that girl's mouth?"

He looked at me. Or maybe it was Dirk. Guess it didn't make a difference to him. Also, I didn't know what girl he was talking about.

"You know what else has no permanence?"

I took a wild guess.

"Everything but The Mathematics?"

"Life, after life, death, birth, heaven, hell, eternity, sin, forgiveness. All illusion."

"I guess the past can't be retrieved?"

He made a loud guffaw kind of sound of total paternal disgust.

"Only as illusions. And they don't stay. Either does the mind that kicks out the illusions."

"I'm full of illusions, Dad," I moaned, surprised at my own tears.

He studied me closely as if I were a test tube and he was waiting to see what a catalyst would do.

"You'll get over it. Nothing more impermanent than emotions. In short, The Mathematics can't help you. Use words. Write her a letter. It's what inferior minds resort to."

"Write her a letter?"

I looked over at him.

I heard him snoring.

I left silently, last rays of the winter afternoon sun's particles dancing toward him and all around him. Star particles.

"Love ya, Da."

Write her a letter?

CHAPTER FORTY-FIVE

MY DEAR BETTINA

My Dear Bettina,

I hope this finds you well and not dead.

At any rate, I hope what I am writing here finds you wherever and, however.

It's funny what you find when you're looking for something.

Not some thing but a person or an answer.

For instance, I'm looking for you for sure.

But I run into a question: What is Death?

This question only comes up because, one, I think you're dead

And I think that because I see myself leaning over you in our bed

Giving what I hope is CPR

And I'm calling to you but . . .

You died as I was looking at you.

I see this again and again in all weather and all times and places.

I see your face overlaying all faces.

Thus, the question: What is Death? And if you are dead, where are you now?

I know. That's two questions.

I go in search of you and two questions are raised.

And these questions trigger questions I'm not interested in, questions I am not asking.

I see them as blockades thrown up to detour me.

Substitutions when there are no substitutions. No supplements to Death. No matter how many times you supplement the words you use with other words all you have are words. Death escapes you.

Fronts and alibis, analogues, and addendum.
For instance, I want to talk about dying
And the talk is of treatment.
It means nothing to me if I'm told I will see you in the Afterlife
As represented by this or that religion
That each has its own questions
Eternity, Heaven and Hell, Paradise, Reward, Punishment
Are real to you only if faith makes them real to you
Death is different
You don't need faith
I saw it arrive in your eyes and then close them forever
I say I'm not interested in the carrots and sugars of the Afterlife
I stand where Ivan Karamazov stands
When he asks what price do we pay
For the harmony and bliss of the Afterlife?

"Look: if everyone must suffer in order with their suffering to purchase eternal harmony, what do young children have to do with it, tell me, please? It is quite impossible to understand why they should suffer, and why should they have to purchase harmony with their sufferings? Why have they also ended up as raw material, to be the manure for someone else's future harmony?"

The plot here is thick and deep and for me beside the point, the point being Death.

Suffering and redemption? The grounding Truth of human existence reached through such suffering and redemption. The many live in high anxiety hoping for something better in the Afterlife while the few flourish in a life here that is for them more certain than the unknowns of the Afterlife.

What do I care if those who cause others to suffer receive their "just punishment" in the Afterlife? Why would I go along with anyone suffering and anyone being punished? Will I feel good about all the son of a bitches of history, right up to Farabutto, burning in Hell? How is this in anyway an answer to Death?

What's it matter to all those slaughtered, executed, gassed, and blown up if the perpetrators get punished somewhere else and later. Is that an answer to Death?

Why all this scripting of scenes of suffering and redemption that stand like a scaffolding concealing the clear reality of Death? So much wordage, plotting, staging, good and evil drama, clever beginning and ending, punishment and reward. An elaborate conceit that never reveals the reality of Death but instead detours our attention away from it.

Ivan, again:

"And if the suffering of children has gone to purchase the truth, then I declare in advance that no truth, not even the whole truth, is worth such a price."

I am not as heated about all this as Ivan Karamazov or his creator Dostoevsky. It's all a kind of smokescreen, chatter about how your taste buds are excited by this dish and how much you love it when all I want is the recipe.

Forgive me, dear Bettina, for myself going down a road ending in a ditch.

This is a lousy love letter. I am being difficult. But you know that about me.

What I see regarding Death has nothing to do with tales of Afterlife but how I see something of the dead not ever leaving us.

This also answers the question of where you are. Something lingers here in the world. Call it your soul but not the soul that Plato envisioned in its home in an Ideal world. That's the same pot of tea as finding relief in knowing people will be punished somewhere we don't know but not here.

Is the Christian Heaven an Ideal world? Where else would the idea come from? But I tell you, Bettina, I am not interested in any of that because here is where I knew you, here is where you enchanted me, here is the body I love, the eyes I see looking at me. I don't want you transformed or transported to any place where you are not what you are here. Is that a terrible thing for me to say? And if you were to be purified into an ideal, heavenly self, how would I know you? Why in heaven's name would I want you to be different in any way? We recognize everything about each other, the virtues and the vices, the faults and the true. So, if these were washed away, we would be like strangers, unknown to each other. I find that unbearable, my dear Bettina. So very, very unbearable.

Maybe the soul that lingers here with us is not imperishable but penetrated by other such souls so that the idea of an autonomous soul, your soul alone is lost in a tangle of other souls, like lost in a mosh pit at a Justain Peeber concert.

Everything organic is interfused and infiltrated by all other life forms but that sounds like compost to me. All life is holy as William Blake writes but why does the holy die and you never see her again? Where is the holy in that?

Bettina, if your goodness did not linger with us, if Death as oblivion had consumed you, then all stories of love would have become extinct, that love itself would be inconceivable, that all windows to joy and peace of mind, would have never ever been opened. We would have forgotten how to love eternally.

But such is not the case.

I find you everywhere. I find you everywhere because you are alive everywhere.

An idiot would exonerate Death by thinking dying is a replenishing of all the beauties I found in you. I don't think this. I am not consoled because I cannot ever again hold your physical presence. That your spirit lingers and infuses the world is an excellent thing. But it does not satisfy me.

Eve Solly recommends I seek out a twelve-year-old Influencer with more followers than Mohammed to get my head on straight. I need to see that Death is just a lifestyle choice of the geriatric.

Please forgive, if forgiveness goes on where you are, the irrelevances and detours of this letter to you.

Remaining confident and in good health, I am, humbly yours,
Theodorus Bratter

CHAPTER FORTY-SIX

DAN TWO

"So, you are saying that it's up to me to decide whether she is alive or dead?"

"That and all of it. Whether you loved her, married her and lived with her for sixty-five years."

"Fifty-six. So . ."

"You know why idiots say 'so' all the time, Dan?"

"It was explained to me, but I forgot."

"It's not a summary of what's been said or a next step taking into account what's been said. It's a 'whatever.' Whatever you just said but this is what I have to say. It's a disjunction in conversation. A break with what's gone before as if what's gone before wasn't heard. In short, it's the end of communication because it ends the continuous development of thought. It's a click to a new screen, a scroll down to something else. A real 'so' builds and takes on and responds to what's already said."

I nodded. So, in all these pages I've never used a 'so' as it should be used. So, you see, we get nowhere.

"So, you know I was told not to come here to Prospect Park and sit on this bench because you would show up and I was advised not ever to speak to you again."

"Well then, just shut yourself up. It's your interior monologue."

"It can't be. I don't know all that crazy shite you just unrolled about saying the word so."

Dan laughed. It's too scary for me to think that I was laughing. I would then be two screws away from screw loose.

"Look Dan, if you relied on what you knew, you wouldn't be in search of what you don't know if you knew or didn't know. Too many knows in there. Sorry."

"So…I'm to take it that you know what I don't know I know?"

"That's it. You need me for the words. Nobody is schizoids because they can face what they have to tell themselves. They need the tough stuff to be shoved off on somebody else this way they can listen to the tough stuff and just say 'That guy is an idiot or out of his mind.'"

"You're a project of my own mind then? A homeless guy with some stank sitting on a park bench? Why would I think anything you had to say is credible?"

"I don't know but you're here and we're talking. Actually, I look like this because I can't seem credible to you. Your conscious mind won't allow it. It's like the way dreams show up as absurd cartoons. What's on your mind?

"I guess I want to know why you think what happens to Bettina is up to me."

"Good. That's a start. I was afraid you were going to multiple schizoid."

"What's that?"

"Let's say you're Dan one and I'm Dan two. Now I might bring you to a place that churns up more negatives than you or me can handle so I need to talk to Dan three to distance myself from the stuff I can't deal with. Of course, you come along on that because I'm already here because you can't talk to yourself and when I can't talk to myself, we're both going to Dan Three."

"You lost me. Where is he?"

"You'll probably put him on another park bench not too far from here. But not to worry. You and me. We can get a breakthrough here. We won't need Dan Three."

I have to confess I was craning my neck looking around for the guy. I did realize how stupid that was.

Dan was talking.

"Let's say the past is fluid, not done and the whole concept of a final judgment comes down not to an up or down transport but a retrieval of the dead so what was not complete or recognized, somehow fucked up in their lives, is amended and made whole and they know and everyone else knows it. "

Somehow this made me angry.

"She doesn't need forgiveness. She doesn't need to be fixed. She was whole. Always. She doesn't have to wait for some final judgment."

"Then why are you?"

"I'm not."

"Then your past relationship with her is not waiting to be known. She is not waiting for you to find her or to find proof that you both loved each other for a long, long time. The way you know all that you know about her now in the present is how she comes into the present and never dies. Doubt and fear have kept you from knowing this. It put you in search of what was never lost to you, what never had to be found."

I shook my head. Not because I didn't believe what Dan Two was saying but because I didn't know what he was saying.

"About that forgiveness part," I said, or mumbled.

"The guilty always want to be forgiven," Dan said, nodding.

That bent me the wrong way too.

"I don't feel guilty," I said, angrily.

"Okay. So why not tell me that dream you had so we can both review it?"

"You know about that?"

"I was listening in you could say. Go on. Spill."

I didn't want to, but I did.

"It's raining hard, really hard and I'm aware I have no rain gear. Everyone is gone. I open a closet. There's just this one odd looking big coat hanging there. Kind of a retro style. Designer quality. I grab it and put it on. I know it's theft because I'm escaping. On the loading dock, somebody says 'Nice coat.' Now I'm standing under an awning of a luncheonette. Ernie's. I know it. She knew it. I pull an itinerary out of the coat pocket. A long trip planned. I can't read the date when it's going to happen. And in an envelope, I find eight Benjamins. $800. I've got to return this coat. It's a trousseau coat. That word comes to me. A whole future begins with that coat. For somebody. It's precious. This is a birthright coat straight out Biblical. It's the promise of a future for someone. I am filled with a need to return it, but I can never amend the theft. I stole it. That act was done. I interrupted its destiny. I am the thief of a soul I said to myself. The aura of the coat should have told me right off that it was spectral with all the luminosity of a numinous entity. A living soul. And I stole it. I am in tears. How blind can you be that the transcending magnificence of this coat was not seen, not understood. 'The owner of that coat died. She doesn't need it anymore.' The words come. I protest. 'How can she have died?

There wasn't enough time.' In fifty years, I never found a way to give it back. I need to bring it back is an urgent demand I can never fulfill. There is no more time to do it. Time has stopped."

"She didn't own it. She was what you stole."

"And I needed you to tell me this?"

He laughed. I laughed. We both laughed. We had the same fucked up sense of humor.

"Guilt. We presume only because it's probable. But it's a feeling. There is no probability with feelings."

"They have no logic."

"Exactly. We're like of one mind."

"Yeah, one mind talking to itself."

"Two observations. One, the coat was brilliantly numinous, right?"

"Throughout."

"So, clearly it wasn't a coat. Two, you had a dream about a friend, a real upbeat friend who pops up in your head as if she were right there coming into the room. And she says 'I had a good day. A really good day.'"

"Yeah, I remember that. I remember her. Peggy. I remember that dream too. Right after the theft dream. I didn't know what it meant. I hadn't thought about Peggy in years."

"She loved her good days."

He said this very slowly. I got the thought. Why not? It was mine.

"Not Peggy? Bettina?"

He nodded.

"She's telling you that she loved her life. Brother, you can't rack up in your own mind what her life was to her. It was her composition."

"I won't ever know."

"Except she tells you. And you hear it. Or one of us does."

"I don't know. Me telling me. What are the chances there?"

"It may take, and it may not. We still might need to schizoid Dan Three for an assist."

"Jeez, I hope not. You're already wracking my brains and I skipped levels in school."

"Yeah, you probably should get over that. You wouldn't be talking to yourself on a bench in Prospect Park right now if your brain hadn't already been weaponized to fuck you up."

CHAPTER FORTY-SEVEN

A CERTAIN SLANT OF LIGHT

"How do you remember me?" she asked, at sixteen, in her two-piece which I called a bikini, lying on our blanket which was stretched just below the point where the sand swept upward affording us a protective wall.

"What do you mean?" I asked, lying next to her, observing the way her chest moved as she breathed.

"In all those years you imagine we lived together. Isn't that what you said? That we married and had a life together. And then I became ill and died."

I sat up.

"I never said that. That you died. You didn't die."

"I can hear it in your voice," she said.

"What?"

"That I died. You sound so very sad. You're crying, aren't you?"

"It's the sun. I've got the sun in my eyes."

She reached out and put a hand on my back. I lay back down.

"But it was all lovely, wasn't it? When you don't think I died."

"It was. When I think of you. You were perfect. Always. So lovely. Mind and body. I always felt you were the perfect example of the better angels of our nature. A rare visitation on earth."

She laughed.

"What if I don't grow up into being anything like that? I can be naughty you know. Very stubborn. If I don't like something, I walk away. I don't see why I should listen to anybody just because they're loud and keep talking or stand in front of the room or sit there and ask me questions when I didn't ask them to ask me anything? Why should anyone presume what they must tell me is what I want to hear? If I'm told this is what I must know, it doesn't mean anything to me unless I'm hearing it in my own head, in my own time. Most of what's told to me doesn't ever reach me."

"I don't know. Maybe you need all that to reach such a quiet, alluring independence. It's just beginning stuff."

"So, I remain alluring all the time? I mean in all those years you dream we are together?"

"Truth is I'm aware of you fully rarely. That is very hard for me now. It's as if I missed the incredible fineness of your spirit because I was looking the other way."

"Where was that?"

"Inside my own head."

"You were selfish. I can see that."

"Not in the sense that I only cared for anything if it did something for me. Or I had to push my vanity up front for everyone to see and admire. I never thought the whole world was here for my personal use and other people just audience to my own life."

"You fooled a lot of people then. I mean that's the kind of way your brother describes you, isn't it? You don't treat your twin very well, do you? Isn't it very selfish to think he's just, well, you and not him?"

"Yeah, he's not me. The whole world is not me. He's different. I just don't understand him."

"You don't have to understand him. Or anybody. It's not required for you to understand them for them to exist. But you are an inside your head egoist. Not being selfish there. But still, I was there. Wasn't I?"

That was true. I don't think I ever heard her reveal so much about what she felt and thought about me. Was that the only way I could see her? I mean through me? I thought that truly sucked.

"I think I'm slowly getting outside my own head."

She laughed.

"Now? You mean now talking to me here? I do think you are very aware of me now. You're not inside your head now but I'm dead. So, it doesn't matter, right?"

I realized I was running one hand along her thigh.

"I think all of you is in here now with me."

I tapped my head.

"We got married?"

"We did. I have wedding photos in my head. You had auburn, dark honey colored hair, soft, gentle eyes, a sweet smile of wonder.

A small clutch of flowers in your hand. I see the tips of your white shoes peeking out from the bottom of your dress."

I knew I was tearing up.

"There was a kindness to your presence that I feel I damaged over the years. I am and always have been compared to you like a dark cloud sweeping across a bright sun. Not a total eclipse but a darkening, nonetheless. You once wanted to know how you had wound up with me. You were in a passion as if you were feeling that something so good inside of you had been worn down and you knew I had done that to you. I never forgot that. I had no answer, but I knew the answer. I was bent and deformed inside where the meanings are. You know that Emily Dickenson poem?

There's a certain Slant of light,
Winter Afternoons –
That oppresses, like the Heft
Of Cathedral Tunes –

Heavenly Hurt, it gives us –
We can find no scar,
But internal difference –
Where the Meanings, are –

None may teach it – Any –
'Tis the seal Despair –
An imperial affliction
Sent us of the Air –

When it comes, the Landscape listens –
Shadows – hold their breath –
When it goes, 'tis like the Distance
On the look of Death –

"That certain slant of light in winter afternoons has the look of death. There's no sun behind it or in it. But where you are and always have been is in the total light of the sun. I saw that too late. I'm like that cartoon character who always has a dark cloud over his head."

"Why is it too late if you know that our life together is not over and done? We're at the beginning. Or could be if you woke up. You know it is selfish to think what you think in your head about my life is true. And I'd say crazy too if you tell me now you don't think all these memories you have of a past we haven't yet lived aren't crazy."

"Yeah, they're crazy. But I have to tell you that I was given some advice I'm following right now."

"What was that?"

"Pick a time when I know for sure you and I were together and go there."

"Did you?"

"Yeah, I'm here right now."

"Who gave you this advice?"

"Eve Solly."

"Oh, God. You know Eve loves to wind up people on her show. She messes with their heads just to amuse herself."

I shook my head.

"I don't see how she's messing with me."

"I'm not here right now."

A hand reached out for mine. I took it.

As I looked at her, I thought that if she had died would she know that I was with her like this, here at our favorite spot? Would I be holding her hand right now?

What would she know? It came to me that she existed as long as I did and when I too died, we both would truly be gone forever. The way in which we grew together over so many years, all the challenges we met and disasters we outlived, everything that we shared when our eyes met. All of that would have no existence. We would make room for others to go through their own journeys together. Would they see it all as it rushed by, or would they, like myself, suddenly without Bettina see so much of what was unseen and burn in the fires of time till I too ceased to exist?

"You know what I've never learned?"

She shook her head.

"Do we have time?"

"I have never been able to find the present moment. I'm always a day late or now I think years late. Or I think it will be in the future, but it never comes."

"Come here," she said, reaching out for me. I went to her.

I kissed her.

"See?" she said, pulling away from me. "That is here. All that matters happens out here. Not in your head."

That made me smile.

"You're very wise for a sixteen-year-old. And kind of a mystery. I mean you just said you weren't here."

She let that go.

"What was I like when I was twenty? Middle aged? A pensioner?"

I sat up and cradled my knees.

"When you were in your twenties, you had a laughing fit when someone came by looking for Dr. Nutley. You called me that for a long time. Middle aged? You had intraocular surgery and you didn't need your glasses anymore. You shouted, `I can see!' You did that one morning upon awakening. I said, amused, `Good' and you looked at me and said 'Idiot. I've woken up and needed to put on my glasses to see since I was twelve.' And you exulted being retired. You'd suddenly shout, `I'm retired!" I didn't catch the thrill there either."

"You sound very uncaring. And I sound very simple minded. Is that what I became in your mind?"

"Your doctor wrote on a prescription `This woman is perfect in every way!' And you were. Gorgeous and courageous. At every stage."

"And then I died?"

My whole body shuttered and shivered.

"I don't see why you have to keep coming back to that."

"I don't. You do. I don't come back."

Tears again. I was a mess. It was like I had never jumped several grades in school due to my superiority. I was the yolk. Dirk was the runny white. Now I was a joke.

I felt defiant.

"You do. You never went. You wouldn't be here if you had died."

"I'd be in your mind though, wouldn't I?"

"Yeah, always."

"Maybe I'm there now."

They say absence makes the heart grow fonder. But Eternal Absence? What about that?

CHAPTER FORTY-EIGHT

APART

I am in a waiting room
I hear a clock ticking
The time it tells is timeless
For there are no more clocks ticking
I don't know if it will be a long time
Or if I have been there a long time
Or if I have just arrived
I don't know what or who I'm waiting for
You see, she is dead
And no matter if I wait for eons
Grow hoary and decrepit old
She will be dead
But I am waiting for her nonetheless
For you see I don't know
Where I end and she begins
Where I begin and she ends
And so will never feel
Apart

You know how sometimes things in life happen so fast that you don't know they've changed you completely until sometime later?

Dirk calling me and telling me he had accidentally killed a guy who had killed his girlfriend was such a time.

No, not Eve Solly. Gretchen, whom he had met during one of the frequent time-outs in his relationship with Eve. Nothing had been consummated, in Dirk's words, but this Gretchen had sent him a

"Help!" text and my noble brother had shown up to find her dead and the killer lounging on the bed. This killer had assumed Dirk was the clean-up guy he had called. Dirk disabused him and after a scuffle sent the guy's head into a wall. He died.

I couldn't make Dirk understand why I was going to take the rap for him because I didn't understand it myself. Maybe I was trying to make up for having derided and ridiculed my twin for so many years. Maybe I felt I deserved the punishment, and he didn't. For a fuller account read *Between Dog & Wolf*.

Dirk and I were sitting in a courtroom. Arraignment hearing.

I heard the charges brought against me. Did I have a lawyer? I did. Did I plead guilty or not guilty to the charge of murder to which my lawyer, Summer Arpeggio said that I would plead guilty to a voluntary manslaughter charge.

"Mr. Bratter, did you kill the now deceased, the victim, to protect the also now deceased whose life was threatened by the victim? Or was she already dead on your arrival to the scene?"

"She was dead," Dirk told the judge, Judge Trudi, although he had been told by Summer to keep his mouth shut.

The judge peered at Dirk and then at me.

"Which one is being arraigned?" she asked a clerk.

"Mr. Theodorus Bratter."

"Okay. Will the guy with that name stand up."

I did.

"Okay. Court officer. Escort the clone who yelled out she was dead out of the courtroom."

"Wait!" Dirk yelled. "There are things Theo doesn't know."

"You were at the scene also?"

Summer tugged at Dirk's sleeve.

"No, your highness, I wasn't."

"He's spectral," I told the judge.

"He means spectrum," Summer corrected.

"Take spectrum out of the courtroom, thank you. Now, Mr. Theodorus whatever, was the dead woman dead when you arrived?"

"Yes."

"So, you had no reason to protect her as she was already dead and beyond needing your protection. Am I right?"

"I couldn't do anything for her."

"So, why did you kill the deceased Mr. Whatever?"

"Because he killed her."

"So, that's what you presumed. So, then you didn't call the police and say Mr. Whatever may have killed this woman but instead you killed Mr. Whatever yourself. In a fit of rage because you walked in on your wife lying dead on the floor and Mr. Whatever standing over her. It makes sense. You went after him, and he wound up dead. How much do you weigh, Mr. Theophilus?"

"About 15 stone."

"About seven feet tall, right?"

"Six foot five."

"And Mr. Whatever? The dead guy. Where's the body photo? He looks about half your size. You went mano a mano and his head wound up in the wall. Is that right?"

"She wasn't my wife. And he was lying in bed. Smoking and playing with his cell phone."

"Girlfriend?"

"We had one date. Unconsummated."

"Poor her. So, why did she call you for help if you hardly knew her?"

I shook my head.

"I don't know."

"But you showed up and killed Mr. Whatever because for reasons we will never know he had killed your girlfriend. Unless of course you killed them both because you found them doing what you said you didn't do with her. Consummating. She didn't text you. You were following her. And you walk in and she's consummating with Mr. Whatever, and you kill them both in a rage of passion? No, I don't think so. You knew what you'd find behind that door. You had a plan."

"It's voluntary manslaughter!" Summer yelled.

"You'll have a difficult time proving that Counsellor."

"My client is not a flight risk."

"That's because I'm not granting bail. He'll be nice and safe in the U.S. Marshall's custody until trial."

"It's a deep, dark never-ending tragedy when someone you love dies," I told Dirk when he came to visit me in City Jail, awaiting trial.

"But it's a much darker tragedy, a tragedy *de Profundis* when you know you were with this courageous, lovely, sweet natured woman for many, many years but you really weren't there at all."

I was tearing up. I reckoned that my schmaltzy self would be a big hit in Federal Prison.

"Where were you?" Dirk asked, his voice cracking. One thing that has always been true about Dirk is that he tears up at more than at a hand puppet's funeral.

He's always copied me, as if I were a template of great behavior.

"I didn't see what was there to see is what it was. And she was so lovely I should have never taken my eyes from her."

"Bettina? I remember she was a little passion-aggressor with you, wasn't she?"

I let that confusion alone. I now knew the heart behind the words.

"I live now in a vacant place like leaving a motel room and turning back for what you left behind and you see the vacancy. There's that sadness you catch as you see yourself gone as were so many before you. You see what it's like when you're not there or anywhere. When she's not in the bathroom taking a shower. Beautifying. By all that's right and holy, you shouldn't have rushed back because you missed something. You shouldn't be now in that vacant room that was once filled with your life together with her. And, the hateful thing is, brother, you can't ever walk out of there and into a non-vacant place again. There is a vacancy sign over your head that will be there for as long as you live."

"It can't be filled again?"

"There's no hope of that, brother. It was a one time around and through and over thing. That's why my going to jail in your place doesn't matter to me. The thing about the vacancy I'm in is that it fills jails and palaces alike."

"But you haven't been with Bettina for many, many years like you say? I mean she's probably still waiting for you. She's like early twenties?"

I nodded.

"And she'll always be that brother. That's the heart of it. I can always find her there."

He started to tap his knees and move his feet and shake his head up and down. Dirk did this when stuff was coming at him, he couldn't understand or even identify.

"Summer thinks you should get Dr. Fraud to testify."

"As to what? Plead insanity?"

"Temporary, Summer says."

"He's been disbarred or whatever it is they do to psychiatrists. He's a greeter at WallMarx. He wouldn't carry much weight with the jury."

"Unless he had greeted them personally. They do make personal connections. You know, we could get Dr. Wrong. She always said you were batshit crazy."

"She told you that? She told me you were bat shit crazy. She's in an asylum anyway."

"She is? How do you know?"

"I got a Christmas card."

"You know, I bet if I find Bettina, you won't want to go to prison."

"She's gone, my brother."

"What if the one you imagined you spent your life with . . ."

"And failed to cherish every moment."

"Yeah, and that. That one could be dead because you know, Theo, she could be anything like anything not real but just in your head could be anything."

He paused. I could see he was tying himself into a knot.

"And so?"

"But the real one. She's young. Most likely she's alive because, you know, she's young. The young don't die young. It's like you find the real one, and the other one, the one in your head, has to step back. She disappears."

"You know, brother, what I keep asking myself is where has she gone?"

"Probably not dead is what I'm saying. Did you ever think she got married and has a different name and that's why you can't find her? That's what I'm thinking. Maybe she's not Bettina anymore."

What I saw in Dirk's face just then was what I saw in everyone's face when facing the fact that someone alive was now dead. They hold on to medical reasons, lab results and so on. The disease as a cause that somehow explains this death which is so far beyond any cause that your mind boggles, your sense of justice collapses, your soul is crushed.

What justified an Eternal Death? What kind of sentence is that and what kind of crime need be committed? Why is there such quaking fear in a handful of dust? Is it as Whiteman felt to the very core of his being that out of this dust the grass he loves grows? "*You will hardly know who I am or what I mean/But I shall be good health to you nevertheless/And filter and fibre your blood.*"

I realized I was talking out loud. Dirk was a pitiable sight, his love for this twin, me, under attack by my words which flew beyond his grasp.

"All I'm asking, sane or not, where has she gone? Do I side with Plato? An immaterial soul free of a mortal body? I see a final justice in that as would Bettina. This cancer pursued her body for so long now burnt to ashes, her soul free at last."

"She had cancer?" Dirk asked, stunned.

"In our long life together, she did. It finally killed her."

"Wow!" Dirk exclaimed. "That's dark, brother. You dream up some very dark shit."

"I lived it. I was her caregiver. It riddled my soul to see her in so much pain. And now her soul is released from all that."

Dirk was twitching around in his chair, none too comfortable these jail chairs.

"But then again, maybe none of what you imagine is true. Realness is someplace else. And that's where Bettina is. Not sick or dying or dead."

"Did you ever think, Dirk, that Plato was wrong?"

"Not a thought I had."

"There's no soul that springs out of cremation. No. I ask. Is mortalism her fate here? No escape from the oblivion of death?"

"You know what The Pater once told us? The dead don't know they're dead, but the living know they're not dead. That's the living speaking of themselves."

"So, you think Bettina is forever lost in the Void?"

Dirk flushed.

"No, Theo. I think the real, young Bettina ain't there. The other one, like I say, you could put anyplace cause she's only in your head."

"Only in my head? I see her now coming down the stairs, her small basket of laundry in hand. I see her back to me in the kitchen making coffee. I see her sitting across from me at dinner. I see her at the tub giving our daughters a soapy bath. I see her seeing me."

"Wow!"

"I see her drive her car up our dead-end street. I see her looking straight into my eyes as if I need to see something in her eyes, but I can't. I see her ahead on her Fitbit walk as I rush to catch up. I see her looking at the birds and squirrels swarming the bird feeder and environs. I see her beside me unsteady walking to the cancer center entrance asking to hold my hand. I see her hand reach back seeking mine. I see her doing the crossword puzzle or at her desk handling the bills. 'I see you looking at me,' she says, and it is true. I see her on the deck looking lovely calling to me telling me she'll be gone for a time to meet with friends. 'I'm going,' she calls out.

For a time that now opens to eternity.

I paused. I knew I was tearing my poor twin apart with all of what he saw as my illusions. But I could not help myself.

"Time is the fire in which I now burn," I told him, and I saw tears in his eyes. It is indeed very true that identical twins reach out to each other in mysterious ways.

He reached out and put a hand on my arm.

"I wish I could make you less sad, brother. I wish I could make you smile and laugh. You always found me funny. Right?"

I did smile.

"I do sometimes ask myself can any entity exist that has no origin? For I see now what was in Bettina points to such a loving kindness and compassionate concern existing somewhere not natural to us but from which she came and to which I know is now her home. And in her magnanimous way she comes to see me. She takes my hand, Dirk, because I'm unsteady now but she will not leave me. That makes me happy, Dirk. You see? It doesn't matter if I'm in jail. She comes to me. She makes me happy just to see her."

"I'm glad you're happy, brother, but it makes me very sad."

I could see he was. He wore his heart on his sleeve, as they say, which I see now is a good thing.

"We're apart spatially. She and I. Maybe the space is all terrestrial. Or maybe it's terrestrial/celestial. Doesn't matter. It means nothing. "

CHAPTER FORTY-NINE

NUMINOUS

The thing I always wondered about Homer's *The Odyssey*, which I read in classical Greek, has to do with how Odysseus's desire to get back to Penelope isn't given full play.

I thought that a fault, a failure in authenticity and I came to that opinion after one of my own star-crossed voyages back to Bettina.

Something of a voyage from Istanbul to Thessaloniki and then railing from there to Sofia and onto Belgrade to Zagreb to Ljubljana to Trieste to Venice and then Milan where I flew to Frankfurt and then back to the U.S.

There were mishaps all along that way back to her, so threatening that at times I felt I was not destined to return to her. And that feeling of not returning, of something happening to me preventing me from ever seeing her again seized me like a fever, a delirium of anxiety and a terrible sense that no matter how I pushed to get back to her, how furiously I strove to make all my connections, to fight for passage, to give up eating and sleeping in my mad rush across the great distances between us, I was shadowed by the fear that it could not be done, that this was a journey never to be completed.

Not ever seeing her again was the greatest fear. And it possessed me.

You don't see that in Odysseus. He's calculating, clever, manipulative, shrewd, undeterred. But never frantic, never obsessed with the fear he'll never see Penelope again, that she could have died while he was gone, that he could die on the way back to her.

After Bettina died, this dream came to me almost every night.

I think she sent it to me to comfort me. How? Because I had only miles, many hundreds, and thousands of miles, to go before I could be back to her. Only geography separated us. I could rail, sail, fly, drive, walk, run, skip back to her. It could be done.

As long as she and I shared the same finite, physical realm of this world, we could find each other. I could cover the distance, complete the journey, measure the miles already behind me and those still ahead.

But if she were dead.

If she were someplace else, not in this world any longer, not on any map, not miles from me but distanced from me someplace that cannot be measured, someplace on no map. . . What then? There was no return journey, no way back. And if there were, she would no longer be there.

Do you know how a traveler feels when he suddenly becomes aware that the person he is rushing back to is gone, is not there, has not been there for a long time, will never be there again?

One of the gifts of a long journey is the return to the person you love. Maybe it was foolish to go on such a long journey from that person, foolish not to expect that something bad would happen to you or her when you're apart. But in my dream, there was always an irrefutable necessity to be on a journey away from her, a kind of unspoken naturalness to it.

I think that was the way dream tells us that no matter how happy we are together that we are each on a lonely, divided journey that is our individual lives. Just as there was a time before we met, a time when we did not know of each other's existence, a time when we walked alone, there will be a time when we are once again not together but apart in such a way that we can never rejoin.

That is the time in which we burn because we yearn for what can never again be.

Each night, nevertheless, I am frantic to return to her and as terrifying and dark this dream is, it is one in which I have not given up yearning for her.

That is the way I live now, that she is not gone forever but rather there is always my hope that I can find her again, that I will return, and she will be there.

Then too, I have this sense that she never left me, that she is always with me.

This is not a state of being that any words can reach, in any of the Romance languages I know. Not even classical Greek or Latin. They get me nowhere. They are like whatever sails in the breeze looking and not finding, floating eternally without anchor, no place to rest, never a journey's end. I read no language in any way that reveals what I seek.

I am listening to this song as I drive, going someplace I am not interested in, someplace I would not be going to if I had been able to find Bettina, and I hear the words "till the end of time."

He'll love her to the end of time, which means until she dies, until she goes out of time, literally runs out of time. The thread of her life Odin has given her has run out, has dropped from the spool, from the wheel and drifted to where I can no longer see it.

Right now, I am doing something else. I am doing this. I cannot do something else, something you want me to do because right now I am doing the something I want to do.

That time is over.

I no longer have a "right now" and I no longer do something else because there is only one never to be detoured from, or discarded, or disremembered thing. Not some unexpressed unknown thing but only one thing: that she died, and I'll never see her again.

This alone, that I'll never see her again, never talk to her again, never hold her again are thoughts which I feed the fire in which I burn, this imperishable timber of my mind which fuels the fire in which I burn, which I cannot stop doing, probably till the end of my own time.

I am lost in this dark world until she is there in the way this dream presents her to me.

I know I am somewhere and then she is there, smiling, her face radiating such loveliness.

It is as I remember her. But I do not recognize what she is wearing. At first it seems something like the skirt and blouse she wore when I was first alone with her, that quiet winter afternoon, that archetypal place where the young embrace and from that moment on are tied to each other in a way time cannot erode or erase.

I hold on to her when I awake because I know she wants me to remember her so brightly there for me beyond the end of time. I don't know how I know that, but I do. I have never seen her clothed like that before.

When I awake, I feel so suddenly that she was clothed in the earth itself, before time began, vestments primordial, expressions of an archetype whose potency has never died. She was calling me to attend to it, see it as a sign of something she has come to tell me.

Then I suddenly know what she has come to tell me. I instantly know her because I have seen her smile that way; I have seen her eyes gleam with a joy of just being there, her laughing mouth, a radiance that thrills me. It is her. I have found her. But where she is and how she is, I cannot know. She is clothed in a mystery.

All of it is nothing I can know.

I cannot know the way she is now because I am somewhere radically different. I am alive. I am in a state of being in which she now has no place. Her surround is not anything I can recognize. And there she is showing me she likes being a mystery to me. What fun she always had in telling me that. She's not teasing me, my stupidity in living with her for so long and not knowing her at all.

I am awake and I feel reassured that I will see her again, not in the way I see now but in the way she exists when time has ended. I will recognize what she is wearing then because I will be where she is.

I will have the eyes to see.

"I know you <u>have</u> to tell me what you were thinking."
"Death. Your death. I threw a hundred thousand words at it."
"And now your mind is at peace?"
"I didn't get anywhere close to it. The words? They hurt more than anything else. They mock the effort. Break out in ridiculous absurdity when I'm deadly serious. It's all I can do with them. I circled in dreams. I ran the same clips over and over again *ad nauseum*. I wore out the patience of anyone who listened. The reality of it, of what happened to you when you closed your eyes, of where you are now. I never saw the real of it."

I'm terribly sad and know that I will be for the rest of my life.

Then I hear her voice, never muted, never late:
"Come here and sit with me, Joe."

Library of Congress Control Number: 2021920062
ISBN 978-0-578-99984-5

Bad Animal Books

Time is the Fire completes *The New Utrecht Avenue* trilogy begun with *Get Ready to Run*, and *Between Dog & Wolf*. Some characters die, some die and reappear, one never dies.